JUDAS
HORSE

Lynda La Plante was born in Liverpool. She trained for the stage at RADA and worked with the National Theatre and RSC before becoming a television actress. She then turned to writing and made her breakthrough with the phenomenally successful TV series *Widows*. She has written over thirty international novels, all of which have been bestsellers, and is the creator of the Anna Travis, Lorraine Page and *Trial and Retribution* series. Her original script for the much-acclaimed *Prime Suspect* won awards from BAFTA, Emmy, British Broadcasting and Royal Television Society, as well as the 1993 Edgar Allan Poe Award.

Lynda is one of only three screenwriters to have been made an honorary fellow of the British Film Institute and was awarded the BAFTA Dennis Potter Best Writer Award in 2000. In 2008, she was awarded a CBE in the Queen's Birthday Honours List for services to Literature, Drama and Charity.

✉Join the Lynda La Plante Readers' Club at
www.bit.ly/LyndaLaPlanteClub
www.lyndalaplante.com
⬛Facebook @LyndaLaPlanteCBE
⬛Twitter @LaPlanteLynda

Lynda La Plante

JUDAS HORSE

ZAFFRE

First published in Great Britain by Zaffre in 2021
This edition published in the United States of America in 2021 by Zaffre
Zaffre is an imprint of Bonnier Books UK
80–81 Wimpole Street, London W1G 9RE

Hardback ISBN: 978–1–8387–7441–7
Ebook ISBN: 978–1–8387–7442–4

For information, contact
251 Park Avenue South, Floor 12, New York, New York 10010
www.bonnierbooks.co.uk

For my sister Gilly, my best critic and casting director, who is always encouraging and positive, and never negative.

CHAPTER 1

The Cleveland Nature Reserve was a cluster of lakes situated between Cirencester to the north and Swindon to the south. The reserve was just a small section of the Cotswold Water Park which consisted of hundreds of lakes with fishing sites and water sports, intercut with cycle paths, farms and walking routes. Home to thousands of species of flora and fauna, it was only marred by the presence of the occasional, unexpected area of quicksand – proving that even the most beautiful things can hide a more dangerous side.

Jamie and Mark often cycled along Spine Road which, as the name might suggest, ran through the centre of this cluster of lakes. They'd go fishing, watch the people on jet skis and beg free cans of pop from the Waterside Café. But today, they were distracted by a strange sight in one of the lakes: dozens of crows on the surface of the water! The brothers, aged 12 and 13, didn't know much about biology, but they did know that crows could not land on water. Each time the wind blew tiny waves across whatever they were standing on, the birds panicked for a second and created a cloud of black wings all flapping at the same time. But they didn't fly away; something was keeping them there, in the middle of the lake, on their strange, out-of-place platform.

Twenty minutes later, Jamie and Mark had cycled round to a small rowing boat that they'd hidden many months ago, tied to the low, overhanging branches of an old tree. They slid it into the water and set off. Mark, being older and stronger, always did the rowing.

As they got closer to the mass of birds, it became clear that the crows were standing on the roof of a horsebox, most of which sat just above the surface of the water, by no more than an inch. They began to shriek and flap in a unified show of force, endeavouring to keep their prize – whatever it was. The boys could now see that the birds were focussing their attention on a tear in the metal roof, about six inches in diameter.

'Climb up then,' Mark instructed. Then he swung one of the oars through the air and the crows flew away in all directions, creating such a foul-smelling down-draught as they went, that the boys screwed up their faces and held their noses. Jamie thought he was going to puke and said he didn't want to climb on top.

'I'm scared it's gonna sink!'

'Don't be daft,' Mark said. 'It must already be sitting on the bottom, so it can't possibly sink any further.'

Reluctantly Jamie removed his T-shirt and tied it round his face like a mask then tentatively climbed onto the roof. He shuffled towards the six-inch hole, trying to keep his balance as the roof began to wobble, and peered down into the pitch-dark water.

'Nah, there's nothing,' Jamie quickly decided, desperate to get back to dry land or at least into the rowboat. But Mark wasn't prepared to give up that easily.

'Push it with your foot and make the hole bigger,' he said. Above them, the crows circled and cawed angrily.

Jamie pushed his toe into the hole, trying vainly not to get his trainers wet. Egged on by his brother, he began stamping down as hard as he dared on the ripped edge of the horsebox. Finally, it gave way by another inch or two, sending a bubble of old, trapped air up into Jamie's face. The stench was so rancid, that Jamie immediately bent over and puked into the lake, while his foot slipped through the hole filling his trainer with filthy water.

Mark started laughing, But Jamie did not see the funny side. 'I only just got these trainers for my birthday! I'm coming back . . . this is stupid!'

'You're wet now,' Mark giggled. 'Stamp on it, go on. Make the hole big enough to see inside. Go on, Jamie! Don't be a baby!' Mark knew exactly what to say to rile his younger brother.

Jamie angrily started jumping up and down on the roof of the horsebox, splashing Mark in the process. They were both soaked now, but it didn't matter – despite the horrible smell, they were having fun.

With each jump, Jamie brought his knees up to his chest, getting as much height as he could. And each time he landed, the hole opened up a little more. Until, with one jump too many, the roof finally split completely and gave way beneath his weight.

To Mark's horror, Jamie disappeared beneath the surface and into the submerged horsebox.

The next five seconds seemed to last forever. Not knowing what else to do, Mark held his breath, as though he too was underwater. Finally, Jamie bobbed back up, gasping and slapping the surface of the water with his palms. He snatched at the air, trying to find the oar being waved above his head until Mark managed to guide it into his hands, pulling his little brother to the wall of the horsebox. Jamie draped his armpits over the top of the wall, wiped his face and gradually let the wonderful realisation that he wasn't going to die sink in.

Mark was as white as a sheet, as the thought of what could have been spun round in his head. But Jamie, knowing that he'd now earned enough cool points to last a lifetime, began to laugh and this finally gave Mark permission to relax. The boys grinned at each other then started laughing hysterically – until Mark's expression suddenly changed when something broke the surface of the water behind his brother.

Mark couldn't see what it was at first, but gradually the thing bobbing about, just inches away from the back of Jamie's head, turned and twisted in the water until it was suddenly, sickeningly, recognisable. The human skull didn't have much flesh attached, but it was enough to drive the carrion crows crazy as they wheeled about in the sky above, so near and yet so far away from such a tempting feast.

'Jamie . . .' The serious tone in Mark's voice made Jamie stop laughing and pay attention. 'Grab the oar. I'll pull you over the side, then you swim to the boat.' The old, rotted corpse bobbed back and forth as Jamie kicked his legs, and then he jerked as he felt something cold and slimy brushing against him. Feeling suddenly sick again, he turned his head to see what it was.

Jamie's scream was loud enough to finally scatter the crows from the sky.

*　*　*

After solving the Rose Cottage murder, whilst also bringing to a close the investigation into the biggest train robbery ever seen in the UK, Detective Sergeant Jack Warr's reputation for doggedly following his instincts, regardless of how dubious that course of action seemed to everyone else, was known and respected through-out the Met. He was the detective who assessed people quickly and read them accurately; he could be hands-off one minute, and in-your-face the next; but he always seemed to know how to find out if you had anything to hide. Above all, he was uncannily adept at predicting what criminals were going to do. It was almost as though he could think like them.

His boss, DCI Simon Ridley, known to be one of the most anal men on the force, continued to be the perfect counterbalance for Jack's gut instinct and, together, they now made a formidable team. Jack was exactly the type of intuitive officer that the Wimbledon Prowler case needed. Above all, the Wimbledon Prowler case seemed to simply need a fresh pair of eyes. And Jack's eyes were particularly attuned to finding the right detail, at the right time, in the most unlikely of places. So DS Jack Warr was sent on loan to Wimbledon.

Through the summer months, the Wimbledon Prowler brazenly walked the streets with a tennis racquet in his hand, blending in with a thousand other part-time sports fans. And in the winter months, he hired a mobility scooter and moved freely around the Common being ignored by everyone because no one wants to get caught staring at a disabled person. Two disguises allowing him to hide in plain sight, so that any CCTV that did happen to capture him would not provide the police with an accurate description of 'their man'. He was smart, bold and arrogant. He knew how people behaved. And he knew how to manipulate them. So, for five years, the Wimbledon Prowler evaded the police and all of their endeavours to catch him. The case had gone stale.

Between 2016 and 2021, the Wimbledon Prowler systematically terrorised this area of South West London. Sometimes there were months in between burglaries, but DS Richard Stanford always recognised the MO within a minute of entering any targeted house and could separate the Prowler's burglaries from any others.

'When you walk into a burgled property,' he would say, 'you can tell who's done it quick enough. Some sneak in whilst the family sleeps, showing off how bold they are; some break in when the house is empty. Some cause as much damage as possible, to make evidence collection and fingerprinting a nightmare. Look in the fridge – if the food's gone, we know it's likely to be Jacko. Big Tony nicks kids' toys for himself, along with small electronic items that are easy to sell on for a tenner a pop. Some villains go straight for the car keys. Some focus on jewellery, meaning they've probably already got a fence lined up. And if the house looks like it's not been burgled at all, apart from an attic window being forced . . . then we know it's more than likely to be the Wimbledon Prowler.'

The Prowler's MO was to target houses where the roof was accessible via a lower extension, and people who owned a cat. When the owners were out, he'd enter through an attic window, as they were rarely-to-never attached to the security system. And all internal alarms would normally be off to allow the cat to move freely around the home. Once inside, he'd disarm the security system and eventually leave via the back door. Sometimes he got it wrong, of course. Sometimes the attic window was alarmed. Sometimes the cat was confined to the downstairs, so the upstairs sensors were active, but he'd discover that within seconds and manage to escape via a door before the police got close. DS Stanford's biggest problem was that the Prowler was patient. He could go months without burgling. Which meant he could easily fall off the police radar and his escapades just be added to the growing pile of unsolved crimes.

The first thing Jack did after getting up to speed with the Prowler case, was call a retired detective constable called Mike Haskin – the man who'd spent three weeks chasing down the Alley Burglar back in 1995, to tell him what he could remember . . .

* * *

After three weeks of sitting on gravelled rooftops and behind thorny bushes, DC Mike Haskin's team was tired, cold, pissed off and the laughing stock of the station. But they followed him regardless, because they were certain that he was right.

Mike had returned to each of the burgled premises and inter-viewed the owners for himself, learning along the way that, as well as the twelve burglaries they knew about, another seventeen had gone unreported. This was down to the fact that this working-class community did not believe for one second that the police were capable of finding their own arse with both hands – let alone find-ing a burglar who had already evaded them for several months.

Tonight, Mike's team were just forty-eight hours away from having the plug pulled on the investigation – something they would never live down. The Alley Burglar was now just two days away from getting a free pass by having his escapades scaled right down from a full-on surveillance op to a distant memory.

The target zone was in lockdown, with a covert officer on every possible ground exit. They knew the footprint of his target zone but had no intention of going in after him – his nickname of Alley Burglar was well-earned. The vast expanse of shops and residential properties gave him far too many unlit escape routes, places to hide and short-cuts to take.

It was the 'rat in a maze' principle – if you follow the suspect into the maze, you'll get lost; so, you tactically cover all exits because, eventually, the suspect has to come out.

With rooftop vantage points and ground-level runners ready for their moment in the spotlight, Mike was confident this time they'd get their man. He had to be. He was running out of time.

Mike's team were all using basic-issue radios, meaning that their communications were competing with every other officer's on duty that night, and 'radio silence' was impossible. So, the volume was turned down on everyone's handset until the second the chase was on. They needed to be invisible and silent.

The rooftop lookouts were so far away from background noise such as traffic and footfall that every crinkle of their jackets could *be heard in the surrounding silence. This meant hours of sitting in exactly the same position in the hope that, when the time came, they'd still be able to move their legs and run.*

Operation Midnight progressed through its first week and into its second. Then at 3 in the morning, on the final night of the longest stakeout Mike had ever been in charge of . . . it happened. As the metallic noise echoed round the empty streets, it was impossible to work out where it was coming from, so the team stayed put. And listened. Their minds filled in the blanks as they each tried to figure out what they were hearing and which direction it was coming from – the consensus being that someone was standing on a dustbin and scrabbling up hard guttering.

Mike's heart was beating out of his chest as he stretched his cold, seized-up leg muscles, getting ready for action. 'All units stand by, stand by. Radio silence.' His eyes scanned the darkness as he listened and his brain automatically filtered out the sound of foxes feeding, rats foraging and the homeless turning over in their sleeping bags – so that all that was left was the sound of his burglar creeping around his well-trodden rat-run.

Then there was an almighty crash, forcing Mike to instruct his men to go overt: torches went on, and everyone came out of hiding and raced towards the noise, while black-clad police officers looking like ninjas scrambled across rooftops.

Beneath them, their burglar was on the run. The officers covering the ground exits resisted the instinct to close in and help; instead they held their positions and waited for the perp to come to them. Radios burst into life with a running commentary of street names and compass directions. Occasionally, Mike heard the words 'lost him, lost him' but they were quickly followed by 'chasing suspect, chasing suspect' as another officer took up the pursuit. It was thrilling and excruciating at the same time. Mike wasn't near the actual chase; he was on one of the exits with a couple of his men, willing the burglar to come his way so he could be the one who physically caught their man. But then he heard 'suspect detained' And it was all over.

Every officer now left their position and headed for the rendez-vous point, all wanting to see who they'd spent three and a half weeks hunting. In the back of an area car sat a small, wet, dirty man, hands cuffed behind his back. He smelt of beer and BO and, as Mike shone a torch in through the window, he could see that the man was crying. He figured he was a druggie, stealing to feed his habit. He'd targeted a working-class area because it meant that there'd be no alarm systems to bypass. He was a nobody who would not be missed.

Many officers would have seen this man as small-fry, almost harmless, but looking at him Mike knew the truth: when a person commits crime for fun, they can take it or leave it; but when a person commits crime because their life depends on it, they can become a killer in the blink of eye. If you don't catch them in time, they can be the ones you read about in the news.

*   *   *

Ridley had attended Mike Haskin's retirement party some months earlier and had spoken so highly of Mike's dogged determination and unwavering self-belief, that Jack had remembered his name. Ridley had even mentioned the Alley Burglar case, explaining how Mike had stuck to his guns, even when his DI had lost faith in him. If Ridley had taught Jack anything over the years, it was to respect the talents of others and to be humble enough to surround himself with exceptional officers who shone in the areas that he did not. Ridley had wanted Jack on his team for this very reason, and now Jack wanted Mike on his.

DS Richard Stanford was personally grateful for their help on the Wimbledon Prowler investigation, but unlike Mike Haskin, he had struggled with the silent derision from others on the force because he hadn't yet got his man. He knew it should be water off a duck's back, but, for some reason, it cut deep. The Wimbledon Prowler case was becoming the bane of his life and, worse, he'd lost the enthusiasm of his men. On one occasion, a cocky little PC by the name of Denny McGinty had loudly fake-yawned during a morning briefing and Stanford had gone ballistic in frustration and embarrassment. That was the moment that his boss had called Ridley, and Ridley had called Jack.

Jack Warr and Mike Haskin sat quietly and patiently in front of Stanford as he laboriously laid out all of the details of the investigation. It was clear he'd done nothing wrong as such, he'd just lacked imagination and the ability to step outside the rather sterile and restrictive box of police procedure and into the dirtier, messier world of the career criminal.

'Sir . . .' Jack interrupted during one of Stanford's pauses for breath. 'Mike has been where you are, and he got his man. Now, he's going to help us get yours.' Jack smiled, making sure that his deep brown eyes smiled too. 'When going forwards isn't working, go back.' For the first time since they'd arrived, Stanford dared to relax and sit down.

For the next two hours, Stanford gave Mike the floor and he talked them through the Alley Burglar case. Stanford made copious notes, highlighting potential new approaches. Mike drew a map showing where all of the burglaries in his operation had occurred and, by the time he'd finished, a familiar fish-shape pattern was clear to see. Mike explained what Jack and Richard were now looking at. 'The first burglary we knew about wasn't the first one he did, our second wasn't his second and so on. It was only when we caught him that this fish-shape emerged. Our perp lived in a squat situated right in the middle of the fishtail. His first burglary was the closest to his squat, out to the left – the top of the tail fin. His second burglary was the closest to his squat out to the right – the bottom of the tail fin. Then he went further and wider as he got ballsier, until he drew a fish across his self-selected patch. This pattern allowed us to predict roughly where his next burglary would take place . . . and that's how we caught him red-handed.'

Mike could see the fascination on Stanford's face.

'Weird, innit, Rich. But this sort of subconscious pattern is very common according to the boffins at Bramshill. They're the brains who spend their time making sense of the senseless, so I can stand here sounding clever. After we'd caught him, this pattern also allowed us to go back and find every single burglary he'd committed and do him for the lot. Your man won't be being random either, Rich.'

Jack loved that Mike, as retired Job, was able to call DS Stanford 'Rich'. It brought an informal friendliness to a situation full of tension because of the hole Stanford was in. Mike ended his stint at the evidence board with 'I'm gonna need a cuppa soon, Rich, if that's OK with you, mate'.

Energised by Mike's informal approach and easy confidence, Stanford had suddenly found a new lease of life. 'Take yourselves to the canteen and bring me back a tea, will you?' he said. Jack and Mike threw each other a quick grin. They knew that when they returned, there'd be a second fish scrawled on the evidence board.

The canteen was empty, and the cleaner was taking advantage of the fact that most coppers were out on patrol. From the doorway, Jack and Mike could see the glistening wet floor and they wondered why on earth she'd started mopping from the doorway, ending up in the corner of the room with no way out other than back over her pristine floor. They watched in silence as she walked backwards towards the serving counter, sweeping broadly left and right, leaving the lino as clean as the day it was laid. The only marks that defeated her were the black rubber heel scuffs from police issue boots.

Then, without slowing, she dipped under the serving hatch and reappeared behind the counter. That's why she'd started mopping at the doorway, because this cleaning lady was also the serving lady.

Mike looked at Jack. His face was serious, and his expression clearly said, 'I may have been a copper for thirty years, dealing with the toughest of the tough, but there's no way I'm going to be the first one to walk on her wet floor.' So, Jack took Point, and ventured forwards. For some reason, Jack thought it best to take huge strides towards the frowning woman behind the counter, leaving behind as few dirty footprints as possible.

As they sat with two pots of tea and two full English breakfasts, they talked like old friends. 'Are you gonna be at the birth?' Mike asked, as he slurped his piping hot tea through pursed lips. 'I was there for all of mine. It's the most disgustingly fabulous thing you'll ever see.' Mike, it turned out, had six kids – 'two of each,' he joked. 'Two girls, two boys and two as-yet-unidentified. They're amazing. Have more than one, Jack. Mine fight now, 'course they do, they're still young, but it's good to know that, when me and the missus have gone, they'll have each other.'

'Maybe we'll see how we cope with one first,' Jack replied. And then, quite unlike him, Jack found himself talking about very personal things, to this relative stranger. 'We left it quite late,' he explained. 'Maggie's a doctor and, with me being Job, we always seemed to be working towards something, rather than arriving. Moving to London, her promotion, my promotion. The baby wasn't planned, which, if I'm honest, was the only way it was ever going to happen.'

Jack smiled an unexpected smile as he recalled the moment Maggie had told him he was going to be a dad. They were on a flight to St Lucia, to collect his own dad from a cruise and bring him home to die. It wasn't a morbid memory. It was a moment that told him to live life to the full, because, all things considered, it's so very, very short.

When Mike took over the conversation again, he went into great detail about the birth of his third and Jack tried to filter out some of the more gruesome parts of the story as he was still eating. 'He was blue 'cos the cord was round his neck. I tell you, Jack, there's nothing more terrifying at the birth of your baby than silence. *Scream!* I was thinking. And he did. Then the little bugger carried on screaming for the first seven months of his life!'

Jack nodded, as if he'd been paying attention. 'When your wife was pregnant, did you . . . did you . . .' Jack searched for words that didn't make him sound like a complete bastard, but he couldn't find them. 'Did you enjoy being at work, more than being at home?' he said finally.

'I loved being at work,' Mike laughed and he could see how relieved Jack was to hear a wiser man's experience. 'We love 'em, Jack, but, fuck me, being pregnant affects a woman's senses. Fact! She can suddenly see every knife you put into the fork section, she can smell your fear when she mentions a shopping trip. Work was my sanctuary.'

After this twenty-minute breakfast session with Mike, Jack found he had spoken more about the upcoming birth of his first baby than he had in the previous eight and a half months. But then, who did he have to talk to? Ridley was his boss, not his friend; DS Laura Wade was his partner but had shown no interest in the pregnancy at all – possibly because it drew a solid line under her fantasy of ever stealing Jack from Maggie; and DC Anik Joshi . . . well, Anik had become a bit of a dick since Jack got the Sergeant's position instead of him. Jack's only real friend, in fact, was Maggie. But he could hardly talk to her about how he felt like he was drowning. Which is why it had been so liberating to speak with Mike: he was a safe pair of ears, who Jack would know for a week or so, and then never see again.

* * *

Stanford had forgotten he'd asked for a tea, so was pleasantly surprised when Jack and Mike returned with one for each of them, plus some cakes which the cleaner/serving lady had joyfully gifted to Mike once she'd discovered he was a devoted father of six. Sure enough, there was a second fish-shaped drawing on the evidence board. It sprawled across the whole of Wimbledon Common, plus all of the surrounding streets. Stanford's target zone was now huge.

'The CCTV for this area has been looked at a dozen times,' Stanford was saying, eager to crack on and get the most out of Mike and Jack whilst he had them. 'No cars or people consistently appear on the nights the burglaries took place; no one who doesn't belong, that is. All residents and visitors have been checked and cleared.'

'Extend the perimeter?' Mike politely put this as a question, but it wasn't. 'The Common is throwing any pattern out of whack 'cos, as far as potential targets go, it's a worthless area, but as far as cover goes, it's invaluable. So, you've got to extend the perimeter beyond the Common. I suppose CCTV inside the Common is a hope-in-hell, right?'

Stanford shook his head. 'There's no CCTV in the majority of the Common. In the summer of 2018, a wildlife survey was done, mainly around the ponds and in the deeper areas of woodland. There were some cameras placed in trees hoping to catch owls by night and kestrels by day doing their thing. We got all of that video footage, but it gave us nothing. We've tried, Mike, we really have. This sneaky little fucker is driving me crazy.'

Mike smiled and repeated his advice to extend the perimeter. The only advice he then added, was that Stanford should review all CCTV footage himself, because you can't buy experience; and besides, the neck that's on the line should be the one to do the make-or-break work. That was Mike's philosophy and it had always served him well.

By nine o'clock, Jack, Mike and Stanford had burned up the carbs from a heavy meat feast pizza and were trying to find their third wind with slow-release energy from nuts and fruit. But it was no use. They were about to call it a day and head for the pub, when Mike piped up, 'Who's this guy on the mobility scooter, Rich? He's around every day in the winter, but not the summer. Is he cutting through the Common to get somewhere? Does he live or work nearby?'

At eight the next morning, four uniforms were working alongside Jack, Mike and Stanford, tracking the flat-cap-wearing man on a small red mobility scooter and a hooded man in tennis whites carrying a racquet case. They seemed to be the same build and, crucially, both carried an identical rucksack. One or other of these men, it turned out, was seen during the day of each burglary – but never both at the same time. Jack was certain this was the same man, using two different disguises, to hide in plain sight and recce the target house before coming back to burgle that same night.

The man, regardless of how he was dressed, behaved in a very specific manner. He would disappear into the Common and then emerge at another exit hours later. But the *final* time he emerged, whether dressed as a wannabe Nadal, or as an innocuous disabled man, was always at the Copse Hill end of the Common, where a light grey Mercedes was waiting for him. It was parked on a different street each time, always with a heavy treeline to hide the number plate from prying CCTV. But *this*, they now realised, was the centre of Stanford's fish tail – the Merc.

Nadal or Ironside, as their Prowler was now affectionately nicknamed, would stay in the Merc until the dead of night. Then, dressed in dark clothing, he'd head back into the cover of the Common. From there, he could pop out anywhere.

Stanford split his team into two. Some uniformed officers were tasked with using the date and location of each burglary to track their suspect in and out of the Common: burglary after burglary, month after month, year after year, from the Merc, to the victim's home, back to the Merc. Meanwhile, other officers were tasked with using backdated CCTV and Police National Computer checks – if there were any – to track the Merc in and out of London and try to establish if the car was definitely present in the capital on the night of every single burglary.

One of the uniformed officers helping Stanford now was McGinty, the fake-yawner he'd torn a strip off days earlier. Today, however, McGinty was a different man. He seemed to know his place and his role, and he was doing his job enthusiastically without question or back-chat. Mike caught Stanford watching him. 'Is he the kid that yawned at you?' Stanford's rather embarrassed look confirmed that it was. 'Get him transferred to your team, Rich. The worst trait in a police officer is apathy. That boy will give you cheek and challenges, but that can be useful.' As McGinty left the room, he turned and gave Stanford a little nod, then he disappeared like an enthusiastic child on a mission to please a parent.

Whilst the uniforms were doing all of this arduous but vital screen work, Jack, Mike and Stanford were checking out a fish and chip shop in Manchester.

Damien Panagos was a 52-year-old, second-generation Greek immigrant, now running The Codfather in Wythenshawe with his wife and son – and the registered owner of the light grey Merc that was so often parked at the Copse Hill end of Wimbledon Common. His parents had come to the UK in the 1960s and his dad had worked as a sparky, teaching his trade to young Damien. Jack speculated that this is where he'd learnt his party trick of being able to bypass the average home security system.

Stanford was chomping at the bit to head north and get Panagos arrested, but Jack slowed him down. 'We're ahead of him and he's going nowhere. Work the CCTV cameras and gather the evidence. If, while we're doing that, he heads to us, we'll nick him in the act. If he's having some down time, we'll nick him at home when we're ready. Either way, we'll nick him. And when we do, it'll be watertight.'

Stanford was given four more uniforms, so that the hours of CCTV dating back to 2014 could be viewed on a 24-hour rotation. While that was going on, Mike took Stanford and Jack to the pub. 'If all we can do is wait, we might as well wait with a pint in our hand.'

'The thing that . . . gets me,' Stanford slurred three hours later, 'is the community bloody naysayers. I mean, I get it, I do. Some-one comes into your house and takes your stuff . . . that's terrible. It's like house rape, that's what it is. But, fuck me, Jack, people soon forget all the good you've done for them, just 'cos you let one little northern Greek bastard slip through your fingers.' Mike and Jack sniggered into their pints as Stanford went on. 'We'll get this Panagos prick and they won't say "thank you", they'll say "about time". Because this one cuts deep. This one has impacted an entire community for far too long. They're scared, and that's my fault. It's not my fault, but it is my fault. I really, really appreciate you coming here. Both of you . . .' Jack took this as his cue to get Stanford home before he started telling him and Mike that he loved them.

Stanford was first in the following morning, and he was raring to go. He looked as bright as a button, as fresh as a daisy and, as long as you didn't stand too close, you'd never know that he was probably still too drunk to be at work. Jack and Stanford set off towards Manchester, where they were due to be met at midday by DI Leticia Margate. The plan was for them all to go to The Codfather and arrest Panagos as he prepped for the lunchtime crowd. However, at half past eight, before they'd even hit the M25, Stanford got a call from DI Margate, to say that Panagos was heading south. Stanford's excitement was palpable – he was about to get the opportunity to arrest his nemesis on his own patch.

A few hours later Wimbledon Common was scattered with undercover officers disguised as dog-walkers, joggers, litter-pickers, duck-feeders, young lovers . . . all lining the pathways just waiting for a red mobility scooter to trundle past. They communicated back and forth for hours as Panagos weaved around the Common, then out into the streets, then back into the Common. After four hours, it became clear that Panagos had his sights set on one particular house on Parkside, just along from the private hospital: by early evening, the owners of this property were making no secret of packing their BMW with small suitcases for a weekend away. As expected, Panagos made his way back to his Merc parked on Copse Hill, he folded his scooter and placed it in the boot, then got into his car, made light work of a packed lunch and took a nap.

As night fell, Panagos, dressed in dark clothes and carrying a rucksack, set off again through the Common back towards Parkside, strolling unhurriedly as if he didn't have a care in the world.

After arriving at his destination, Panagos jimmied the skylight in the loft conversion and made his way downstairs. On the landing, a cat's cradle was hooked over a radiator and, as he stroked the tabby in passing, it stretched and purred loudly. By torchlight, Panagos made his way into the hallway and towards the front door, where the alarm box was situated. He got his toolkit from his pocket and . . . suddenly the hall light flicked on.

Stanford stood tall in the kitchen doorway, PC McGinty at his shoulder.

A key opened the front door and Jack stood in the porch, flanked by four more officers. Panagos froze in silent shock for a second, then, with a banshee wail, he dipped his head and charged at Jack. Panagos's broad shoulder hit Jack in the ribcage, lifted him off the ground and out into the front garden, knocking the four officers over like skittles. Panagos dumped Jack hard onto the lawn, flat on his back, knocking the wind out of him. The four officers scrabbled onto Panagos, grabbing any moving limb and holding it to the ground. Panagos roared and fought as the officers held on for dear life, making no attempt to cuff him until he'd completely run out of steam.

Upstairs lights from neighbouring houses flicked on and faces appeared at windows. As Panagos finally slowed to a stop and sank back onto the grass panting for breath, Jack crawled out from underneath the scrum of sweaty bodies. McGinty stepped forwards and, using two sets of handcuffs to stretch across Panagos's broad back, he finally secured their man.

*   *   *

Stanford walked calmly past the mayhem, towards Mr Liam Newark-Bentley, the owner of the property, who was now standing in the middle of the street. He and his family had not gone away for the weekend as planned; they'd got as far as the end of their street before being pulled over by Stanford, who'd explained the situation. Newark-Bentley had quickly agreed that the Met could use his house as bait, as long as not one single carpet fibre was left out of place. 'Thank you very much, sir,' Stanford now said politely. 'We're grateful to you for agreeing to allow us to use your home like this. The skylight will be fixed now. If you're happy to stay in the hotel we've provided, just for tonight, you'll be able to come back tomorrow.'

And then Newark-Bentley said those words that Stanford had waited five years to hear. 'We're very happy to help, DS Stanford. And thank you for keeping us safe. You have a very difficult job.'

On the periphery of the action, Mike got out of an area car and walked towards Jack, who was still seated on Newark-Bentley's front lawn trying to breathe. 'Well done, Jack. I love the way you distracted him so the uniforms could pounce.'

Jack held his ribs as he squeezed out the words, 'Fuck off, Mike,' then Mike's hand reached down and dragged Jack to his feet. By the time Jack was fully upright, Stanford had joined them.

'PC McGinty, read him his rights,' Stanford instructed. The look of excitement on McGinty's face gave Stanford a far better feeling of satisfaction than he would have got if he'd taken the honour for himself. Mike beamed his approval and shook Stanford's hand. Mike thanked them both for a great few days and for being allowed to briefly feel like a copper once again. 'If you ever need my old brain again, you have my number. It's been a pleasure, boys.' And, with that, Mike returned to the area car and was driven away.

Later that evening, the squad room was buzzing with the over-lapping chatter of invigorated officers reliving their exciting evening and comparing scrapes and bruises. 'Thank you, Jack.' Stanford's tone was sincere. Although he knew that Ridley had an inter-station duty to help when help was requested, he also knew that Jack's input was above and beyond anything he'd expected. 'DCI Ridley's lucky to have you.'

Jack's eyes twitched in pain as the adrenaline began to fade and his body started to complain about being slammed to the ground, then jumped on by four policemen. 'Enjoy your victory, sir. It was hard-earned.'

Jack turned and, to a chorus of ''Night, sir,' he headed home for a hot bath, a glass of wine and a cuddle with his beautiful, beached whale of a fiancée.

CHAPTER 2

Jack got home around nine. As he turned into the end of his street, he was still imagining the fantasy evening ahead of him: Penny would be out, Maggie would be in her pyjamas, the wine would be open, and the dinner would be in the oven ready for him to serve. He was exhausted from the obbo with Mike Haskin and Richard Stanford but also elated from their success and subsequent arrest of Panagos. Stanford would be dining out on that one for years to come.

This part of Twickenham was lovely compared to where their old flat had been in Teddington. They'd purchased the three-storey terraced house just under four months ago. It was a doer-upper. The kitchen, lounge and master bedroom had been the priority – these rooms were now painted plain white with cheap, mis-matched furniture that would ultimately be replaced when they'd had time to decide on the 'look' they wanted to go for. The second bedroom would slowly become a nursery but, for now, was nothing more than a pink-plastered box. The top floor had two bedrooms and one bathroom – this was his mother's domain. She'd moved in with them at the old flat within weeks of Charlie's death, as both Jack and Maggie were absolutely insistent that she was not going to live on her own. They initially assumed that, regardless of the love they had for her, Penny would be an added 'burden' – for want of a better word – but, in truth, she'd been the one to hold everything together.

Since moving to the Twickenham house, Penny had been a godsend. She stepped into Maggie's life at exactly the moments when Jack wanted to step out – the nestbuilding, the conversations about pelvic floors and piles and sickness, the fear and trepidation about life after the baby was born. All of the things Jack would have been totally crap at, Penny was in her element. And when it came to the everyday stuff, Penny made Maggie's life easier and better than Jack ever could – and being constantly occupied helped Penny to rally from the death of her beloved husband far more quickly than if she'd been allowed to wallow in some supervised-living accommodation, full of other old people with dead partners. She had a new generation to live for now and she was going to love the new baby with all of her heart. Penny likened waiting for the birth of Maggie's baby to waiting for Jack to be handed over from Social Services all those years ago.

Jack was very lucky that Maggie and Penny got on so well, but Penny was also surprisingly astute about their need for privacy. She'd signed up for a couple of evening classes and had even bought herself a little TV for her bedroom, turning the top floor into a proper little granny flat. She was secretive about the evening classes, prompting hours of humorous speculation, Jack eventually deciding that Penny was doing pole dancing and woodwork.

Jack loved returning of an evening to his ever-changing home. This house, or one like it, had been their dream ever since they moved from Totnes. They'd been priced out of the London market for so long, but after Jack's 'windfall', they jumped on this property by quickly offering £15k below the asking price, in cash. Within a week, they were in. The windfall was attributed to an impulsive lottery ticket purchase, which Maggie never questioned. Jack didn't know whether she thought he was lying, or whether she was just too scared of hearing the truth. All Maggie knew for sure was that her husband was a changed man after the Rose Cottage case. He was *found*. He now knew where he belonged and that, for any person, was life-changing.

* * *

Penny didn't know that Jack had even looked for his real dad, let alone that he'd found out he was the son of Harry Rawlins, one of London's biggest gangsters in the 1980s. That was Jack and Maggie's secret. But the 'gift' of £250,000 was Jack's secret alone. Jack knew it was the proceeds of crimes from back in the '80s; he knew it was untraceable; he knew the thieves were long gone; he knew the case file was closed. No one knew or would care . . . and all that made it easy to keep, and easy to spend.

The money had now dwindled, but Penny's pension and Jack's sergeant's wages kept them ticking over. As a new young family, they were firmly on the social ladder – they wouldn't fall off unless Jack got sacked, but on the other hand they wouldn't climb unless he got promoted. For the first time in years, it felt as though life was where it should be.

The baby would complete the family, and Jack and Maggie would get married once she'd got her figure back – her words, not his – he was loving her big breasts and ample backside . . .

But Jack's dream evening vanished in a split second when he saw the car parked in his space on the street. They had visitors.

Jack recognised the deep, howling laughter as soon as he opened his front door. Regina was a nursing auxiliary in the same hospital as Maggie and they'd bonded over both being pregnant. She was nice enough, but loud. The moment the front door closed, Maggie was out of the kitchen and in Jack's arms. 'I'm sorry, I'm sorry, I'm sorry . . .' Her words were punctuated with a kiss. 'She's had a rough day and I wanted to cheer her up.' Maggie dragged Jack down, over her heavily pregnant belly and hugged him tightly round his neck. He could have fallen asleep on her shoulder right there, but instead he allowed himself to be led into the kitchen where he would spend the next couple of hours pretending to want Maggie's friends in his home.

Regina and Mario were both drinking non-alcoholic wine, and there was a buffet-style feast on the table. Jack briefly raised his dark eyebrows; widening his beautiful brown eyes at Maggie with the unspoken message: 'We're not a food bank.' Maggie had previously told Jack that Regina and Mario were struggling financially in the run-up to the birth of their baby, so he knew why Maggie had taken it upon herself to treat them to a feast every now and then. They'd also be forced to take home doggy bags, whether they were embarrassed to or not.

Regina had been to the house numerous times, but tonight was Mario's first visit. Jack knew it was his job to talk 'man stuff' with this stranger and as Jack got himself a beer from the fridge, Mario made a comment about abstaining from alcohol in solidarity with Regina. Jack quickly assumed that his evening would go downhill from there.

In fact, Mario was decent company and, by ten o'clock, he was on the beer too. Mario was a painter and decorator, existing on word-of-mouth recommendations. It was a tough job, with long hours and no security, but he had the sort of friendly demeanour that won people over quickly. Slowly but surely, Jack began to understand why Maggie gave so much to this couple and was happy to get nothing practical in return. They were worth helping.

At 11.15, Regina and Mario said their goodbyes at the front door, and Jack confirmed that he'd be in touch to talk about dates and times for decorating the nursery. The men shook hands, the women hugged, and Jack finally had his wife all to himself.

Maggie brought Jack a whisky and they settled into their newly adopted positions on the sofa. Before Maggie was too pregnant, they'd sit close together, using only one half of the sofa, but these days, they sat at opposite ends so that Maggie could bring her feet up and rest them on Jack's lap. 'Was it your idea for Mario to paint the nursery?' she asked. Jack's smug little smirk told her that it was. 'I love you, Jack Warr.'

'I know.' From where he sat, he could hardly see her face above her bump. He stroked his hand across her belly. 'Ah! She's a footballer!' Jack closed his eyes and felt his baby slowly turn and stretch and kick. 'There is only one in there, isn't there, Mags?' For a moment, there was genuine worry on Jack's face. 'Regina's much smaller than you and I can definitely feel three legs.'

'She's only five months, you idiot; I'm close to my due date. And I imagine that third leg might be an arm.' By midnight, Maggie was hauling herself up the stairs by the bannister, and Jack was pushing her bum skywards from below. They were both giggling as quietly as possible, so as not to wake Penny. 'That doesn't actually help, Jack.'

He knew. She told him every night. But he liked doing it.

At the top of the stairs were three boxes from Amazon. Maggie went into the bathroom, leaving Jack to have a nosy at what she and Penny had been buying. With no distinguishing pictures on the delivery boxes, Jack scrabbled about on his hands and knees trying to decipher the labels. Nursery stuff was about all he could discern.

As he knelt on the third stair down, his elbows on the landing floor; he smiled. Penny and Maggie's nestbuilding had accelerated over the past few weeks. They'd shown him material swatches, paint charts, online nurseries and asked his opinion, which they didn't really want or need, and Jack didn't want to give. Being asked his opinion put Jack in very dangerous territory: if he said it was up to them, he'd be scolded for being uninterested; but if he offered an opinion that differed from theirs, he'd be scolded for not understanding the needs of his unborn child. Jack much preferred the mind games of criminals to the mind games of his wife and mother: they mercilessly ganged up on him all the time. But the masochistic part of him adored being bullied by the women he loved – and it was tragic that Charlie wasn't here to share the burden. He deserved to be here. He'd worked hard all his life to mould Jack into a man to be proud of and now, when Jack needed his dad to be on his side against 'the women', Charlie wasn't around. The very thought of Charlie brought tears to Jack's eyes – the pain stage of his grief was merging with the anger stage and resulted in short-lived, intense moments of heightened emotion. Jack deep-breathed through it and the tears subsided.

Then a strange memory popped into Jack's head and he sat on the stair to relive it.

* * *

The sonogram burst into life and showed them an indistinct, grainy picture like something on a water-damaged VHS tape. In this uniquely beautiful moment, Jack's mind leapt to one of his first cases for the Met, in which he was asked to watch illegally produced porn tapes found in a toilet cistern, to see if any of them starred James Daniels, a well-known, yet highly elusive local pervert. Jack closed his eyes – 'For fuck's sake!' he thought as he desperately tried to get rid of the memory. Maggie squeezed his hand, and he was back in the room.

She repeated the question they'd been asked and which he hadn't heard: 'Do we want to know the sex?' The romantic in Jack didn't want to know, but the practical decorator in Maggie definitely did. So, for the sake of painting the nursery in the appropriate colour, they both said yes.

'It's a girl!'

The tears welled up in Jack's eyes. He had no idea why and he could do nothing to stop them. He and Maggie looked at each other through the blur of tears, and they laughed with joy, hysteria, fear, anxiety, anticipation. 'She's amazing' Maggie blubbed, as she looked at the grey snow on the screen with a black bubble, inside which was their baby. But all Jack could see was James Daniels' bare arse bobbing up and down . . .

When they got home, Penny had made spaghetti bolognese and opened a bottle of non-alcoholic wine. With only two places set at the table, they knew that this meal was for them and that she'd retire to her granny flat to watch reruns of Lovejoy. *In the centre of the table was a large white box tied with a bow. 'You don't have to use it,' Penny said before heading upstairs and leaving them to serve themselves.*

Inside the box was the most stunning christening gown either of them had ever seen. On the hem, in faint, worn lace, were the letters P and C. 'Oh my God.' Jack's words fell from his lips in a long, exhaled breath. 'This is her wedding dress. Her mum made it – look, she sewed P and C just above the hem. Penny and Charlie. No one knew the letters were even there apart from the three of them. It was for this moment, Mags, it was so that when Penny made her wedding dress into her own baby's christening gown, the initials would sit on the hem of that too. And I didn't even know Mum could sew!'

'She couldn't.' Maggie smiled. 'I guess she wasn't learning how to pole dance at her evening class, after all.'

* * *

The toilet flushed, Maggie came out of the bathroom and waddled past Jack towards the bedroom. In bed, Jack snuggled in behind her and kissed her neck. She stirred in his arms, her hand reached back and settled on his naked thigh. Within minutes, they were both asleep.

* * *

Ridley hadn't accounted for Jack returning from Wimbledon quite so soon. He'd received a phone call late the previous night from Richard Stanford, thanking him for sending such a diligent and astute DS to help catch the Prowler. As Jack walked into the squad room, Ridley was still deciding how much of Stanford's praise to pass on.

Ridley nodded Jack into his office. 'You OK?' Ridley had never asked Jack if he was OK, not even at Charlie's funeral, when Ridley stepped in to carry the coffin on account of most of Charlie's friends being too old to do it. 'DS Stanford said you were hurt during the arrest.' Jack assured Ridley that he was fully recovered and fit for work, regardless of the fact that, this morning, his back was as stiff as a board and he felt like he'd played forty minutes against the All Blacks. 'You've got two weeks Maternity Support Leave to take, half on full pay, half on statutory pay. You have to take it soon, or you'll lose it.' As Jack stood silent, Ridley could see the fear in his eyes. 'The baby's coming, Jack, whether you're ready or not.'

CHAPTER 3

Within three days, Jack's decision about when to take his Maternity Support Leave was made for him, when Maggie went into labour. She waddled up and down the kitchen, stopping every ten minutes or so with her palms on the cool fake-marble worktop and her forehead on the back of her hands. Whenever this pause occurred, Penny rubbed circles into the small of Maggie's back and both women breathed noisily as they waited in horrible anticipation for the building pain to peak and then left Maggie alone for another ten minutes. The women were like a finally tuned partnership – both knowing exactly what to do, when, and for how long.

Jack stood in the kitchen doorway with a birthing bag in one hand and the car keys in the other, waiting for the signal. After two hours, Maggie said she was ready to go to hospital.

* * *

In the delivery room, Jack knew the nurse's chant of 'breathe, breathe' wasn't for his benefit, but it was working, so he went with it. He was completely out of his comfort zone and, worse than that, had no idea what his purpose was in this room – he wanted, needed, to be in control, but he was a million miles away from that. He was annoyed with himself for being this useless. *This is why expectant dads are told to stand at the head of the bed and hold the mum's hand: it's to keep them out of the way!* he thought to himself.

Maggie, on the other hand, was being wonderful and strong. She didn't seem to be frightened, and calmly did exactly what she was told, when she was told. As Jack watched her prepare to push out the baby's head, his mind raced. He'd witnessed many a police officer run towards danger in the name of the Job, but he'd never seen anyone face this degree of pain, with such unfaltering bravery. Maggie had no choice, of course, he knew that, but still – the pride he felt at this moment for his amazing wife swelled in his chest and ended as tears.

Maggie caught sight of Jack's face. 'What the fuck are you crying for?!' she screamed. Her scream turned into a grunt of pain, then back into a scream. Then a higher-pitched, gurgling scream joined hers and it took Jack a few seconds to realise that his baby had arrived.

The baby's head was covered in a thin layer of white, paste-like vernix and her face was screwed up so tight that it was nothing more than a lumpy red ball. But once on Maggie's chest, the baby stopped crying and her little face took shape. She was beautiful, Jack thought, beaming at her through his tears. Maggie was beautiful, too. The baby seemed to look around the room, her eyes rolling in their sockets as though she had no control over them, then they settled on Maggie's face. Seconds later, Maggie's smile and warm body making her feel safe, she fell asleep.

In the corridor of the maternity wing, Penny flicked through pictures on her mobile. After Charlie's death, Jack had scanned every grainy old photo she owned, going right back to when Jack was little, onto her mobile so she could reminisce whenever she needed to: Charlie teaching his boy to ride a bike; Jack, aged ten, blowing out the candles on his birthday cake; Penny crying at his graduation; Jack, Maggie and Charlie, complete with paper hats and eggnog, celebrating a long-ago Christmas. Penny could feel the love in her heart as it yearned for Charlie at this moment – it was physical, like a lump. Penny was so engrossed in her reminiscing that she didn't immediately see Jack walking towards her. Then she saw the bundle of handknitted blankets in his arms, gasped, leapt to her feet and rushed to his side. From beneath the patch-work blankets, two big puffy eyes were closed tight shut. The vernix had gone, and the baby's skin was now a mix of perfect pink with the tiniest tinge of yellow. 'She's got hair!' Penny screeched, making the baby jump and her eyes flicker. Penny toned her excitement down to a whisper. 'Sorry, my darling. I'm just so thrilled to meet you. Oh, Jack, she's . . . Oh, Jack.'

'I've got to take her back in, Mum, to get properly cleaned up,' Jack said gently. 'Go up to the ward. We'll be with you in a bit, then you can have a hold.' Penny watched Jack walk back towards the delivery suite, moving so slowly and carefully, as though he was holding the most precious cargo in the world.

Thirty minutes later, Maggie was one of four new mums on B Wing of the maternity ward. Families gathered, bringing tears, laughter, balloons, cards and babygrows. The 'two visitors per bed' rule was blatantly flouted – but there wasn't a nurse in the hospital brave enough to make any relatives leave. Penny sat in a high-backed chair, with a pillow under her elbows and the baby in her arms. 'She's so interested in what the world has to offer,' Penny whispered. 'All the other babies are sleeping but look at ours . . . it's like she wants to know what's next.' Jack always knew that Penny would be unable to stop herself from comparing her grandchild with every other baby; but he had done her the disservice of assuming that her comparisons would be silly. Now he found himself nodding at her words, feeling their rightness.

'Do you have a name?' Penny asked.

Months earlier, Jack and Maggie had each made a list of names and then compared to see how in tune they were. Maggie had gone a bit highbrow and literary with some, such as Orson and Agatha, while Jack, in contrast, had gone old-school, favouring names like Alfie and Alice. But there were several names common to both lists. 'Charlie' had been on both, of course, for a boy or a girl. Then there was James, Emily, William, Hannah, Max – and unexpectedly Elsie had appeared on both lists too. When Penny asked if they'd decided, the truth was that they hadn't – but Jack now glanced at Maggie, giving her full permission to be the one to finally choose. 'She looks like a Hannah,' Maggie said.

Penny looked down at the sleeping little bundle in Maggie's arms. 'Hello, Hannah,' she whispered. 'You know, your name means "grace". You've graced us with your presence, Hannah. That means you make us happy simply by being here.'

*　　*　　*

Over the next week, Penny went into overdrive with the cooking, cleaning and washing, while Maggie's sole job was to keep Hannah happy. Jack's job was to open all of the Amazon boxes and build whatever was inside. And Mario's job was to design and create a woodland scene on the long wall of the nursery, using stickers that Maggie and Penny had chosen. They'd decided that Hannah should appreciate nature from a very early age, a decision that had come from reminiscing about living in Totnes. They had been so incredibly lucky to have had beaches and wilderness right on their doorstep. Growing up in London would be different for Hannah, but they still wanted her to learn about nature. And they'd take her back to Totnes when she was older, so she could see where she was truly from.

Within a week of being home, Jack couldn't remember what life had been like without his baby girl, and having three generations of Warr women under the same roof felt like the way it was meant to be. He thought about Charlie every day but, the truth of it was that if Charlie were still alive, then he and Penny would be

200 miles away in Totnes. As Jack hung a little picture of Charlie on an unobtrusive corner of the nursery wall, he smiled. 'Keep us right, eh, Dad.'

In the master bedroom, Maggie was sitting with Hannah on a V-pillow on her lap. Both of them were asleep. There was a milk-soaked pyjama top on the floor, along with three dirty babygrows and several wet muslin cloths. Two mugs of tea had been allowed to go cold on the bedside table alongside a blackening, half-eaten banana. Maggie's right breast was out, and there was a streak of milk on Hannah's cheek.

The scene was a strange mixture of blissful calm and utter chaos, and Jack felt certain he would never, ever tire of being a parent.

CHAPTER 4

It wasn't long before Jack was desperate to go back to work. And it wasn't as if he was even doing a third of the parenting, as Maggie and Penny had everything in hand, but, even so, Jack quickly found himself yearning for the peace and sanity of a murder investigation.

Quite how one tiny baby could run rings around three adults was beyond him. He was a smart man. He could manipulate the sharpest of criminals into a confession, so why the hell couldn't he convince a clean, fed, winded baby to go to bloody sleep at three in the morning?

But lack of sleep wasn't the real problem: the truth was he found the endless routine tasks mind-numbingly boring. Jack hadn't been surprised by anything for as long as he could remember.

He'd been given the job of wheeling Hannah around the neighbourhood in her pushchair, because Penny insisted that she needed a 'daily dose of fresh air.' Jack knew this was probably just a ploy to get him out of the house, so that she could do all of the noisy chores such as vacuuming, but he didn't mind as it was his opportunity to breathe too. He'd sit on a bench in the park and check his emails because even though he wasn't involved in any active case, he sometimes got cc'd into the round robins. This at least gave him a welcome sense of the outside world he so desperately missed, but Jack didn't dare say anything to Maggie about being bored, for fear of upsetting her. He would have been surprised to hear what she and Penny were saying back at the house.

'Tell him!' Penny giggled in her easy, matter-of-fact way. 'If he's getting under your feet, kick him back to work. He's bored, Maggie. I never had this with Charlie, 'cos we got Jack once he was old enough to be interesting.' Penny laughed. 'Babies don't do much, and the novelty quickly wears off.'

* * *

It was 9.30 p.m. and Ridley was in his office, arranging statements into chronological order for a court appearance later in the week. His obsessive nature came into its own when prepping for court and this showed in his track record. The very sight of Ridley taking the stand made defence lawyers tremble, because they knew they'd not be able to shake his testimony or him. He was rock solid.

Ridley's satisfying evening of paperwork, however, was interrupted by a phone call from DI Joseph Gifford, from Chipping Norton. 'Simon,' Gifford boomed down the line. 'Couple of minutes for me?' Gifford didn't introduce himself, nor did he need to. His deep, resonating voice had an upper-class tone, but his tendency to lengthen the last word of every sentence betrayed his Midlands roots which he was clearly ashamed of. 'Got this bugger of a case, not unlike your Wimbledon Prowler and I'm after a bit of advice.' Reluctantly putting his court case preparation aside with a sigh, Ridley listened.

'Three years ago, there was a burglary in Kingham. Big house set back off the main through road, no CCTV.' Gifford always used short, clipped sentences, leaving the listener to fill in the blanks. 'These people, Simon . . . too much moolah. Losing the odd item of jewellery means nothing. Insured to the hilt. They just want to move on, you know. So, these bloody criminals are getting away with it. No one's on my side, that's the problem. Privacy, you see, that's the currency here. The victims won't even give statements half the time. Rentals as well, that's another problem. Some bloody actor or singer or somesuch will hide away in a rental – top secret, like anyone gives a shit. They'll tell me nothing, bring their own protection team, not let us do any security checks and then, when they get targeted, it's my fault!'

'This is still going on, then, is it?'

'Every few months. And they're just the ones we get to hear about. Could be more. It's a political balancing act. Iron fist in a velvet glove was never more appropriate than right here, right now. But . . . things have just got more serious and something needs to be done. Fast.' Ridley sipped his tea as Gifford described the scene at the last house that had been burgled.

* * *

Mick Arbrose needed just four hours sleep every night, starting at one and ending at five. He was a well-respected businessman living in the village of Churchill who, each morning, would walk his Labrador the twenty minutes into Chipping Norton to collect the morning paper before the newsagent's had properly opened, and then walk back. Part of the walk had no footpath, forcing Mick onto the narrow road, but so early in the morning, he always felt perfectly safe. On this particular morning, however, when Mick walked down the oak staircase, his old Labrador, Jonty, was not sitting in the hallway waiting to greet him. Mick went straight into the kitchen and looked under the breakfast bar, where Jonty's night-time bed lay empty. Jonty's routine was as rigid as Mick's, so now Mick was beginning to worry. The only other place the old Lab could possibly be was in his daytime bed, which was under Mick's desk in the office.

As soon as Mick entered the office, his blood ran cold. The safe in the wall was open and had been emptied of around £100,000 in cash, a Hamilton watch and the keys to the never-used Bentley that sat under a tarp in the garage. But Mick wasn't looking at the open safe. His attention was fixed on the golden paw draped over the edge of the lavish tartan dog bed. He knew Jonty had to be dead because he always, always got up to greet Mick when he walked into any room. As Mick crept round the side of his desk, he could see that the red and green tartan at the front of the dog bed was now no longer tartan, but solid red. Mick's breathing became audible as he fought back tears. A few more steps forwards revealed that Jonty had been stabbed through the ear with Mick's silver letter opener, the ornate handle still poking out of his skull. Mick began to gasp for breath as a panic attack dropped him to his knees. He reached out his hand, placed it on the ribcage of his beloved companion, and kneaded his fingers through the cold yellow fur. He knelt there for the twelve minutes it took for the police to arrive. And he knelt there for the further thirty-seven minutes it took for the family vet to arrive. Only when Jonty was safely in the care of someone he knew, did Mick allow the police to get on with their job.

*   *   *

'Mick said that Jonty would have greeted the burglars,' Gifford continued. 'He wouldn't have barked. He was a soppy companion, not a guard dog. So there was no need to kill him. They did it because they wanted to.'

'I could come and bounce some ideas around with you?' Ridley suggested, but Gifford didn't want that.

'Don't get me wrong, Simon, but ... well, you might get me wrong when I say this, actually ... but the locals will spot you a mile away. You look like Met. It'll panic everyone. I was thinking about your boy. The one you lent to Wimbledon. He's used to rural policing, isn't he?'

'He's just become a new dad, Joe. He won't want to be assigned to a potentially lengthy job out of region.'

* * *

Jack snuggled behind Maggie and nuzzled her neck. The faint smell of sick filled his nostrils and he rolled over to face away from her. She'd changed her top, but it was still in her hair. Never before, in all their years of being together, could Jack recall sleeping next to Maggie facing outwards. It was one of the recent changes he hated most.

'You should go back to work, Jack,' Maggie whispered. 'We're OK, me and Penny.' Jack felt the bed move as Maggie rolled towards him and curled her arm around his waist. 'If we snuggle this way round, you don't have to inhale the smell of second-hand breast milk.'

Jack hesitated, unsure whether Maggie really meant it. 'Are you . . .?'

'Jack, I love you, but if you don't go back to work soon, Ridley will be arresting *me* for murder.'

* * *

Ridley wasn't surprised to see Jack walk through the squad room door, bright-eyed, bushy-tailed and raring to go; although he was surprised when he volunteered for the Cotswolds consultancy job. Jack had been sitting at his desk like a spare part when he overheard Ridley briefing Anik on the job. Ridley even gave Anik the name of Mike Haskin and instructed him to liaise remotely as the Met hadn't cleared any official funds for outside help. Jack had quickly interjected, 'You won't need funding for Mike if I'm assigned to the

Cotswolds, sir. In fact, you won't need Mike at all.' And that's all Jack had needed to say: his experience with rural policing, together with his time in Wimbledon and his knowledge learnt from Mike made him the perfect choice. Ridley sent a disgruntled Anik back to his desk.

Anik was bored of being a policeman. He constantly looked to the future, rather than focussing on the case in front of him. He was impatient for the big, decisive moment when he'd shine and get all of the kudos he thought he richly deserved. His youthful ambition had not waned with experience, it had simply become more desperate. Anik had recently started to make mistakes and was now a hair's breadth away from being transferred out of the most prestigious team in the station. Ridley could clearly see that he'd offended Anik, but was in no mood for temper tantrums. He shut his office door firmly, leaving Anik to sulk on his own.

'Your senior officer will be DI Joseph Gifford,' Ridley told Jack. 'He's based in Gloucestershire, but he and his team are working this case from Chipping Norton. Over the past three years, there have been thirty-four known burglaries, but, in the past six months, there have been eleven. So, they're either getting cocky, or they're blitzing the place before moving on. And Gifford knows they're not cocky, so he's potentially on the brink of losing them.'

Jack sat with the Cotswolds file open on his lap. It was clear that he'd already got a good steer on the case. 'DI Gifford has got some big names to deal with around here,' he mused. With ex-prime ministers, famous authors, actors and half of the *Top Gear* present-ers all owning homes inside the target area, kid gloves would be needed if he was to successfully help a community that demanded solutions whilst also insisting on privacy. 'His biggest problem is surveillance,' Jack surmised. 'The Wimbledon Prowler used the Common as cover; DI Gifford's crew have got half of the Cotswolds to hide in. No CCTV, houses several miles apart, long driveways that aren't overlooked on any side for at least half a mile. This will be all about thinking like them and making them come to us.'

'How's Maggie?' Ridley's question had another, unspoken question attached, and that was the one Jack heard and chose to answer.

'She'll be glad to get rid of me for a while, sir. I'm best out of the way whilst they establish a routine for Hannah.' Jack stood. 'I'll discuss it with Maggie, of course, but she won't say no.' Ridley remained silent as he sensed that Jack had something more to say. 'Hannah's not going to be christened exactly, 'cos we're not religious, but there'll be a naming ceremony of some kind to celebrate her birth . . .'

Ridley misunderstood, quickly saying, 'I'll make sure you're back in time. What's the date?'

'Oh, nothing's arranged yet, sir. I was actually mentioning it because Maggie and I would like you to be Hannah's guardian. Her godfather, really.' Ridley was visibly shocked; he never imagined in a million years that he'd be asked to do anything so personal by a member of his team, especially not Jack – they'd butted heads numerous times and been firmly on opposing sides in many cases. But their working relationship had always proved fruitful, so perhaps being each other's biggest critic actually made for a closeness that Ridley had overlooked. He sounded nervous as he asked what being a guardian actually meant.

'It means, if you kill me in the line of duty, you have to pay Hannah's school fees,' Jack replied with a grin. Ridley appreciated the glibness of Jack's response. It lightened the moment. 'I guess, sir,' Jack added more seriously, 'it means that if Hannah's ever in trouble and feels that she can't come to her parents, we know that there's a safe pair of hands waiting for her in the wings.'

Ridley cleared his throat. 'I'd be honoured, Jack.'

Jack headed home to discuss the Cotswolds assignment with Maggie. Once Jack had gone, Ridley took out his mobile and opened his photo album. It was clear to see that he only had around ten photos stored, showing no private moments or special memories. But the last photo was from Maggie. It was an image of Hannah, fast asleep, on the day she was born. There was text accompanying the picture:

Hannah Penelope Warr. 15 May 2021. 6lb 4oz.

The corner of Ridley's mouth curled with a pride he'd never felt before. This precious baby was being entrusted to him, in the unlikely absence of her parents. Adrenaline started coursing around his body as he experienced a sensation that had been alien to him for years: he felt nervous.

CHAPTER 5

Jack watched Maggie from the lounge door as she breastfed Hannah. It seemed clear that sucking and breathing at the same time was impossible, so Hannah would noisily drag air in through her nose in between guzzles, while something sounded like it was gurgling at the back of her throat – milk? Phlegm? It sounded horrible. 'She's so noisy,' he said with a frown.

'She's this noisy at midnight, and 2 a.m., and 4 a.m. Doesn't seem to disturb you too much then,' Maggie replied. She said it gently, but Jack knew she was exhausted and couldn't help pointing out how easy Jack had it in comparison.

Maggie looked down at Hannah, their eyes met and they gazed at each other. Maggie had once told Jack that a newborn baby's eyesight was only clear between eight and twelve inches; beyond that everything was blurred. Eight to twelve inches was the distance between the faces of mother and baby when feeding, so nature had very purposefully designed a baby's vision to see Mum far more clearly than the rest of the world. As Jack watched Maggie interact with Hannah so naturally, despite himself his thoughts drifted to Trudie Nunn. Jack's inadequate birth-mother had clearly had none of the maternal instinct he was watching at work here. She'd walked away from him as a baby, leaving him with his Aunt Fran who, after months of struggling to look after him in addition to her own family, had finally handed Jack over to the fostering system. How fickle they must both have been to walk away from their own flesh and blood, he thought. And how incredibly special Charlie and Penny Warr had been, to love a baby that wasn't theirs.

'What are you grinning at?' Maggie's question broke into Jack's moment of reminiscing.

'I was thinking about Dad.'

There was such a soft, loving look in Jack's eyes that Maggie knew he was talking about Charlie Warr, not Harry Rawlins. Maggie held out her hand and Jack moved to her side. He leant in and kissed Hannah's forehead, then rested his own head on Maggie's shoulder. Hannah's eyes moved to Jack and explored his face with such intensity that it felt as though she was staring into his soul. Jack whispered to his daughter, 'I'm going to tell you all about your grandad when you're older. I hope I can be half the dad he was.' Maggie stroked Jack's hair as Hannah continued to take in every inch of his face. Then Hannah smiled and Jack gasped. 'Look, Mags. She smiled at me.' Maggie lovingly kissed Jack's head and decided not to tell him that Hannah had just farted on her knee.

* * *

DI Joseph Gifford was outside the police station, waiting for Jack's taxi to arrive. Parked behind him was a blue Vauxhall Corsa that had seen better days: this would be Jack's transport for the duration of his stay in the Cotswolds. This station was tiny compared to even the smallest of London nicks, and Jack's parking space had been stolen from a uniformed sergeant.

Gifford was a short, dumpy man, at least two inches shorter than Jack. His deep voice and rotund appearance gave him the look of an opera singer. He greeted Jack with a handshake that could crush bones, suggesting a streetwise toughness belied by Gifford's rather sheltered upbringing and uneventful rise up the ranks. 'Welcome, Jack. Good to have you on board.'

* * *

The station was a three-storey, characterless new-build forming an ugly blot on the beautiful Cotswold landscape. The inside was as dull as the outside, and the squad room looked like any other office. If it hadn't been for the evidence board displaying crime scene photos, it could easily have been mistaken for an estate agent's. Gifford led Jack to an empty desk near the window, so he could admire the view whilst ploughing through the huge pile of files and statements waiting for him. 'My office is over there,' Gifford said with a frown, pointing to a partitioned corner of the main room, which wasn't really an office at all.

'Oaks!' A young male officer promptly appeared at Gifford's side. 'DC William Oaks, DS Jack Warr from the Met. Oaks will show you round and answer any questions. He's been involved from the off, so he knows his stuff.' Then Gifford pulled his mobile from his pocket and headed to his office to read his messages.

'Drink?' Oaks asked, and, with that one word, Jack knew that Oaks did not want him there. Jack declined the drink and instead asked Oaks to sit and talk him through the case notes. Within minutes, Jack had made Oaks feel so important that the young DC was putty in his hands. Oaks's strong Gloucestershire roots gave him one of those accents that unfortunately made him sound like a yokel; but it was soon clear to Jack that he was as sharp as a tack and had a natural aptitude for the job. And Oaks also clearly cared about the work he did here. That's why he was initially hostile towards Jack, because he was embarrassed that they'd reached a dead end in the case. Jack knew that he'd do well to keep Oaks close, as he'd be far more acceptable to the local homeowners than a stranger from out of town. After an hour of learning, Jack knocked on Gifford's office door. 'If it's all right with you, sir, I'll settle into my digs, then have a look around.'

Oaks had driven less than half a mile down the road, when he pulled into a layby. His head was turned away from Jack. 'Sir . . .' he muttered in a shamefaced tone. Oaks plucked up the courage to look at Jack before continuing, 'I've booked you into a right shithole. Me and the lads thought it'd be funny, see. Well, not funny, just … I don't know. When the Guvnor said a DS from the Met was coming to help out, we … well, we thought you'd come in all bluff 'n' balls, bossing us about and treating us like we didn't know how to do the job. So, I booked you into a shithole.'

Jack wanted to laugh out loud at Oaks's naïve honesty, but instead kept a straight face. 'Why are you telling me?' he asked in the sternest tone he could muster.

''Cos, I changed my mind. This B&B we're heading for now is no way to welcome you.'

When Jack finally smiled, his entire face softened and his eyes glowed. Oaks knew immediately that he was forgiven. 'My cousin, Blair, runs The Fox Hunters in the centre of town. Lovely place. I'll take you there.'

Jack nodded happily. 'Let's go the scenic route, please, DC Oaks. I want to get a feel for the area.'

The Cotswolds were sprinkled with chocolate-box houses, hedged fields and a variety of roaming animals. 'Them hedges look easy to nick sheep over, right?' Oaks's upbeat tone when posing the question made it obvious that *them hedges* held a secret. 'From roadside, they're waist height, but on the field-side most have got a wide trench filled with brambles. No way you can get sheep out over that. I had to cut a tourist's dog out of a bramble trench once. He'd spotted the sheep, leapt the hedge and landed in, well, it's like barbed wire once you're in the middle of it. Poor thing had to be put down … should have been the owner who was put down, in my opinion.'

Everywhere Jack looked there were roads and pubs that gave a proud nod to their long-gone yesteryears – The Railway Tavern was no longer anywhere near a working railway, The Horse and Groom pub had converted its stables into a car park now filled with Land Rovers, and Jack was 100 per cent certain that Oaks's cousin who owned The Fox Hunters was not, in fact, a fox hunter.

All in all, old and new seemed to co-exist relatively neatly. Even old decommissioned red phone boxes had been reassigned and most now contained defibrillators – presumably to save the lives of overweight, city-dwelling ramblers when they succumbed to heart attacks after thinking that one week of healthy living in the fresh air could make up for fifty-one weeks of a sedentary lifestyle.

Jack noted that a lot of the villages and small towns tended to be served by one main road, meaning there was only one way in and out, so, unlike London burglars, the perpetrators here would not be able to escape like rats in a maze. Which prompted the question, why had Gifford and his team not caught them yet?

As Oaks turned the next corner, he was pulled up by temporary traffic lights. From the opposite direction, three lorries carrying farming equipment and supplies rumbled past, followed by a couple of horseboxes and a half dozen cars. 'Where's all of this traffic coming from and going to? How do you keep track of these bigger vehicles?' Jack asked. 'Do you recognise all of them?'

'Most,' Oaks answered. 'The riding schools have their logo on the side of their horseboxes, so they're easy to spot. The unbranded horseboxes belong to renters; I wouldn't know who's got them week to week. Horse shows bring thousands of outsiders in, of course; some rent boxes, some bring their own. And the lorries . . . some are transporting big equipment to and from local farms; some are European, passing through. We've seen dozens of local petitions asking us to force the lorries to go around, but we can't.'

Jack was intrigued by just how confusing this community actually was. There were so many people who didn't permanently belong. He speculated that a stranger would certainly be noticed, but also ignored, as they'd be assumed to be one of the numerous transients who pass through every week. Jack's view of the investigation had radically changed in a moment. Now he was thinking, *How on earth could Gifford and his team be expected to keep track of everyone?*

'Now I can see your big problem, Oaks,' he said thoughtfully. 'You live in a moveable community. Private renters with their own staff coming and going every week, famous faces taking a break from life, weekend wanderers, second homes, tourists, horse shows. Fuck me.' Oaks snorted out a laugh at Jack's profanity. 'These burglaries are quick and slick, right?' Jack continued as the lights finally turned green and Oaks pulled away.

'Yes, sir. I'd say they were targeted but, truth is, you could break into any of these out-of-the-way houses and you'd probably hit the jackpot. The gang definitely has electronics knowledge 'cos security systems and safes don't cause them any bother. We had one old fella last month, took him days to notice he'd even been robbed. They went straight for his collection of watches in the dressing table, see, and he never knew till he was getting ready for some golfing awards ceremony. He called his insurance company before he called us. The problem with that burglary, sir, and one of the reasons my guvnor called yours, was that the old fella reckons he must have been asleep in bed on the night they robbed him, 'cos he'd been ill with flu. They wouldn't have known that, and thankfully he was dosed up on Night Nurse, so didn't wake up. But it's only a matter of time before they bump into a homeowner, and I reckon they'd not think twice about killing someone. I mean, if you can stick a letter opener into the ear of old Jonty, you can kill a man ...' Oaks shook his head sadly. 'How does all that compare to your burglaries in Wimbledon, sir?'

'These are worse,' Jack said grimly. 'Because you're right, if this gang comes up against a homeowner, things could get out of hand very quickly.' Jack glanced at Oaks and noted the new worry on his face. 'But burglars always exhibit patterns of behaviour. What we need to do is find the pattern your guys are leaving behind. Then we can get ahead of them.'

The Fox Hunters was an old sandstone building with wonky walls and small, cross-hatched leaded windows that no longer fitted into their frames. In the reception area, the exposed stonework and wooden beams were tastefully maintained and minimally decorated . . . but in the bar, the homage to the past had gone into overdrive. The walls here were almost completely covered with sepia photos, horse brasses and tack, and old leather 'things' that Jack couldn't even begin to identify. But the deliberately antiquated feel of the place was in stark contrast to its current incumbent, the 20-year-old, much-tattooed Blair, who looked exactly like a pretty, feminine version of DC William Oaks.

Jack sat on a narrow, creaky bench to call Maggie whilst his new best mate booked him in. Maggie quickly answered, told him to FaceTime, then hung up.

Hannah's face filled the entire screen! 'Can you see her?' Maggie's voice was unnecessarily loud. 'Say hello to Daddy.' Jack looked around the bar. It was scattered with older men nursing pints and reading the newspaper whilst on a long lunch and they could hear Maggie as clearly as Jack could. 'Hello, Daddy. Talk to her, Jack. She knows your voice.'

'Mags,' Jack whispered, unsuccessfully trying to turn the volume down on his mobile, 'Mags, I'm not talking to the baby. I'm not . . . Mags, please.' Jack glanced up to see Oaks dipping under the doorframe and openly sniggering at him. 'I'm hanging up, Mags.'

* * *

Back at the station, Jack told Gifford that he'd like to start at the beginning by re-interviewing one of the very first victims, Maisie Fullworth, as she was their one and only eye-witness to any of the burglaries. Gifford shook his head. 'Can't. Maisie's a delicate girl and has a very overprotective mum. Currently, she's with her aunt in Swindon.' Jack's face showed little sympathy. He accepted that Maisie was only 15 at the time of the burglary, and it would have undoubtedly been traumatic to wake and find a man standing in her bedroom. But that was back in 2018. 'This is a perfect example of what we're up against, Jack,' Gifford explained. 'Mrs Fullworth is a high court judge in Oxford. If she says we can't interview Maisie, then we can't interview Maisie. Her statement's here, but that's all you'll be getting. Oaks!'

Oaks interpreted the booming of his name as an instruction to relay Maisie's statement.

'Maisie was woken at 2 a.m. by a noise that she said sounded like someone standing on the creaky floorboard just outside her bedroom. She sat up in bed and, in the mirror of her open wardrobe door, she saw the outline of a man. From the description, which wasn't bad actually for a scared young girl, he was of medium build and over six feet tall. She guessed his height based on looking at me. He got away with a diamond engagement ring and £500 in cash.'

Gifford looked over Jack's shoulder at his small team of six men and women. Jack followed his gaze. 'Why don't you introduce me before curiosity kills them?'

In the squad room they sat low in their seats, arms folded, ready to be told how to do their jobs by 'the man from the Met'. But Jack's opening words instantly threw them off-balance. 'Thank you for welcoming me to your patch. Don't get me wrong, I'm the one in charge now and I'll lead from the front until this gang is behind bars. But I recognise that I'm coming to this case with all of the excellent groundwork already done. So, thank you.' Then Jack went in for the kill. 'This gang *will not* move on and disappear for good. They *will not* escalate to murder, which I know is your biggest concern. We *will* get them. And you *will* have your moment.'

A hand reached out for Jack's. 'Thank you, sir. It's good to have you here.' Oaks spoke with all the maturity of a seasoned detective constable. Jack took his hand and, with that single act, he was accepted into the Chipping Norton team.

CHAPTER 6

The next morning, half of Jack's new team were at their desks wading through all of the evidence, specifically looking for people or vehicles present in the vicinity of all of the burglaries, while the other half were out taking fresh statements and asking all known burglary victims if they knew of anyone else who'd been targeted and not actually reported it.

The pinging of Gifford's mobile could be heard two seconds before he himself appeared in the squad room carrying a mixture of hot and cold breakfasts for everyone. He was clearly surprised to see only three of his officers at their desks. 'The others are re-interviewing, sir,' Jack explained quickly. He knew Gifford would be unhappy that this order had been given without being run past him first. 'We know that some burglaries have not actually been reported and that's no use to us. We need the whole picture, so we can see the pattern – if there is one. We'll get nowhere by being reactive; we must be proactive. And any pissing off of bigwigs we do now will be forgotten once we catch this gang.'

Without replying, Gifford handed the hot breakfasts to those of his officers who were present and put the cold breakfasts on the desks of those who were out and about. He was giving himself time to consider Jack's rather insubordinate first order of the day.

'They have gone plainclothes, sir,' Oaks added once the silence got too much for him. 'So, they shouldn't get too many curtains twitching.'

Gifford had no choice but to go along with the decision for now. 'Well . . . we'd better have something to show for it by the time the complaints hit the DCI's desk.'

'We will.' Jack took a deep breath before delivering his next sentence. Gifford's response would tell him whether this case was winnable or not. 'Oaks and I are on our way to re-interview Maisie Fullworth.'

Gifford slammed the tray of drinks down on the nearest desk.

Jack was prepared for this reaction and he already knew what he was going to say. 'I won't work with one hand tied behind my back, sir. Mrs Fullworth does not know what's best for this community – we do. The fact that she can't see it is not my problem.'

Gifford pursed his lips, stuck out his chin and nodded. Then he took his perpetually pinging mobile out of his pocket, went into his office and shut the door. As the disgruntled DI sat down at his desk to read his messages, Jack saw right through the fat man's suddenly very transparent façade. Gifford was not a leader, but a follower in disguise. Jack would be gentler with him from now on – not out of pity or guilt, but because he knew that there was no need to be pushy with a man who wasn't going to push back.

*   *   *

Mrs Fullworth wasn't happy to see the police on her doorstep again and made it very clear from the outset by not stopping what she was doing. She moved around the kitchen, sweeping zig-zag-shaped chunks of mud into the corner nearest the back door. 'I tell Mr Fullworth to kick the step before he comes in, so that his boots drop their mud outside, but he always forgets.' Then, almost without taking a breath, she began recapping how incredibly cooperative she'd been so far. 'You have the contact details for all staff – the pool maintenance chap has died since then, so you can strike him from your list. You have the insurance details for the £2,000 ring – that payment took several months to arrive with me, now there's a crime for you. Not that the ring can be replaced. That's the crux of it all with a robbery, isn't it? It's so bloody personal. What else, oh yes, the cash; well, I'll not see that again. Never mind. It was only £500 for housekeeping and the like—'

'Mrs Fullworth,' Jack interrupted. 'When is Maisie back with you?' Jack knew it was important for him to gain control of the conversation. So far, Mrs Fullworth had not stopped talking, in an endeavour to assert her authority, and although Jack could see it working with Oaks, it definitely wasn't going to wash with him.

'My daughter . . .' Mrs Fullworth emphasised her words to indicate her ownership over Maisie. 'My daughter has suffered with anorexia for much of her teenage life, but since the burglary, it's got worse. She is currently with her aunt, my sister, Lisa, in Swindon. Lisa is an art therapist. Maisie's going through a rough patch and it helps her to be away from here. Away from all of the traumatic memories.' Jack asked again when Maisie was due to return, but was told that it would be open-ended. 'Healing has its own timeframe.'

'Unfortunately, Mrs Fullworth,' Jack replied firmly, 'we also have a timeframe. These burglars are working their way through your community, your friends. They're making fools of us.' Mrs Fullworth's eyes narrowed and her knuckles turned white as she squeezed the handle of the broom. 'They know you value your privacy as highly as your possessions, and so they force you to choose.' Jack took a step towards her, getting closer than she was comfortable with, so he could see that she wasn't arrogant at all. She was scared. Now he knew what to say. He promised to give her the one thing he knew she'd genuinely lost. 'My intention is to take control away from them and give it back to you. Your daughter can return to her home, unafraid. Do you have a first name I could use, Mrs Fullworth?'

Within seconds of Mrs Fullworth blushing like a schoolgirl and announcing that her first name was Eloise – 'you can call me Elli' – she'd revealed the guilt she felt for having been at her weekly bridge game at the time of the burglary. She and several female friends met every Tuesday and on this particular night, Maisie had been home due to her school's mid-term break. Elli had still gone out, because it was her one night off and she worked so hard the rest of the week. So Maisie had been left home alone, to be confronted by a man in her bedroom. Elli had almost cried at the thought of what could have happened to her little girl on that horrible, terrifying night. As a family, she was thankful they had got off very lightly.

Oaks couldn't stop grinning as they walked back to the car. 'Sirrr!' he laughed in his West Country burr. 'That was fucking awesome.'

Jack leant against the passenger door of the car and looked out over the endless chequerboard of fields. Oaks, oblivious, got into the car and started the engine. Then he stopped the engine and got out again, unsure as to why Jack had paused. 'Never stop looking at this,' Jack said, looking towards the horizon. 'I was brought up somewhere similar to this, but my daughter will grow up in London. It's an amazing city, but, shit . . .' He spread his arms. 'Look at this.' Oaks's brow furrowed as he desperately tried to see what Jack was seeing. 'You have to understand what Mrs Fullworth values, in order to get her to do what you want.'

'So, we're manipulating her?'

'Of course. As long it's for the right motive, it's fine. This . . .' Jack looked to the horizon again. 'This is where Elli's anger and fear comes from; from losing this. Losing it to scum. This countryside is Maisie's. How dare anyone take it from her? Maisie's in fucking Swindon. Have you ever been to Swindon?'

The furrow on Oaks's brow disappeared and his eyes opened wide. He got it. Then Oaks's mobile rang and he stepped away to answer it.

Jack took this moment to take a snap of the view and text it to Maggie. She immediately texted back.

Wish we were with you xxx.

'Sir,' Oaks cut in. 'Charlotte Miles owns a plant nursery and gardening business just outside Churchill. It's in the grounds of a smallholding – pigs, chickens, ducks, goats, that sort of thing. She has two vehicles: a van for delivering veg and plants, and an old pickup for the garden maintenance side of things. Between those two jobs, she works for most people round here. Either her van or her pickup was at each of the properties, a couple of nights before it was burgled.'

Although Oaks was telling Jack that they'd found a common denominator, he wasn't confident that Charlotte was *the* common denominator. Oaks explained how she had already been interviewed and eliminated as she had a solid alibi for each burglary. 'And besides, sir, Charlotte definitely isn't a six-foot-plus bloke,' Oaks added.

Jack pointed out that, although he agreed Charlotte could not be involved in the burglaries themselves, she could still be a scout of some kind, potentially recce'ing properties before they were hit. Oaks was doubtful. 'Well, yeah, she could. But then, so could John – he's our postman. And so could June – she's our 50-odd-year-old paper girl. And so could . . .' Jack walked away. He didn't want to listen to Oaks listing everyone who visited houses on a weekly, if not daily basis.

*   *   *

Ridley stood erect and motionless in the witness box, arms behind his back. His suit jacket hung perfectly off his shoulders and you could hardly see him breathing. His face was unreadable as he listened to every syllable of every word of every question the defence lawyer asked. And whilst Ridley was thinking of how to answer, his eyes did not move around to suggest a faulty memory or any kind of elaboration. He was statuesque. DS Laura Wade couldn't take her eyes off him.

Once she realised she was staring, she began to blush. *Jesus Christ!* she thought to herself. *Ridley looks as hot as hell up there!*

Ridley wasn't Laura's type at all. Jack was her type. She and Jack had been partners for just over a year and she'd fancied the pants off him for every second of that time – his dark, bohemian looks and effortlessly rugged appearance made her heart beat faster whenever she saw him. Laura had hoped this feeling would abate once Maggie became pregnant, but it didn't; she just became better at hiding it.

Ridley, in contrast to Jack, was skinny and boring. But seeing him so composed and convincing in the witness box made her realise just how smart he was. Laura had never before found 'smart' attractive, but maybe she was maturing, she thought.

She found herself defending Ridley against her own preconceptions: in her mind, she replaced 'skinny' with 'athletic'. 'Boring' with 'smart', and suddenly . . . Ridley was a catch!

The judge's gavel came down and Laura's dream bubble burst. Ridley stepped down from the witness box and Laura followed him out into the courthouse corridor as he took a call on his mobile. He smiled at Laura, indicating that he'd be with her in a minute. 'Trust me,' Ridley said into his mobile, 'DS Warr never dismisses anyone until he's 100 per cent certain that they're not involved. Let him backtrack. Let him double-check. Go with him, Joe, or you'll regret it.'

Once he'd hung up, Ridley headed for Laura, seated alone on the corridor bench.

'You look nervous, Laura. There's no need. Be concise, be confident. We've got this.'

A thought popped into her mind – an old conversation she and Jack had had months ago whilst taking the piss out of the fact that Ridley prepared for every case and every raid so slowly and then delivered so quickly. Laura had made a flippant comment back then: 'Do you think he's like this in the bedroom? Prepping at the speed of a tortoise and delivering at the speed of a train!' But now the joke had morphed into an exciting image that Laura couldn't get out of her head. Her name was called by the Court Clerk – she was next to take the witness stand. Ridley threw her an encouraging smile. 'Just focus. Don't be distracted by anything.'

Yeah, right! she thought.

* * *

Charlotte Miles's property was exactly as Jack had imagined. The fence marking the perimeter was high and solid to protect the free-roaming sheep, ducks and chickens, but the inside fences were makeshift. The pigpen's structure was a mix of recycled wooden and metal gates from other areas of the smallholding, strapped together with wire; this was home to three very large pigs. And the extensive veg and fruit fields were protected by chicken wire and plastic zip ties. In what must have once been the back garden, greenhouses were filled to bursting with plants that grew out of the tiny gaps between the glass and its frame, and beyond that there was a stunning orchard boasting lemon, apple and pear trees.

The exterior of the house was shabby and weather-worn, with windows so dirty they were impossible to see through. Oaks knocked on the equally dirty door.

A woman in her thirties opened it. She was slender and pretty with long, messy hair tied in a knot hanging between her shoulder blades. She wore a vest top and dungarees cut low at the side, so they revealed the top of her hips. On her feet, she wore thick green knitted socks, designed to fit snugly into the Hunter wellington boots behind the door.

'Hi, Annie. This is Annie Summers,' Oaks announced. 'Annie, this is DS Jack Warr from the Met in London.' As Annie smiled and stepped back to allow them in, Oaks added quietly, 'Take your shoes off, sir.' It was only now that Jack caught sight of his once-black brogues, thick with what he hoped was only mud. Oaks, on the other hand, was wearing brown boots with soles so thick that the leather uppers were hardly dirty at all.

Beyond the muddy porch, the outwardly mucky farmhouse was immaculate. Dark wooden ceiling beams split the large reception room into lounge, dining area and kitchen. The lounge was cosy, with plush cream carpets and modern furniture complete with numerous cats scattered about the place, while the dining area and kitchen were more like a typical farmhouse with an Aga, hanging pans and heavy terracotta floor tiles.

Oaks told Annie that they were here to see Charlotte; they did try to call ahead but received no reply.

'Lotte's useless with her mobile,' said with a smile. 'She's with the horses, so it'll be on top of a hay bale somewhere. She won't even know it's not in her pocket.' As Annie spoke, she texted. This was quickly followed by an electronic whistle from somewhere near the kitchen windowsill. Annie headed for a flowerpot by the side of the sink, and there was Charlotte's mobile. 'See! Didn't even make it out of the house. Do you want me to take you over, Will, or can you make your own way?'

Oaks assured Annie that he'd be able to escort Jack to the stables, no problem.

Once they had their shoes back on, Jack asked how well Oaks knew the two women, seeing as Annie referred to him by his first name. Oaks reiterated what Jack already knew – that everybody knew everybody round here and things could get incredibly messy if they discovered that one of their own was in league with the burglars.

Around the back of the farmhouse, not visible from the road, were two stable blocks with space for four horses in each. One block was currently full, the other empty and being used as storage for animal feed and the equipment that Charlotte used for her gardening business. As Jack and Oaks approached, Charlotte was guiding the four horses into a neighbouring field. They raced excitedly into the open green space where they bucked and kicked, before settling to feed on the fresh grass.

Charlotte was a bigger woman than Annie, but not fat; she looked strong and athletic from working the land and tending animals. She had thick curly brown hair tied back with a yellow ribbon, similar dungarees and Hunter boots to Annie's and a longer T-shirt underneath that hid her midriff. A large red checked shirt finished the look, and Jack would have assumed by its size that it belonged to the man of the house, if he hadn't already been told by Oaks that Annie and Charlotte were a couple. Once the horses were in the field and the gate securely fastened, Charlotte started searching her pockets in vain for something that clearly wasn't there.

'It's in the kitchen, Charlotte!' Oaks shouted, so she turned to face them.

Charlotte had the lightest blue eyes, framed by long black lashes. Her petite nose and big lips made her face effortlessly pretty, although not beautiful in the truest sense of the word. She was riveting to look at. Oaks introduced Jack, and Charlotte asked if they minded her continuing to work whilst they talked. This simple gesture of courtesy immediately set her aside from the likes of Mrs Fullworth – Charlotte was naturally confident, and so could also be polite without fear of seeming submissive. She did not need to assert her position with anyone. Charlotte disappeared into one of the stables and reappeared carrying a pair of men's wellingtons. She handed them to Jack – 'They were my father's once upon a time.' Now Jack knew the owner of the oversized shirt.

Jack propped himself against a tractor tyre, swapping his ruined shoes for a dead man's wellies, and watched Charlotte stride back and forth stocking up the feed for when her horses returned to their stables, clearly not fazed by having two police officers in her stable yard. She then collected two bridles and headed for the field where the four horses she'd just let out were enjoying the freedom of the open land.

'Watch this.' She grinned with pride as she raised her hand and let out a soft whistle. A big dapple-grey mare pricked up her large ears and galloped towards them. The grey stopped right in front of Charlotte and lowered her head to allow the bridle to be slipped into place. 'Have you missed me, Florrie? She has the sweetest temperament. Perfect for children. She's going to spend a couple of hours helping out at the riding school later today, because one of theirs has gone lame.'

Jack found himself in awe of the relationship Charlotte clearly had with Florrie, seeing this animal, standing head and shoulders above Charlotte, doing as she was asked out of something other than ownership or duty. It seemed to him that the horse respected, trusted, maybe even loved Charlotte. Jack found it inspiring to watch. She then took the second bridle, climbed the gate and ventured into the field. At the far end, a chestnut brown beast of a horse grazed on his own. Charlotte raised her arm high in the air and kept it there until she had his attention. Once he'd seen her, she made a swift gesture to come forwards. The chestnut reared up for a second, like a bucking bronco, then galloped towards her at a frightening speed.

Even from the safe side of the gate, Jack could feel the ground shuddering underfoot. Charlotte gave Jack a glance over her shoulder. 'He's showing off.' The chestnut raced past her, looped, circled and eventually came to rest by her shoulder, head held high. 'He's a mustang. A rescue from some prat from the US who brought him over here and then couldn't train him. They gelded him, but that didn't help. They saw him as no practical use to anyone, so they neglected him. I saw him in their field as I was passing one day and – my God – he was magnificent. Underweight and unkempt, but still magnificent. See how he's not giving me his head?'

This mustang stood far taller than the grey, towering over Charlotte. Then his head turned and his dark, frightened eyes focussed on Jack. He let out a jet of hot air from his nostrils that blew loose hair across Charlotte's forehead. She looked up and whispered, 'Judas.' The mustang lowered his head and allowed her to put on his bridle. That's all it took. The right word, at the right moment.

'Do you know what a Judas Horse is?' Charlotte asked as she buckled the bridle into place. 'When the wild mustangs are running free, you corral one and train it. It can take weeks, even months, but when he's ready, you can release him and he'll bring his team back into the corral like Judas betraying them.' Charlotte looked thoughtfully at Judas. 'We're waiting for the vet to come and give him his regular medical. He's not yet as strong as he should be. But he's getting there. Shall we go for some tea? Annie will have the kettle on.'

In the kitchen, Annie did indeed have tea on the go. Hunks of white bread were roughly cut and laid out waiting to be smothered in homemade jam or honey. Jack declined, but Oaks tucked in. 'Annie makes the most amazing bread,' he said, cramming in a huge mouthful.

Once the niceties were done, Jack asked Charlotte about Eloise Fullworth.

'Mrs Fullworth is one of my clients.' Charlotte was candid about how well she knew the family. She answered quickly, without pausing, which suggested she wasn't thinking about what might be the best thing to say. This told Jack that she probably had nothing to hide. 'I do her garden; keep it tidy, that sort of thing. I change plants I think need changing, trim what I think needs trimming; she lets me decide. I do one afternoon a week for her. Tuesdays normally, but that can shift depending on when Maisie's home. When Maisie's there, it's their time. Mrs Fullworth is very protective.' When Jack asked what Maisie was like, Charlotte suggested that she was probably much stronger than her mother gave her credit for.

Jack went on to ask more generally about Charlotte's clients. 'I meet the staff at residential properties,' she explained. 'But the rentals tend to bring their own people with them, and they rarely use me as they don't stay long enough. The full-time staff are often Eastern European. Lovely. Well, I like them. Not that I'd be able to spot a wrong-un if they were standing in front of me, I don't suppose. I can spot a bad horse from a good one a mile away, but people . . . I'm sorry but I'm not much use to you, DI Warr.'

*　　*　　*

Back in the squad room at Chipping Norton, all six of Gifford's officers were now at their desks, eating the cold breakfasts they'd been bought hours earlier. One of the men who'd been out and about re-questioning victims had brought back a Tupperware box full of scones from old Mr and Mrs Gaddas. He'd also been provided with a jar of jam and a tub of clotted cream. Mrs Gaddas was housebound due to illness, but she was still able-bodied and loved baking for visitors.

Jack respectfully popped into Gifford's office to update him, before the rest of the team. But Gifford was not in the mood for pleasantries. 'I've been on to DCI Ridley,' Gifford said as if this would knock Jack off-balance. Jack reckoned Gifford must have complained about Jack double-checking all of his hard work, but he knew Ridley would have politely but firmly put him straight. 'You better not be dragging your feet now you've started this messy little ball rolling,' Gifford continued. 'Remember what I said about getting answers before the complaints start hitting the DCI's desk.'

'Elli – Mrs Fullworth won't be complaining, sir. I can assure you of that.' Jack left it at that and headed for his team. Jack had 'accidently' used Mrs Fullworth's first name, so that Gifford knew the kind of relationship Jack had been able to establish in just one ten-minute visit.

In the squad room, Jack asked each officer in turn to introduce themselves, and then share any relevant discoveries. As this began, Jack sat his desk, got out a brand new pair of brown boots, just like Oaks's, and swapped them for the muddy shoes he was currently wearing. He then binned the shoes.

His team were brimming with a new enthusiasm, stemming from a couple of pieces of additional information that had been uncovered. As people spoke, Oaks wrote everything on the evidence board: four more burglaries had now been unofficially reported, with no one wanting their house to be treated like a crime scene at this late stage. They'd moved on and would not be dragged back. But the dates, times, methods of entry and items taken were all new and potentially important information.

Most re-interviewed burglary victims had put their ordeals behind them, upped their security, claimed on their insurance and got on with their lives. Although this made little sense to Jack, he understood that it was all relative – losing £50,000 of insured property here would be like him having his bike nicked.

Within the hour, the whiteboard was full and a second had been borrowed from another department. They now had a comprehensive list of all properties that owned updated security systems, new CCTV, guard dogs and, in some cases, security guards.

Oaks walked backwards away from the evidence boards, until he was in his newly adopted position right by Jack's side. Jack immediately noticed that he was now a good half inch taller in his new boots, which he liked the feel of. That morning, Oaks had been a fraction taller than him; now they were the same height. Jack was average, just shy of 5'10", but in this job, he knew he was considered to be on the short side.

They still had no prints, no damage for the sake of it and no alarm systems tripped. What they did have was one dead dog and a sick old man who was in bed during his break-in.

'It's my belief,' Jack started, 'that this gang is getting inside information from someone you all know and have probably already interviewed. I want a calendar on this whiteboard showing all upcoming social events – golf tournaments, harvest festivals, school plays, walking groups, theatre groups, bridge nights – let's see if we can predict when they might hit next.'

Oaks immediately picked up the whiteboard pen and got to work, and soon everyone was chipping in. It turned out the social calendar for residents in and around Chipping Norton was a busy one. Most residents were out more than they were in, which was a boon for burglars.

But Jack's biggest problem came from those property owners who still wouldn't give up the names of the famous people renting at the time of a burglary. It meant that apart from the unfortunate Maisie, there were no witnesses at all.

As Oaks filled up the whiteboard, one thing was abundantly clear: this gang was bold, because they came prepared with transport big enough to cart away antique furniture and paintings; they weren't restricting themselves to easier, smaller items such as jewellery and cash. And they hadn't been caught in more than three years of activity, meaning every one of them was a professional. Except, that is, for the person caught creeping up Maisie's stairs. This discrepancy was bugging Jack.

Were the people who stuck a knife into the ear of a dog the same people who ran when a teenage girl spotted them in the mirror of her wardrobe door? And, perhaps more to the point, were the people who had never once been caught on camera, or left a single fingerprint, the same people who allowed Maisie to spot them so carelessly? Jack was beginning to think that Maisie's burglar was someone else entirely.

CHAPTER 7

Gifford's team was pleasantly surprised to see Jack mucking in with the laborious background research connected to this case.

'Nothing's irrelevant,' Jack had told them. 'If it's in this room, we need it. We might not know why yet, but we do need it.'

Barbara from the canteen was under orders from Gifford to keep his team and his guest topped up, so a steady stream of pastries and hot drinks were brought up every couple of hours. Within a few days of arriving, Jack could tell whether Barbara was having a quiet day or not, depending on the variety of homemade biscuits and pastries. Jack sometimes thought she looked like a gnarly old witch, but her baking was fabulous, and her tea was to die for. She was also a mine of information.

Barbara walked into the squad room just as Jack and Oaks were discussing Charlotte and Annie's financial situation. The two women were still of interest based on Charlotte being in the employ of all the burglary victims – but it was a tenuous link at best, seeing as Charlotte was also in the employ of half the station. Most of her customers had not been burgled, so she was looking more and more like a stray statistic that would come to nothing.

Four years earlier, Annie's father had passed away and left her £200,000. Their smallholding had been mortgaged to the hilt, so this money rescued them at exactly the right moment. They paid off the mortgage and were now living a much more comfortable life. Charlotte's earnings peaked at around the £30,000 mark; most of that came from the gardening work, with a little extra from produce sales, but nothing life-changing. Charlotte sold fresh fruit and veg direct to her gardening clients and Annie sold the rest at a farmer's market each Saturday morning. They also both had part-time work at the Soho Farmhouse, a 100-acre luxury retreat in the Oxfordshire countryside.

Their bank balance fluctuated seasonally, which made sense to Jack, and currently it was low – but a cash amount of almost £2,000 had gone out just three weeks ago and this was an anomaly. Jack had just instructed Oaks to find out what that money was for when Barbara chipped in, 'That's her new mower. Big green thing it is. Noisy as hell. Got it second-hand for £1,800 from James Somerset. She gets a bargain and he gets free mowing for the rest of his life. Not that that'll be long. He's got cancer of the pancreas . . .' Jack had stopped listening just after Barbara said that Charlotte had bought a new mower for £1,800, which Jack thought was good, because he liked them and didn't want them to become persons of interest.

By early evening, Oaks and Jack were the only ones left. Oaks watched Jack's silhouette as he paced up and down the wall of windows, the rolling hills beyond reddening under the setting sun. 'Maisie's burglary is confusing us,' Jack finally said. 'It's not the same. It's clumsy, amateurish. I know real criminals, and the man who allowed himself to be seen by a teenager was not a real criminal.' Oaks listened intently. He'd learnt so much from Jack already about how to read people and events properly. 'Oaks, find out if Maisie can come back. If she can't . . . we'll go to Swindon and interview her there. I'm popping to London tomorrow, but I'll be back the day after.'

Then Jack said goodnight and headed to his B&B.

* * *

Jack returned to London with an empty suitcase and a list of items he needed to bring back with him – top of which were his wellies. He called Maggie from the M40 to ask if she needed anything bringing home for tea – but in truth, he was checking to see whether any stray pregnant couples had been invited over to eat his food and drink his beer. Maggie confirmed that not only were her friends not going to interrupt their evening, but Penny was also out with a friend she'd met at her needlecraft class. Jack ended the call by saying that he'd bring home a takeaway and a bottle of wine – so Maggie was under orders to express enough milk to get Hannah through the night, because this evening she was going to learn how to drink again. He'd be with her by seven.

Jack could have been home by five, but he wanted to detour via the station to catch up with Ridley.

'How's it going over there?' Ridley asked when Jack walked into his office, though he already knew the answer. Gifford had called him the second Jack left for London and bent his ear – again – about the dangers of ruffling delicate feathers.

'The gaps between burglaries is interesting, sir.' As Jack spoke, Ridley invited him to sit and then set about making two mugs of tea. 'These guys were in no rush, doing an average of one or two burglaries every couple of months; then all of a sudden they're doing one every two weeks. Gifford was getting nowhere fast due to the lack of a pattern, lack of MO, lack of resources. But I think he's right to assume that this gang is working up to something big before disappearing for good.'

From the squad room, her chin resting in the palm of one hand, Laura faced her computer screen, but her eyes were definitely looking at Ridley. Anik could feel the jealousy rising in his chest and burning in his face. It wasn't pure jealousy, because he didn't fancy Laura; it stemmed from being overlooked in general. Anik wheeled his chair across to Laura and stopped at her shoulder, making her jump. He spoke in a spiteful whisper. 'You don't always have to fancy someone from this squad room, you know.' Laura looked him dead in the eyes and told him to fuck off. Which he did.

Twenty minutes later, Anik watched Jack stand, shake Ridley's hand and head for the office door. Jack paused when Ridley said something, the men smiled, shared a private joke and then Jack left, giving a general wave and a 'Night all' to the squad room.

'What a prick,' Anik mumbled under his breath.

* * *

Jack arrived home bang on seven, as promised. The plates were in the oven, the wine glasses were out and two bottles of breast milk were in the fridge door. Maggie was sitting cross-legged on the floor of the lounge, surrounded by christening paraphernalia – even though it wasn't going to be a proper christening. Propped on the coffee table was an iPad showing Hannah on her nursery camera, sleeping in her cot.

Jack sat on the floor next to Maggie and laid the takeaway out on the coffee table for her to help herself. Maggie had become an eclectic eater since Hannah arrived – she'd learnt to eat on the run, grabbing bites of this and that as she ran from the washing machine to the dishwasher to the steriliser. Jack had ordered his usual chicken madras with steamed rice, while Maggie had gone for several starters that she could pick at.

Maggie swept the invitations, guest list, car list, booking confirmation, food confirmation and gift receipts to one side, so as not to get any of her hard work stained with curry sauce and Jack stared at it all in trepidation. Considering this wasn't even a proper christening, there seemed to be a hell of a lot of prep to be done.

Through the onion bhajis, lamb samosas and kakori kebabs, Maggie never stopped talking. Such overt excitement was very unlike her and Jack wondered whether lack of sleep might be sending her a little manic. Then he spotted that she was drinking at her pre-pregnancy pace, which, after nine months sober, probably wasn't a good idea.

He listened to his beautiful, exhausted, drunk wife and tried not to laugh. 'The hotel in Richmond is booked, we got a discount on that so actually it's the same price as the hall down the road. They said there's no untoward reason, just a promotional thing. Anyway, it's done now. There'll be four babies and three kids there, so I've got them all gifts. Just a little something. Penny's getting there in Mario's car. The only thing left to sort is, I want some of those disposable cameras, so guests can just snap away.' Jack didn't express his curiosity about the price and instead smiled at Maggie's unbridled enthusiasm.

When Maggie asked what he was smiling at, his next words came without having to think about them. 'I'm happy, that's all.' The tears immediately welled in Maggie's eyes. Jack put his food down and crawled across the carpet towards her. He wrapped her in his arms and held her head to his chest. She put her arm around his waist and gripped his shirt, screwing it tightly in her fist.

'You OK?' Jack whispered.

Maggie slid one leg across his thighs and sat on his lap. Her smile told him that nothing was wrong and that these were happy tears. When she kissed him it wasn't passionate, but slow and loving. Her hands explored him, as though rediscovering every curve. Jack didn't touch Maggie, he simply enjoyed being touched by her. It had been so long.

As her hands slid down his torso and began unbuttoning his trousers, Hannah stirred. They froze and looked at the iPad, holding their breath. It took a second for the crying to begin.

Jack kissed Maggie and told her to 'hold that thought'. He grabbed a bottle of breast milk from the fridge, blitzed it in the microwave and headed upstairs.

Maggie sat sideways on her hip, head resting on the sofa's seat cushion and watched the grainy, black-and-white image of Jack feeding Hannah. In less than three minutes, Hannah was asleep in his arms. Maggie watched him put the bottle down, run his finger over the contours of his daughter's face, down the bridge of her tiny nose, across her chin, and gently over her closed eyes. He put his finger in her hand and she closed her tiny fist. Jack stayed with Hannah for another ten minutes, just looking at her face and listening to her breathe.

As he walked back downstairs, he imagined Maggie would by now be comatose on the sofa. In fact, she was still on the floor, with her head on the seat cushion. Fast asleep. Jack sat back down on the floor and finished his now-cold chicken madras.

* * *

Back in the Cotswolds, George and Sally Barrowman's house was dark apart from the hallway light, which suggested an empty home pretending to be occupied. Security lights flicked on and off, as foxes moved freely through the extensive grounds. The garden was rustic and rambling compared to its neighbours, but that's how the Barrowmans liked it – the idea of wildlife sharing their habitat was important to their son, Mathew, so they had purposefully asked Charlotte to use plants that would naturally come and go with the seasons, with little intervention. This four-acre garden was home to mice, foxes, hedgehogs and an unknown number of bird species. It was a beautiful space.

Around the back of the property, there was a swimming pool housed in a glass conservatory and an area for playing various outdoor games such as football, basketball and putting. When George had got this part of the garden levelled and turfed, it was his honest intention to play sports with his son, but this had never quite worked out. Mathew's autism meant that while as a very young boy football occupied his every waking minute, once he reached the age of eight or nine, his obsession became chess, and by the time he was in his late teens, things had changed again to fantasy and science fiction. Since then, Mathew focussed on the comings and goings of TV shows, such as *Dr Who* and, more recently, *Game of Thrones*.

The Barrowmans' next-door neighbour, Essie Blaketon, was walking her four Jack Russells past the Barrowmans' home, when her attention was caught by the fact that the electronic driveway gate was wide open and, more disturbingly, there was movement coming from the overgrown garden – and she knew it wasn't foxes because they always made her dogs bark like crazy until they'd walked beyond the Barrowmans' boundary. This time, her dogs did not bark at all. Essie paused and she gave her eyes a couple of seconds to adjust to the darkness away from the streetlights – then she saw it. A man was in the bushes of the Barrowmans' garden. Essie got out her mobile and was just about to dial 999, when the figure emerged and started to sprint in her direction. Once he was out in the open, she could immediately see that it was Mathew – his height and frame were distinctive and, when he moved quickly, the top half of his body seemed to get ahead of the bottom half. When he used to play football day and night, he always ran like he'd tripped over something and was about to fall flat on his face. Mathew stopped and turned and changed direction, as though he simply couldn't decide on where he should be heading. He was crying, clearly distressed and confused. Essie immediately texted Sally.

George and Sally were less than ten miles away at the local golf club, hosting their annual charity auction to raise funds for St Barnabas's, in Gloucester, the special school that their son had attended until he was 16. George was on stage, talking up the sale of a vintage SylvaC collection, when he happened to glance down at his wife, who was standing by the edge of the stage supervising the order of the lots. Her face was lit well enough by the light of her mobile phone for him to see that she was ashen. Within minutes, George and Sally were driving home.

'We should never have left him on his own!' Sally cried.

'What else could we have done, Sal?' her husband countered. 'He refused to come, and when he gets like that, there's no shifting him. Tonight was an annual commitment. Once a bloody year! He picks his moments, I'll give him that.'

Sally's mobile pinged and another text came through from Essie: Mathew was still circling the garden and was still incredibly distressed about something. George and Sally knew that Essie wouldn't approach Mathew; she was unsure of him at the best of times. But she'd not leave him on his own either. Mathew was rarely aggressive but when he was, it was terrifying; and as an 18-stone, 26-year-old man, he could be hard to deal with. Another text:

Mathew's come out onto the road and someone's called the police!

It was another seven worrying minutes before George and Sally pulled up next to a patrol car parked across both lanes of the narrow road outside their home. Sergeant Fiona McDermott held up her hand and made a turning motion with her arm, telling them to go back the way they'd come. George and Sally got out of the car and raced to the blockade. 'Oh, it's you, Mr Barrowman. Thank goodness for that. I've not seen Mathew like this in years.'

In the distance, George could see a second police car blocking the road at the opposite end and, right in the middle, Mathew was pacing back and forth, shoeless, with his hands pressed tight over his ears. 'I can't get him to move off the road.' McDermott's tone was concerned but kindly. 'If you could get him back into the garden and close the gates, that'd be perfect. Then I'll need to talk to you.'

George called Mathew's name as he approached and he immediately stopped pacing and lowered his hands. 'Come on, lad,' George said. 'Let's go home.'

Mathew's voice quivered as he spoke. 'No, thank you, Dad. No, thank you. I'm not going home. The police can go away now. I'm OK here.'

'They're here because you're in the middle of the road. If you want them to go away, then you have to come home with Mum and me. You can't be on the road, Mathew. It's dangerous.'

Mathew strode towards the open gates, faltered as he got closer, then continued into the grounds of his home. George and Sally followed him, and three police officers on foot followed them. George clicked the button on his car keyring and the gates began to close. At the same time, from the darkness of the road, the police cars could be heard pulling out of the way and the traffic began to move again.

Mathew turned at the sound of the gate closing and, for reasons unknown to everyone but himself, his anxiety levels soared. He headed quickly back towards the road, in a race against the closing gate.

'Matty, what's wrong?' Sally shouted. 'Calm down, darling, calm down! I'll make you a hot chocolate.' But not even the promise of his favourite drink was going to stop him from trying to escape.

Sergeant McDermott held up her hand, palm towards Mathew and shouted 'Stop!' but he wasn't listening. Driven by an inexplicable fear, Mathew barged past her, knocking her off her feet. George raced forwards, worried that now he'd technically assaulted a police officer, they'd try to arrest him. 'Don't grab him! It'll make him worse! He's just frightened! Please don't grab him!'

Cars were now speeding down the long, straight stretch of unlit road beyond the still-closing gate. Mathew was head down, tilted forwards as he ran. He had no comprehension of the danger ahead, George was too far away to help and the police were out of options. Officers stood, arms wide, shouting for Mathew to stop, but he couldn't hear them above his own prolonged, high-pitched squeal. Then, in a flash, Mathew was on his belly with a police officer pinning each arm to the ground. He screamed at the top of his lungs in utter terror. Sally fell to her knees by Mathew's head and stroked his hair as his screaming turned to sobbing. 'OK, darling. OK. It's over.' Sally glanced up and could now see that the frustratingly slow-moving gates were finally closed. 'They'll let you up now, darling. And you'll come with me into the house. It's over and you're fine. I'm not going to leave you. I promise. I'm not going to leave you ever again.'

Inside the Barrowmans' house, Mathew helped Sally to make hot chocolate, while George placated the police in the lounge. They were very reasonable, mainly because Sergeant McDermott, who Mathew had pushed to the ground, knew him from a chess club they had both attended as children. McDermott declined to pursue charges against a man who clearly acted out of no malicious intent, and she also said she'd write a statement explaining the situation. 'I truly am sorry for his behaviour,' George said gratefully.

'Don't do that, George,' Sally interrupted from the doorway. 'Don't apologise for him.' She looked at the grass stains on all of the police uniforms. 'It was awful, of course, and I am sorry this happened. But Mathew's not a violent boy. He didn't try to hurt anyone on purpose.'

'Darling, they've already said there'll be no further action,' George said with a sigh. 'Sergeant McDermott knows Mathew. She understands.'

It took a while for Sally to get her emotions under control. 'Oh, my goodness, Fiona!' Sally's relief brought on more tears. 'I didn't recognise you. Thank you, thank you so much. I'd be happy to pay for your dry cleaning, of course.'

Sergeant McDermott said that wouldn't be necessary and the police showed themselves out.

George poured two very large single malts, handed one to Sally and then stood stiffly in front of the open fireplace, as though he was standing to attention. He took a couple of sips of his whisky before speaking again. 'He worries me, Sal. He's not a child any-more. Tantrums from a child are very different to tantrums from a strapping young man. He'll get himself in trouble one day and then what? We should be very grateful that it was an old friend he sent flying across the front lawn!'

But Sally was thinking about something else. 'I wonder why he didn't want to come back in?'

George tutted and headed for his study. 'Go to bed. I've got a couple of hours' work to do.'

When George entered his study, he noticed a faint sulphurous odour, as if something had been burning. The only thing out of place was an ornate mirror which now sat on the floor, propped against the desk, rather than on the wall behind it. The safe which was normally hidden behind the mirror had its door ajar and there was a blackened hole next to the dial from a high-powered laser. George hurried over, slamming his whisky down on to the desk as he passed. All the valuables were gone: three gold bars, three pieces of jewellery and nine stacks of £50 notes amounting to £9,000.

Sally sat beside Mathew in his bedroom. He had his headphones on, watching an episode of *Game of Thrones* on his computer. The volume was so loud that she could hear what the characters were saying. Mathew blinked slowly as he gradually calmed. 'Nothing to be scared of, darling,' she whispered. 'Nothing to be scared of now.'

*   *   *

Jack lay in bed, hands behind his head, staring up at a small, grey stain in the corner of the ceiling. 'I think Penny's shower's leaking,' Maggie slurred. Jack looked over at her. Maggie was sitting propped up by several pillows with a huge V-shaped one on top of her on which Hannah slept soundly. Jack promised that he'd ask Mario to recommend a plumber, then got up to put the kettle on.

In the kitchen, Penny was flicking through the scanned family photos on her mobile, whilst sipping a fresh cup of tea and nibbling on a cold samosa. Jack pressed the button on his charging mobile: 4.20 a.m.

Their kitchen was a 'happy mess', as Penny called it. If it had been a crime scene, Jack thought, he'd have been able to tell everything about the occupants: the bottles of pills said 'old lady'; the dirty babygrows on the floor said 'newborn'; two used wine glasses said 'couple'; dirty dishes in the sink said 'too tired to care'; and the fridge door, with its mother-and-baby pamphlets, take-away menus, evening class leaflets, paint palette charts, packed calendar and notepad containing numerous messages to each other, said that this was a family who were trying to do too much all at once. But there was also a lot of love in this room: the photos on the fridge showed a close family who adored each other.

While the kettle boiled, Jack leant on the back of Penny's chair and looked at photos with her. She paused on one of Charlie, aged about 60, but still looking as strong as an ox. 'He was the most handsome man I've ever seen in my life.' Penny reached back and stroked Jack's face. 'Second most handsome,' she corrected. 'I hear him at night. I lie in bed and I hear him breathing in the darkness next to me. He was such a gentle breather for a big man; you'd think he'd snore like a bulldozer, but he didn't.'

At this intimate moment, Jack's mobile buzzed. Without taking his attention from Penny, he read the text from Oaks:

There's been another.

CHAPTER 8

Jack and Gifford stood in silence, watching George Barrowman pacing furiously up and down with a look of thunder on his face. 'Three years, Joe,' he boomed, 'three fucking years these burglaries have been going on, and what have you got? Piles! From sitting on your arse! That's what you've got.'

'Sir . . .' Jack started.

'And I only want to hear from you,' Barrowman interrupted, jabbing a finger in Jack's direction, 'if it's to say, "We've arrested the bastards and have found your property, Mr Barrowman." Anything less than that and I'm not interested. I work in gold in the City, so I know people in the Met, but I don't know who the hell you are. Just write this down: three gold bars, one emerald necklace, one string of pearls, a diamond tiara and nine grand in fifties.' George then turned his attention to Gifford. 'You have one week, Joe. Then I'll be bringing in my own investigators to do your job and I'll be sending you their bill.'

Without a word, Jack walked away. He wasn't going to get anything remotely useful from George Barrowman in his current frame of mind, so he went in search of Sally instead. In the kitchen, Sally was preparing a large but very healthy breakfast. She was a sophisticated-looking blonde, wearing designer clothes, probably in her mid-40s, but the likelihood of cosmetic surgery made it hard to be sure. She was slim, toned and barefooted, with toenails painted bright red and Jack was surprised to see that she wore a toe ring and ankle bracelet. Clearly Sally Barrowman had been a freer spirit in her time.

She saw Jack looking at her. 'Mathew has Prader-Willi Syndrome on top of his autism,' she explained. 'He has no trigger that says "I'm full. I should stop eating now." He just carries on. It's more complicated than that, of course, but that's the gist of it. It gives him the habit of biting the inside of his mouth until it bleeds and chewing the skin around his fingers.'

Jack nodded sympathetically and looked around the extensive kitchen. Everything was exactly where it should be, and every surface shone like new. Certain cupboards had locks on them, as did the fridge. Nothing in this room was homely; it was clinical, like a lab. And as Sally weighed some porridge oats, Jack thanked God for his small 'happy mess' of a kitchen. He was just about to ask Sally a question when he heard George Barrowman's angry voice.

'Did you just walk away from me?'

Jack glanced over his shoulder, purposely not bothering to fully turn and face George. 'Yes, sir, I did. I decided that yours would not be a productive interview right now, so came to see if I could chat to your wife.'

George came and stood right in front of Jack. 'How dare you presume to do anything in my home without my express permission!'

'Mr Barrowman,' Jack replied calmly. 'If I'm to ask your permission before I can make a move, I'll head back to London now.' Sally froze, mouth open, with a spoonful of oats hovering in the air. Jack continued whilst he had George's full attention. 'I'll be respectful of your position, your property and your family, sir, but I won't be slowed down by unnecessary formalities.'

Stumped by Jack's firm response, George then resorted to the oldest cliche in the book. 'I want the name of your superior officer!'

'DCI Simon Ridley of the Metropolitan Police is not technically my superior, but if you want to speak with him, you can use my mobile. His direct line is in there.'

George adjusted his stance, shoulders back, chest out, chin up, making himself look as threatening as possible. Jack returned his eyes to Sally for a second and smiled, as if to say, 'Pardon me one moment whilst I put your dickhead of a husband back in his box.' Jack had seen this kind of hollow bravado a thousand times before. Barrowman was a bully, and because his bullying worked with Gifford, he assumed it'd work with Jack.

'You don't know who I am,' he said, right in Jack's face, 'but, my God, you're about to find out.'

Jack waited for a moment then said, 'George Barrowman, 56, ex-Corporal in the Coldstream Guards, wealth management advisor for high net-worth individuals, your speciality being the global gold market. Net worth, including assets, close to the fifteen-million-pound mark. You were investigated back in '07 for tax fraud, but the case was dropped due to lack of evidence.'

Whilst Jack was speaking, George's shoulders dropped, his chest deflated, and his chin dipped without him being aware of it. 'Sir, I can waste time explaining to you why your wealth gives you no special privileges in this investigation, or I can interview your wife before the details of last night fade from her memory. Which would you like me to do?'

Seconds passed as George tried to figure out how to respond. Then he turned on his heel and marched out of the kitchen.

Jack and Sally sat at the heavy walnut kitchen table, making their way through a pot of tea and a plate of assorted shortbread biscuits. Up close, he could see she had delicate features which made him think of Felicity Kendal in *The Good Life*, which he used to watch with his mum and dad. As she explained about the standoff between Mathew and the police in the middle of the road, Jack began to understand why she was with George. She clearly loved looking after people – a husband, a son – and George, although a hard-working businessman, probably wouldn't know how to turn on a toaster. They seemed to be perfectly suited.

Sally went on to explain what jewellery was missing from the safe. 'A diamond tiara bought for my niece's wedding; some gold bars, three, I think; cash, you'll have to check with George how much, and an emerald necklace once owned by the infamous Barbara Hutton, the poor little rich girl, who had everything except happiness. She was married seven times, you know. When she died of a broken heart, her jewels were auctioned at Sotheby's and . . . I got the necklace for my fortieth. It gets talked about a lot at parties, but I've never actually worn it outside of the house. Far too valuable.'

There was a sadness in Sally's words. Jack thought she didn't really want all these trappings of wealth; she was a much simpler soul than her husband. 'Oh!' Sally suddenly burst back into life as she took a sheet of paper from her pocket and handed it to Jack. 'George said you'd need a list of staff.'

Jack speed-read the list: a housekeeper, a pool cleaner, three domestics, a tutor for Mathew, one full-time gardener and the seemingly ubiquitous Charlotte Miles who came three after-noons a week to deliver fresh fruit and veg as per Mathew's strict dietary regime.

Jack thanked her and asked if Mathew normally stayed in the house by himself.

'Rarely,' Sally explained. 'He was meant to attend the charity auction with us last night, but then he watched the episode where Ned Stark gets beheaded. He always watches the "death" episodes twice, which put him an hour behind and, well, we couldn't wait for him as we were hosting. I started to keep track of where the "death" episodes were, so we could plan around them but there are so many! Have you watched *Game of Thrones*?'

'People talk about it so much I sometimes feel like I have!' Jack joked. 'But no, I haven't watched it.'

'Mathew is . . .' Sally faltered. At first Jack assumed she was going to open up about how hard he made life, but she did the exact opposite. 'He's wonderful. People think he's to be pitied because he has an illness, but Mathew just is who he is and will be for the rest of his and my life. I love him without question, DS Warr, as you love your children, if you have any. Yes, there are rules, routines, dos and don'ts, behaviour charts and coping techniques that most parents don't need to consider, but . . . it's just horses for courses.'

Jack allowed Sally to continue telling him about Mathew, not because the details were important, but because her cooperation was. He needed her to like him, just as he'd needed Eloise Fullworth to like him, so that from this point forwards they were allies in his investigation. Sally spoke of how Mathew was not allowed a bank card, as his urge for instant gratification was too strong for him to control. And although he often experienced erratic mood swings, he'd rarely in his life been physically violent. Medication tended to keep him on an even keel.

'He can't ride a bike, or swim, and he hates almost all sport. Of course, that could all change depending on what takes his fancy next. He adores walking, though, and can be out for hours with Nathaniel just looking at the world around him. Nature fascinates him. Nathaniel's his tutor; I'll introduce you to him shortly. *Game of Thrones* and nature are his current obsessions. And I mean obsessions!' Sally lowered her eyes to her china cup, turning it gently on its saucer. 'I couldn't make him come with us last night, DS Warr. So, I left him . . . all on his own.'

Sally got up and rinsed her cup under the tap, so that she didn't have to see the disapproval on Jack's face. But he was actually full of admiration for her parenting skills. 'Mathew wasn't diagnosed until he was seven,' she went on, 'but I always knew. George just thought his son was the quiet, unaffectionate type but deep down he knew too. I go to bed an hour after Mathew every night and, whilst he's in his drug-aided sleep, I sneak into his room. I hug him and I kiss him. He's not keen on me doing that when he's awake. Do you have children, DS Warr?'

'A daughter. Just a few weeks old,' Jack smiled.

'Oh, how lovely!' Sally said warmly. 'Smother her with love . . . whether she likes it or not!'

Jack caught himself hoping to God that his little girl remained fit and well, and did not end up having a life as complicated and as confusing as Mathew's.

'What do you think about me . . . interviewing Mathew?' Jack asked hesitantly.

Sally didn't seem fazed by the request. 'He's far more amenable after food,' she explained. 'It's not that you can't talk to him now, it's just that I doubt you'll get much from him. I mean, you can try if time is against us, or . . .'

'Mrs Barrowman, I'll fit in with Mathew. It's not a problem,' Jack assured her, and he could see the relief on her face that he understood.

* * *

Later that morning George sat alone in the conservatory. It was half past ten and he was on the single malt. When Jack entered, he acted as though they'd never had a single cross word. 'Mr Barrowman, would you mind escorting me around the outside of your property, please?'

The CCTV cameras around the outside of the building were all situated just below the first-floor windows, and yet were still disabled by being sprayed with paint – an achievement in itself.

Jack wasn't sure how the burglars managed to reach them, unless one of them was into rock climbing.

In the secure porchway by the front door, a top-of-the-range alarm system was still switched off. Attached to the right-hand side of the property was a triple garage housing a red Ferrari and a black Range Rover. The garage doors were open, but both vehicles were untouched. The car George had driven to the charity auction, a dark green BMW, was on the gravel driveway. Jack noticed all three vehicles had tinted windows. 'Tinted windows mean it's likely the burglars couldn't see that Mathew wasn't in the car with you. They'd have presumed your house was empty,' Jack reasoned.

'Mathew watches television with the lights off, door closed and headphones on. He must . . .' George sipped his whisky, which he'd brought with him, before continuing. 'He must have been scared shitless when he saw them, otherwise why was he flapping about in the middle of the road with no shoes on?' George's voice deepened into a low growl. 'How dare they? How fucking *dare* they?'

He drained his glass and, without thinking, headed for the front door. A young PC dutifully stepped in his way. Beyond the police tape on the front door, George could see dozens of paper-suited and masked CSIs, painting everything he owned with fingerprint powder. He looked and felt helpless, no longer master of his own domain.

'Sir.' Jack's tone respectful. 'Let's go back in the way we came out.' As they walked back towards the conservatory, Jack asked George to repeat the list of stolen items. 'The written list your wife gave me, sir, doesn't include the string of pearls.'

'Oh, my mistake,' Barrowman said. 'Her list is correct.'

He didn't flinch, didn't smile. Jack instantly knew he was hiding something.

* * *

DC Cariad Bevan stared at her computer monitor watching CCTV footage, whilst simultaneously typing a report on everything she was seeing. After leaving the incandescent Barrowman in Jack's hands, Gifford had returned to the station and immediately tasked her with trawling through CCTV, because of her known talent for being able to do the most mundane of tasks with the enthusiasm of a newly adopted Labrador puppy. She was one of those officers who was thrilled just to be there.

There was no CCTV on the quarter-mile driveway up to the Barrowmans' house, nor on the first ten-mile stretch of road. The cameras only kicked in two miles outside Chipping Norton and there were a couple of turn-offs before that, so the burglars could have bypassed Chipping Norton altogether.

However, on CCTV from some of the surrounding villages, Bevan had managed to get footage of an unmarked, three-horse trailer driving past the same camera a number of times. What really caught her eye was the muddied number plate. In itself this wasn't unusual as most horseboxes were constantly sprayed with dirt and muck from the stables. But she knew that if this horsebox had been to a stable, it should have been muddy everywhere; and this horsebox had no mud on the wheel arches, sides and tail ramp. Just on the number plate.

Bevan played the CCTV footage for Gifford and he agreed that this could be an ideal way to transport a team of burglars and an array of stolen property. Then Gifford started to get ahead of himself. 'Ay! Remember that biker we clocked on a number of the burglary nights? We thought he was a tourist. Paid him no heed 'cos of looking for a big vehicle.' Gifford tapped the screen of Bevan's monitor, leaving a buttery fingerprint from one of Canteen Barbara's pastries. 'Bet he'd fit in that horsebox. Could be a scout. Doing recces.' Gifford grinned. He didn't get them often, but he knew a good idea when he had one.

Bevan's smile slowly faded and was replaced with a frown, as a thought was being dredged up from the depths of her mind. Gifford was walking away by the time Bevan's thought was fully recalled. 'Sir . . . Oaks's cousin, Blair . . . Did I ever tell you about that thing she said about her mum's neighbour's kids finding a horsebox in a lake?' Gifford turned with a blank expression. 'Sorry, sir, I'm just trying to remember it properly. About eight months ago, two kids found a horsebox submerged in a lake out Cirencester way. They rowed out to it and found a dead body inside. Well, it was more of a skeleton. Blair's mum reckoned the horsebox was just dumped; it happens sometimes out there. It could have been fully submerged until the water level dropped for some reason and its roof broke the surface. Once the carrion crows got wind of a free dinner, they came down in a flock. It was like that Hitchcock film, she said! Anyway, Blair says that her mum said it was a tramp who crawled into the horsebox for warmth and then died. Then, I dunno, maybe kids pushed it into the water not knowing he was there? But what if he wasn't a tramp?'

Gifford paused for a moment, then nodded. 'You better get on to the Wiltshire lot and see what you can find out.'

* * *

By early afternoon, George was allowed back into his study to collect his computer and any paperwork he needed. He then brought it all into the kitchen to catch up with his work. Sally pottered around making enough sandwiches to feed an army.

Jack stood right in the middle of the wide hallway and turned on the spot taking in every detail. All of the furniture in this house was immaculate, but none of it looked *used*. It certainly didn't feel like a home. Even the family portraits looked as if they were just for show. Jack also noticed how much artwork had been left hanging on the walls and wondered why the burglars had not stripped the place bare as they had done in other properties. Perhaps the unexpected presence of Mathew had forced them to cut their losses; or perhaps George Barrowman's artwork was as fake as him.

Sally went to the kitchen door and shouted, 'Who's hungry?' Masked heads popped up from beneath desks and windowsills, and around doorframes. Sally then headed upstairs, past Jack, saying, 'Mathew should have showered by now. I'll see what's keeping them.'

Back in the kitchen, George was distracted from his work by a seemingly endless stream of CSIs and police officers who had swooped in to snaffle sandwiches and then scurry back out. Seeing as the heavy police presence was already disturbing George, Jack decided to try and build some bridges by asking him about the gold market.

For the next ten minutes, Jack listened to George explain its ups and downs in various countries across the world. Jack could see that George was very good at what he did. And he had to be. He worked in a high-stakes world, where one false move could destroy a fortune. Jack figured that's why he'd had a go at Gifford – because Gifford wasn't as good at his job as George was at his. So, Jack knew that all he had to do to keep George cooperating was to measure up to his standards.

Suddenly Mathew raced into the kitchen, looking very agitated, arms in the air, shouting, 'Masked men! Masked men!' He flapped his hands just above his shoulders, grimaced as if he was in pain and, in between words let out a high-pitched 'eeeeee' sound. As soon as he saw Jack, he headed straight for him. As Mathew was over six feet tall, Jack's instinct was to bring his hands up to defend himself against a possible attack – but by the time Mathew had moved across the kitchen, George was standing in between them. 'Calm.' George spoke in a slow, quiet voice. 'Calm. What's the matter?'

'Masked men! Masked men!' Mathew repeated. Although an adult, right now Mathew seemed like a little boy needing his dad for comfort. George took Mathew by the wrists and explained that the 'masked men' were policemen and were nothing to be afraid of. Mathew put his hands heavily on George's shoulders and squeezed in a pulsating, grasping motion. Jack could see this physical contact was comforting and regardless of the discomfort, George put up with it.

Within seconds of Mathew entering the kitchen, he was followed by Sally and a handsome young black man. He was tall and muscular with wide, body-builder's shoulders. 'This is Nathaniel Jones,' George said. 'He's Mathew's tutor-cum-carer-cum-minder-cum-anything else he might need. This is DS Jack Warr from the Met.'

Nathaniel gave Jack a backwards nod, then focussed on calming Mathew down. He put his hands firmly on Mathew's shoulders and squeezed hard, just as Mathew had done to George. 'Come on, Matty. Shower.' Nathaniel glanced at Jack. 'I'll give you a shout when we're done. Sorry it's taking longer than usual.'

In the study, Oaks was in his paper suit with his mask tucked under his chin. He stood in the centre of the room, on a twelve-inch-square metal plate so as not to make footprints in the thick carpet. Four CSIs meticulously worked their way from the study door to the open safe. As the sun shone in through the tall sash windows, it glistened off a small patch of something shiny at the top of George's tan-coloured leather office chair. The shiny stain was around the area where a person's head might touch when leaning back, or where you might grasp the chair if walking behind it.

'What's that?' Oaks said to the room in general. The CSI nearest to him followed his pointing finger to the chair. They then dipped their head and moved from side to side until the sun caught the shiny patch, and they were able to see what Oaks was seeing. They agreed that the substance looked oily, which seemed out of place in such an immaculate study. 'Take a sample, please,' Oaks requested.

The CSI collecting the sample from the office chair tugged an imaginary forelock, saying, 'Yes, Willy. Right away, Willy.'

Oaks blushed, smiled and turned towards the door where Jack was now looking in at him from the hallway. Oaks moved across the metal plates towards Jack and dipped under the police tape. 'That's my Auntie Helen. Well, she's my cousin really, but 'cos she's got twenty years on me, I've always called her Auntie.'

Jack laughed. 'Everyone knows everyone. I get it. You're doing fine, Oaks. Listen, when you get back to the station, I need you to do something for me. Get a warrant to check George Barrowman's accounts. You're looking for a jewellery purchase – a string of pearls.'

Oaks shuffled uncomfortably, saying that he'd need to ask DI Gifford to authorise the request, and he was fairly sure that he wouldn't do it.

'No worries,' Jack said. 'I didn't mean to put you on the spot. I'll sort it myself.'

Oaks's eyes lifted and looked over Jack's shoulder. Jack turned to see Nathaniel standing behind him with a look of simmering anger on his face. He held out his mobile phone and Jack saw a photo of Mathew, shirtless, towel round his waist, hand in the stream of shower water, as though checking the temperature. On his back, he had four dark, deep-red bruises, each one was eight to ten inches long.

'They weren't there yesterday,' Nathaniel said. 'He showers every night, so I know they weren't. And, before you ask, Mr and Mrs Barrowman have never laid a finger on him. Nor have I.'

Jack and Oaks looked intensely worried. Was this why Mathew raced into the road screaming? Was he brutally attacked by the burglars? 'I need to speak to him,' Jack said.

Nathaniel held Jack's stare.

'No. Matty will be able to recall the events of last night, for forever and a day, so you don't need to worry about that. But right now I'm going to break this news to his parents and then get him to hospital. Come back tomorrow.'

Jack was about to protest when Nathaniel went on. 'I've been Matty's carer for seven years. We're mates after all that time and he trusts me to look after him. I get that you've got a job to do, but so have I. Believe me, you get one chance with him, DS Warr. If he decides not to like you, you're screwed. I want him to talk to you and give you everything you need to catch the bastards who hurt him. That's why I'm saying you have to wait.'

Nathaniel didn't give Jack the opportunity to reply. He took his mobile back and headed upstairs.

Jack turned to Oaks. 'Get everyone down here. Tell them we're looking for a weapon that matches the length and width of those bruises on Mathew's back. A baseball bat, maybe? Garden rake or spade? Go with him to the hospital in case he says anything. I trust Nathaniel, but if Mathew opens up, you need to hear it.'

As Jack thought about the violence Mathew must have experienced at the hands of strangers, his eyebrows furrowed and his eyes darkened. Oaks recoiled, ever so slightly, as he saw something in Jack that had not shown itself before. Oaks thought that if the burglars walked into the room at that moment, they would not leave alive.

CHAPTER 9

On the way to the hospital, Oaks got a phone call, which Jack answered as Oaks was driving. Jack put the phone on speaker and, before he could say anything, DC Ronnie Davidson's voice piped up, "'Ere Will, I got a message for your new girlfriend. *Elli* called and said . . .' At this point Davidson started to mimic Eloise Fullworth's voice. 'Oh, Jack, Jack from the Met, it's Elli. Maisie's home if you'd like to come and speak with her. And when you're done with my daughter, maybe you and I can . . .'

Jack interrupted before Davidson said something that crossed the line between taking the piss and rank insubordination. 'Thank you, DC Davidson. I'll interview Maisie on the way back to the station. Oaks is going to the hospital with Mathew. And you, Davidson, when the rest of the team get the order to go to Barrowman's house and search for a murder weapon, you're going to stay there and finish the social events calendar.'

Davidson spluttered for a reply, as Jack continued. 'I don't have many rules, but not taking the piss out of the victim is definitely one of them. If you'd like to argue your case when I get back to the station, I'm happy for you to try.' Jack ended the call and put Oaks's mobile back into the money tray in between the front seats. He looked over to see Oaks's face in a fixed grimace of embarrassment.

'Tell you what, Oaks, come and interview Maisie with me. You won't be allowed in the clinical areas whilst Mathew's being examined anyway, and you were the officer who originally interviewed her, right? You'll know if her story has changed in any way.'

* * *

Maisie was a beautiful, slender girl with an extraordinary amount of curly, jet black hair. She looked like she was making no effort at all with her appearance, right down to wearing a tracksuit that was far too big for her. Jack knew this look: Maisie was scruffy-by-design – setting the bar low so when someone told her how terrible she looked, she could just say, 'Yeah, I know.' In his time as a police officer, Jack had come across many women with self-image issues and, seeing as he already knew Maisie had struggled with anorexia in the past, her appearance was no surprise to him.

Mrs Fullworth, however, clearly found Maisie's appearance embarrassing. 'Maisie's a little under the weather,' she explained. 'So, she's having a tea-and-sympathy day in the house, aren't you, darling? Not going out, so no need to make an effort.' Maisie looked away and said nothing.

Jack ignored her mother's words. 'Maisie, could you show me your bedroom?'

Mrs Fullworth quickly cut in. 'Maisie can't go in that room anymore. So, I'll come with you in case she gets upset.'

Jack kept his attention focused on Maisie. 'Do you want an appropriate adult, Maisie? You don't need one, but of course your mum can come if you'd like. It's completely your choice.'

Maisie's eyes twinkled and she headed upstairs. Jack turned to Mrs Fullworth. 'DC Oaks will keep you company down here.'

When Jack got upstairs, Maisie was sitting on her old bed quietly waiting. This room was childish, as though stuck in a time-warp. The only mature things were several pieces of artwork torn out of a sketch pad and stuck up with sellotape but, to Jack's untrained eye, highly accomplished. 'Mum says this tracksuit makes me look like I belong in a young offenders unit,' Maisie said.

Jack snorted, which immediately put Maisie at ease. 'I can't remember much about the night it happened.'

Jack nodded. 'I'm going to try and help you but, if you can't remember, it's no problem.' He didn't want Maisie to think any less of herself than she already did. 'Can you sit where you were sitting when you saw the intruder, please?' Maisie scooted up the bed, until she was seated on top of the pillows. Jack then moved to her wardrobe and opened the door, so that the mirror reflected the stairway just outside Maisie's bedroom. It was a shorter mirror than he'd expected, not quite full-length; to fit the whole person in, they'd have to be standing a good distance back from it.

Jack asked Maisie where the burglar was when she noticed them, and she directed him to the second stair down. This wasn't helping: he needed to be seeing what Maisie was seeing. Jack shouted down to Oaks to join them, then told him to stand two stairs down while Jack moved to the bedside. He said, 'May I?' and Maisie got off the bed so he could sit where she'd been sitting.

'You told my officer – this officer in fact, DC Oaks – that you thought the burglar was over six feet tall. You said that because DC Oaks told you that he was 5'11", you thought the burglar seemed to be a couple of inches taller than him. Is all of that correct?' Maisie nodded. Jack looked at Oaks in the mirror. His head was bowed in shame as his rookie interview mistake quickly sank in. 'How about now, Maisie?' Jack stood up and Maisie sat back down on the bed. 'Look at DC Oaks in the mirror – lift your head up, Will – and tell me how much he differs in height from the burglar.'

Maisie grappled with the memory of that night and, as she took herself back in time, her breathing became more rapid.

'There's no difference. I can't see his hair. The top of DC Oaks's head is cut off by the top of the mirror, just like the burglar's was. If anything, DC Oaks is a little taller than the man I saw.' Jack then asked about size and shape and Maisie confirmed that Oaks and her unidentified burglar were of a similar build.

Back in the kitchen, Oaks remained silent as he prepared himself for a well-deserved bollocking on the drive to the hospital. Jack thanked Maisie for being so helpful and then, quite out of the blue, he asked her what she wanted to be. Maisie glanced at her mum before saying that she'd probably go into the law, like both of her parents. Jack was not deterred by her passionless answer. 'Your mum mentioned that your Aunt Lisa is an art therapist. Is the artwork in your old bedroom yours?' She nodded with a tentative smile. Jack knew full well that it was, and he also knew that Mrs Fullworth would hate what he was about to say. 'You're very talented. What does your Aunt Lisa think?' Maisie confirmed Jack's suspicions that no one outside of the house had ever seen her work. 'You should show her. I don't take after my parents. I take after my Uncle Simon. Took me a long time to find my path, Maisie, but, when I did . . . it's liberating. Take very good care of yourself.' Jack threw Maisie a wink, which made her smile properly. 'Smile more, Maisie Fullworth. It suits you.'

On the drive to the hospital, Jack had no time for Oaks's apologies about his error in interviewing Maisie.

'We now know that the person who broke into Maisie's house was about my build but was probably shorter. I'm so sorry, sir. We've been on the wrong track with this for months.'

'Get over yourself,' Jack said briskly. 'You'll make worse mistakes than that. Anyway, you didn't waste my time, you wasted DI Gifford's.' He thought for a moment. 'Maisie could even have seen a woman, don't you think?'

Oaks pulled up just outside the A & E department of Cheltenham General. 'Tread carefully with Nathaniel,' Jack warned as they got out. 'He's protective of Mathew, so he'll let you know he's in charge. And that's fine. Your presence is to let Nathaniel know that the second Mathew's ready to speak, we're ready to listen. Ignore George

Barrowman altogether – he'll no doubt ignore you. He's not the one we need to keep on-side anyway; that's Sally.' Then Jack got back into the driver's seat and Oaks headed for A & E. As Jack pulled away, he shouted one more instruction. 'Text me every hour. Whether there's anything to say or not.'

* * *

At the station, a calendar of social events for the next twelve months was plotted out in great detail on one of the whiteboards, an over-lapping, chaotic mess that would be a nightmare to police. The most obvious problem was the upcoming annual equestrian event that lasted for an entire week and was, at some point, attended by everyone in the local area.

Gifford stood in front of the whiteboards with DC Bevan, admiring their hard work. Davidson avoided Jack's eye by burying his head in a computer screen. The rest of the desks were empty as everyone else was at the Barrowmans' searching the property for the weapon used on Mathew. Gifford seemed to be on a high from his productive afternoon so, for now, Jack kept quiet about Maisie's revelation regarding the height of her burglar and allowed Gifford to go first.

Bevan started by explaining how she and Gifford had uncovered two new key pieces of evidence: an unmarked, untraceable, uni-dentifiable horsebox with dirty number plates; and a motorbike from out of town, with false plates. 'Both vehicles can be seen driving up and down the stretch of road that runs by the Barrowman house. So, I went back to the CCTV footage from the other burglaries, and they both pop up in and around each target house on one, or all, of the three days before each burglary.'

Jack waited patiently. Bevan was clearly laying the groundwork for her big reveal.

'If we accept that this gang uses rented horseboxes as one of their getaway vehicles . . .' Bevan paused to look at her notes. 'Eight months ago, a dead body was found in a submerged horsebox just south of Cirencester. According to the autopsy we have a white male, mid-30s, of South American descent. No ID. No criminal record. Dead for approximately three years. His hyoid bone was snapped, indicating manual strangulation probably from behind. In the pocket of his trousers was a pair of 18-carat white gold oval cufflinks, with inset diamonds, worth around £2,000. These cufflinks were on an insurance claim list from 2018 made by Mr Bright-Cullingwood; he's a writer of kids' books, lives in Kingham. He was our first known burglary victim.'

Bevan couldn't help but look up to see how people were reacting – all eyes were on her. But now she'd paused for slightly too long . . .

'You after a round of applause, girl?' Gifford's words nudged her back on track.

'Er, no, sir. Sorry.' Bevan found her place in her notes again. 'The horsebox, I think – I'm checking – was stolen from a livery stable in Cirencester, which could be why we never got wind of it. Wherever it's from, there's no forensics. It remains an open murder case with them.' Bevan put her notes away. 'Sirs, I chatted to Mr Bright-Cullingwood on the phone about an hour ago and he said that the day after the burglary he locked his office, which is located at the bottom of his garden, as the "contaminated" space was no longer an inspiration for his writing. He's not been in it since. So, I thought maybe . . . it might be worth sending forensics over?'

She looked at Jack for approval, but he remained silent and thoughtful. When he did speak, he said something sobering: 'Looks like Mathew Barrowman got off bloody lightly then, didn't he?'

Jack walked to the bank of windows overlooking the idyllic views beyond. He recalled one of the first things he ever said to his team of Chipping Norton officers: 'This gang will not move on and disappear for good. They will not escalate to murder, which I know is your biggest concern. We will get them.' But the truth now, it seemed, was that this gang were already killers.

'Right . . .' Jack turned and addressed the expectant room. They were subdued after Bevan's diligent research into an eight-month-old murder case, so Jack had to kickstart them. 'Fundamentally, nothing's changed in terms of the investigation. More seems to be at stake now, I understand that, but we can't deviate from the path we're on. Bevan . . .' She stared at him expectantly, like a child who'd been ignored by her parents. 'Well done.' The tension immediately drained from Bevan's face. 'You should go with forensics and supervise. After you've finished briefing the team and after you've done one job for me – which I'll tell you about in a minute. Carry on . . . horseboxes and motorbikes.'

'Oh, right, sir. Yes, well . . .' Bevan took a deep breath and began again. 'The big problem is that from the weekend after next, we'll be inundated with horseboxes and motorbikes because of the equestrian event. Tens of thousands of people will descend on the Cotswolds.'

Jack held up a hand. 'What's the relevance of the biker? Why are they suddenly of interest?'

'Well, sir . . .' Bevan started to falter. Being faced with having to justify a new angle of enquiry to a Met man was daunting. She looked to Gifford for backup, but he didn't offer any. His silence was the first piece of direct leadership Jack had witnessed: Gifford knew Bevan was doing fine without him, so he wanted her to be the one to answer Jack's question. She started again, 'It's possible that the biker is acting like a scout. To recce the properties, collect information about the owners' routines and such. He'd easily fit in the horse trailer.'

Jack nodded. 'Good shout.'

Jack then changed the subject to Mathew. This was the other job he needed Bevan for. It was important to know for certain that their burglars were responsible for such a brutal attack. He wanted to exclude every other possibility before concluding, 100 per cent, that this gang had assaulted him.

'I need the bodycams from all officers who attended the Barrowmans' early yesterday morning. I need to know—'

'Set up and ready to go on the computer at your desk, sir!' There was no stopping Bevan now. 'I downloaded the footage from all three cameras into the same file and cut it down, so you've just got the Barrowman incident. There's nothing on it, though, sir. The traffic was held back by police vehicles, so you can't see anything clearly.'

'I'm not looking for the vehicles, Bevan. I'm looking to see if any of the officers drew their batons and used them in self-defence.'

This instantly got Gifford's attention and prompted him to chip in, 'Now, wait a minute. If there's been a complaint . . .'

All Jack had to do to stop Gifford in his tracks was hold up his mobile and show him the images of Mathew's back that Nathaniel had forwarded to him. Gifford physically flinched at the sight of the bruising on Mathew's torso. Jack assured them that there had been no complaints and that he didn't doubt the officers for one second, but they had to be certain for their own peace of mind.

The collated footage from the bodycams all showed the same thing: Mathew sent Sergeant McDermott tumbling backwards, then raced towards the busy road. When he refused to stop for the other officers, they made the decision to take him to the ground and restrain him for his own safety. No batons were drawn. Jack watched the footage from McDermott's bodycam: once Mathew was down, she crawled across the lawn and talked soothingly, assuring him that he wasn't in any kind of trouble. All the while, Sally could be seen stroking Mathew's hair and repeating the instruction for him to be calm.

Gifford was relieved. 'When we got bodycams, I thought they were a waste of time but, my God, they just earned their slice of the budget.'

Jack asked Bevan to contact Sergeant McDermott. 'I've just seen her in the canteen, sir. I'll go get her.' Then Bevan bounced out of the squad room.

Jack and Gifford looked at the frozen image of Mathew, pinned to the lawn outside his own home, sobbing and petrified. 'I don't know this boy well, Jack, but I know his parents. Yes, George can be a pompous arse, but he's a good dad. For the past twelve years, at every one of Mathew's annual reviews, the authorities have suggested that his "challenging behaviour" is too much to handle at home. But George and Sally refuse to let Mathew be admitted into an institution. They'd do anything for him. So this must be killing them. It'd kill me. Look at him, Jack . . . look what he does when he's scared. He doesn't fight, he runs. The bastards who did this to Mathew don't think like normal human beings.'

This was the most Jack had ever heard Gifford say. It reminded him that anyone can surprise you under the right circumstances. Gifford was a family man, Jack realised; that was why he had allowed Bevan to shine in front of Jack. Gifford might well have stopped learning, as Ridley suggested, but he was still capable of teaching.

'Sir . . .' Jack had to ask Gifford to authorise the accounts search on Barrowman and wasn't sure how. 'Do you think Barrowman was guilty of tax fraud back in '07?'

'What the hell's that got to do with the price of fish?' Gifford responded.

'Nothing. I want to know if you think Barrowman is an honest man. He could be generous and loving to his family and still have strayed onto the wrong side of the law.'

Gifford was becoming familiar with Jack's methods. 'What's the real question?'

'His list of stolen items differs from his wife's. He included a string of pearls; she didn't. She also didn't know how many gold bars were in the safe or how much cash, so, I'm inclined to believe that his recollection is more accurate. But when I double-checked, he backtracked and said there were no pearls.'

Gifford slowly put his hands into his pockets. 'You can't think he's our inside man. *He* was targeted!'

Jack shrugged. 'This gang is capable of anything. Maybe it was a warning. Or maybe there were no pearls and Barrowman was mistaken. I don't know, sir. And I hate not knowing.'

Bevan scurried back into the squad room with Sergeant McDermott in tow. She had half a sandwich in one hand and a cup of tea in the other, so Bevan had clearly dragged her from the canteen. 'DS Warr from the Met wants to talk to you about Mathew Barrowman.' Jack couldn't hide his grin. Since arriving in the Cotswolds, it seemed that his surname had become 'Warr-from-the-Met'. Bevan then scurried out again, to take a forensic team to the secluded office of Mr Bright-Cullingwood.

Ten minutes later, McDermott was sitting with Jack and Gifford, whilst Davidson gathered together all the statements from Barrowman's employees.

Jack had just asked McDermott to fill them in about Mathew and the time they'd spent together at chess club. 'It was an after-school club for 10 to 16-year-olds. Although Matty stayed till he was 18, I think. He joined when I was 12, so I guess I knew him for about four years. We weren't friends, we just played chess together. That's as good as it got with Matty. He needs a reason to be with you, see; if he has that, he'll keep coming back. Till he gets bored.' McDermott smiled fondly. 'It's nothing personal.'

Jack was encouraged to know that he and Mathew had the shared skill of being able to play chess. This would be his way into Mathew's world. But McDermott quickly brought him down to earth.

'Nah, he's passed that. Do you know anything about *Game of Thrones*?' Jack's blank expression told McDermott that he didn't. 'Oh, I'm a huge fan,' she continued. 'Me and Mathew are soulmates when it comes to hobbies. It takes a bit of work to get him on-side but, once you've got him, he'll not forget you.'

Jack thanked her very much then let her go so that she could finish her sandwich.

Jack looked at Gifford and was about to return to the subject of Barrowman, but Gifford spoke first. 'I'll do that check. But only to prove you wrong.'

* * *

Annie was in the pigsty, mucking out. She spotted Jack heading towards her and her eyes immediately went to his shoes, but when she saw his new boots, she smiled. Not that Jack could see her face, as it was hidden behind a scarf to keep out the stench that she was stirring up each time her spade disturbed the crust on top of yesterday's pig shit.

'Still can't get used to the pong,' Annie shouted. 'I don't normally do the pigs, but we need the money from sending one of them to slaughter and Charlotte won't choose.' As Jack got closer, the smell hit him too. 'Stay there. I'll come to you.'

Annie propped her spade against the fence and headed to the stables where she washed her wellies beneath the outside tap. The diluted pig muck ran downhill towards Jack, so he moved with it, keeping out of harm's way until Annie was done. 'Charlotte's delivering plants at the moment. Was it her you came to see? I'll have to carry on if you don't mind. I need to get Alec boxed up before she gets back.' Then, in a whisper, she added, 'He's the chosen one.'

Jack was happy to chat to Annie whilst she worked. 'Could you tell me where you were last night? I'm asking everyone.'

Annie's interest was instantly piqued. 'Has there been another?' Jack remained silent and she immediately knew that there had. 'I often look at these big houses with envy, you know. I'd love a swimming pool; that would be my indulgence if I had money. But every now and then we're reminded how wealth brings its own problems. Jealousy is very destructive. Taking instead of earning is . . . well, I just don't understand it.'

As Annie continued, she casually got a sheet of tablets from her pocket and took one.

'We were at the Soho Farmhouse from seven till just gone midnight. I wait tables and Charlotte's a commis chef. We don't normally work that late, but there was a private function for a group of Londoners who've just bought themselves a racehorse. It's the same every year when the annual equestrian event comes around, and it'll stay this busy for the next couple of weeks. Sertraline.' Annie was telling Jack the name of the tablet she'd just taken, even though he'd not asked. 'I get a bit antsy some-times. I'm an insulin-dependent diabetic. It's under control now, but when it first started, I wasn't great at adapting to the new regime. And it *is* a regime! Charlotte keeps me on track. But I do stress about it. "Antsy" is her word for me!'

Jack thanked Annie for her honesty and then asked her what they did beyond midnight, once they'd stopped work.

'We spent an hour or so helping to tidy up, then drove home. Well, no actually, it took us another half hour to get out of the car park because one of the diners, who hadn't booked a room for the night, tried to drive back to Chipping Norton to find a B&B and the manager took their keys off them. There was a bit of a ruck and he had to call the police. Ronnie Davidson took the call. Charlotte and I had a chat with him, so he'll be able to confirm all of that.'

Jack rolled his eyes. Davidson could have bloody mentioned that he was part of Charlotte's alibi, but no, he was too busy hiding. Jack swallowed his frustration. 'Thank you, Annie. I'll let you get back to Alec.' Then curiosity got the better of him. 'What are the two survivors called?'

Annie said that Charlotte had named the pigs Alec, Billy, Daniel and Stephen as she was a huge fan of the Baldwin brothers. Stephen had met his maker a year ago, which had been so traumatic they'd vowed never to slaughter another Baldwin. But needs must . . .

* * *

Back at the station, Jack headed straight for DC Ronnie Davidson. 'Have you read all of the witness statements?' Davidson's silence told Jack that not only had he not read every statement, but he also didn't know why Jack was asking. 'Read them. Then come and tell me why it's essential for every officer to be up to speed with every aspect of my investigation.'

Bevan waited patiently by Jack's desk. As he turned in her direction, Ronnie made a 'wanker' motion behind Jack's back, which she ignored. She was enjoying the investigation too much to join in with any unprofessional mocking, and besides, by now the entire station knew that Davidson had been caught taking the piss out of the fact that Mrs 'call me Elli' Fullworth fancied Jack. The only way Davidson knew how to save face was to pretend he didn't give a damn.

'Sir,' Bevan said. 'Elaine Thorburn, the Barrowmans' house-keeper, wanted to speak to someone about the case. She said it was important. I knew you were on your way back, so I put her in the canteen and said you'd be with her as soon as possible.'

Jack asked what had happened at the home of Mr Bright-Cullingwood.

'Forensics are still there. I interviewed him formally, but then I was just twiddling my thumbs.' She said she'd left a couple of experienced uniformed officers at the house to continue supervising, but that she thought she'd be of more use in the squad room.

'Good,' Jack agreed. 'Right then: Elaine Thorburn. Come on, Bevan. You lead.'

* * *

Elaine was a short, stocky woman with broad shoulders and muscular arms. She certainly looked like the kind of house-keeper who led by example. Jack and Bevan sat opposite her, and Bevan was clearly waiting for Jack to start the interview, so Jack asked them what they'd like to drink and left them alone. By the time he returned, having left their order with the lovely Barbara, Elaine was mid-explanation as to why she'd taken it upon herself to come to the police station. Her voice was soft and gentle, belying her sturdy appearance completely.

'Your policemen told me that I wasn't allowed to do anything or touch anything, as you'd expect, but while I was waiting to be told when I could come back to complete my duties, I got all caught up with watching your CSIs work. Ooh, it was interesting. Anyway, one of them, poor girl, was going through the bin and that's when I saw the folded-up pizza box. It definitely wasn't there the night before, 'cos I empty the bins every evening on my way out, so it must have been delivered on the night of the burglary.'

'Mathew got a pizza delivered on the night of the burglary?' Bevan didn't yet understand how important this detail was.

'I don't know if you've seen their kitchen,' Elaine continued. 'But all the food cupboards and the fridge have got locks on them. Mathew's on a constant diet, you see, on account of his condition. Takeaway food is a definite no-no. But, well, between you and me, being left on his own is often a temptation too far. He's capable of being very independent, is Mathew. I hear he's got autism and they think he's some sort of simpleton, but he's a smart boy with a lovely manner. I've taken him shopping to Banbury before now and all people see is the flapping hands and funny noises. Then when we sit with a hot chocolate – don't tell his mum – and we chat about *Game of Thrones*, people are surprised that he can hold down a conversation. He's very intelligent; he's just selective about what he learns . . .'

Elaine had definitely lost her train of thought, so Bevan nudged her back on track.

'You were telling us about the pizza box in the outside bin.'

'Oh yes! So . . . well, yes, that was it really. He had a pizza delivered. Probably by Idris Jackson . . . he's a little shit, if you're interested. But he might have seen something useful. That's what I came to tell you.'

* * *

When Jack arrived back in the squad room with Bevan, Davidson was waiting for him. He was holding all of the witness statements and looking sheepish. Jack repeated the question he'd asked about half an hour ago: 'Why is it essential for every officer to be up to speed with every aspect of my investigation?'

Davidson now knew that if he'd read Charlotte's statement about being at the Soho Farmhouse at the time of the Barrowmans' burglary, he'd have been able to verify her alibi and save Jack a trip to their smallholding.

'Exactly,' Jack replied. 'Talk to each other. All the time. Right, DC Davidson, go and pick up Idris Jackson, please. He delivered a pizza to Mathew on the night of the burglary. I want you to interview him here.' Davidson was stunned that a day that started with a double bollocking was about to end with him leading his first interview.

'Got to start somewhere, Ronnie.' Jack's tone was glib. 'Bevan's just led her first, now it's your turn. When you get him here, make him a drink. Let him do most of the talking. Don't be afraid of silences; they're useful, because he'll instinctively fill them. We need every second accounted for – from the moment he headed down that unlit stretch of road towards the Barrowmans', to the moment he left. Don't let him leave out a single detail. He's not suspected of anything, so you'll be fine. You're only interviewing him here because I'm here. If you need me, just shout.' Then Jack turned his back on Davidson and sat down before the poor lad could doubt himself any further.

*　*　*

In A & E, Mathew was in a high dependency side room, despite the fact that he wasn't actually high dependency; not medically anyway. The room was away from the hustle and bustle of the waiting room and cubicles area, so it was perfect for keeping Mathew relaxed. When they'd first arrived, and had walked through the bleeding, swearing, vomiting, drunken crowd of people, Mathew had kept himself calm by repeating, 'Don't worry, Nate, these people are poorly at the moment, but they'll be fine. They'll be fine and I'll be fine.' George Barrowman had led the way, followed by Nathaniel and Mathew, followed by Oaks. Oaks had always recognised Barrowman's social 'pull' but did wonder how he'd managed to bypass the extensive queue and secure a private side room. This was the NHS after all, not a private hospital. But then, seconds later, just outside the high dependency room, Oaks found his answer: a sign that read 'The Barrowman Room – dedicated to Mr George Barrowman in recognition of his generous support of our autistic community'.

'It's a social room,' Nathaniel explained when he caught Oaks reading the sign. 'Toys, board games, pool table, library, sensory stuff, computer games. There's even a mini cinema in there. Mathew's been in and out of hospital since he was a nipper and he needed a safe space to play.'

Oaks was shocked – he had no clue Barrowman had a generous side.

Barrowman now stood in the corner of the high dependency side room, keeping himself out of the way and leaving Mathew in the very capable hands of Nathaniel. Oaks was outside the room, watching through a clear horizontal gap in the otherwise opaque window. Nathaniel helped Mathew to remove his T-shirt so that the medics could examine his wounds. One of the strikes to his back had broken the skin and, just beneath his hairline, there was a small, open gash. There were two or three minutes of chatter and conferring, before Barrowman popped his head around the door. 'He'll have an X-ray as a precaution, but they think he'll be fine. Maybe some hot drinks while we wait? Mine's a coffee, black, no sugar. Nathaniel's a tea, no sugar; and Mathew's a hot chocolate. Oh, and not the vending machine. Use the canteen.'

Oaks texted Jack to get him up to speed and headed for the canteen. Oaks couldn't help but grin as he mumbled to himself, 'I know your secret, Barrowman. You're a closet nice guy.'

* * *

Jack sat listening to Davidson relay his interview with Idris. He had taken the instruction to not let him leave out a single detail very seriously indeed.

'The pizza arrived at a quarter to nine. It was a large chicken and bacon, with double cheese and extra mushrooms. Idris rang the bell at the gate and Mathew buzzed him in. The gates opened, he drove his scooter to the kitchen door, where Mathew paid him and then he left.'

Jack fired some important additional questions at Ronnie: why did Idris use the kitchen door? Where's the gate buzzer located in the house? Did Idris see the gates closing behind him when he left? But Ronnie had all the answers. 'Idris had delivered to Mathew before, so he knew to use the kitchen door. That's where the gate thingy is . . . by the kitchen door. And Idris didn't see the gates close after he left, but he heard them.'

Jack stood and headed for Bevan's desk, where she was going through the hundreds of horseboxes that were registered to attend the annual equestrian event – they all needed their own parking space allocation, so that the vet could find them quickly if necessary, and she was creating a file containing a photo, owner details and registration for every single one. Bevan was good at doing the dull, routine work with enthusiasm, but right now he needed her to shift to a different train of thought.

'Bevan, start the Barrowmans' CCTV from the night of the burglary at eight, please.' Jack glanced back, expecting to see Davidson at his shoulder, but he'd returned to his desk thinking that he was no longer needed. 'Ronnie!' Jack snapped. 'Don't wait to be invited, this is your investigation too. Get over here.' Davidson was on his feet and at Jack's side before he'd finished speaking. 'I want it quarter-screen, with the two external gate cameras and the two internal gate cameras playing simultaneously.' It took Bevan a few seconds to get the screen as Jack had requested. As the action played out, initially showing nothing but the odd fox, Jack started the brainstorming. 'Ronnie, if this gang uses scouts and if Mathew ordered himself a pizza . . .' Jack left his sentence unfinished and stared at Davidson, forcing him to think for himself.

'Oh, er . . .' The waiting was painful, but Jack knew that this was the best way for any copper to learn. 'Oh! If a scout saw Idris arriving, they'd have known Mathew was at home. But then they still went in? They've never done that before, have they, sir? Gone into a house they knew was occupied.' Jack headed back to his desk, leaving Davidson and Bevan to watch all four screens between them and note down every detail of every second between 8 p.m. and the moment Mathew ran from the house screaming.

* * *

Maggie took so long to walk to the front door that she thought whoever it was would have gone by the time she got there. She held the baby bottle under her chin, so it stayed in Hannah's mouth; she had a dummy hanging from her finger, a muslin cloth over her shoulder ready for burping, and the bottom half of Hannah's baby-grow was unfastened ready for a quick nappy-change before nap time. Hannah's chubby bare legs flapped about and occasionally kicked Maggie in the chin.

She somehow managed to open the door and Ridley smiled over the top of the biggest bunch of flowers Maggie had ever seen. Then he held out a bottle of red wine, label facing Maggie for her approval. Châteauneuf du Pape! Maggie didn't know a lot about wine, but she'd heard this one mentioned on TV by Nigella Lawson, so she knew it must be good.

Maggie sat on the sofa with Hannah's head resting in the palm of her hand, as she rubbed and patted her back. Hannah stared at Ridley through a deep frown, framed by her ever-darkening brow – she was looking him up and down, as though working out who the hell he was and what he was doing here.

Shit, Ridley thought to himself. *She looks at me like Jack does!* Then she burped and smiled, making Ridley grin.

Hannah's eyes closed and she arched herself backwards in a long stretch. Maggie deftly caught her, then laid her down on the sofa so she could join Ridley in a well-earned glass of wine. Now that Hannah was asleep, Ridley didn't actually know what to say. Small talk wasn't really his thing. Eventually he said, 'I wanted to say thank you. For the compliment of asking me to be Hannah's guardian.'

Maggie smiled. 'Honestly, Simon, we couldn't think of anyone better. Don't worry, though; it doesn't mean Hannah has to move in with you if we both pop off. Just that we trust you to make the right choices for her. To be on her side.'

Ridley nodded. 'I can do that.'

Maggie looked at him and gently shook her head in disbelief. 'My God, Simon, why aren't you married?' Ridley laughed, to cover his embarrassment. 'I've never heard you say much, if I'm honest, but what you do say is always so lovely. You're very kind.'

Ridley had no idea how to respond, so he sipped his wine instead. Maggie could see she'd caught him off-guard. His humility was heartwarming. As Maggie looked at him, she realised that she actually had no idea whether Ridley was married or not. He could even be gay for all she knew, although he had more of a celibate vibe about him. But whatever the truth, it was clearly not something he was prepared to elaborate on.

They talked for another twenty minutes, mainly about whether or not parenthood was how she thought it would be. Then Ridley excused himself and got up to leave, saying Maggie should take advantage of Hannah napping. She looked so tired, Ridley reckoned she too would be napping within seconds.

* * *

'Guv!' Davidson shouted loudly across the squad room, bringing Gifford out of his office. Jack joined them at Davidson's side and for a few seconds, they both watched Bevan getting all four screens to the right time-code. Then Davidson narrated as the action played out in front of them.

'Idris arrives bang on 8.45, just like he said. He presses the buzzer, and the gate starts to open pretty much straight away, so Mathew must have been waiting in the kitchen. The gate takes twenty seconds to open fully, then stays open for about a minute before Idris heads back out again. But look, sir . . .' Davidson pointed to the bushes just outside of the Barrowmans' property. During the minute the gates were open and unattended, a figure dressed in black biker leathers, wearing a black balaclava and carrying what looked like a torch, crept out of the bushes, entered the grounds and hid in the bushes on the inside of the gate. Then Idris rode his scooter out, and the gates took another twenty seconds to close behind him.

Bevan fast-forwarded all of the recordings thirty-seven seconds and pressed play. The biker stepped out from his hiding place and got on his mobile phone. Whilst he talked, the biker paced in front of the camera, not remotely bothered by the fact that he was being recorded. He then put his mobile away and walked towards the house. Bevan fast-forwarded a further one minute and twenty-six seconds. The gates opened. Two masked men nimbly climbed the stone walls and spray-painted the camera lenses, exactly as Jack had suspected. These two masked men then disabled the inside gate cameras in the same way. Then just before the final camera lens was covered in spray-paint, a fourth masked man walked past in the background. In his hand, he brazenly carried a crowbar. Following him in was a car pulling a double horsebox. Bevan paused all four screens.

Jack's mind raced as he finally made sense of something he'd heard Mathew say. 'Masked men,' he said to himself. Then he closed his eyes and bowed his head, almost in shame. Bevan and Davidson couldn't bring themselves to interrupt Jack's moment of self-reproach. He then quickly stood upright and strode away across the room. He stood, hands on hips, looking at Gifford who was now leaning against his door frame.

'When I was at the house, sir, Mathew rushed into the kitchen, frightened, shouting about "masked men". Seeing as his home was swarming with CSIs at the time, everyone thought he was talking about them, but he was talking about the burglars. The masked burglars.' Jack paced, trying to put the chain of events together. 'The scout opened the gates for them. They brought weapons with them, meaning they've *always* been prepared for confrontation. What else? What else? There's something I need to remember . . . come on, Jack . . . Yes! The oily stain. Bevan, get on to forensics and fast-track the results on the stain that was collected from the back of the chair in Barrowman's study. Ronnie, we need that pizza box . . .'

'I'll call forensics. They'll be quicker for me.' Gifford was on his mobile before Jack had time to thank him. 'What are we thinking the oily stain is going to turn out to be?'

'If these cocky bastards were in the house just seconds after Idris left . . . if they took Mathew by surprise and took him out of the equation quickly, what would they do next?'

Davidson replied instinctively. 'I'd eat his pizza.'

Jack clicked his fingers at Davidson. 'So would I. They had all the time in the world. The house was empty for hours, Mathew was under control. This gang comes tooled up, ready for anything, but this is the first time they've actually had to fight – and *that's* exciting. The adrenaline would be pumping. They'd have felt invincible. That's what violence does to people like this. The good news is that adrenaline can also make us do stupid things . . . like nick Mathew's pizza and, hopefully, leave a dirty great DNA profile on a leather office chair.'

Right on cue, Gifford received a call-back from forensics confirming that the oily stain on the back of the chair in Barrowman's study was indeed from the cheese topping on a pizza. It seemed this astute, experienced gang of burglars, who hadn't put a foot wrong in three years, had taken off their gloves to steal and eat the sneaky bootleg dinner of an autistic man.

* * *

Mathew paid Idris for the pizza with three £5 notes, and then handed over another £5 in coins. This was their routine. Their arrangement; £15 for the pizza, and £5 for Idris to keep his mouth shut. And for

Mathew it was worth every penny. There was plenty about life that Mathew didn't understand, but he understood bribery: if he's a good boy, he gets ice cream; if Idris keeps their secret, he gets £5. Idris said goodbye, jumped onto his scooter and skidded away down the gravel driveway. Mathew pushed the gate button, knowing that the twenty seconds it took to close was plenty of time for Idris to get out onto the road.

Mathew headed for the stairs, pizza in hand, making a low, involuntary humming sound; this was how he contained his excitement and controlled his urge to eat the pizza on the way back to his bedroom. God, it smelt so good! The humming wasn't loud, but it was loud enough to mask the sound of biker boots approaching across the tiled kitchen floor.

The first blow from the heavy torch came down hard across Mathew's shoulder blades, forcing him down onto his knees and then forwards onto his hands. The pizza box shot across the highly polished floor, out of reach. The second blow came from the man with the crowbar. The crowbar hit Mathew's ribs and forced him to drop onto his side, curled up in the foetal position.

Mathew made no noise at all as the blows fell; shock had rendered him silent. From his position on his side, Mathew looked up to see what was to come next. Four masked men surrounded him. The closest was holding the crowbar, a second twisted a foot-long metal torch in his hands and the last two were unarmed, but their gloved fists were clenched so tight that Mathew could see their knuckles. Mathew desperately tried to make sense of what was happening, why they seemed so angry with him, but it didn't make any sense. He'd done nothing wrong, except order a pizza behind his parents' backs, but he was certain that had nothing to do with these men being in his home.

As Mathew hugged his aching ribs, a third blow from a boot struck him in the backside. The men laughed, which, again, Mathew couldn't understand. He even said as much: 'Not funny!' The giggling stopped and the beating began. Boots and weapons rained down on his body, all the time Mathew shouting, 'I'm sorry! You can laugh! I'm sorry, I'm sorry! You can laugh if you want to!' The man holding the crowbar then stood back and watched the others continue the beating. When this man finally stepped towards Mathew, all of the others immediately stopped hurting him, and Mathew was grateful. This man was in charge; he could tell. 'Thank you,' Mathew whimpered, and blood spilt from his mouth. The man's head cocked to one side, his part-hidden mouth smirked, and he raised the crowbar. Mathew cried out in fear, screwed his eyes tight shut and wrapped his arms around his head waiting for the blow to land. Nothing. Mathew opened his eyes to see what the man in charge was doing. He was standing, arm frozen in the air, crowbar poised. 'I promise to only hit you once more,' the man whispered. 'But where? Where shall I hit you?' He shifted the position of the crowbar, as though he was going to strike Mathew on the legs. As Mathew flung his arms low, the man seemed to change his mind and instead aimed for Mathew's head, then his chest, then his legs again. And so it went on, with the man pretending to strike Mathew, and Mathew desperately trying to follow his movements and defend himself against the one final blow that never came. As Mathew writhed about like a dying fish, the gang laughed at him and called him the most terrible names. Finally, when the man was bored with his game, he sharply brought the crowbar down in a fake blow towards Mathew's legs, then quickly diverted upwards and cracked him round the back of his skull. Mathew stopped moving, his eyes open, but expressionless. Shock had taken over. Mathew's brain refused to acknowledge the pain and made his body play dead, whilst it worked out what to do next.

Through blurry eyes, Mathew focussed on the pizza box lying about five feet in front of him. It made him feel happy. He didn't take his eyes off it. Not for one second. Not until the man who had hurt him so badly bent down and picked it up. Mathew stared at the empty spot on the floor and imagined his pizza.

* * *

Within the hour, all of Gifford's team was back in the squad room, having been stood down from pointlessly searching for the weapon or weapons used to assault Mathew. The atmosphere was electric. Gifford stood in his doorway, leaving the floor to Jack, as had become the norm. Gifford couldn't help feeling jealous: he'd never before seen his team so together and so pumped. Jack saw it. It was the same look he'd seen on Ridley's face in the past, so Jack went and stood firmly by Gifford's side before addressing the room.

'There are at least five people in this gang, and there's also an inside man. This gang went to the Barrowmans' thinking the place was empty, so there's also an electronics expert, because they expected to have to bypass the high-tech security system. They use a scout on a motorbike to clear the way, and they use a horsebox to get the bigger stuff out. They wouldn't have known till they arrived that Barrowman's artworks and furniture weren't worth nicking, so let's assume they came prepped with a horsebox.'

Gifford piped up. 'We've got our biker and our horsebox on CCTV, but it gives us nothing useful as yet.'

'It does,' Jack explained. 'It gives us patterns. The roads round here are straight and long. No back alleys and a limited number of short-cuts. They have to be staying somewhere. They have to have a base. There will be a geographical pattern that our biker and our horsebox are drawing across your landscape. We just need to find it.'

Both men looked at Bevan. 'I'll find it, sirs,' she said with a grin. Then she spun her chair round back to her computer and began furiously tapping away.

* * *

In the next thirty minutes, Jack and Gifford worked together to allocate the right job to the right officer. One was tasked with enhancing CCTV images of the men who entered the Barrowmans' property to establish height and build. A second was tasked with trying to track the horsebox. And two were sent back to the house to supervise the CSIs in cordoning off the bushes either side of the driveway gate so they could be examined for footprints at first light. The only fly in the ointment was the arrival of the forensics report on Mr Bright-Cullingwood's office space, which revealed one set of unidentified fingerprints, which showed no match to anyone on the CRIMINT database.

A text message from Oaks pinged through:

Mathew's got the all clear. They're heading home in an hour.

'Bevan,' Jack said. 'Find Sergeant McDermott for me please.' It was seven o'clock and Jack wanted to be at the Barrowmans' house by eight the next morning to interview Mathew. 'She's got twelve hours to teach me everything she knows about *Game of Thrones*.'

CHAPTER 10

At the station, Gifford was running the show. At the Barrowmans' house, Jack was the one leading the investigation. And Oaks had stepped up to lead the charge on the streets.

An hour and twenty minutes away from Chipping Norton, in Newbury, DC William Oaks and DC Ronnie Davidson were arriving at a racing stables owned by the aptly named Steven Goodwin. The closer examination of CCTV from the Barrowmans' home had revealed a safety label on the tailgate of the horsebox, with a code number on it that ultimately identified where and when it was given its annual once-over. Oaks had already spoken to Goodwin on the phone and he'd confirmed that three days earlier, he'd rented a three-horse trailer to a Mr Smart. The trailer had been returned in the early hours of that morning and was now tucked away behind the stables waiting for Oaks and Davidson to take a look at it.

Oaks walked up the ramp of the suspect horse trailer. 'Can you smell that? Disin-fucking-fectant. Jeez, Ronnie, the floor of this trailer has got less trace evidence on it than my bog seat.' There were four other identical trailers in the main yard, all of which had been rented out to Mr Smart on numerous occasions over the previous three years. He always paid in cash and the keys were always left underneath a wheel arch, as he always collected and dropped off in the early hours.

As Goodwin approached, Oaks tried to hide his disappointment. He didn't want Goodwin thinking he'd done anything wrong by cleaning the trailer so thoroughly, but Goodwin realised his mistake. 'I'm sorry,' Goodwin started, 'if I'd known, I'd have left it as it was. But it's booked out again this afternoon, so I . . . I cleaned it about an hour before you called.' Then he quickly added that he'd of course cancel the afternoon booking and the trailer would remain where it was until Oaks was done with it. 'It smelt of petrol,' Goodwin said, desperate to make up for destroying all of their evidence. 'And there were muddy tyre tracks inside.'

Oaks shared their suspicions that one of the gang rode a motorbike. 'Yes, they could have been motorbike tracks,' Goodwin agreed. 'But there were also double tracks. Like a quadbike.'

Davidson stood in Goodwin's yard, holding his mobile away from his ear. 'A fookin' quadbiiike!' Gifford's Midlands accent came to the surface as he ranted. 'That means they had two recce vehicles, one of which can approach any property, over any nobbin' terrain!'

Goodwin kept detailed records of everyone who hired his horse trailers, so he was able to provide a driving licence and phone number for Mr Smart. Oaks knew that both would be fake, but at least they would provide a starting point for two new lines of enquiry.

'So, you left the keys under the wheel arch as requested and, in the morning, the horse trailer was gone?' Oaks asked.

Goodwin confirmed that Mr Smart paid in full upfront, so he was more than happy to accommodate his requests. It wasn't unusual for people to collect hire-vehicles during the night, because driving on empty roads was better for the horses and many of the local events and competitions started early. The trailer had been returned in much the same way: in the dead of night, with no witnesses.

'I saw them.' Oaks spun round to see a young lad with a broom in his hand. He was small, wearing tight clothes that showed off his lean body. Oaks guessed that he was in his late teens and definitely a jockey in the making. 'I didn't see them bring the trailer back, but I saw them pick it up.'

The stable boy's name was Justin Estrada. It turned out he was of Guatemalan descent, born in Gloucester and had always yearned to be a jockey. He was the perfect build and temperament. He flowed as he walked, almost as if he was floating, and the animals adored him. He explained how he'd been woken at around two in the morning by the sound of a motorbike. He got up and looked out of his window, as he was worried that the noise might disturb the horses. As he looked down into the yard, he saw a figure get off the back of the motorbike and head straight for the keys under the wheel arch. By the time the keys were retrieved, a car had reversed into position in front of the trailer. It took them no more than five minutes to hook up – then they were gone.

Oaks asked Justin if he could describe any of the men he saw, but he shook his head. 'I didn't see much. The guy who got off the back of the bike was just ordinary. He was average height and build, and he never took his helmet off. The guy who drove the car was wearing a dark hoodie and dark jeans. I never saw his face, but he was heavy-set, you know. His hoodie was tight on his biceps and around his chest. Oh, and he wore black Adidas NMDs. With the red sole. The R2, I think. Could have been the R1, but I think it was the R2.'

Oaks stared at Justin, open-mouthed. The kid had said he hadn't seen much and then narrowed the perp's footwear down to a specific design of trainer. Justin grinned, knowing he'd done well. 'I sell collectable trainers online, see. The R2 isn't collectable yet, it's too new, but it will be.' Oaks double-checked that Justin was certain about what he'd seen. 'The security light went on when the bike pulled into the yard. Definitely Adidas NMDs.' Oaks shook the lad's hand and wished him all the luck in the world in his endeavours to be a jockey.

* * *

Ridley called while Jack waited in the kitchen for Sally Barrowman. Jack opted to call him back after he'd spoken to Mathew. There'd hopefully be more to say then. Mrs Thorburn, the housekeeper, put a plate of biscuits and a pot of tea down in front of Jack and then began unloading the dishwasher. She clearly wasn't in a good mood and when Jack asked what was wrong, she said she'd been given a verbal warning by Mr Barrowman for keeping Mathew's contraband takeaways a secret for all these years. After giving her statement, she'd had to admit to finding takeaway containers in the bin on numerous occasions. She wasn't bothered about the warning itself, though; she was more worried about having to tell tales on Mathew from now on, knowing it would damage their relationship, possibly beyond repair.

When Sally Barrowman joined them, Mrs Thorburn kept her head down and neither woman acknowledged the other. 'Mathew's ready.' Jack could hear the unease in Sally's voice.

'Mrs Barrowman, I won't do anything to knowingly upset Mathew. But we can't lose sight of the fact that your son is the only person to have had any direct contact with the—'

'*Contact?*' she almost yelled. 'Is that what you're calling it? He was assaulted. He's traumatised. He's tremendously vulnerable, and the second I think he's had enough of you, you will leave his bedroom. If you can't promise me that right now, DS Warr, then you can get out of my house!'

The gentle, subservient housewife had gone, to be replaced with a ferociously protective mother. Jack wondered if perhaps George Barrowman was not the head of this household after all.

Sally went on to explain how, at the hospital, even though Mathew was escorted straight through to a side room, he had still been scared and agitated by all of the people and all of the beeping machines they were trying to attach him to. It took them hours to examine him properly and, when it came to persuading him to go into the X-ray room, it was an almost impossible task. 'He's had so many bad experiences with hospitals and doctors . . . he can't help the way he reacts. It's the same with the police. Matty has been horribly mistreated by some of the police in his time, because they've assumed him to be naughty instead of poorly.'

Jack remained respectful in the face of Sally's motherly fears, but he wasn't going to completely give in to her. 'I'm in your home, Mrs Barrowman, asking to interview your vulnerable son; so, you're the one who's making the rules here. Create an environment that Mathew will be happy with, then tell me how to behave and I'll do it. I'm not going to go against your advice. But I'm also not going to leave without speaking to him.'

By the time Jack had finished speaking, Sally had tears in her eyes and he wasn't sure why. 'I'll stay down here.' Her voice had become nothing more than a whisper. Jack felt compelled to ask her if she was OK. 'Mathew said he didn't want me at the hospital, so I haven't seen his injuries and George won't tell me anything. Are they terrible? Was he frightened for long, do you think?' Sally's eyes begged Jack to say something comforting.

'I think it was over quickly. I think he didn't fight back and gave them no reason to continue hurting him. With professional gangs like this, they just want to get in and out as quickly as possible. They would have wanted Mathew to be scared and be quiet . . . which he was.' Jack hoped she believed him. In reality, he suspected the gang took pleasure in beating Mathew and stealing his pizza, and from the extent of his injuries, that once Mathew was on the ground, the gang continued to beat him.

Sally shook her head sadly. 'I wish I'd never gone to that fucking charity auction.' She sighed. 'Nathaniel is already upstairs. Knock and he'll let you in.'

Jack headed up the winding, double staircase, pausing to look at the family portraits lining the panelled walls. Mathew was in most pictures, but his face was always turned away from the camera and he rarely smiled. Not that he looked sad; it was just as though he was in a perpetual state of deep thought. One photo, taking pride of place on the landing where the staircases met, was of Sally, George and Mathew, aged about eight, running around the garden playing what looked like a game of tag, and it stood out from the rest. The glee on Mathew's face was so animated and unrestrained that Jack couldn't take his eyes off the image. It was slightly blurred and the composition was awful, but this photograph was clearly positioned there to be the first one this family saw in the morning and the last one they saw at night.

Jack felt his heart quicken with parental understanding, and once again he thanked his lucky stars that his daughter was, as far as he knew, a healthy little girl who was on track to live a normal, happy life.

'Took two hours to get that, apparently.' Jack turned to see Nathaniel standing outside Mathew's bedroom. 'It took Matty a while to get the hang of why he'd want to run away from his parents but, once he twigged that dodging a touch from your mum or dad was actually fun, there was no stopping him. Matty's in a good mood and is looking forward to your chat. Give him his space though, and please don't touch any of his things.'

Mathew's bedroom was bright and light. It was really just a white box; a blank canvas on which he could display his obsession with *Game of Thrones*, with myriad posters, character figurines and other merchandise, as well as DVDs, well-thumbed books and T-shirts. Mathew sat at his desk, playing *Game of Thrones Ascent* which was being displayed simultaneously on two large Mac screens and was hooked up to surround sound, though at the moment the sound was nothing more than a dull buzzing coming from the headphones which were hooked over the back of Mathew's chair.

Mathew paused his game and spun his wide, heavy leather gaming chair, so that he was side-on to Jack. 'Well, well, well.' Mathew's deep, resonating voice was a surprising contrast to the high-pitched screaming Jack had heard on the police bodycam footage. 'It's the diminutive Detective Sergeant Warr.'

Nathaniel leant close to Jack and explained in a whisper that Mathew had a thing about height: anyone perceived to be below around 5'10" was referred to as 'diminutive', and anyone above 6'5" was 'Hodorian' after the *Game of Thrones* character, Hodor. Anyone in between those two heights was of no interest to Mathew at all. Mathew stood, walked over to Jack and, whilst keeping his eyes averted, offered his hand. Mathew's grip was uncomfortably firm and accompanied by one single, violent up-and-down shake. Then he let go and returned to his chair. 'What do you want to talk about?' he asked.

Jack glanced at Nathaniel for any indication that Jack shouldn't start his questioning, but Nathaniel had his hands in his pockets and was smiling, so Jack took a deep breath and began. 'Thank you for agreeing to meet with me, Mathew. I'm loving your *Game of Thrones* stuff. Have you played *The Sword of Darkness*?'

Nathaniel's smile disappeared and he audibly groaned.

As Mathew began talking animatedly about *The Sword of Darkness*, he swung back and forth in his chair, shifting between the different voices as he recounted the entire game narrative. At certain moments, Mathew even stood up and excitedly acted out some of the most thrilling fight scenes. Jack could see he had forgotten himself – just like the little boy in the picture at the top of the stairs, playing tag in the garden with his parents. Exactly thirty-two minutes later, Mathew stopped talking as suddenly as he'd started. He then sat perfectly still, like a wind-up toy that had finally run down.

Nathaniel breathed a sigh of relief and threw Jack a warning look that very clearly said, 'Don't ask him anything else about *Game of bloody Thrones!*'

'Mathew,' Jack began, 'will you talk to me about the night the men broke into your home?' Mathew laced his fingers together, sat forwards in his chair and bowed his head. His eyes remained open and he looked as if he was concentrating, waiting for a question to be asked. 'Can you remember how many men there were?'

Mathew briefly raised five fingers.

'Were the men diminutive or Hodorian – or neither?'

Mathew thought for a moment, then said that three men were diminutive and two were neither.

'Were all the men masked?'

Mathew nodded

'OK, Mathew, then—'

'Oberyn Martell,' Mathew said quickly.

Jack stopped and let him continue.

'Oberyn Martell took his mask off.'

Jack looked around the bedroom walls, desperately trying to recall what the hell Oberyn Martell, who he knew was a character from *Game of Thrones*, actually looked like. His eyes paused on a poster of the House Martell family tree: Oberyn was a handsome young man with Mediterranean looks and a perfectly trimmed jawline beard and moustache.

'He couldn't eat my pizza through the hole in his mask, so he lifted it up.' Mathew put the palms of his hands tightly over his eyes and his voice shot up in pitch. 'If he wanted me to share, he should have asked!'

Nathaniel nodded to Jack, indicating that Mathew was OK: he was getting upset, but he was coping.

Mathew's tearful, increasingly frantic voice spat out words through his fingers. 'They hit me and hit me and hit me. And then Oberyn Martell promised to only hit me one more time, but that was a lie.' Mathew dropped his hands and leapt to his feet, his face wet. He looked towards, but not directly at, Jack, stepping quickly from foot to foot as he inched forwards. 'I was so still, DS Warr, as still as a sleeping lion. For a long time. All the while they ate my pizza, I never moved.' Jack had been told not to invade Mathew's personal space but now Mathew was invading his. What should he do? Nathaniel once again gave a reassuring nod, so Jack stood his ground.

As Mathew continued, he began to sob, loudly and painfully. 'And when they left, they took the pizza box with them and I shouted, "Please put that at the bottom of the bin!" 'cos Mum doesn't let me have pizza. But Oberyn Martell just hit me again really hard on my back and shouted, "I'm the boss!" And again. Before running out of the house to catch up with his friends. I got up and I ran after him. "Please give me the box," I said. "My mum will be so cross!" And do you know what Oberyn Martell did, DS Warr?'

Mathew was now standing so close to Jack's face, that Jack's eyes couldn't bring him into focus. Jack shook his head.

'Oberyn Martell put the pizza box in the bin for me. Right at the bottom, so Mum would never find it. That was nice of him.' Mathew returned to his chair, put his headphones on and pressed play on his game.

CHAPTER 11

Ridley was stuck behind a 'car v cyclist' Road Traffic Collision near Vauxhall and hadn't moved in over thirty minutes. All around him, irate drivers shouted at their passengers or into their mobiles or at the inconsiderate dead cyclist lying under a white sheet in the road ahead. Ridley was comparatively serene: he was working on his mobile, making lists and planning his day.

When his mobile rang, number withheld, he expected to have a short, one-sided conversation with a PPI salesperson; instead he found himself talking to DCI Louisa Hearst from Gloucester. It seemed that the complaints that Gifford had predicted would hit the DCI's desk had finally started coming through, and when George Barrowman's complaint arrived, Hearst had no option but to pick up the phone. Ridley had never met Louisa Hearst, but her reputation for being a man-eating bitch preceded her.

'Your man is causing problems,' she told him firmly. 'We're a microcosm here, Simon; everyone knows everyone else's business, so diplomacy's the key. And your man is not diplomatic.'

Ridley knew that Hearst was referring to Jack as 'your man' so that he would feel the weight of responsibility for Jack's actions, but he didn't.

'One of our most prominent residents, George Barrowman,' she continued, 'has made an official complaint about your DS Warr, and I have to be seen to be doing something about that. Barrowman is neighbours with ex-prime minister Cameron, so on the one hand he has an inflated perception of his own impor-tance, and on the other hand he may have a point. He says that your man interviewed his disabled son without his permission.

Now, I happen to know for a fact that the mother was present, but to a man like Barrowman, that's like saying "the cat was present". He's demanding that you replace your DS with a more experienced officer . . . and that request didn't land on my desk, by the way, it landed on my boss's desk. So . . . what do you suggest I do?'

'What would you like to do, Louisa?' Ridley had all the time in the world right now, so he was up for an argument if that's the way the conversation was destined to go.

'I'd very much like to get Seb from his stable and ride him over to Bledington to meet an unhappily married man I know, but I'm doubtful that'll happen this side of the weekend. So, for now, I'd like to have your assurance that DS Warr knows what he's doing.'

'I trust him with my life,' Ridley replied evenly.

'But are you sure you want to trust him with your reputation, Simon?' she asked pointedly.

'Absolutely. Jack will get results for you. But I'm afraid he won't suffer any fools along the way. Is Barrowman a fool?'

'When threatened. Which I think is all that's happened here, really. I don't know the reputation of Jack Warr, but I do know the reputation of Simon Ridley from a mutual friend. So, I'm inclined to trust you.'

'Sounds like I owe Joe Gifford a pint, in that case. How's he doing?'

'The word perfunctory springs to mind.'

For the next hour, Ridley listened to Hearst share her derogatory opinions of every mutual acquaintance they had, and it turned out she was hilarious. Surrounding drivers, who were becoming more irate with every passing minute, stared daggers at Ridley who was sitting there, windows up, laughing his arse off. It was one of the most enjoyable conversations Ridley had ever had with a woman.

* * *

Over in Chipping Norton, the squad room was a hive of activity and Jack was right at the heart of it, scribbling furiously on the whiteboards. He noted that the height of Maisie's burglar was now more likely to be around the 5'10" mark, and that one of the men who broke into Mathew's house was identified as Mediterranean in looks. Gifford doubted Mathew's reliability as a witness, but Jack had absolute confidence in him. 'Mathew has an eye for certain details. In this case, one of the burglars lifted his mask and was described as looking like Oberyn Martell.'

'I don't know the name,' Gifford frowned. 'Does he have a criminal record?'

'He's a character from *Game of Thrones*, sir,' Jack explained, ignoring Gifford's look of incomprehension. 'Mathew is an expert on the subject. If he says that the man looked like Oberyn Martell, then he did. And we also know that one of the men was heavy-set and wore Adidas NMDs, probably R2s because of their red sole, and that the gang is using a quadbike as well as a motorbike. Sir, the case was always going to get messier before it got neater. But everything will fall into place.'

Jack then turned his attention to Bevan and asked if she'd made any progress with finding the submerged horsebox and the owner of the cufflinks. She was disappointed to say that the cufflinks had been a dead end, with no known burglary victim claiming them. And the submerged horsebox containing their eight-month-old dead body was probably, but not definitely, hired from a small-scale

livery stable just outside Aldsworth. She'd come to this latest conclusion because, three years ago, the owner had passed away and
his children had sold the property almost immediately. It was now
a B&B, with all evidence of its previous working life gone without
a trace. It was the only place Bevan could find that could possibly
have hired out a horsebox and then lost track of the fact that it had
never been returned.

'Fantastic work, Bevan.' Jack's upbeat response was a surprise to
her seeing as, to her mind, she'd delivered nothing of value. 'Loose
ends are a distraction. So, thank you for tying those up.'

Gifford's mobile pinged.

'Here's another loose end tied up,' he said, reading the message,
then indicating to Jack to follow him to a more private corner of
the squad room. 'I've got Barrowman's credit card statement: one
string of pearls, £900. Purchased a couple of weeks ago. The next
purchase is a meal for two at The Ivy last Wednesday, and the next
purchase is a red satin negligée.' He gave Jack a sorry smile.

'So it's not a pay-off for inside info from a gang of murderous
burglars, I'm afraid. It's a birthday surprise for his secretary in
London. Apparently her name is Sherry and she turned twenty-
seven last Wednesday.'

* * *

At that moment, Ridley walked into the squad room.

None of Gifford's team knew who he was, but they could tell
he was a copper, and an important one. Ridley looked seriously in
Jack's direction.

Jack, intrigued by Ridley's presence, picked up the pace.

'On top of everything we've already discussed, we need to track
the high-end items, especially the Barrowmans' emerald "Barbara

Hutton" necklace. They won't be able to fence it here, so it'll end up in London. We know this gang is transient, so it makes sense that they come here, stick around long enough to commit these burglaries, then disappear again. This further supports the theory that, as outsiders, they'll need local knowledge to help them choose their targets.' Jack then turned to Ridley. 'You here to see me, sir?'

Ridley's silent, stern-faced nod suggested that Jack might be in trouble. Since arriving in Chipping Norton, Jack was aware that he'd clashed with Gifford, Oaks, Barrowman and Mrs Fullworth, but none of them mattered a jot to him. Ridley, on the other hand, mattered a great deal.

As Ridley closed Gifford's office door, Gifford made himself comfortable at Jack's desk, with the scenic view to his left and his own glass-walled office in front of him. He might not be able to hear the bollocking Jack was about to get, but he'd certainly enjoy watching it.

Ridley got straight down to business. 'Joe's boss, DCI Hearst, called me today.' Jack opened his mouth to defend himself, but Ridley held up a hand to cut him off. '*Her* boss, DCS Lindgarden, has been getting complaints. Hearst has to be seen to be doing her job, as do I. So, just stand there and listen. Gifford is a cowardly old bastard who should have retired years ago. After today, he'll be able to legitimately tell people like Mr Barrowman that you've been reprimanded. I know you can live with that. But don't change anything, Jack. You're doing a good job. What's he doing now?'

Jack's eyes flicked to Gifford for a split second, then back to Ridley. 'He's grinning.'

Ridley frowned. 'Prick. Your gang's getting restless, that right?'

'They've severely beaten a young man with autism, and they've killed a pet dog. And they're more than likely connected to a murder committed about eight months ago; probably one of their own. I know it doesn't sound like much compared to the stuff we get every day in London, but the reason both of the "innocent victim" attacks are so worrying is that neither was necessary. The burglars had the upper hand in both situations. They turned to violence because they wanted to. As for the dead guy in the horsebox, I don't know; maybe he pocketed the cufflinks and, in return, got what was coming.'

Ridley shared Jack's concern. 'Sounds like they've got a taste for it. Like a psychopath moving on from killing animals to killing people.' Ridley slid his hands into his pockets and thought for a second before continuing. 'Detective Chief Superintendent Lindgarden wants to bring in two DIs from Oxford Robbery to help you.'

Jack's face tensed and his cheek muscles twitched.

'Something's happened out their way, which links them to your case, so they're coming whether you like it or not. Use them, Jack; this is their world. But if they get in your way, you let me know.'

Just as Ridley walked out of Gifford's office, Hearst entered the squad room with two men. At the sight of her, Gifford and his team all stood. Jack sighed. Keeping one senior officer off his back was going to be time-consuming enough; three would slow him right down.

Ridley and Hearst shook hands like old friends, even though this was actually the first time they'd met in person. Their one-hour, traffic-jam chat had clearly been a bonding experience. She was petite, with broad shoulders like a swimmer, and an impressively slim waist, and her suit was subtly tailored to set off her athletic figure. After greeting Gifford, she introduced her two companions: the Oxford Robbery boys.

DI Eamonn Lee was a sandy-haired man with stubble, brows and lashes so fair in colour that his face looked hairless. And this made his piercing blue eyes stand out. DI Colin Mason looked exactly like a thicker-set version of President Obama, but with a strong Welsh accent.

While Mason introduced himself with little fuss, Lee practically recounted his entire Robbery CV, as though wanting to make it very clear that he was the most experienced person in the room. This told Jack a lot about both men: confidence whispers, insecurity shouts. 'It'll be good to work alongside you, sirs. Your expertise will be very much appreciated,' he said politely.

'Thanks, Jack,' Lee replied in a voice that was deeper than he expected. 'We lead from the front, so don't you worry about being left to do all of the legwork. All we ask is that you keep up.' The last was said through a big, toothy grin. Jack smiled back; he just found this sort of posturing amusing. Jack hoped that Lee was simply nervous about being on someone else's turf and would ultimately prove to be an asset to the investigation.

Gifford, as obsequious as expected, silently deferred to the Oxford boys without the slightest hint of independence. He invited everyone into his office and then sent a message to Canteen Barbara, asking her to provide the obligatory tea and pastries.

Ridley could see Jack's disappointment in Gifford, as if he was ashamed to even call him a fellow officer. In a moment alone, Ridley explained a few home truths:

'You've heard Gifford's mobile pinging all the time?' Ridley kept his voice low, so that only Jack could hear him. 'That's his race results coming through. He used to be a good enough officer, but he got left behind. Now, he's a gambler. This will be his last case, Jack. Get him through it, so he can retire with his head high and his pension intact.'

Jack felt the pressure of being in a no-win situation and at that moment he wished he'd never volunteered for the bloody Cotswolds job in the first place. He was now stuck between the useless Gifford and two Oxford Robbery guys he knew he didn't need.

'You're all on the same team,' Ridley soothed. 'Play nice, at least to their faces – you're good at that.' Ridley gave Jack a knowing smile. 'Go and talk to them. Share information. Then leave them doing all of the cross-referencing and I'll drive you back to London to recharge your batteries over the weekend.'

'I won't leave now, sir, this is my case! Are you sidelining me?' Jack asked quickly.

Ridley couldn't believe that he even had to say the words. 'No, Jack, I'm not sidelining you. It's the naming ceremony for your firstborn tomorrow.'

CHAPTER 12

Jack knew a grand total of seven people in the crowd of about fifty who were currently milling around the conference room and adjoining patio, gulping down Pimm's – which Jack assumed he'd paid for. The conference room had been disguised well, behind lavish lace drapes and silver 'baby' balloons. Only the projector, stuck underneath a table in the corner, gave the game away. As he swapped his empty glass of orange juice for a full one, Jack imagined that at the same time tomorrow this room could be full of arseholes like Barrowman, talking pompous horseshit to each other about the price of gold bullion.

Jack moved out to the patio and stood away from the smokers to enjoy the view of the stunning grounds of this five-star Richmond hotel. Maggie had been right to book it. Turning, he could see her chatting to a group of people he didn't know, work colleagues from the hospital, he guessed. Penny was by the gift table peering through a tiny rip in the paper on one of the presents, trying to work out what it was. And Ridley ... Ridley was surrounded by cooing women, being force-fed Pimm's as he cradled a sleeping Hannah in his arms.

An hour later, DCI Simon Ridley, the stiffest man on the force, was attempting to sing a lullaby that he only knew half the words to.

Hannah was riveted by Ridley's out-of-tune rendition. And, although he was surrounded by ladies, he only had eyes for the one in his arms.

In the far corner of the room, out of Jack's eyeline, Laura was being chatted up by a doctor giving her the full 'their beating heart was in the palm of my hand' story, but although she was smiling in all the right places, she wasn't listening to a word. Instead she was listening to Ridley singing.

Laura, like many people who worked all the hours God sends for the emergency services, had been single for a long time, and every married police officer she knew, male or female, was with someone else from the emergency services. Not surprisingly, since there was no time to meet anyone outside of the job. She even went to the pub with people from work, so how on earth was she ever going to meet anyone new?

Her life was full and exciting, but it was repetitive. She'd been out with paramedics, firemen, policemen, so perhaps this handsome but boring doctor was going to be next? There was a time when Laura would have begun a relationship with an attractive man like this in a heartbeat, but today she felt like walking away.

She turned and, right behind her was Ridley. He put a sleeping Hannah into her arms and said, 'Just have to nip, you know.' He smiled his thanks, put his hand on Laura's elbow and, as he walked away, his fingers slid down her bare arm and to her fingertips before he walked out of reach. Goosebumps immediately broke out over her entire body and she could feel herself blushing and heart palpitating.

Sadly, she knew that Ridley would not have had the same reaction from her touch. Laura looked down at Hannah and took advantage of the fact that a woman close to tears in public was perfectly acceptable if she happened to have a gorgeous baby in her arms.

On the patio, Penny had appeared by Jack's side. 'Hannah's been given four cot quilts and three mobiles. You'd think people would confer.'

'Why would you give a baby a mobile?' Jack asked.

'Not a mobile phone, darling. A dangly mobile. For above her cot.' Penny wrapped her arm around Jack's waist and, together, they watched the room. They were amazed by the number of people who wanted to say hello to their little Hannah. It reminded Penny of the number of people who had turned out to say goodbye to their Charlie.

'A funeral, a christening and a wedding all in the same twelve months,' she said, thinking out loud. Jack squeezed Penny's shoulder and she rested her head against his chest.

'I think the wedding will be next year, Mum. I'd like to take Maggie back to St Lucia for the honeymoon and, well, it's not cheap. Plus Maggie wants to get back down to a size ten.'

'Oh, she could do that in a couple of months if she put her mind to it.'

'She's a hormonal woman with a currently insatiable craving for Chinese takeaways and red wine . . . are you going to tell her to "put her mind to it"? 'Cos I'm bloody not!'

* * *

Although Hannah had slept through much of her big day, she still went straight down as soon as they got home. As did Penny.

Jack hadn't drunk a drop of alcohol at the naming ceremony because he was the designated driver but once safely back home, he sat down on the sofa with Maggie and poured himself a large brandy. Maggie ventured to ask how his assignment to the Cotswolds was going and he told her how he felt he'd been shafted: 'First of all I get personally requested because of my experience in similar cases, then I'm outranked by a couple of Oxford Robbery guys. And Ridley's playing both sides. He bollocked me for show, so that Chipping Norton thinks I'm on some kind of fucking leash, but then, he's also told me to bypass them and report directly to him.'

'You get the same sort of political games in the NHS,' Maggie shrugged. 'It doesn't mean Ridley doesn't trust you.'

'I know that,' Jack conceded, 'but sometimes I wish he'd just stand up and be counted.' Maggie moved closer to Jack and gently laced her fingers through his. 'I don't know, Mags. It's bad timing, I guess. The team over there are just starting to respect me and . . .' Maggie leant over and kissed him.

'Does that mean shut up?' he asked, laughing. She kissed him again.

Jack seized this rare intimate moment. He picked Maggie up, making an 'ooomph' noise as she settled on his hips and linked her ankles behind his back. Three stairs up and Jack stepped on a pile of ironed babygrows, which sent him tumbling forwards onto his left hand – while his right hand stayed firmly around Maggie's waist so that he didn't drop her. They giggled as quietly as possible, trying not to lose the moment.

Jack stood up, leaving Maggie sitting on the stairs. 'Get me a brandy,' she instructed. 'Then get your arse upstairs before I fall asleep.'

Not needing to be asked twice, Jack raced down to the kitchen.

It was the first time that Jack and Maggie had made love since Hannah was born – and the quickest. As they lay together after-wards, relaxed in each other's arms, it felt like a new, exciting chapter was about to begin. Maggie declared that she was happier now than she had ever been in her entire life. And part of her happiness came from Jack finally finding his place in the world.

'Go back to the Cotswolds with your head high, Jack. Whether they know it or not, they're lucky to have you.' Maggie was clearly in a soppy mood, but her words were sincere and made Jack feel better about the awkward situation he was in. Maggie propped herself up on Jack's chest, so she could look him in the eyes. 'You're a special copper, you know that, don't you? With the mind of Harry Rawlins and the heart of Charlie Warr.' Jack was surprised to hear Maggie speak Harry's name. He assumed that Maggie had erased him from their lives as a long-dead, bad influence. But apparently Harry Rawlins popped into her mind every now and then, just as he popped into Jack's. 'They make you who you are. *Think* like Harry, *act* like Charlie, and you'll be invincible. You are the very best of two strong and memorable men. You are a force to be reckoned with, Jack Warr.'

CHAPTER 13

In the forty-eight hours Jack had been in London, both teams – Oxford and Chipping Norton – had shared all the intel from the past three years and were now completely up to speed.

Before he'd left for his daughter's naming ceremony, Jack had contributed one vitally important instruction: to keep this case on a 'need-to-know' basis. The general public already had little-to-no faith in the police's ability to catch this gang, so if they found out about the growing physical dangers to homeowners, they'd be up in arms. Jack advised that, although the Barrowman burglary itself would inevitably become public knowledge, 'Mathew's assault should remain a secret. And, most importantly—'

Lee had interrupted at this point to say that he'd personally go and see Mr Barrowman to explain. 'Barrowman will be fine once he sees you've brought in the big guns. And I'll give an edited statement to the press, to keep them out of the way.'

Jack waited until he'd finished. 'What I was going to say was that we still don't know who the insider is, or if there's more than one. Any gossip on the streets could be fatal.'

* * *

By the time Jack got back to Chipping Norton, DIs Lee and Mason had got their feet firmly under the desk and Jack was now the one playing catch-up.

Lee and Mason sat opposite Gifford in his office. Oaks perched on the windowsill and a small, low office chair had been provided for Jack. He opted to ignore the obvious symbolism and remain standing in order to assert authority, whether he actually still had any, or not.

Lee took the lead. 'There's a livery stable in Oxford renting horseboxes, trailers, tractors and farm equipment. The owner, Jacob Mulhern, has it on record that, in the dim and distant past, he rented a three-horse trailer to a Mr Smart. I believe you know the name. It's the same MO – fake ID, paid in cash, collected and dropped off in the dead of night.'

'Apologies if this has already been covered in my absence, but how come this wasn't flagged when DI Gifford originally shared Mr Smart's name with you?' As soon as Jack had said it, he knew the answer. Gifford never had shared the name of with Oxford Robbery. Everyone in the room silently decided to ignore Jack's question. It was pointless raking over old mistakes; they had to move forwards now. And they had to move together.

Lee continued: 'As soon as we did realise your gang had rented trailers in Oxford, we interviewed Mulhern. We've had two burglaries, both about a year and a half ago. They were picked up by uniform and, because the owners just wanted to claim on the insurance and forget about it, they weren't escalated to us. This, in itself, is nothing unusual – if the victim doesn't pursue, we can't pursue. Anyway, the name Smart was on file, so here we are.'

Oaks piped up, wanting to be an active part of the handover to Jack. 'Because of Bevan's mastery of the whiteboards, it was a quick and easy job to compare the Oxford robbery dates with our Chipping Norton dates and see that this gang has never actually had any down-time, as we originally thought. When they weren't in one place, they were in another. They never stopped.'

'Great.' Jack felt he was having his own investigation explained to him. 'So, we now have all information pertaining to these two old burglaries and trailer rentals, do we?'

'We've brought you more than that, DS Warr.' Lee's smug tone made Jack lean forwards in anticipation; something good was about to be shared. 'Mr Smart has just rented another trailer from Mulhern.'

Jack's eyes widened. Oaks stood up, full of excitement. 'So, they're gonna hit again!' He realised for the first time in three years, they were ahead of the gang.

Mason spoke for the first time in his soft Welsh lilt. 'We've got it covered. We're watching the most likely targets, based on the geography of the two known incidents.'

Jack's demeanour immediately shifted from confident to concerned. 'Sir, two incidents can't give you any kind of a pattern, it's statistically impossible, so there's no way for you to know if you're protecting the right target homes. You have to watch the livery.'

Mason frowned and his voice took on a deeper, darker tone. 'I can assure you we know how to do our job.'

But Jack stood his ground. 'Scattergun policing won't work with this gang; they're too organised. You have to be precisely targeted and the only thing you know about for sure is the livery stable.'

Mason shook his head. 'That would mean allowing the burglary to take place.'

'It's the only thing you can do.' Jack looked to Gifford for some kind of support, any kind of support, and when he didn't get it, Jack finally snapped at this poor excuse for a police officer. 'Tell me I'm wrong if you think I am, sir. Or tell them they're wrong!' Jack tried to regain his composure. 'DI Mason, if you follow them into the rat-run, you will get lost. You have to wait for them to come out. At the livery stable.' A troubling thought brought a deep frown to Jack's brow. 'How did Mulhern know to call you about Mr Smart? Does Mulhern know that Smart's name is directly connected to the burglaries? Because if you've told him, then he's definitely the one you should be protecting!'

Before Jack had finished his sentence, Lee was on his feet. 'DS Warr, that's enough! We've just brought you the best lead you've had in three years. We fully intend to return to Oxford and interview Mulhern. If you want to remain part of this investigation as we finally close in on Mr Smart, I suggest you toe the line.'

Jack's jaw clenched and his nostrils flared, but he didn't say a word. At that moment, he wanted to arrest Mr Smart slightly more than he wanted to hit DI Lee.

CHAPTER 14

The Oxford livery stables were in darkness by the time Mason's car pulled up across the uneven driveway. Lee had returned to their Thames Valley Police Station on Abingdon Road, to get his DCI and local councillors up to speed, which told Jack all he needed to know about where Lee's priorities lay; placating the elite was clearly more important than making sure Mulhern was safe and then laying a trap at his livery stables to be triggered by the gang when they returned the horse trailer in the dead of night.

The fifty-minute drive to just past Abingdon in Oxfordshire had been deathly silent. Jack and Lee had clearly not got off to the best of starts, which irked Mason who hated any kind of confrontation within his team. He'd decided that the best way to handle the tension was to say nothing.

Mason had just received a phone call from Lee to say that a patrol car had attended Mulhern's livery stables less than an hour ago and had been unable to get an answer. But all was quiet, and the house was secure, so he was probably out. Lee's insinuation that they were on a wasted trip didn't allay Jack's fears that something could be very wrong.

Mason knocked loudly on the front door to Mulhern's home for the third time. 'Looks like uniform was right,' Mason shrugged. 'He's just out. It's all good.'

Jack peered in through the lounge window for signs of life as Mason headed towards the stables just across the yard. Jack shielded his eyes from the glare of the security light. 'There are coats and boots inside the front door.' Jack shifted position, so he could see the other end of the lounge. 'There's a half-eaten sandwich on a plate perched on the arm of the sofa. And a mug of tea on the floor. Not touched by the looks of things.' On the kitchen table was a carrier bag, rolled down to reveal a potted plant inside. Although partly obscured, Jack could just make out the business logo on the side of this bag: the word 'Miles' inter-twined with leafy graphics. Charlotte Miles again.

Jack turned to share his discovery, but Mason was standing frozen in place, staring in through the open top half of a stable door. Jack moved swiftly to his side.

Mulhern's body was on the floor. He was gagged and his arms were bound behind his back with rope. He was lying in the middle of a large blood-soaked pile of hay and a huge grey stallion stood within inches of Mulhern's head, eating its fill of the crime scene. Jack moved quickly past the seemingly catatonic Mason, opened the lower half of the stable door and led the grey away from the body. Once the horse was secure, Jack turned to Mason with every inten-tion of tearing a strip off him for freezing, DI or not, but from the expression on Mason's face as he stared down at the body of the man he'd failed to protect, Jack knew that shouting wasn't necessary. Mason already knew this was his responsibility.

'Call it in,' Jack instructed, 'DI Mason! Call it in!' Mason snapped out of his horrified trance and got out his mobile phone.

Mulhern lay on his right side, with his left arm pulled so far round his back that his shoulder was no longer in its socket. His right shin bone was so badly crushed that it lay almost flat against the concrete floor, and the bloodied hoof prints on his shredded trouser leg suggested that the grey had been encouraged to trample this part of Mulhern's body, over and over.

Torture. Brutal, excruciating torture. Jack crouched down, care-ful not to touch anything, and examined the body more closely. Someone had carved gouges out of Mulhern's forearms as well as cutting out little squares of skin. Finally, they'd brought his pain to an end by shattering his skull, most likely with the same crow-bar they used on Mathew. Mulhern's crushed and misshapen head now lay in a pool of dark red gore. Only his thick blond hair and the coagulated mess of hay, blood and brain matter, held his skull together.

Jack heard repeated heavy exhalations as Mason breathed himself calm over Jack's left shoulder. 'Ambulance . . . is coming,' he managed to say between breaths. 'And DI Lee . . . Fuck . . . Mulhern didn't know anything. They'd have known that in seconds, so . . . why this? Fuck.'

Jack spun round and looked into Mason's panicked eyes. Then Mason uttered completely the wrong words: 'Right . . . well . . . we need to get our story straight with this one, DS Warr.'

If Mason had shown any sign of guilt, instead of the desire for self-preservation, things might have gone differently.

Jack jabbed Mason in the stomach with his clenched fist, sending him to his knees, then grabbed him tightly around the neck from behind, forcing his head up so he had no option but to look directly at the mangled body in front of him. Mason desperately tried to force his fingers into the gap between Jack's forearm and his own windpipe, so he could breathe. Jack squeezed his words out through gritted teeth: 'You sent all of your resources to pro-tect the most *important* homes in the area! Those who shout the loudest, right, Colin? Fuckwits like Barrowman, the man who pays your wages. Well, Jacob Mulhern paid your wages too! And look at him . . . *Look at him!*'

Mason's eyes bulged and reddened as oxygen left his panicked brain, but Jack continued, calm and terrifying. 'You're thinking, how do I get out of this fuck-up? Well, I'll tell you. *Me!* I'm your only way out of this now.'

Jack threw Mason forwards onto his hands, where he retched and gasped for breath while distant sirens filled the air. Jack spoke calmly. 'This gang has gone beyond the point of no return, because after murdering an innocent man, they know they have to get out quickly and with enough money to go to ground. So, they'll hit the annual equestrian event back in Chipping Norton, and they'll hit it hard. I know this gang, and I know how to track burglars. I will fight the likes of Barrowman to get my job done, but I won't fight you. From this second forwards, you're on my side, *sir*, or I'll ruin you without a second thought.'

Jack turned on his heel, closing the lower half of the stable door behind him, and walked towards Lee's unmarked police car, which was followed in by two marked patrol cars and the forensics van.

Mason, still on his hands and knees, wasn't visible to anyone outside of the stable. He crawled to the wall, pushed himself to his feet and brushed his trousers clean of hay; he took in several deep breaths, loosened his tie and opened the top button of his shirt. He heard Lee and Jack talking as they approached. He finally managed to compose himself, and then appeared round the doorway as though nothing at all had happened.

Lee was immediately thrown by the sight that faced him, but he was a calmer, colder man than Mason so recovered his senses quickly and quickly started barking out instructions to the uniformed officers and forensics team. But Mason didn't hear any of it. He was too busy staring at Jack, his dark eyes now hooded by his thick brows and divided by a deep furrow. Looking at him, Mason knew that every threat made by Jack a moment ago had been genuine. But more than that, Mason also knew that every accusation Jack had thrown at him was justified.

* * *

From the outside, St Aldates Police Station in Oxford could just as easily have been a library or public baths. It was a beautiful old building with centuries of city life etched into its sandstone walls. Only the numerous CCTV cameras and modern windows made it look as if it belonged in the twenty-first century. Inside, however, it was a typical police station; far more high-tech than Chipping Norton and more heavily manned, but a typical cop shop nonetheless.

Gifford, Oaks and Davidson had driven across from Chipping Norton and were now waiting to be brought up to speed. They were each nursing a machine-dispensed hot drink in a paper cup but none of them were drinking the contents. Canteen Barbara had spoilt them rotten and now there was no going back.

As DI Lee spoke, Mason sat at his laptop and got all of the crime scene photos up on the interactive whiteboard that covered one complete wall. Once the images were uploaded, Lee could then move them around, enlarging and reducing, as he referenced each one. For Davidson, this was his first murder. The gruesome nature of the images didn't bother him, as he'd seen numerous farming accidents in his time. But the deliberate brutality of one person taking another's life in such a cruel way was shocking to everyone.

Lee's succinct and emotionless summary of Mulhern's murder was impressive. 'So,' he concluded. 'The burglaries and the murder are intrinsically linked. Because the crime scene is so vast, covering both our jurisdictions, we need to work very closely together now and constantly share intel. I propose that DI Mason and I lead the murder angle from Oxford, and DI Gifford continues to lead the burglary angle from Chipping Norton.'

Jack knew that Lee wanted the far sexier murder investigation for himself, which was fine by him. All Jack wanted was to make sure that no one else died. 'Sir, of course DI Gifford and yourself should lead this now dual investigation, but perhaps we should

shuffle the teams to make best use of accumulated knowledge.'
Out of the corner of his eye, Jack could see Davidson twitching
and fidgeting like a child desperate to be chosen first for a game of
five-a-side. 'DC Ronnie Davidson would be an asset to you, sir.'
Jack glanced casually at Mason. 'And DI Mason would be invaluable to us. If you're amenable, DI Mason?'

Mason knew he had no choice but to back Jack's decision and
claim to be more than happy with the idea of joining the Chipping
Norton team.

*   *   *

Mason and Jack drove back to Chipping Norton together. 'When
I said you'd be invaluable to this end of the investigation, I wasn't
blowing smoke. I don't really know what kind of a copper you
are. But I do know what kind of a man you are. Finding Mulhern
was . . . well, just hang on to those feelings of guilt and horror,
because you'll need them to catch this gang. You've got to feel
in this job, Mason. Lee doesn't, but you do. Guilt. Horror. Anything. Without feeling, there's nothing pushing you on. Nothing
that's worth anything, anyway.'

By eight o'clock, Jack and Mason were in the bar of The Fox
Hunters sipping their first pints of the evening. 'So, who's this
inside man you were on about?'

'Inside woman,' Jack said with a smile, opening a packet of
crisps.

'Charlotte Miles has a smallholding and runs two businesses,
a gardening and landscaping sort of set-up, and a fruit and veg
delivery service. Her name crops up in every burglary, though
to be fair, there's a lot of names connected to every burglary; it's
a small, tangled community in that sense. But . . . on Mulhern's

kitchen table there was one of her delivery bags with a potted plant inside. She's involved. I know she is.'

Mason, overwhelmed by his personal need for redemption, wanted to get over to Charlotte's right now and bring her in. But Jack assured him that she wasn't going anywhere.

Oaks joined them carrying a very cloudy-looking pint of cider and dragging a bar stool, as it was the only unoccupied seat left in the place. Oaks relayed all of the information that had just been sent through to him. 'Jacob Mulhern: widower, two daughters, three grandkids. Nothing from his CCTV. It had been disconnected, but not in a "burglar" kind of way. It looked like Mulhern did it himself. His phone records show he was getting quotes to have all of his security replaced . . .'

Jack wrinkled his brows. Why was Mulhern updating his security?

Oaks was too focused on reading from his mobile to notice. 'Post-mortem's booked for first thing tomorrow morning, but initial observations are crushed skull leading to exsanguination.' Oaks took a gulp of his cider, then picked a speck of apple from his tongue. 'It's a bit on the gritty side. Worth the effort though. Did you see Ronnie's face when you said he could stay there? He'll never see the outside of that station! He'll be glued to a computer screen watching CCTV and doing PNC checks. He'll bloody hate it!'

Oaks then excused himself and headed towards the toilets, but not before posing a couple of key questions to think about. 'I wonder why they tortured him? What did they think he knew?'

'What do you think, Mason?' Jack's question was accusatory, and Mason knew it. 'This is exactly why need-to-know was so important.' Jack didn't wait for Mason to deny yet another mistake. 'Someone at your end told him way too much. He knew

"Mr Smart" had more than a passing connection to a couple of old Oxford burglaries. He was scared. That's why he was taking extra precautions.' Jack shook his head in disbelief. 'One look at Mulhern's face and they'd have known he'd had the cops round asking questions. That's why they tortured him. To find out how much you knew. And Mulhern would have told them everything before they made the second cut . . . Everything else was sadistic.'

Mason touched the rim of his pint glass. He just wanted to be able to do something to make his guilt vanish.

But Jack pushed him further. 'Carving him up like that. Getting his own horse to trample his bones.'

Mason squeezed his eyes tight shut. 'Enough! You're right, is that what you want me to say?! This is on us. On *me*, OK? My God, he must have been terrified.'

Now that Jack had Mason stoked up, he presented the solution. 'OK. Tomorrow, we target the weakest link. Charlotte Miles. And we *make* her tell us everything.'

CHAPTER 15

Jack had been parked up in his blue Vauxhall Corsa hire car at the end of the driveway to Charlotte and Annie's smallholding for about an hour. The Corsa had been another one of Oaks's 'jokes' intended to make Jack feel unwelcome, just as the original, dingy B&B had been. But whereas Oaks had been able to change the B&B to his cousin's pub, he had been unable the change the hire car.

Mason, slumped low in the passenger seat, looked like he hadn't slept. He gazed out of the side window, but his eyes couldn't focus on anything. He was miles away, still thinking about Mr Mulhern.

The lawnmower that, according to Canteen Barbara, Charlotte had bought from James Somerset for £1,800, was parked underneath the kitchen window. The known finances of this small cottage industry swirled around in Jack's head: Annie's father had died, leaving them £200,000 which allowed them to make up their mortgage payments and keep their home – but only just. Charlotte earned, on average, £30,000 a year and Annie's sporadic wages seemed to come from her one or two shifts per week at The Soho Farmhouse. Was he right about Charlotte? Or was he about to accuse a completely innocent woman of something she knew nothing about?

Jack felt a small grin forming at the corners of his mouth. He'd underestimated seemingly hard-working, low-income women before. He couldn't take anything at face value here.

Jack had parked so that he could see the pigsty. He knew that Annie would by now have sent Alec to slaughter, so he assumed Charlotte would be taking extra care of the others. He was right. Within ten minutes of arriving, Charlotte emerged from the house and wandered, head down and dragging her feet, towards her pigs.

'That her?' Mason asked eagerly.

'Don't get out of the car taking it for granted she's complicit and that she'll lead us directly to Mulhern's killer. *If* she's our connection between all of the burglaries, I doubt she fully understands how important she is. We're not here to scare her. OK?'

As Jack and Mason approached, Charlotte was bent over with her back to them, raking the slurry into a corner, while the remaining pigs constantly got in her way. Charlotte put her hand onto the back of the biggest pig and leant heavily on it. The pig just stood there, as though it knew that she needed support. Charlotte then put the broom into the crook of her elbow, covered her face with her hand and began to sob. Jack and Mason stopped dead in their tracks.

Jack looked away in an attempt to give her a moment of private grief. Mason, on the other hand, had no clue why she was crying. 'What's up with her, Jack?'

Jack was looking along a dirt path that cut down the side of the smallholding. He walked in that direction, and Mason followed. The dirt path ran the length of the house before disappearing into the back field. What had caught Jack's attention were the parallel tyre marks; too wide to be a car, and too narrow to be the lawn-mower. These were quadbike tracks. As Jack followed the path a little further towards the building, he crossed Charlotte's eyeline.

'She chose Alec!' Charlotte was so desperate to talk to someone – anyone – other than the murderous Annie that she didn't even say 'hello'. She didn't seem to be embarrassed by her show of emotion, even though she was still crying quietly. 'I nursed Alec from the day he was born. He was the runt, so he's the only one I had to do that with. Pigs are very intelligent animals, DS Warr. And they bond with us. Like dogs.'

Mason shook his head in disbelief: this seemingly heartbroken woman was crying over a pig! Jack could hear Mason take a long, slow breath to keep himself from smirking.

'This is DI Mason,' Jack said. 'From Oxford. His investigation has crossed with ours, so he's down here for the time being, helping us out.' Mason tried to redeem himself by smiling sympathetically.

Before Charlotte could reply, Annie appeared with a farrier come to re-shoe Florrie and Judas before their appearance in the annual equestrian event. If looks could have killed, Annie would have dropped dead right there in the slurry.

'I'll show you through, James,' Charlotte barked to the farrier. Clearly she was not going to stay in Annie's company for a second longer.

'Can I help?' Annie ventured.

Jack wasn't sure what Annie knew, if anything, so he suggested that they all go to the house and wait for Charlotte there. Mason grabbed Jack by the arm. 'If she won't talk to us – right now – we should arrest her for obstruction.'

Jack shook his head. 'We're not going to do that, because if she's the person I think she is, she's desperate for someone to show her that there's a way out of the mess she's in. How the hell does a gardener from Chipping Norton get tangled up with a gang of burglars? She's not connected emotionally or professionally – so we're missing something. Once we have that, we have her. Look, Mason, if you want to take the car back to the station, you do that. I'll make my own way back once I've spoken to Charlotte.'

Every instinct told Mason to go. He'd felt as though he was Jack's 'bitch' ever since finding Mulhern's dead body and he hated it. He only faltered because the ache in his neck was a constant reminder of Jack's violent warning: *From this second forwards, you're on my side, sir, or I'll ruin you without a second thought.*

Mason followed Annie and Jack to the house.

In the kitchen, Annie made a pot of tea, then covered it with a woollen cosy in the shape of a hen, and poured a selection of biscuits onto a large plate, telling them to help themselves while she busied herself with tidying.

Jack was content with the silence while his eyes explored the kitchen, as he intuitively assessed their target's home for psychological clues that could help them in the questioning.

Jack's silent train of thought was broken by his mobile buzzing, and he quickly saw that it was Maggie calling. The fact that Maggie was calling instead of texting when she knew he was at work made him instantly worried. He excused himself and stepped outside.

Maggie's first words were, 'We're all fine.' She then fell silent and her noisy breathing told Jack that she was crying. 'Take your time,' he said gently. 'I'm here.'

After a long silence, Maggie eventually said, 'Regina's been taken into hospital. Her baby's going to come three months too soon.' Jack said nothing as there was nothing to say. 'I'm going to go and be with her and Penny's going to look after Hannah. I just needed to hear your voice . . . I miss you.'

'I miss you too,' he said. 'But you're not crying because you miss me.'

'We're so lucky, Jack. Yesterday, Hannah was lying on her tummy and pushed herself up on her arms all by herself and I . . . I called her a clever girl and clapped my hands. These milestones . . . the same milestones that, for Regina, may never even be reached and I . . .'

'Mags, Mags, Mags . . . she'll be thinking about all of the worst-case-scenarios; she needs you to remind her of the best-case stuff.'

'What if I can't? What if she sees that I know the stats and the problems and the—'

'Go and be with her. You've got this, Maggie. You're not her doctor, you're her friend. This is the woman you not-so-subtly feed when she hasn't got the money to feed herself. You love her, so this is easy, Mags. You're exactly who she needs. And before you ask me how I know, I'll tell you: because that's what you are to every-one in your life.' Maggie came out with a snotty sounding laugh. Jack could then hear the clatter of her mobile being put down and the distant trumpet of her blowing her nose.

As Jack waited for Maggie to return, he saw Charlotte walking back towards the house, still looking furious. Jack smiled at the thought of Mason having to referee these two feisty women as they tore into each other over the recent murder of Alec the pig.

There was another clatter in Jack's ear as Maggie picked up her mobile. 'Right,' she spoke with renewed strength. 'I'm going to be at the hospital for the rest of today, but I'll text you later to let you know what's happening.' Jack said he'd look forward to the update, which Maggie knew was a lie; but she appreciated him saying it.

As Jack approached the house, he was a expecting a scene of mayhem. In fact, Annie had left the room, Charlotte was washing her hands furiously, and Mason was drinking tea he clearly didn't want just to avoid saying anything.

Before Jack could speak, Charlotte turned to him with an angry look. She was clearly up for an argument and if Annie wasn't going to give it to her, then Jack would do. 'I'm not speaking to you today, DS Warr. You already know that I work for all of the burglary victims, just as most local produce suppliers do. I don't know what else you need to ask me. If you do need to speak to me, perhaps call ahead next time. I have two businesses to run and Annie has now left me on my own for the rest of today it seems.'

Jack listened intently. Not to the words Charlotte said, but to the audible quiver in her voice. She was flustered and he wanted to know why, so today was exactly the right day to talk to her. 'Charlotte, I'm happy to talk here, if that suits you better, but we *will* be talking today. Because I know we can help each other.'

There was a flicker of fear in Charlotte's eyes. She quickly turned away, but she knew that Jack had seen it. She started talking nineteen to the dozen about needing to ride Judas's new shoes in once the farrier had gone, and Jack now knew that she was scared and had no idea how to get herself back to a safe place. She was stuck and needed his help, and although she would not see it as help, Jack did the only thing he could under the circumstances: 'Charlotte Miles, I'm arresting you for obstructing police enquiries.' By the time Jack had recited her rights, Charlotte was shaking and sobbing.

* * *

Jack didn't handcuff her. In the car, he sat in the back with her and, at the station, he escorted her towards the purposely scary back cage that led into the processing area. They were met by Bevan, who was given clear instructions that Charlotte wasn't to be left alone. Jack wanted Charlotte to fully experience the frightening truth of what it was like to be in police custody, and he wanted her to look to himself and Bevan for comfort. Jack wanted Charlotte to need him.

'DC Bevan will stay with you until you're processed,' he told her gently. 'And then she'll take you to the interview room.'

As Charlotte was led away, Mason nodded his appreciation of Jack's psychological tactics. 'You think you're good at manipulating people, don't you, Jack?'

'I know I am,' Jack said with a straight face, and Mason laughed.

'What's funny?' Mason turned to see Gifford standing behind him. Mason shook his head. 'Nothing.'

Gifford grunted, nodding towards the Vauxhall Corsa. 'You got the keys to that shit-heap? You could come with me and meet Mr

Barrowman. He's a big player round here, so I want to keep him on-side.'

Mason, to his own surprise and certainly to Gifford's, declined, saying that he wanted to sit in on Jack's interview with Charlotte.

'Fuck's sake, Mason, she's been interviewed! Twice! He's going over well-trodden ground, whilst the rest of us are pushing ahead. Well, don't say I didn't warn you.'

Gifford got into the hire car and slammed the door.

Annie had stormed out of the house after Charlotte had had yet another go at her for murdering Alec the pig. She'd then stocked her basket with the day's deliveries and headed off into the village via the riverbank path. At the craft shop, several women had delighted in telling Annie that, not five minutes earlier, they'd seen Charlotte being driven down the main street in the back of an unmarked police car. By the time she arrived at the station, she was in an anxious state.

Jack put her mind at ease straight away. 'Charlotte is here to speak with us, Annie. I expect her to be back home with you by this evening . . . as long as she answers our questions, that is.'

'Can I see her?' Annie asked.

Jack shook his head. 'This is official. She refused to speak to me at the house, which is why I had to bring her here.'

Annie's mobile rang. She glanced at the screen and sent it to voicemail. 'I doubt she refused to speak with you because she has anything to hide,' she explained, trying to help as best she could. 'It'll be because I killed Alec. When she feels like she's losing con-trol, she shuts down, you see. She's always been like that. Awful at expressing her feelings. She's a brooder. What I'm saying is . . . she's not a bad person, she's just upset.'

Annie's mobile rang twice more while she was talking. Her caller was so persistent that she eventually answered it, snapping, 'Dad, not now! Sorry. Yes, well, I'm in the middle of something and you're only calling about your honey, I suppose. Well then, wait! Give me five minutes and I'll call you back.' Then she hung up.

Jack explained that he'd be careful when speaking to Charlotte and take into account her emotional state, and when she realised she was not going to be able to speak to her, Annie sighed and said, 'Tell her that I'm thinking of her then and that I'll be at home. Waiting.'

Jack promised and Annie cycled away, with her mobile still beeping away in her pocket.

Jack headed towards the back cage, where Mason was patiently waiting for him. He slowed, with a frown on his face. 'I just remembered something . . .' Jack thought for a moment. 'Charlotte and Annie told me that when Annie's dad died he left them £200,000, which they used to pay off the mortgage. But that phone call was from Annie's dad.'

Mason grinned. 'So, where did they get the two hundred grand from?' He clearly thought the money was Charlotte's pay-off for being their gang's insider.

Mason and Jack stood in the observation room, behind the two-way mirror that allowed them to watch Charlotte and DC Bevan in the interview room. Bevan stood just inside the door, like a sentry, while Charlotte sat at the table, fingers lightly touching the rim of a polystyrene cup of tea.

Jack entered the interview room and took his seat opposite Charlotte. She sat up straight in her chair, like a schoolgirl when a teacher walks into the classroom.

'How's Judas? New shoes OK?'

Charlotte looked confused. She wasn't expecting small talk. 'I'll try not to keep you from him for too long. I expect you have a lot to prepare before the upcoming equestrian event. So . . .' Jack turned the tape recorder on and introduced those present in the room. He then reminded Charlotte that she was under caution and that she'd declined legal representation, although she could change that any time she wanted. He then asked her to verbally confirm that she'd understood everything he said. 'I saw Annie outside.' Again, Jack's words threw Charlotte off-balance. 'She's gone home to wait for you. I said you'd more than likely be back later today. As soon as we've finished talking.'

In the observation room, Mason grinned and nodded to himself. Jack was promising Charlotte something he knew she wanted: he was promising Annie. The reward of being back home with the woman she loved, dangled in front of her like a carrot on a stick . . . and to get her reward she had to tell Jack what he wanted to know. It was a cleverly veiled threat because the unspoken flipside of heading home 'as soon as we've finished talking', was that she would stay in custody if she refused to talk. Charlotte was becoming putty in Jack's hands, whilst Jack, to the untrained eye, still remained very much 'the good cop'.

When Jack started the interview in earnest, he was straight to the point. 'You told me that four years ago Annie's dad passed away and left you £200,000; is that right?'

Charlotte nodded.

Jack looked at her. 'Only, when Annie was outside the police station earlier, she received a phone call from her dad.'

Charlotte was quick to answer. 'That's Bob. Her stepdad. Annie's real dad passed away four years ago. Him and her mum split back in, oh I don't know . . . I've never known them be together. He had a poor relationship with everyone in the family but, still, when he died, he left everything to Annie. Her mum has been with Bob for as long as I've known them. Lovely man. His memory's not so good anymore. It would have been Bob who phoned her. I imagine he called a few times times,' she smiled. 'He usually does.'

Jack instinctively believed Charlotte's story, and although this line of questioning had come to an unexpectedly abrupt dead end, it did serve to tell Jack what Charlotte looked and sounded like when she was telling the truth, so it wasn't time wasted. Now he'd be able to recognise a lie when she told one.

Jack moved on to the subject of Maisie Fullworth, watching her carefully to see if she shifted from being confident to being frightened. 'We now know that the person who broke into Maisie Fullworth's house was not necessarily a member of this gang of burglars, nor were they necessarily male.'

And there it was! Charlotte's face drained of blood and Jack imagined that her skin was now clammy to the touch. She swallowed noisily and looked down at the cold cup of tea in her hand.

'This person,' Jack continued, 'whoever they were, was frightened away by a teenage girl. That's the action of someone who is capable of empathy, it's not the action of a heartless killer.' Charlotte's eyes flicked to Jack's face, then down again, then to Bevan, then the mirror. She didn't know where to look as the word 'killer' echoed round the room. She was clearly desperate to ask who had been killed, wondering frantically if she was responsible. As she struggled with the impossible task of hiding her feelings, the blood raced back to her face and she flushed bright red.

'Do you know Jacob Mulhern, Charlotte?'

Charlotte's eyes stopped on a small scratch on the desk where the laminate had chipped and she seemed to become transfixed by this tiny flaw. Jack's voice continued, slow and deliberate. 'He owns a livery stable in Oxford, and he ordered a plant from you recently. Do you remember delivering that to him? It doesn't matter if you can't. We are just trying to find the last person who might have seen him alive.'

It was at this point that Charlotte actually seemed to stop breathing.

Her wide eyes, full of tears, looked imploringly at Jack, and he reached out and wrapped her trembling hands in his own. 'I know your role up until this point, Charlotte, but I also know what's coming. So, I need your help. Today.' The tears finally rolled down her cheeks. As they did, it was as though she became free, and she started to breathe again.

As Jack entered the observation room, Mason couldn't hide his admiration. 'Nice interview. She's gagging to tell you everything she knows.'

Jack didn't smile. 'She's not a criminal, Colin. She's just got herself into something that she can't get out of. I've now given her that way out, so she was bound to jump at it.'

Mason shrugged. 'Well, either way, you've got her where you want her . . . just like calling me "Colin" is your attempt to keep me where you want me.' Mason shifted his position, so that he stood square-on to Jack. 'Let me tell you this, *Jack* . . . it might just be working on us both. The difference, of course, is that I know what you're doing.'

Jack gave Charlotte fifteen minutes to gather her thoughts, take a toilet break and be given a fresh cup of tea. When he went back into the interview room, he started the tape, re-introduced everyone present and reminded Charlotte that she was still under caution. He then said six more words – 'Tell me how this all started' – and he sat back.

* * *

Charlotte sipped her tea and began.

'We were behind with the mortgage. I knew that the Fullworths' house was ... I *thought* the Fullworths' house was empty because Mrs Fullworth plays bridge on Tuesdays.' The next words were whispered, as Charlotte chastised herself for her carelessness. 'I don't know how I could have forgotten about the school's mid-term break.' Then she seemed to remember that she was talking to Jack. 'I knew Mrs Fullworth paid all of her staff in cash, I knew about the diamond engagement ring and I knew that she didn't wear it because it needed resizing.' She fell silent as she began to relive the moment. 'I honestly don't know who was more fright-ened when I reached the top of the stairs.'

In the observation room, Mason grinned. They had her! *She* was the perpetrator of the first burglary and she'd just confessed.

'I waited for Annie to be working overtime at The Soho Farm-house,' Charlotte continued, 'and I took the engagement ring to London to see if I could sell it. Anyone from Chipping Norton would have recognised it as belonging to Mrs Fullworth.'

Charlotte explained how she used to work tables in a bar along the King's Road in Chelsea and, on her way home, she'd cut through the huge antiques emporium on the corner of Lots Road. She'd fantasise about one day being able to afford the stunningly delicate earrings and gold twisted-wire anklets she saw there – her biggest fantasy-buy being an upper-arm cuff fashioned from twisted and pressed gold into the shape of ornate leaves. 'It looked like a delicate tree, reaching out, enveloping and growing with you. Back then, it cost a week's wages; now, you can get them for a tenner on Amazon.'

Jack let her reminisce unhindered. He thought it was good that she was associating her past with a purity that she'd now lost – reminding her of how guilty she felt. But he also recog-nised that she was delaying: she was about to give Jack a name and this petrified her.

Instead of pushing her, Jack paused to ask if she'd like a fresh cup of tea. As the words left his lips, Jack could almost hear Mason gasp in despair from the other side of the mirror. Bevan left to put the kettle on, leaving Jack and Charlotte alone.

'The stupid thing is,' Charlotte continued, 'if I'd held on for another couple of months, Annie's dad would have died and left us all the money we needed.' She shook her head, laughing at her own terrible luck. But she knew there was no stopping now. 'Michael De Voe,' she said, almost in a whisper.

Jack's expression didn't show his excitement, but on the other side of the mirror, Mason flung open the door to the observation room and grabbed Bevan, who was busy pouring one mug of tea from Canteen Barbara into two polystyrene cups. He told her as soon as she'd delivered the teas, she was to get DI Gifford back to the station and get DI Lee down from Oxford. They'd just learnt the identity of the man behind their gang.

Charlotte held Jack's gaze. She felt oddly relaxed in his company; which was good because she now had no option but to trust him with her life. 'De Voe was very interested in the diamond ring. But he knew as soon as he looked at me . . . he knew it wasn't mine. He asked for provenance knowing I wouldn't have any. I was about to leave, thinking he wasn't going to buy stolen goods, or that he was perhaps going to stall me and call the police – but instead he asked if I'd like to be paid in cash! I was so relieved. But I was scared too, and I just wanted to get out of there so, when he asked for ID, I handed over my driving licence without even thinking. 'Course, now he had my name and address. He told me it'd be OK. He told me he wasn't the kind of man to judge. He could see that I was a good person, just trying my best to survive.' She shook her head sadly. 'I'm so stupid.'

Charlotte's words tailed off and she began sobbing. Bevan entered with the teas, put them both in front of Jack and then left again.

Jack tried to be reassuring. 'This man, De Voe . . . he trapped you. I know men like Michael De Voe, Charlotte. They prey on innocent people without a second thought. And you're not stupid.' Jack slid Charlotte's cup towards her, making her look up. 'You're doing really well. Together, you and me can stop this gang from killing anyone else . . . and then I can give you back your life.'

Charlotte laced her fingers around the warm comfort of the cup and found the strength to continue. 'He went into a small back office, he said it was to get the cash from his safe. But when he came back, he was different. Hard. I suddenly felt like, I don't know, for a second, I actually thought he was a copper and that he was going to arrest me. The look on his face was like he'd won, you know. I wish now that he *had* been a copper.' Again, Charlotte bowed her head in shame and self-pity. What De Voe had actually done in his back office, she explained, was to check a list of property registered as stolen from the Chipping Norton area. As a noted, *reputable* jeweller, his local bobby had already visited, and asked him to look out for the ring as they knew that it was unlikely to be sold locally. De Voe had then put £1,000 on the desk in front of Charlotte, which was far more than she had expected to get. But instead of feeling buoyed up by the money, she was frightened. De Voe didn't threaten her directly, but he did say that he would keep her secret as long as she understood that she now owed him. All she had to do was answer his phone call and do what he asked when he decided it was time to collect.

By now, DC Bevan was standing alongside Mason in the observation room. Gifford, who had been placating Barrowman at the Wychwood Golf Club, had been called back to the station as a matter of urgency, but the Vauxhall Corsa hire car had finally given up the ghost, so he was currently stranded in the middle of nowhere waiting for a uniformed officer to go and collect him. All of which made Bevan secretly smile.

Back in the interview room, Charlotte was getting to the crux of her involvement with the gang. 'I told De Voe about Mr and Mrs Bright-Cullingwood's annual boat trip. They've got a yacht moored in Bristol Marina and they . . . well, I don't think they take it anywhere, actually. After Mr Bright-Cullingwood's heart attack, I don't think he can sail anymore. But they still go over there. They were the first house to be robbed, back in the summer of 2018.'

Jack suddenly realised something. He tapped on the mirror and, within seconds, Bevan appeared at the door. 'Bevan, Charlotte can give us all of the burglary victims. So the ones choosing to hide behind their insurance can now be approached.' Bevan sat down next to Jack, pen in hand. But Charlotte had gone ashen white and she'd stopped breathing again. Suddenly she leapt to her feet and pushed her fingers into her tangled hair.

'Oh my God, they'll know. They'll all know. I can't . . . Annie! She won't be able to cope. She's ill. She has anxiety. She'll never forgive me for this. We'll have to move. And she won't move. She was born here. It's her home! That's why I stole from Mrs Fullworth, to save Annie's home. She needs stability. Oh, God . . . our neighbours, our friends, our families will find out that I betrayed them all! I did this! Jacob Mulhern . . . that was me! It was all me!' Charlotte backed herself into the corner of the room and slid to the floor. Her body trembled and she gasped for breath. 'I'm not talking anymore. I take it all back. Please! Please let me take it back!'

Jack and Bevan calmly watched her meltdown, knowing that all of this raw emotion was better out than in. When he felt she was ready, Jack spoke. 'There's no going back, Charlotte.' Jack's voice was filled with a simple honesty. He wasn't going to lie to her.

'The only thing you can do now is make amends. Accept what you started – and work with me to end it.'

Jack paused for a minute or two, allowing Charlotte to fully take in her situation.

'I tried to get myself out of it,' she said finally. 'When he called and asked me for the second address, I said no.' Charlotte kept her head bowed as she spoke. 'He was so calm. He said something about having to live with the decisions we make. He called me a good person. And then he hung up. I was out of the house for six hours, doing my deliveries, and when I got home, Annie was in tears. She'd found our cat on the doorstep. Dead. He'd been caught in barbed wire, she said. And he'd walked home to die. His body was in a shoebox. As I was burying him in the orchard, I got a text message: *We live with the decisions we make. . .* The next day he called again and I gave him the second address.' Charlotte glanced up from the safety of her corner. Her damp hair almost covered her eyes.

Jack spoke softly.

'When you're ready, I want you to tell DC Bevan the name of every address you gave De Voe. I know you can remember them all, Charlotte, because they weigh heavily on you. Charlotte, I am on your side. But I will not allow you to clam up now, because there are lives at stake. So . . . and think about this very carefully before you answer . . . are you sitting there telling me that you have nothing more to say? Are you telling me that your "what will the neighbours think" fears are more important to you than another human life? Are you telling me that you're choosing to continue to protect Michael De Voe? Or are you going to do the right thing?'

Charlotte stared at Jack for what seemed like minutes. Bevan felt increasingly awkward, whereas Jack was more than comfortable to just stare back. Eventually, Charlotte dragged herself to her feet and retook her seat at the table. Bevan maintained the official tone of the interview: 'For the tape, Charlotte Miles has returned to the table.'

Jack was different now and Charlotte knew it. If she didn't play her part, he'd see her go down for whatever he could convict her of. In his way he was just as remorseless as De Voe, and she was just as trapped.

For the next three hours, Jack asked questions and Charlotte answered them. He was pleased to discover that she hadn't accepted any kind of payment from De Voe for the information she fed to him, even when it was repeatedly offered. Charlotte took a while to get started but, once the floodgates opened, there was no stopping her. She explained how she had recommended livery stables and given advice on what sort of horseboxes could carry the weight of a quadbike and motorbike; how she had informed De Voe of all roads that had no CCTV and of all back routes into and out of target properties. She passed on information about residents' holidays, day trips, nights away, empty rentals, as well as staffing levels and security systems. And she talked of how, each time a target was identified, the gang would recce the area for three full days before deciding whether or not to go ahead. Charlotte also mentioned how, when she'd once been talking to De Voe on the phone, he'd taken a second call. Because he'd kept her on the line, she could hear his side of the other conversation. He'd spoken about flights and about buying airline tickets so that 'his people' would be in and out of the country before the cops even knew what had happened. And she also heard him mention a second jewellery shop in Camden, although he didn't mention the exact location. She said he had no problem at all stealing from rich, insured people. In fact, he regularly used the words 'victimless crime'.

As the interview came to an end, Charlotte and Bevan looked exhausted, whereas Jack still looked as fresh as a daisy and raring to go. Jack's final question was whether Charlotte knew where the gang stayed during their regular, three-day recces. She shook her head.

'What happens now?' she asked, realising the interview was finally over. 'I mean . . . can I see Annie, please? She'll need to know . . . that I'm not coming home. I want to be the one who tells her.'

Jack didn't immediately answer her question. 'The annual equestrian event starts next week. That'll be something De Voe won't be able to resist. So, he'll be contacting you shortly in order to do his three-day prep. Bevan will see if De Voe is in the system and, if he is, we'll need a positive ID please . . .' Jack paused before delivering his bombshell. '. . . then she'll drive you home.'

Charlotte's jaw nearly hit the table. As did Bevan's, as she wondered on whose authority was he about to release their only connection to the leader of this elusive gang.

'Charlotte, I need you out there, not in here, Jack continued. 'I will keep you and Annie safe, but you must trust me. Do you trust me, Charlotte?'

The tears once again began to flow, quietly and softly this time. Charlotte nodded.

Jack sealed the deal with one final sentence that only he and Charlotte knew the meaning of. 'Charlotte Miles, for three years you've been De Voe's Judas Horse; now you're mine.'

CHAPTER 16

Jack and Mason entered the squad room to find Lee had just arrived from Oxford and was itching for a full handover. 'DI Mason and I will go through the details of his interview and then communicate the next course of action to the team,' he announced.

During his drive from Oxford to Chipping Norton, he had coordinated a series of background checks on De Voe, but it turned out he was not in any system and did not have a criminal record. However, his name was now in capital letters right in the centre of the evidence board. Jack was horrified. 'We can't show our hand yet, sir.'

Lee shrugged. 'We've got no IDs, no court-reliable witnesses, no prints, no DNA . . .'

Gifford chipped in. 'Even the greasy fingerprint on the back of Barrowman's office chair doesn't belong to anyone in any system, here or internationally. They're all clean, Eamonn.'

'All we have is one scared woman who's confessed to a burglary-gone-wrong from three years ago,' Jack went on.

Lee ignored Jack and was looking at Mason to see if he was going to back him up, seeing that Gifford now seemed to have gone over to the other side. But Mason simply said, 'Just listen to him, Eamonn.' Lee frowned. He knew nothing of the violent confrontation between Mason and Jack when they found Mulhern's mutilated body in the stable, but he could sense that Jack now had some kind of hold over his Oxford partner.

With Gifford and Mason providing backup, Jack continued. 'If we go after De Voe now, we lose the gang, and we can't allow that to happen just because we're itching to move. I want the man who can push a letter opener into a dog's brain, and who can beat Mathew with a crowbar over a pizza, and who can torture and murder Jacob Mulhern. I want Mr Smart. Look at how much we *do* know, sir. We've been right about everything: how they used an insider, how they move around, how they avoid CCTV, how they select their targets, the fact that they're transient and not from around here ... and now we know where they come in from and disappear to. We're ahead of them.'

Lee looked at Jack warily. 'What do you suggest then? And remember the final decision lies with Oxford Robbery.'

Jack thanked Lee for his trust and stepped forwards to address the room. Mason was glad to be on Jack's side; he reckoned being against him was probably a dangerous place to be.

'The annual equestrian event next week is too good a target for them to resist. We have time to get this right. Charlotte will need looking after, so she should stay in the care of myself and Bevan. Bevan has a good rapport with her and won't take any shit from Charlotte when she falters, which she will. The only thing we don't know, and I'm sure Charlotte doesn't either, is when this gang is here, where do they hide? Why haven't we noticed them?' he turned to Bevan. 'We still need to check out the transient communities and visitors that move around the Cotswolds unseen; bus drivers, casual labourers, road workers, lorry drivers, tourists.'

Bevan nodded eagerly. 'Yes, sir. We can track and collate visitor parking permits, temporary council contracts and acquisitions, B&B booking systems—'

'Do this for me as well, please,' Jack interrupted. 'When I first arrived here, Oaks and I stopped at temporary traffic lights – there are loads of them all over the place, but why? Are they legitimate? I didn't see any roadworks being done. Has this gang got the balls to actually control the fucking traffic to clear their escape route? I wouldn't put it past them.'

Lee held a hand up. 'I get the impression, DS Warr, that you're giving all of us orders, while having another plan for yourself.'

Jack ignored the sarcasm. 'I know the world De Voe lives in. I suggest that I go back to London and get on the inside. From there, I can do more. Oxfordshire is your territory, DI Lee. London is mine.'

Lee was clearly finding it difficult to fault Jack's logic, so Jack gave it one final push. 'Ex-prime minister Cameron is opening the equestrian event. His property hasn't been hit yet – for one thing Charlotte doesn't work for him – but I think all bets are off now, don't you? Everyone will be out of their homes. Everyone is a target. Sir, if you think Barrowman will be grateful when we catch these bastards, just imagine the praise that'll come our way from someone like Cameron.'

Lee didn't respond immediately, asking Jack to pop into Gifford's office with him whilst they discussed a few details.

Once the door was closed, he let rip. 'Is that how you see me, Jack? With my head halfway up the most important arse in the county? You don't understand: I'm not in this for the fucking kudos; I'm just seeing the bigger picture. The bigwigs that you insist on ignoring are the same people who have the ear of the DCI. That matters because, whether you like it or not, we're answerable to them. One of us has to keep that in mind.' He gave Jack a hard stare. 'So, you go back to London, Jack. But you report to me daily and you don't act without my say-so. This must be coordinated, or it goes tits-up in the blink of an eye. This gang has taken the piss for three years – they hire horseboxes from right under our noses in the name of Mr Smart, for fuck's sake! We're different coppers, me and you, and that's fine, but if you can't work under my lead, now's the time to say so.'

Jack gave him his sincerest smile. 'I can, sir.'

Lee nodded but still looked at him suspiciously, suspecting that Jack had somehow got the better of him.

* * *

Before Jack headed for London, he had one final conversation with Bevan. 'I'm going to give Charlotte my mobile number and I want you to give her yours. But Charlotte's not the weak one; Annie is and Charlotte will do anything to protect her. She needs to feel safe, so I want her to only communicate with us in the first instance. I'll then feed the relevant information on to everyone else. I'm also going to get a burner phone; you'll have that number, too. But just you.' Although Bevan was listening intently, Jack could see that she wasn't sure about the ethics of following his instructions above those of his senior officers. 'Bevan, you're one of the smartest, most painstaking officers I've ever had the pleasure of working with. We're so close to the end. I need you to be my patient, logical brain over here, whilst I'm in London. Please. Help me to help Charlotte get out of this in one piece.'

CHAPTER 17

Jack let himself into the house and was met by silence. He didn't call out in case Hannah was sleeping, but as he was hanging up his coat, Hannah's little smiley face appeared around the door frame, floating about four feet off the ground! Penny was hiding as best she could, but Hannah was heavy and so her 'little joke' didn't last long. Jack rushed forwards and scooped Hannah into his arms – she beamed and gurgled and kicked her legs so hard that she pushed herself away from his body. Although Jack and Hannah saw each other on Maggie's phone daily, he hadn't held his daughter for days.

'She changed, hasn't she?' Penny said proudly. 'You don't think they can change much in less than a week, but . . . I'll put the kettle on. You two catch up.'

Jack followed Penny into the kitchen, as she nattered away. This was something Penny always did when there was a serious conversation to be had at some point in the immediate future. She had to work herself up to it. When she was ready,

Penny turned towards him. 'Now then . . .' Penny waited until she had Jack's full attention. 'Maggie is at the hospital with Regina . . . she left the car for you. Join them if you can but, if you don't have time, she'll need a lift back at least. Regina went into very early labour. The baby was breech to begin with . . . upside down.' Jack nodded. 'Now, this is no one's fault really; well, it might have been, I don't know, because Regina was being seen by a junior doctor and they . . .' Penny looked annoyed with herself and pulled a piece of paper out of her pocket. 'I can't remember the bloody name . . . Ah, right, so, the junior doctor used forceps, and doing that, they think, has caused bilateral Erb's palsy. That's damage to the nerves in the shoulder. So, the poor little mite is in a bit of a state at the moment. Oh, and she might be deaf, but they won't know for a while. She's in an incubator for the foreseeable.' Having finally managed to deliver the terrible news about Regina's new baby, Penny gratefully snapped back into grandma mode. 'Bath time! You carry her up. Then I'll put her down and you can go to the hospital if that's your plan. Visiting starts at six.'

It took a while for Jack to trust that the little seat in the baby bath was capable of supporting Hannah without his help – and he was even more sceptical when Penny said that he could pour the water over Hannah's face and she wouldn't mind. But once he relaxed and realised that both he and his daughter would be fine, he began to enjoy bath time. He waved a plastic boat in front of Hannah, then he waved a fish and made a popping sound with his lips, then finally waved an octopus and made a clicking noise.

Penny suddenly howled with laughter as a memory popped into her head. 'That's from your dad!' she laughed. 'He didn't know what noise an octopus made either, so he clicked and thought, *that'll do.* I'd forgotten all about that. He could tell you anything and you'd believe him. That's why he never lied to you about important things.'

The phone rang just in time to save Penny from another spontaneous crying session. They were far less frequent these days; but the grief still surprised her every now and then.

From the bathroom, Jack heard her tell 'Simon' that Jack was busy bathing Hannah, but that he'd return the call as soon as they'd finished. Jack gently chastised his mum when she returned, saying that Ridley was his boss and had every right to ask to speak to Jack during the working day, but he couldn't help smiling nonetheless.

* * *

On the way to the hospital, Jack called Ridley back. Ridley was concerned whether Jack could safely get on the inside of De Voe's operation in the space of a couple of days. 'I'm going to go in as a buyer, sir,' Jack reassured him. 'Meet De Voe and assess the situation from there. He's clearly a smart guy who keeps a good distance from the sharp end, so I'm going to take my lead from him.'

'Fair enough,' Ridley conceded. 'Oh, and well done for sticking to your guns with Charlotte, by the way. But be careful, Jack. Stubborn self-belief can come across as insubordination with you. I can hear you smiling, but you know I'm right.'

Jack was smiling now. 'If you're around tomorrow morning, sir, I'd like to come in for a proper tactical briefing.' It was quickly agreed that Jack would be in Ridley's office by seven. Jack then disconnected the call and pulled into the hospital grounds.

*　　*　　*

Maggie had her professional doctor's head firmly on as she sat by Regina's bedside in the small, four-bay ward, talking her through the potential complications she might expect in the coming months. But when she saw Jack at the window, a lump immediately formed in her throat, forcing her to excuse herself and leave the room. Taking Jack by the wrist she dragged him out of sight of Regina and then she leant heavily against the wall, and exhaled. Jack pulled Maggie's head forwards onto his chest, supporting her weight as she sagged against him. 'I've got you. Don't do too much, Mags. You're no good to any of us if you're worn out.' Maggie leant back, so they could look at each other.

'How are Regina and the baby? Mum mentioned Herb's palsy or something,' Jack said.

'Erb's. E-R-B-S. There could be the option to operate but, if not, then it'll mean paralysis. And it's bilateral, so it's affecting both arms.' Maggie put the palms of her hands flat against Jack's chest. 'She won't be able to lift her arms.' Maggie put her hands round Jack's waist to hug him tight.

When Maggie and Jack went back onto the ward, Maggie was surprised that Jack wasn't saying comforting words to Regina; he just hugged her. Perhaps he didn't know what to say, or perhaps he thought actions spoke louder than words – either way, Regina seemed grateful for his kindness, as waves of worry ebbed through her mind. Jack then asked the one question that Maggie had forgotten to ask.

'How's Mario?'

Regina had spent the past few days talking non-stop with various people about herself and the baby, but this was the first time anyone had asked about Mario, and she immediately burst into tears.

'He's working all the hours God sends, because if the baby turns out to be as poorly as she could be, we'll need money. Truth is, he can't earn enough in one lifetime to pay for all of the treatments, and carers, and medicines. And when he's not working, he's researching. Yesterday, he was telling me about a new, ground-breaking treatment in the US, where Doctors re-train the brain to use areas that are damaged. I don't even know if that's what we need! Maggie, do you know?'

Maggie assured Regina that no one knew enough just yet. For now, Mum and baby would be watched and looked after, day by day. And so would Dad, she added.

On the way out to the car, Maggie took Jack past the neo-natal unit. It wasn't usual for non-relatives to be allowed in, but as Jack was with Maggie, the charge nurse made an exception. There were four incubators in the one room and the one nearest to the observation window held Regina's baby. She was tiny, Jack thought, so tiny that instead of feeling how cute she was, he just felt fear for her future. 'Jeez, Mags.' Jack's mind flashed back to two hours ago when he was holding Hannah in his arms. The baby he was looking at now was half Hannah's size, if that. There was so much equipment surrounding her, so many tubes and lights and sounds. It looked like chaos. But all of the tiny, doll-like babies in the unit seemed to be sleeping soundly, oblivious to how precarious their hold on life actually was. 'Is she . . . I mean, apart from her arms and the deafness, is she OK? Will she be OK?'

Maggie linked her arm through Jack's and rested her head on his shoulder. She didn't have an answer.

That night, Jack just watched Hannah sleeping for over an hour. He thought about Mathew and about Regina's new baby, and how he and Maggie were so incredibly lucky.

* * *

Ridley pulled into his parking space at six thirty and then spent thirty minutes getting ready for his meeting with Jack, who walked into the squad room bang on seven. Ridley put two freshly brewed cups of tea on his desk and they got down to work.

'Michael De Voe. I can confirm "no criminal record" – and that's all I can tell you about him. I hoped to have been able to prepare a file for you, but there's nothing.' Ridley handed Jack a map of the Chelsea Emporium. 'This indoor space houses thirty-four high-end shops and eateries. De Voe's Jewellers is on the second floor. Shop number twenty-one. His other shop was out Camden way, but has recently closed down. I don't have a picture of De Voe for you: there's no social media, no local-interest news pieces on him – he keeps below the radar. Not what you'd expect for a man who's just been accused of masterminding the biggest burglary racket this side of the Pennines. Or maybe it's exactly what we should expect? Did you know that the total insurance claims from the Cotswolds burglaries over three years is estimated to be £7.6 million?'

'But I think a murder means they have to wrap up and get out,' Jack said. 'One more big score. If we miss them at the annual equestrian event, that's it. They'll disappear forever.'

Ridley nodded. 'So, what's your plan for getting on the inside of De Voe's world?' Ridley looked Jack up and down. He was wearing the boots he'd bought for wandering through muddy farmyards out in the Cotswolds, along with jeans and T-shirt.

Jack grinned. 'I'll look the part, sir, don't worry.'

*   *   *

That afternoon, Jack sat down to a full chicken dinner, with five different vegetables, gravy and bread sauce. Even though Maggie was the one who served it up, he knew this meal was Penny's creation, as he believed no one else on the planet still knew how to make bread sauce from scratch. Penny sat with them to eat and then took Hannah out for a walk.

'So . . .' Maggie knew her husband inside out. '. . . are you playing nicely out in the country?'

'Well, I met the Oxford Robbery DIs. One's arrogant, the other's a prick and, so far, they're both guilty of culpable manslaughter. But, apart from that, yeah, it's going well.' Maggie refilled Jack's empty wine glass. She then made a gentle observation about Jack always having had problems with those above him. She reminded him of how he once described Ridley as an anally retentive jobsworth, who couldn't exist outside of the bureaucracy of law and order. Now, he was their daughter's godfather!

'Ridley didn't change, Jack. You did. You grew to respect him. And you were very lucky that he's a patient enough man to have waited for you to do that.' Jack loved the way Maggie could tell him off so gently. Whenever they argued about unimportant things, like dirty socks being balled up and thrown behind the washing basket instead of inside it, she could be as loud and belligerent as the next woman, but when she had something serious to say, she was quiet and calm. This made Jack listen attentively to every word she said. 'Who *do* you like?' she asked.

'DC William Oaks; I like him. He's honest and eager. DC Cariad Bevan is a tour de force. I'd bring them both back here in a heartbeat. And there's a uniform, Sergeant Fiona McDermott: she knows people. I don't mean that she knows important people; I mean she knows her community.'

Maggie knew that Jack rarely butted heads with lower-ranking officers; he was great at both teaching and learning from people who were no threat to his position. But with the higher-ups it was different. 'It's just egos, Jack, and I include you in that. When there are too many in one room, sparks are bound to fly.'

Jack smiled in consternation. 'How can you be so clever one minute and, the next, you're putting the TV remote in the dishwasher?'

Maggie mopped her gravy with a slice of bread. 'It's a gift.'

CHAPTER 18

Jack beat Maggie downstairs for the first time since Hannah was born. He was dressed in clothes that suggested he was about to do some gardening. In fact, he was off on a surveillance mission, to get his first look at Michael De Voe.

From Google Maps, Jack had identified a small café directly opposite the Chelsea Emporium which catered mainly for tradesmen on their way to and from work – hence his choice of clothes. When they first moved to London, Jack and Maggie didn't have a garden, nor did they think they'd ever be able to afford one; so, Jack resigned himself to never owning that long yearned-for, middle-class status symbol, gardening clothes! But since Jack's 'lottery windfall' all that had changed. Their garden was an eight-metre-square lawn, with beds down either side waiting for plants; and a small area of decking with loose panels that bounced as you walked across them. It was north facing, and too short to ever get the sun, but they loved it and Penny promised that come the summer, she'd plant the borders and make it into a beautiful safe space for Hannah.

Jack sat in the café, wearing a battered old baseball cap and nursing a cup of tea. He wasn't actually drinking, because he didn't know how long the surveillance would last and he didn't want to have to keep going to the toilet. By eight o'clock, the emporium shop owners began filtering in to receive deliveries and stock shelves. By nine, most shops were open for business. The emporium was an impressive glass-fronted building with advertisements in the windows for all of the shops inside. The advertisement for De Voe's Jewellers marketed him as a 'high-end dealer and maker of new and redesigned second-hand pieces'.

There was a security guard on the main door and a second security guard stood outside the attached underground car park.

Jack had Charlotte's description of Michael De Voe, but no photo; he'd seen several men so far who could possibly have been De Voe, but he'd only know for sure by going inside and heading for shop twenty-one.

Jack left the café with the intention of first of all wandering around the emporium to get a sense of the layout and where all of the exits were on the off-chance that something had already gone wrong and they knew he was coming. He didn't want to be stuck inside a rat-run with no way out. He decided that, once he felt safe, he'd do a couple of passes of shop twenty-one, before actually going in. He didn't want to look purposeful; he wanted to appear as though he was browsing and had no specific destination.

As Jack stepped out into the street, he heard the unmistakeable deep throbbing of a Ferrari. Like most other people in the street, he stopped and stared to watch the red 375 MM Coupe Scaglietti slow down and pull into the underground car park. And there it was. A personalised number plate: VOE 1. Behind the Ferrari was a white convertible Mercedes. Both cars paused just outside the car park and waited for the barrier to rise for them. The female driver of the Merc got out of her car, strode over to the Ferrari, and bent down to speak to the driver. As she did so, her short, figure-hugging red dress pulled tight across her backside, briefly drawing all the male attention away from the cars. All male attention, that was, except Jack's. His eyes were fixed firmly on the driver of the Ferrari. But from where he was standing, all he could see was the back of the driver's head. The woman then returned to her Merc, allowing the Ferrari to drive down the darkened slope and disappear into the underground car park. She then did a clumsily executed U-turn, temporarily stopping all traffic in both directions, and sped away.

As the Merc disappeared, Jack took a quick snap of the number plate, then headed back into the café and ordered another cup of tea.

Jack accessed the HOLMES database on his mobile and checked the details of the white Mercedes. It was owned by a 28-year-old Brazilian woman called Betina Barro. He got her home address from the DVLA and then went to her Instagram account. Here, he found thousands of selfies of Betina from all over the world, standing next to various iconic landmarks, or on picturesque beaches in a tiny bikini. She was absolutely stunning, but Jack wondered how much of her was real, and how many hours it took her each morning to look that perfect.

In any case, he preferred the more natural look. Maggie rolled out of bed in the morning with no make-up and her hair like a bird's nest, but he fancied the pants off her every single time. She oozed contentment and happiness and that was sexy in a way that Betina, even with her perfect figure, was not. She looked untouchable, like a priceless piece of artwork, and – as such, she was breathtaking at first sight, but wouldn't remain interesting for very long.

From Betina Barro's Facebook page, Jack learnt more about her background: her father owned a chunk of their home country the size of Wales and she had a brother, renowned polo player, Alberto Barro. Alberto seemed to have been a star of the polo world in his younger days, but at 38 was now a player-for-hire with no real loyalty to any particular team; he went where the money took him and, in his career, had played for numerous teams across Europe and in the UK, where he once apparently played against Prince William. It was telling that he didn't stay with one team for very long, suggesting that he perhaps wasn't an easy man to be around.

Alberto's photographs showed a fit-looking, handsome man with coal black hair. But, like his sister, his flawless look made him appear fake. Jack thought the beautiful owner of the Merc, and her playboy brother, would easily blend in among the posh horsey set at the annual equestrian event in the Cotswolds.

Jack made his way back across the road, towards the underground car park, where he was stopped at the barrier by the security guard, who asked him for ID. This was a private car park for Emporium businesses only, and the guard knew that Jack did not belong.

Jack played the affable passer-by. 'No worries, mate, I just saw the Ferrari pulling in and wanted to see if it was a Scaglietti. Never seen one close up . . .'

The security guard assured Jack in no uncertain terms that he wasn't going to see *this* one close up either, and to please move on. He sniggered at his own joke and his friend over on the main door to the emporium, joined in. Jack could see that his tradesman's attire, that had served him so well in the café across the road, was now letting him down.

Jack did as he was asked. But both security guards' faces were firmly locked in his memory. At some point, he'd be back to set the record straight.

On his way to the bus stop that would take him home, Jack popped into a local newsagent where he bought copies of *Vogue, Tatler* and *GQ*. Then he went to a small, pop-up street booth that specialised in selling all of the things you never knew you needed. Jack bought a packet of cigarillos and a fake Bentley key ring. He loved how London catered so openly for those who wanted to adorn themselves with the trappings of wealth, at a fraction of the price. London was all about looking the part: you didn't have to actually have anything of substance to back it up.

Back home, in the little box bedroom on the first floor, Jack pushed all of the boxes still to be unpacked against the wall and laid an old pasting table across the top of them, in order to make a temporary desk. This room was completely Jack's responsibility, as it was going to be his office. Which was why everything was still in boxes.

The only thing that was unpacked and ready to be used was the leather office chair. With his makeshift desk now in place, Jack set about making the longest wall of this room into an evidence board, so that he could run this end of the Cotswolds operation from here. It was at this point that Maggie entered carrying a cup of tea and a sandwich.

'What the hell are you doing?!' Jack didn't understand her dismay, as he thought he'd made quite a good job of things. 'Why are you using a pasting table on boxes as an office desk, when the boxes contain your *actual* office desk?' Maggie continued. Jack had no idea that he even owned an office desk. 'It was one of the first things you bought when we moved in, Jack.'

Jack's mobile phone suddenly started buzzing away to itself from on top of a copy of *GQ* as DI Lee called him for the fourth time that morning. Jack ignored it.

'It's only Lee. Look, Mags, I need your help. I need a surveillance cover so that I can—'

'DI Lee?' Maggie interrupted. 'Is he the arrogant one or the prick? Never mind. But why are you ignoring him? Remember what I said about egos and working out how to deal with them. Ignoring probably isn't the best way.'

'I'm not ignoring him. I'll call him back in a bit. Listen, Mags, Ridley and I are running this end of things and we speak all the time. The Cotswold team's DCI has daily briefings with Ridley. No one's being ignored or left in the dark, honestly. Oh, and you'll like this, Ridley and their DCI, Hearst she's called, fancy each other. I mean, Ridley will take months to do anything about it, so nothing will happen, but at least we know he's human.' Once Maggie had been placated, he steered the conversation back on course. 'So, my surveillance cover. I need to create this sort of look.' Jack dumped all of the magazines into her arms. 'Help me, Mags.'

* * *

Jack had never taken a great deal of interest in clothes, which Maggie didn't mind because it saved them money, and she genuinely thought he looked great in anything. She loved nothing more than looking at Jack's shoulder muscles beneath a tight white T-shirt.

Today, Maggie took Jack into shops he didn't even know existed. He hated all of them from the second they entered, because a sales assistant immediately pounced and then proceeded to follow them around, despite the fact that Maggie said firmly that they didn't need any help. Jack assumed that the assistant suspected them of being shoplifters, who couldn't be trusted to wander without supervision.

In a Paul Smith shop, Maggie picked out a white linen shirt with a rounded collar. An assistant sprang from behind a rack of trousers, slapped the palms of his hands together in excitement and commented on how distinguished 'Sir' would look in this particular shirt, especially if it was underneath a casual navy Harrington jacket. Maggie sniggered as Jack squirmed in the hands of this overzealous salesman, but eventually put him out of his misery by telling the assistant that they did not need the jacket, but that they would buy the shirt. Maggie pointed out to Jack that this particular shirt was in the sale, reduced from £140, to £115. 'Fuck me, Mags!' Jack whispered as they queued to pay. 'I'm not paying £115 for a shirt.' Maggie said that she'd keep the receipt and, once his surveillance op was over, she'd bring it back.

As Maggie really got into the swing of things, Jack's day went from bad to worse. In the next shop, she made him buy a pair of fawn corduroy trousers and a pair of navy suede loafers from Hackett's. Jack couldn't believe how much they'd spent in less than one hour. He had to bring the shopping spree to an end when Maggie tried to make him buy a £20 pair of socks – insisting that it was the latest fashion to go sockless.

Still, on the way home, Maggie spotted a Vivienne Westwood couture shop and tried to convince Jack that he needed a £350 man-bag, but he took her firmly by the hand and dragged her away before she could argue with him.

Back home, Jack put all of his new clothes on and looked at himself in the full-length mirror on the back of their bedroom door. He turned and checked out his backside in the perfectly fitted trousers, and Maggie couldn't resist running her hands over his buttocks just to make sure. As his wife admired his dashing new look, Jack stood tall with one foot pointing forwards and the other pointing outwards, like he'd seen male models do in catalogues. An image, quite uninvited, popped into his head. It was an old photo of Harry Rawlins taken at an art gallery opening back in the mid-80s. As usual, Harry's face had been partially hidden from the camera behind a carefully placed champagne glass, but his clothing was on full display. His camel hair coat had hung elegantly over a dark tailored suit, and he wore brown Christian Louboutin Oxford shoes, that Jack now knew must have set him back somewhere in the region of £500. In that old photo, Harry stood exactly as Jack was standing now, in a pose that said, 'I know I'm worth looking at, but, be careful.' In that second, Jack knew that his temporary new look was exactly right. *This* man could infiltrate De Voe's world. *This* man would be respected. The clothes made Jack look like Harry but, more to the point, they made him feel like Harry.

Whilst Jack had been admiring himself, Maggie had left the bedroom, and now came back. She handed him a fake Rolex watch bought by Charlie when they were in St Lucia. Jack snapped out of his daydream: in a single gesture, Maggie had highlighted the difference between Jack's dads. Who was he trying to kid? He was Charlie Warr, not Harry Rawlins.

Maggie slid her arms around Jack's waist and kissed him. She squeezed his buttocks and whispered, 'Do you know what I want to do to you now?'

* * *

Jack stood in the empty bath like Da Vinci's 'Vitruvian Man', wearing just his white Armani boxers, whilst Maggie spray-tanned his ankles. His face, neck and hands were already turning a healthy shade of bronze. 'When you're dry and you put those clothes back on, keep your sleeves rolled down, 'cos there's not enough left in the can to do your whole body.' Maggie stepped back to admire her handiwork. 'Don't get dressed for twenty minutes or it'll come off.'

'I've got to stand here naked, for twenty minutes!'

Maggie considered Jack's options. Then she locked the bathroom door and started to undress. 'All this James Bond stuff is exciting. People will look at you, Jack. Women. And they'll wish you were theirs.' Jack stepped out of the bath and, as he lowered his hands to remove his white boxers, Maggie took over and did it for him with a seductive smile on her face.

Making love on the bathroom floor felt like a decadence that they'd neglected for months. They took their time, as though they were the only two people in the world. In truth, they weren't even the only two people in the house, but that didn't matter. As Penny and Hannah napped downstairs, Jack and Maggie silently enjoyed each other, for as long as time would allow. Afterwards, Maggie lay on Jack's chest and, as she listened to his heart slowly come back to its normal rhythm, she purred the words 'I love you'.

It was another ten minutes before they heard Hannah's hungry cry from the lounge directly beneath them, and the real world insisted that they return.

CHAPTER 19

DI Lee sat at the desk that used to be Jack's and stared out of the window. The picturesque view did not lighten his mood.

The rest of the room was a hive of activity as they hunted down the gang's bolt-hole. No B&B, no hotel, no caravan park, no camping or glamping site had ever booked them in. No lorry parks had registered any unexpected overnighters. No private landowners reported any unwelcome travellers. The best suggestion was from Bevan, who speculated that they probably bedded down in the trailers they hired, an idea that irritated Oaks, as he recalled the stench of bleach that had come from Goodwin's trailer. If Bevan was right, then he'd missed a trailer full of evidence by one hour! Then Oaks unfortunately murmured a thought out loud: 'We're just not thinking like them. Jack would be able to get inside their heads.'

Lee bounced to his feet, sending his swivel chair sliding into Oaks's desk and spilling his tea. 'If you think DS Jack Warr sees us as anything more than his country bitches, you're wrong.' Lee stormed out of the squad room.

Oaks mopped at his spilt tea with a tissue. 'DS Warr knows his stuff,' Oaks mumbled, not caring who heard. Mason looked at him thoughtfully. He didn't disagree. Outside the window, Lee was pacing the car park, with an unlit cigarette in his mouth. Mason knew he hadn't smoked in seven years and didn't own a lighter, but the feel of a cigarette between his lips calmed him in times of extreme stress. Lee felt out of control of his own investigation and he hated it. Mason knew that, and that it wasn't something he'd tolerate for long.

* * *

Jack took the Underground to the police station. His 'disguise' was neatly contained inside a long suit cover, folded in half.

He'd been awake half the night, thinking of the best way to engage with De Voe. Looking the part was half the battle, but there was no point in just meeting the man by pretending to be a customer. Jack wanted to catch De Voe's eye. He wanted De Voe to think that Jack was a man he needed to know. And the best way to do that was not through his legitimate business dealings.

Jack signed himself into the evidence store.

*   *   *

The Wimbledon Prowler, Damien Panagos, had been arrested back in 2014 and was now serving nine years on seventeen counts of burglary. However, not all of the stolen items had been recovered, as Panagos had already had time to sell some of them on. So, the outstanding items went onto a list that dealers like De Voe would have been asked to keep an eye out for.

One such item was a seven-inch platinum and diamond antique bracelet worth around £2,500. This item had finally been found in Glasgow just one week earlier and was currently in the evidence store waiting to be returned to its rightful owner. Jack knew that De Voe wouldn't know this and would still think the bracelet was missing. Jack pocketed the bracelet and left the evidence store – he'd return it before anyone knew it had gone.

As Jack headed down the corridor towards the main entrance, he was aware of the clock ticking. He wanted to get to the emporium as soon as possible. He also needed to get changed into his 'disguise', which he'd have to do in the public toilets as there was no way he was walking out of his police station looking like a rich playboy. As he walked, he ordered an Uber.

'How's it going, Jack?' Behind him, Laura Wade was closing the door to a small briefing room. As Jack turned to face his partner, her eyes widened. 'Bloody hell, I see you've had time to do a bit of sunbathing over there!'

Jack had completely forgotten about the fake tan. It was nothing over the top – Maggie knew what she was doing on that score – but he was certainly more golden-brown now than when he'd left. Jack laughed it off, saying that he often chose to walk instead of drive when in the beautiful Cotswold countryside. He also confirmed that the case was coming to a head and that, yes, he hoped he'd soon be returning to London, because he was really missing the family. Laura smiled. 'I'm so happy for you and Maggie. Hannah's such a beautiful baby.'

At the end of the corridor, Ridley briefly came into view as he paused to sign something before moving on, but for those few seconds, Laura's attention was fixed on him.

'Laura?' Jack said, but she didn't seem to hear him.

So now she's got the hots for Ridley, he thought to himself.

Laura turned back to him, a flush spreading over her face, as she realised she'd been sussed. Jack's mobile buzzed to say that his Uber was pulling into the car park. 'You'd better be quick, Laura,' he said with a wink. 'Someone else has her eye on him.'

* * *

Lee sat in front of Hearst, relaxed and calm. He knew he was in the right. 'My last instruction, which I made very clear, was to keep me, his DI, in the loop. Now, either his mobile isn't on, or he's deliberately ignoring me.'

Hearst sighed. This part of the job was utterly draining. They were meant to be righting wrongs, not bickering. She sat with her

JUDAS HORSE | 206

elbows on the arms of her chair, and her hands together in concentration. This was her 'I'm listening' pose, and seemed to be working because Lee was still talking. His obviously rehearsed speech finally came to an end. 'If I can't control every aspect of the case, then I can't control the outcomes, so blame someone else if all of this goes tits-up.'

Hearst lowered her hands and laid them flat on the desk. 'You could have come in here and spun a story that left me no choice but to send DS Warr back to London. But you didn't. You don't want me to get rid of him; you want me to show him that you're the boss.' Lee opened his mouth to speak, but she had no intention of letting him. 'Now, my question is, why can't you do that yourself? What I see here, Eamonn, is chest-beating. Showing him that you have the big guns on your side. Well, you do. But I'm disappointed that you feel you need to play that card.' Lee stayed silent, but felt his colour rising. 'There is no blanket approach to command, Eamonn. Treat each officer in the way that you need to, in order to get the best out of them. Some of them walk to heel, like good little doggies and others will need one of those bloody annoying extendable leashes to give them a sense of freedom – but at the other end of that leash is you. Let him run for now. Don't reel him in just for the sake of it.'

Lee nodded curtly and stood up.

Once he'd left the office, Hearst picked up her phone.

*   *   *

Jack, now wearing his posh new clothes, asked the Uber to drop him at the end of the street, just along from the emporium. He didn't want the security guards to see that he didn't have transport – and his own car, which was a perfectly respectable Skoda Octavia, would have immediately told them that Jack's new wardrobe was all for show, while Jack's regular clothes were now squashed into the Hackett's bag he'd been given when he bought his shoes.

Jack headed straight for the security guard on the emporium's main door with a natural swagger and nodded a 'good morning'. The security guard nodded back, said, 'Welcome, sir,' and opened the door for him. It was a small and petty revenge, but it was still sweet.

Inside, the emporium was a dazzling place. Every window was brimming with items that twinkled under carefully placed spotlights.

After his first lap of the lower floor, Jack headed up the central ornate metal staircase. At the top, the shop right in front of him was numbered fourteen; to its left, was number thirteen and to its right was number fifteen. Jack turned right. He took his time, making sure that he paused to look in every window and even go into some of the shops for a quick browse.

Shop number twenty-one had a relatively low-key window display, with far less in it than most of the others. It whispered 'quality, not quantity'. A small brass bell above the door jingled as Jack entered and it brought a young woman out from behind a door in the back. Inside, the shop was again economical in terms of its contents, allowing every item to be prominently displayed in a space of its own.

The young woman went and sat behind the counter and smiled sweetly to let Jack know that she was here if he needed her, then she picked up a book and started to read, allowing Jack to browse uninterrupted.

Some of the locked display cabinets housing the more expensive items of jewellery had mirrored panels to allow shoppers to view them from all sides. In these mirrors, Jack counted seven unobtrusive

CCTV cameras mounted in the corners of the shop and down the centre aisle. It was an impressive set-up. As Jack passed the young woman reading, he glanced up in an attempt to see what was beyond the door behind her, where – thanks to the plan of the interior given to him by Ridley – Jack knew was an on-site office and storage area that was about half the size of the shop itself.

The second-hand section of the shop boasted a few Cartier or Tiffany items, and hand-written notes invited visitors to ask if they were looking for anything in particular, as there was also a select number of Chopard, Vogue and Bulgari items in the back. Jack assumed they were family heirlooms that had been exchanged for more practical cash. As Jack moved around the shop, he could feel the thick maroon carpet sliding beneath the shiny soles of his new shoes.

'Let me know if you have any questions.' Jack looked towards the female voice, expecting to see the young woman peering over the top of her book; instead, he found himself looking at Betina Barro.

She was of medium height and slender in a skin-tight, off-the-shoulder dress with three-quarter sleeves. Her coily black hair sat neatly on her bare shoulders. The only jewellery she wore was a pair of large diamond stud earrings. Up close, Jack thought she was less sexy than in the airbrushed images he'd seen on social media. She wasn't unattractive by any means; she simply wasn't a goddess, with a slightly longer face and more prominent nose than the glossy images suggested. Jack thought that trying to be someone you're not was a shame, until he reflected that he was doing exactly the same thing. But he wasn't doing it out of vanity; it was just part of the job.

The feature that Betina had no need to alter, however, was her eyes – they were astonishingly wide and dark, with large irises.

Betina raised her eyebrows and tipped her head to the side in a silent repeat of her question, as Jack looked at her.

'Just looking,' he said, and she smiled, clearly assuming he was referring to her as much as the jewellery in the display cases, and went back to working on her laptop, which sat on the black velvet and red leather jewellery examination block. Her long, slender fingers barely seemed to move as she typed for a few moments.

'Actually . . .' Jack began. Betina closed the lid of her laptop and gave him her full attention. 'I'm looking for something for my girlfriend.'

Jack assumed Betina would instantly show him the most expensive item in the shop, but instead she asked him to tell her about his girlfriend.

'She's . . .' Jack tried to think of a fictional girlfriend, but couldn't. He could only think of Maggie. 'She's perfect really. Beautiful in an understated way. She doesn't wear a lot of jewellery normally, only items that mean something to her. She *subtly* showed me this photo the other day. The gift is for a very special occasion, so money is no object.'

Jack reached into his pocket, 'accidently' taking out the fake Bentley key ring. Once he was certain that Betina had seen both the keyring and the fake Rolex, he replaced the keys and dipped into his right-hand pocket. From here, he removed a folded page from *Vogue* magazine showing a ring – a large square-cut emerald, surrounded by diamonds, on a platinum band.

Betina looked at it appreciatively. 'Your girlfriend clearly has wonderful taste. Are you specifically looking for an emerald? We have a lovely range of rose diamonds in at the moment. And is her heart set on the square-cut, do you know? It's the most common, of course, but . . . if she's as special as you suggest, perhaps "common" isn't the way to go.'

Jack shook his head. 'Emerald is her birth stone, so nothing else will do. The square-cut isn't important as long as it's around three carats.' Jack continued to talk breezily about jewellery that cost about a third of his annual police salary and began to enjoy the feeling of power it gave him, knowing that Betina totally believed in the fake persona he'd created. When another customer entered the shop, Betina called the young woman from behind the counter to deal with him so she could focus on Jack.

Now that Betina had an idea of Jack's girlfriend's taste, she asked about the special occasion he'd mentioned. This was the question Jack had been waiting for. 'It's to celebrate one of her Arabians winning a European title.'

There was a brief glint of interest in Betina's eyes, but she clearly didn't want to be diverted from a potentially big sale onto the subject of horses. 'I'd estimate the ring in *Vogue* to be priced at around fifteen to twenty thousand pounds. Is that roughly what you expected?'

Jack laughed softly. 'That's a little less than I thought you'd say, actually.'

Betina smiled, as if money was of no importance to either of them. 'We have several rings I think you might want to look at. They won't be identical, of course. We have a couple of the rarer, round emeralds, and we have two five-carat examples that I can show you. We also have some vintage styles. Would you like to see those as well?'

'I'm happy to put myself in your very capable hands,' Jack smiled back. As Betina turned to open the office door, the bell above the door rang and the other customer left, letting someone else in at the same time. A deep, velvety voice quickly echoed around the small shop.

'Your fucking brother has been caught bullshitting his way onto a polo team in the Hamptons with a rather creative CV.

Again! And then he couldn't keep his dick in his pants, so was thrown out.' As the owner of the voice moved round the central jewellery cabinet, Jack came into view from behind a tall display stand. Betina threw an embarrassed and apologetic glance at Jack. 'Oh, my apologies!' the owner of the deep voice laughed. 'I thought the gentleman who just went out was the only . . . I hope you'll forgive my outburst.'

Jack smiled, showing he wasn't offended, and offered his hand. 'Richard Delaware.' Jack had chosen the name of his best friend from school. Richard Delaware had died of cancer at the age of nine. It was a name Jack would always associate with strength and bravery: both qualities he needed for this undercover operation if it was going to succeed.

'Michael De Voe,' the man replied. *Game on*, Jack thought, a flash of adrenaline coursing through his body.

Michael De Voe was an impressive-looking man. He was over six feet, with thick, wavy blond hair and deep blue eyes. At first sight boyish, as he got closer it became clear that he was in his mid to late 40s. His tanned skin was deeply lined, the result, Jack presumed, of years of travelling the world and enjoying outdoor pursuits. De Voe wore a navy blue silk draped shirt and similar corduroy trousers to those Jack was wearing. On his left pinkie finger, he wore a heavy gold carnelian ring. De Voe gripped Jack's hand tight and showed a row of gleaming, perfectly capped teeth in a broad smile. 'Apologies again, Richard. My dear assistant's brother is a constant pain in my derriere. But you don't want to hear about my problems. Come and have a seat, whilst Betina sees to your needs. I don't like my customers to wait standing up . . . or without a drink in their hand.'

*   *   *

As Jack followed De Voe through the office door and into the private space beyond, he knew there was no turning back; now he was in the dragon's lair. Maggie's words echoed in his mind, clear and sharp: *You can't ignore who you are. Think like Harry. Act like Charlie.*

The small office contained a half-sized desk, a desktop computer, a landline and various chargers for devices that were not on display.

An impressive-looking safe was bricked into the wall behind the desk with no attempt at disguise, suggesting that no one came back here without an express invitation, or that the safe was possibly a decoy. De Voe put two single malt whiskys on the desk and sat down in a wide black leather office chair, gesturing to Jack to seat himself on the velvet-cushioned chair on the other side of the desk. 'How did you find us?' De Voe's casual tone couldn't disguise his curiosity about 'Richard Delaware'.

'To be honest,' Jack replied, 'I didn't know you were here. I was just wandering when your displays caught my eye. Some of the other shops seem very cluttered, as though they're trying to make me buy as much as possible. I prefer quality over quantity.'

Jack wasn't really putting on a particular accent for De Voe's benefit, but Penny would probably have called it a 'telephone voice', posh enough to vaguely suggest he was from London and rich.

The conversation drifted from twenty-grand emerald-and-diamond rings, to Jack's girlfriend's wealthy family and stud farm. Jack wanted De Voe to think that Richard Delaware's wealth was not his own, suspecting that De Voe would be drawn more to a cunning charmer who lived off someone else's money.

Jack chose this moment to bring the diamond bracelet from his pocket and ask De Voe if he'd consider it in part-exchange. De Voe took the bracelet and examined it through a small teardrop-shaped magnifying glass. Jack knew from the stolen items log that it was a high quality, beautifully crafted piece of jewellery and when De Voe asked him who the bracelet had belonged to and why he was selling it, Jack said it was an heirloom handed down from his grandmother, and that his girlfriend didn't like – being diamonds rather than her favourite emeralds. De Voe's eyes flicked to Jack and then back to the magnifying glass, and Jack immediately knew that De Voe thought he was lying. De Voe didn't flinch again. He didn't check any police list or ask any more questions: Jack's demeanour was telling him everything he needed to know. He was playing the 'chancer' perfectly and De Voe was falling for it. But De Voe wasn't going to let his guard slip just yet; that would take longer than a short conversation over a single malt.

It took Betina another ten minutes to gather all of the rings she thought Jack might be interested in and, during that time, De Voe took his opportunity to delve deeper into the background of his new acquaintance.

Jack had to have his wits about him. He had no experience as an undercover officer and was simply drawing on his natural instincts to be able to read De Voe's questions and supply appropriate answers. 'Although my girlfriend pointed out the emerald-and-diamond ring, I'm thinking I might also be in the market for a matching necklace.' Jack raised his devilish black eyebrows and grinned his best super-smooth grin. 'She won't be expecting that.'

De Voe did not flinch at the mention of an emerald necklace. And Jack chose not to pursue it further for now, not wanting to be too obvious. He'd planted the seed, and he wasn't expecting De Voe to instantly mention that he had recently acquired a one-off emerald necklace that had been owned by the infamous Barbara Hutton.

But De Voe did do something that, as far as Jack was concerned, indicated his guilt just as strongly: he instantly changed the subject completely and asked what line of work Richard was in.

'Shipping. Import, export. It's a family business that keeps the wolf from the door, but I have no real interest in it,' Jack replied airily. 'The only sea-going vessel that interests me is my father's yacht.' At that moment Betina entered the office carrying a small red leather briefcase, reminiscent of the Chancellor's red box. She placed it on the desk in front of Jack and then left. De Voe invited Jack to open it.

The clasps were stiff and when they sprang free, they did it with such force that the briefcase jumped slightly on the table. Jack lifted the velvet-lined lid, which had 180-degree hinges, so it could then be used as a display tray.

Four emerald rings, each sitting inside its own black velvet bed, glistened at Jack. They were stunning and he knew from his research that he was looking at around £170,000 of jewellery. He quickly dismissed the ring on the lower right-hand side of the briefcase as being too small, then lifted out the other three rings, one by one, and examined them against the light. He gave the impression of being uncertain that any of them were quite what he was looking for. 'You know, the more I look at these, the more I'm thinking that a matching necklace would be the way to really impress her. You know what it's like, Mr De Voe – she's a woman who's used to getting what she asks for, so the trick is to also give her what she's *not* asked for.' Jack returned the rings to the briefcase and flipped the lid closed, hoping the threat of leaving the shop empty-handed would prompt De Voe into action.

De Voe refilled Jack's crystal tumbler with single malt from the matching decanter and looked thoughtful. Jack made himself wait patiently. He'd set the hook; now he just had to sit back and see if De Voe would take the bait.

After what seemed like minutes but was probably only seconds, De Voe finally volunteered the information Jack had been waiting to hear. 'I may be able to help you with an emerald necklace, actually. I have some exceptional stones, although the necklace itself would have to be custom made. But that means it can exactly match the ring you choose. Are you working to a timeframe?'

Jack confirmed that there was no rush and that he was perfectly prepared to wait for any custom design to be made as he didn't need the jewellery for another month, intending to give it to his girlfriend on her birthday. Jack then flipped the small red briefcase open again and pointed at the most expensive-looking ring. 'That one'll do,' he said casually, downing the last of his whisky.

De Voe then explained that an emerald necklace had recently come into his possession, but the stones' settings were damaged and the clasp needed replacing, so he had decided to dismantle the piece and either sell the stones individually or make a new design.

Jack smiled to himself. Of course it would be impossible for De Voe to sell Sally Barrowman's Barbara Hutton necklace in one piece, as it would be instantly recognisable, so breaking it up was his only option.

De Voe was clearly delighted to be shaking hands on such a huge deal, especially since Richard Delaware had not even asked the combined price of the necklace and ring. De Voe asked him for his mobile phone number, and Jack recited the one belonging to the burner phone in his pocket. He also gave his address as a huge property in the Cotswolds. De Voe smiled: 'Lovely part of the world.'

Jack stood to leave, he mentally patted himself on the back for his performance, but then De Voe threw an almighty spanner in the works by grabbing the diamond bracelet from the desk before Jack could take it back. 'If you leave this with me, I'll get it valued and then be able to tell you how much I can part-ex it for.' Jack froze for a second. How could he leave police evidence with De Voe? 'Don't worry, Richard; I'll give you a receipt. Trust me.'

Jack stiffened as he realised that De Voe was testing him. It was Jack's move and there was only one thing he could do. He forced himself to relax and gave De Voe a casual smile, shrugging his shoulders. 'I'm not a man to trust easily, Mr De Voe. But I feel that you and I understand each other, so I'm happy to leave the bracelet with you. I don't need a receipt . . . it's not like I don't know where to find you, is it?' he said with a just a hint of menace. Jack left without another word.

Outside the emporium, he made a quick phone call: 'Are you free to meet?'

* * *

When Mason glanced up from his desk, more than an hour later and noticed that Lee was not back in the squad room, and wasn't pacing the car park either, he started to wonder if DI Lee might have done something rash, and went to look for him. He found him in the canteen nursing a cappuccino and still reeling from his conversation with Hearst.

'We should bring Charlotte Miles in,' Lee said. Mason did not let his worry show. 'I just called her and she's ignoring me. She's picked that annoying little habit up from Jack Warr. We need to bring her in, brief her and get her into protective custody, exactly as we should have done in the first place. Then we're in control. And when De Voe calls, we can guide the conversation instead of leaving it in the hands of some bloody gardener.'

Mason drew on their years of friendship to steer Lee back on track. 'Eamonn, if De Voe suspects anything, we'll lose them all. He won't take any risks. And, this close to the equestrian event, he'll have people here already. What if one of them has eyes on Charlotte? We could put her in danger.'

'She could put *us* in danger!'

'Coerced or not, let's not forget that she's a home invader and she's responsible for aiding and abetting scores of burglaries, one of which led to the death of a dog and another to the severe beating of an autistic lad. *And* she's responsible for the death of Jacob Mulhern!'

'That's bollocks and you know it!' Lee's argument was born out of the sheer frustration at being left out of the loop and being unsupported, as he saw it, by his senior officer. Mason lowered his tone into a forced whisper before he continued. 'We're responsible for the death of Jacob Mulhern. And I don't mean the police force, Eamonn, I mean me and you. We left him to uniform when we should have been all over it ourselves.' Mason watched Lee's nostrils flare and his cheek muscles twitch. He was angry because he knew Mason was right and that hurt like hell. 'I don't give a fuck whether you like Jack Warr or not,' Mason continued. 'He's right about the handling of Charlotte. You should see her, Eamonn, she's putty in his hands.'

'And what about you, Colin? Are you putty in his hands too?'

As Lee stormed from the canteen, he didn't notice Bevan sitting with her back to the table he'd just left. Nor did Mason. She got out her mobile and texted Jack on his burner:

We may have a problem.

Ridley wore a pair of classic blue jeans, a pale blue T-shirt, black trainers and a black leather jacket. He was so close to looking cool, but somehow couldn't quite pull it off. Perhaps because he just didn't feel comfortable. As a man who normally dressed immaculately in a perfectly fitted suit, Ridley now felt very under-dressed sitting in the lounge bar of the Franklin Hotel in Egerton Gardens.

'You said we were meeting in a caff opposite the emporium!'
Ridley looked Jack up and down. He knew the cost of the clothes
Jack was wearing. 'And don't even try to put that lot on expenses!'

As Ridley sipped a £5 lime and soda, Jack got him up to speed,
flitting from subject to subject as thoughts popped into his head,
with Ridley just about keeping up. 'De Voe's definitely our man,'
Jack said. 'I think his main gang might be Brazilian, and they come
and go from the country as and when he needs them and maybe
also as mules to move the stolen items on into Europe. He could be
using different people each time, but I reckon he has a trusted group
that he sticks to. I think Mathew knew exactly what he was talking
about when he described the man who beat him with a crowbar as
being Oberyn Martell from *Game of Thrones*. Alberto Barro is the
spit of him. We need to put plainclothes on De Voe, Betina Barro
and Alberto Barro, from today. And we need to have enough officers
to change about so they don't get sussed. De Voe's got an iPhone and
a Samsung, so you need to track both . . . and he has to have an off-
shore account somewhere to deal with the sales of stolen items. That
won't be in his name, but it might be in Betina's; they're close and he
definitely trusts her. He doesn't trust Alberto, though: he's a liabil-
ity and is probably only being kept on board 'cos of his willingness
to get his hands dirty. Oh, and if you send Alberto's photo to DC
Oaks, he can ask Justin Estrada if he's the guy in the Adidas NMDs.
Estrada's our stable-boy witness. I think it'll turn out that they're two
different men, as Alberto seems to be a smaller build—'

'When was the last time you checked in with DI Lee, DI Mason
or DI Gifford?' Ridley's question stopped Jack in his tracks. Was
Ridley really asking him about pedantic, hierarchical protocol,
after Jack had practically just handed De Voe to him on a silver
platter? Ridley could see Jack's anger rise through his chest and
colour his face, but he didn't falter. 'Don't look at me like I'm the

one who's in the wrong, Jack. An officer not answering his mobile is *the* most infuriating thing. And I should bloody know! Especially when that officer is undercover in the company of a potentially dangerous criminal. Anything could have happened to you.' Ridley paused to sip his drink, giving himself time to formulate his next sentence, while also forcing Jack to wait silently.

But Ridley knew exactly what needed saying and he wanted to get it all out in one go. 'Don't treat me like I'm not on your side, Jack. You now expect me to coordinate the biggest dual-approach operation of my career, align resources, track all the key players using officers from across the south-east and south-west of England, deploy armed response, air support, dogs and the mounted division – all while keeping some of the most prominent names in the UK safe from a Brazilian gang of murdering house-breakers who are about to embark on one last job. A job that'll be bigger than anything they've done to date, with risks and rewards so immense that they'll be armed, extremely dangerous and won't give a shit who they take down as long as they get out alive.' Ridley paused for breath. 'You're about to ask me to do all of that. Whereas I asked you to do one thing, Jack. *Play nice!* Can you just do that for me?'

Jack mumbled the words 'Yes, sir'. They were barely audible but Ridley nodded. 'Good. Because it's embarrassing for everyone when his DCI calls your DCI.'

Jack took a second to catch up. 'Lee reported me?'

Ridley shook his head. 'He stopped shy of that. You're a team, Jack. That can be demanding, I know, but it pays dividends.'

Jack was well aware of his own flaws, which was why he didn't argue further. They were born out of resentment for the red tape and arse-kissing that sucked the life out of being a police officer. It was the best job in the world and Jack *did* love it – but when he looked back at this case, he sure as hell wouldn't remember the tactical briefings and the paperwork in triplicate. But he'd remember the thrill of coming face to face with De Voe in the guise of Richard Delaware; of physically forcing Mason to understand his failure to protect an innocent man; and he'd remember feeling the lust in Maggie's body as his undercover alter-ego made love to her on the bathroom floor, almost as if they were having an affair . . .

Now that they were back on an even keel, Ridley suggested that they both return to the station, so that they could talk tactics before Skyping the rest of the team for an update. Jack agreed but asked if they could change the location to his home address; as he was going to be heading west again soon, he wanted to spend as much time as possible with Hannah first.

The first thing Jack did when he and Ridley arrived was get his main mobile phone out of the kitchen drawer. He had seven missed calls from DI Lee, two from Ridley . . . and a voicemail from Charlotte Miles. *Shit!* Jack put this mobile on speaker and played her message. She sounded frantic. 'DI Warr! He called. Just now. He told me to get my thinking cap on 'cos he'd be calling again tomorrow and, this time, he wants five addresses. The biggest jewellery targets I can think of. He doesn't need horse trailers this time; he's not going for the big stuff. And he didn't ask me about security systems or anything like that; he just wants to hit the biggest houses in Chipping Norton. He sounded . . . he sounded like he doesn't care anymore. I'm scared, DS Warr. DI Lee has been calling every day, asking if I've heard from De Voe. I've done what you asked and called you first, but . . . he keeps calling. I can't ignore him forever. Call me back. *Please!* I need you to tell me what to do. I'm scared and I . . .' The allocated time to record on Jack's mobile cut Charlotte off mid-sentence.

Ridley's face was easy to read: why had Jack asked the case's biggest asset to call him before the SIO?

'She's vulnerable, sir,' Jack explained. 'Through one mistake, she's put herself at the heart of this mess, and I want to protect her. The last time a careless officer overstepped the mark and told an innocent bystander too much, that bystander was tortured to death in his stable. Lee wants to bring Charlotte in and use her like a police informant – Bevan told me – but that'll get her killed. We have to limit what she knows, or she'll end up accidentally saying the wrong thing to De Voe when he calls, and she *will* tip him off. Because she's not a liar, sir. She's not an experienced police informant. She's a farmer.'

Ridley instructed Jack to call Charlotte and together they assured her that although Jack was her primary liaison, in the background the entire force was there to protect her. Ridley's calm voice was exactly what Charlotte needed to hear and his higher rank made her believe that the entire force was somehow right by her side. Once she'd calmed down sufficiently, Jack asked if she already knew the five addresses she was going to suggest to De Voe. As Charlotte reeled off dozens of potential high-end targets, Ridley numbered them and then plotted them on Google Maps. He then gave Charlotte her next instruction.

'Charlotte, when De Voe calls you tomorrow, I want you to give him address numbers one, three, four, seven and nine. Tell him you've chosen these homes because they contain the highest-value jewellery items, as requested. It doesn't matter whether they do or not, because he won't get that far.' Then, after another five minutes of both men telling her what a great job she was doing, Charlotte hung up.

Jack got two beers from the fridge and handed one to Ridley, who thanked him and said, 'He's going for a quick getaway this time. No horse trailers. Just bikes? Quads? Maybe cars? We don't know what to look out for if they're changing the way they move around . . .' He thought for a moment, then chugged down almost half a bottle of beer before he started talking again. 'Well, we've narrowed everything down as much as we can. We've given De Voe a cluster of houses, so they'll be easier to monitor. They'll avoid the A44, I think, and only two other roads link all five properties. From what you'd expect of this gang, they might be using the tactic of holding traffic with temporary lights at certain crossroads to allow them a clear escape route. So, once they have their targets, we need to monitor those roads to see if any temporary lights pop up. That'll give us their likely way in and out. Then all we need to know is when. The annual equestrian event starts next Monday and lasts for a week. So we need to be patient.' He looked at Jack. 'You, Jack, need to be patient.'

By midday the following day, Ridley and Hearst had got substantial teams of officers allocated to this mammoth sting. Their first job was to trace the various travel agencies used by Betina Barro to book flights back and forth to Brazil and occasionally to Europe. From this information, they were able to identify the names on the associated passports and visas, and although these were no doubt all fake, they still provided trackable details that would consistently appear at both ends of the flight. The account used to fund all of these flights was held at Coutts bank in the name of Betina Barro, and although a constant supply of money fed this account, there was no record of where that money came from, as it was always deposited in cash by Betina herself.

There was no evidence linking De Voe to anything remotely criminal, other than Charlotte's statement. During the Skype conference call, Jack suggested that DC Oaks be sent undercover onto Charlotte's smallholding, as a casual labourer. Oaks grew up on a farm, so could act the part. They had to do everything in their power to make her feel safe.

That evening, Jack and Ridley were back at Jack's kitchen table drinking their way through a six-pack of beer. There was a chilli bubbling away in one pan and cooked, drained rice waiting in another. 'I've only met De Voe once, sir,' Jack said, 'but I know he's catchable. I mean, he's smart and we can't underestimate him, but his problem is that he thinks he's untouchable. He's arrogant, and he's greedy. He doesn't need to sell an emerald ring and matching necklace to Richard Delaware, but he will. He can't help himself. Another Achilles heel is Betina. He likes her, trusts her, but she clearly comes as a package with Alberto. He's their weak link. If he's our killer, and I think he is, then he's the one with the most to lose and the most to gain from talking to us. But the best thing about Alberto Barro is his selfishness. If we get Alberto alive, he'll give us De Voe.'

CHAPTER 20

The squad room in Chipping Norton was a hive of activity. Bevan was in charge of updating the information on the whiteboards: one was now dedicated to the timeline, one to the identification of potential gang members and the third board was for outlining the operational tactics that would ultimately catch this gang in the act of robbing five, preselected target houses, all at once. While everyone threw information at Bevan on various subjects, she listened to every word, noted every detail and added it in exactly the right place on exactly the right whiteboard.

When Jack walked into the room, Oaks rushed to his side, eager to get him up to speed on the recent job he'd been personally assigned. 'Justin Estrada couldn't pick Alberto Barro as being the man in the Adidas trainers he saw collecting the trailer from Goodwin's yard. I think, sir, that if the security lighting in the yard was good enough to see that a pair of trainers had a red sole, then maybe Estrada is right. Adidas trainers don't seem very "Alberto Barro" anyway, if you ask me. He's a higher-end designer label man, isn't he?'

DI Lee sidled up and listened with a frown on his face. 'I'd prefer it, DC Oaks, if you relay any relevant information via the proper channels, rather than skip about reporting dribs and drabs to a select few. Inadequate reporting is how cases fall apart . . . wouldn't you agree, DS Warr?'

Fresh from the pep-talk he'd had from Ridley, Jack didn't take the bait. 'Oaks didn't want to waste your time with a dead end, but yes, you're right. Oaks, we know that Adidas Man is a trusted lead player in this gang, so that's the detail we take from this.' Oaks said that he would add this information to the board, and off he went. Then Jack, with a friendly smile, asked Lee to lead a briefing with him: Lee could share all of the Chipping Norton discoveries and Jack would share about his encounter with De Voe. Despite his cooperative demeanour, Jack's intention was actually to irritate Lee. And it worked.

'Oh, so you're affording me some respect now?' Lee said. 'I specifically told you to keep me in the loop whilst you were in London.'

Jack smiled. 'Yes, DCI Ridley did mention that you were unhappy with my conduct.' Then Jack walked away and began the briefing. After getting the attention of the room, Jack invited Lee to stand by his side and speak first, hoping his deferential manner would irritate him even more.

* * *

There was now so much work going on in the squad room that the briefing was allowed to be a bit of a free-for-all.

The research done on Alberto Barro so far was extensive. He'd lost all of his inherited wealth to polo – playing, socialising and gambling – so he was now financially dependent on his younger sister. From checking both of their bank accounts, it seemed that she would intermittently release funds, to help him 're-establish his career'. But it was obvious to everyone that, as soon as Betina's money cleared Alberto's bank account, it went straight back out on living the high life. Including, back in 2008, paying a substantial amount of hush-money after he assaulted a waitress in Virginia for refusing to serve him beyond the point where he puked the previous hour's alcohol into an ice bucket. She'd asked him to leave and he'd reacted by pushing her over a table stacked with glasses. The waitress had hounded Alberto on social media, threatening to report him to the police if he didn't pay her off. He'd de-activated those old accounts, but had not deleted them, so Hearst had got permission to re-activate them and the private messages were now part of their investigation. It seemed that the waitress had eventually gone quiet for £30,000.

Another, equally disturbing allegation of violence made against Alberto came in 2007, when a member of the Canadian Polo Team, who Alberto was due to play against in a winter friendly, found his horse collapsed on the floor of its stable. The Achilles tendon in its left hind leg had been severed. Although the police were brought in immediately, the culprit was never identified, but the very next day, Alberto was removed from the team and he left Canada. Apparently this was the last time any polo team allowed Alberto near a horse.

It seemed that Alberto Barro was a sociopath at best, and a psychopath at worst.

Michael De Voe was connected to a web of small companies that allowed him to move money around. A seven-year-old marketing image of De Voe, from the launch of one of these companies, was pinned to the suspects board. It wasn't ideal, as it had definitely been photoshopped to make him look younger and slimmer, but it was all they had.

It was hard to track all of De Voe's cash flow but, for the most part, it all seemed to involve legitimate payments and purchases. They had discovered that a week or so prior to each robbery, between £30,000 and £50,000 went into Betina's bank account. Lee had used his Oxford leverage to assign a Fraud Squad officer to the highly complex task of following the money but so far, establishing that the money came out of one of De Voe's bank accounts and he was the paymaster had come up blank.

Just after Canteen Barbara had refuelled the room with tea and pastries, Jack got a message from Ridley. The phone tap had picked up a seemingly innocent conversation between De Voe and Betina. The recording began with three minutes of chat about the emporium shift patterns, followed by fifteen minutes about jewellery. But after that De Voe began to talk in an artificial manner usually associated with cagey criminals who were aware of the potential for being bugged. 'That dog of yours, Betina, you have to find a way to control it, you know. I've never been bitten in my life, and that's because I know an untrainable half-breed when I see one. It's in his nature to turn on you too, my dear. I'd hate to see that.' Betina had then defended her 'dog' and reassured De Voe that she could control him. De Voe spoke with genuine concern about her safety, emphasising that some animals are so damaged that no one can truly control them; they want to be liked and loved but, in the end, they don't know how. When Betina again sprang to the defence of her 'dog', De Voe snapped. 'He bragged about Angelo being *alive* when he went into the fucking lake, Betina! Wake up!' And then the line went dead.

This single, spontaneous, ill-considered outburst from De Voe was game-changing. Out of context, it meant nothing but, put together with everything else they knew, it *could* mean that Alberto strangled the man in the horsebox to the point of snapping his hyoid bone, before sliding him into the lake. And, if that proved to be true, then De Voe's recorded outburst just proved that he knew about it. This could link all of the key players to the first murder. They were miles away from this recording being of any use in a court of law but in this squad room, it was invaluable. It gave them a possible name for the man in the horsebox: Angelo. As soon as she heard the recording, Bevan jumped on this lead without being asked, driven by a need to find justice for the dead man she'd linked to their case in the first instance.

This dramatic new angle was then almost trumped when Oaks announced he'd stumbled on another new name: Miguel Delgardo.

He was an Argentinian in his late fifties who had spent time in a Brazilian prison for drug smuggling. He was a skilled criminal who had evaded capture for most of his career; and was only ever charged with a fraction of the crimes that the Brazilian criminal justice system brought against him, serving seven years of what should have been a life sentence. Delgardo was loosely connected to the Brazilian billionaire businessman, Luiz Barro, father to Betina and Alberto, but when Oaks couldn't trace any recent communication between the two men, he decided to add Delgardo's early-90s mugshot to a fourth 'possible connection' board and move on.

Jack was immediately drawn to this 20-year-old image. He wasn't sure why at first. He studied it until his mind made sense of what was nagging at him, then Jack moved Delgardo's image onto the 'prime targets' board, alongside the image of De Voe.

Oaks then asked the obvious question: 'How come he's a prime target when we don't even know who he is?'

'Look at the eyes.' Jack's smile worried Oaks, as it meant that there was something bloody obvious right in front of him and he had no clue what it was. The whole room was now focused on trying to see what Jack was seeing.

Bevan got there first.

'It's him!' She was so excited that she couldn't help shouting it out. 'Michael De Voe *is* Miguel Delgardo!'

Jack grinned. '*Was*. Oaks, we need to know everything about Delgardo. Most importantly, how he worked, his MO, and how he was caught. Listen, everyone! Michael De Voe's real name is Miguel Delgardo. He's not late-40s, as his business CV states, but late-50s. And he's an accomplished drug smuggler. He is exceptional at getting things across borders, undetected. This is excellent work from DC Oaks, because now we can learn our target. Well done, William. Bloody well done.'

Looking on, Gifford appreciated how Jack freely praised his officers. Jack's easy way with his subordinates had niggled Gifford at first, but now he saw its true value. If, or more likely, when Hearst got the next batch of complaints about Jack, Gifford would pull rank on him, but for now he was content to share in the warm feeling that spread around the squad room from the results of everyone's hard work. Even Lee could find nothing to complain about, which, judging from his sour expression, mightily pissed him off. He couldn't stand Jack's easy-going manner, sure it concealed a far more sinister person beneath.

'Bevan,' Gifford interrupted her before she could begin trying to find out who Angelo was, 'get four uniforms and brief them on the recording, the guy in the horsebox, the name Angelo, and whatever else is relevant. Get them to start trying to identify him. I don't want you on the sidelines. We need you front and centre.'

When Jack's mobile rang, he glanced at the screen. 'CM'. He clicked accept and Charlotte began talking before he could say hello. 'He's changed the plan, DS Warr. And I'm scared he knows that I've spoken to you. Meet me at the King's Stone. Just you. Please. Be there in an hour.' Then she ended the call.

* * *

The Rollright Stones, out in the direction of Long Compton, were a series of Neolithic and Bronze Age megaliths, whose mysterious origins made them as revered as Stonehenge. Popular explanations ranged from the stones once being the King and his knights, turned to stone by a witch, to the site being the King's burial ground – all without satisfactorily identifying which 'King' they actually related to. Either way, the myths surrounding the stones brought tourists and film crews from miles around. The King's Men stones stood in a circle; the Whispering Knights formed a huddled group; and The King's Stone stood alone behind a waist-high circular fence. Jack waited in the open field, the cold wind blowing through his coat and straight into his bones. But he hardly noticed, there was so much going through his head. Mainly he was worried that his performance as Richard Delaware had not been as convincing as he'd originally thought, and now De Voe suspected the police were on to him and his gang. And he was worried that as a consequence he'd put Charlotte in danger – the one thing he swore he'd never do.

As if on cue, Charlotte emerged from a distant treeline and started hurrying towards him. He recalled the first time they'd met on her smallholding in the heart of this beautiful part of the world that she so fondly called home . . . *She commanded the space with a confidence that came from being at one with her environment.* Charlotte did not appear confident now. She didn't stride, she scurried. She didn't command the space around her, she feared it. With one phone call from De Voe, her home had been psychologically taken from her and she was scared to the point of wanting to run away and leave it all behind.

'I gave him the five addresses you told me to,' Charlotte began. 'But he's not going to hit them during the annual equestrian event next week.' Charlotte was so desperate to deliver all of the information that was muddling her head, and then leave as quickly as possible, that she hardly paused for breath. 'On the evening before the opening ceremony, there's going to be a launch party. It's not usually part of the proceedings, but Barrowman's organised it as an extra. It's going to be this huge buffet dinner in a marquee, to raise money for St Barnabas's in Gloucester – that's Mathew's old school. Everyone's coming. After the attack on Mathew, I think guilt set in and now he's making amends in the only way he knows how – by throwing money around. So anyway, that's when De Voe will hit the homes. On the day before the equestrian event even starts. That's the day after tomorrow!'

Jack was going to ask how on earth De Voe knew about the last-minute addition of a charity buffet, but he didn't have to; Charlotte was clearly guilt-ridden at having innocently let it slip during their phone call. This sort of rookie mistake was exactly why Jack had worked so hard to keep Charlotte out of the police station, out of Lee's hands and away from the more important details of the case. Jack could only imagine what she would have told De Voe if Lee had brought her in and used her like he wanted to.

'Have I ruined it all? You won't be ready for him, will you? Annie and I are leaving. I can't stay, DS Warr. I've told her it's a holiday, but I can't bring her back. I can't be here when the lives of five more dear friends are ruined by . . . Oh God, the intrusion and the violation . . . I can't live with myself – and, if Annie finds out, she won't be able to live with me either. And she's no good on her own. This will kill her. Please don't arrest me. Please let me go now, before . . .'

Jack placed his hands firmly on Charlotte's shoulders and held her steady, as her body began shaking violently. She was in absolute turmoil.

'Charlotte, listen to me. Are you listening?' Jack then made her a promise that he knew was not his to make. 'The burglary at the Fullworths' house will disappear.' As Jack looked into Charlotte's shocked eyes, he knew that she believed every word he was saying. 'I'm going to tell that to one other person, OK? I'm going to tell DCI Simon Ridley who you spoke to on the phone the other day. I trust him with my life, so I certainly trust him with yours. Don't leave. If you leave, it'll tip De Voe off and he'll disappear. Remember what I said to you: this is your chance for redemption. I can protect you. From De Voe, from the law. I *can*. Charlotte, don't throw everything away just because you're scared. You can't live without redemption. I know you can't.' Jack then let go of Charlotte and put his hands by his sides. 'But if you decide to run, I won't stop you.'

From the darkness of the treeline, Lee watched. He spat the unlit cigarette from his mouth, revealing the scowl behind it. His lips were pencil thin, pursed into a tight line that held his anger at bay. For now. He was too far away to hear anything that had been said, but the simple fact that Jack was out here, privately meeting their informant behind everyone else's back, was enough to make his blood boil.

Hearst's placatory metaphor about dogs on leads popped back into his head and made him smile. She really had no idea.

But she'd soon find out.

*   *   *

Because the name Regina means 'queen', her baby had naturally become known as Princess. Only a few days ago, the ward sister had asked Regina and Mario if they intended to name their baby, but they flatly refused – they knew full well that they were only being pushed into it so that, if things took a turn for the worse, she'd die with a name. Regina and Mario stubbornly backed their newborn daughter's ability to beat any odds and be named when she was ready.

Regina's arm was inside the incubator and her finger was in Princess's hand. She now weighed just over three pounds. She was being ventilated and various machines monitored her other organ functions. But Regina didn't notice all the wires anymore; all she saw was Mario's nose and chin, her own hair and, on the rare occasion that they opened, she saw her dad's eyes. Regina saw a little person – whereas Maggie saw a medical challenge that would go on for years at least and in truth might never end. She sat quietly by Regina's side and read Princess's notes.

'I'm ready to hear it, you know,' Regina said without averting her besotted eyes from Princess. 'Whatever the doctors say.'

Maggie closed the file and said that it was too early for the medics to know anything for certain. 'Remember that shift you did up on my ward, Maggie?' Regina said. 'All those old people heading for the end of their lives, losing so much along the way – continence, movement, cognition. How awful that must be, to knowingly lose all of those things that made your life worth living. Princess will be happy no matter what, because she can't miss what she's never had. I'm going to fill her life with such joy, Mags . . .' As Regina continued, the tears came, but they were accompanied by the broadest, most loving of smiles. '. . . my touch, my voice, my kisses. As far as she's concerned, those will be the only things she'll ever need. She'll think herself to be the luckiest little girl alive. She will know love like most people can't even imagine.' Regina wiped her face clean of tears and took on a more serious tone. 'I understand the possibility of paralysis and brain damage, Maggie – don't think I'm ignoring it. I'm just . . . I'm just . . . we had a three-legged dog when I was a kid and he didn't miss his fourth leg because he never knew he was meant to have it in the first place.'

Maggie tried not to laugh at Regina's analogy, but then the two of them burst out laughing together, making the nurse in the corner of the room glance up from her paperwork. Regina had some awful times ahead, but she was driven by her faith that boundless love would see the whole family through.

Princess's file did not make happy reading. Her traumatic birth and significant hypoxia would more than likely result in kidney and liver damage, if not ultimate failure. And her consultant also suspected that the risk of her developing necrotising enterocolitis was high, although they wouldn't know for sure until Princess was a few weeks older. He was monitoring her closely as it was his goal to avoid invasive bowel surgery on such a tiny body if at all possible.

But physical and emotional exhaustion, plus the exertion of concealing their true fears had made Maggie and Regina slightly hysterical, hence their current laughing fit. And for a few precious moments, the two friends allowed themselves to be happy.

* * *

Jack sat at a corner table, in the bar of The Fox Hunters, nursing a pint of some local bitter with a quirky name. It had an unpleasant aftertaste, but Jack's palate was getting more accustomed with every sip. He was on the phone to Ridley, getting him up to speed with what Charlotte had just told him. While Jack had been with Charlotte at the King's Stone, Gifford had called Ridley to tell him about their De Voe/Delgardo discovery, so now he knew everything.

Jack was careful to accentuate the positive: 'With the resources you and DCI Hearst have got in place, in such a short space of time, we're good to go when De Voe is. Him bringing things forwards won't knock us off-track.' But once he had Ridley placated, Jack threw in the curveball. 'I've promised Charlotte leniency when it comes to it. She's was acting for De Voe under extreme duress, and now she's turned informant; I'll speak up for her.' Ridley pointed out that Charlotte was unquestionably guilty of the break-in at the Fullworths' home. 'I can get Elli not to press charges. I know that won't get Charlotte off the hook completely, but it'll help.'

Ridley was in his office sipping a tumbler of single malt. 'None of this is your call to make, Jack,' he said with a frown. He looked out over London which, at this time of night, was a dazzling display of dancing lights. Ridley didn't normally indulge in whisky unless he had company but, during his telephone conversation with Hearst, she'd asked him to drink with her, so he had.

Jack had expected this by-the-book response from Ridley. 'Maybe not. But I won't let them go after her full throttle. All that'll do is drive her out of her home and lose her the love of her life. She identified De Voe and now she's going to bring him to us. We owe her – for being our Judas Horse, we owe her.'

'Our what?'

'It's a horse that you trap and train to do as you ask. Then you set it free and, because it's trusted by the other horses, it can betray them and lead them back to you. They don't see it coming. That's the gist of it: De Voe will follow her into our trap because he trusts her.'

'So, this is why you're keeping her close and not allowing her to report to Gifford or Lee before she reports to you? You trapped and trained her, so she's yours.'

'Yes, she is. And when all of this is over, I want to let her go,' Jack said firmly.

'Well . . .' Ridley took a moment to empty his glass and pour himself another. 'I can't wait to meet this woman, Jack. She must be quite something.'

Jack's burner phone buzzed in his pocket. Ridley offered to hang up so that Jack could answer it, but Jack said no and let it go to voicemail.

From inside the empty bar, Jack then played the voicemail on speaker, so that Ridley could hear it. 'Richard. Michael De Voe here. So, I've secured the emeralds for the necklace you commissioned, and that's being created as we speak. It'll match the ring you chose in every detail. As a bit of a side issue, my assistant mentioned you were into your horses, said one of your girlfriend's Arabians had just won something or other. Anyway, as you're spending a good chunk of cash with me, the least I can do is stand you a day at the races. What do you say? Oh, and that bracelet you showed me. I've had it valued and it'll bring the price down by £800. Call me back when you get a moment and we'll arrange things.'

Ridley could practically hear Jack grinning. 'Be careful, Jack. He's a game player. And he's used to winning.'

'Not this time, sir. This time he loses.'

Ridley took the opportunity to impart one piece of wisdom that he knew for a fact Jack didn't have. 'I was an UC officer for seven years, back in the day. Don't get too confident. Some UC officers get too comfortable and start seeing the criminal underworld as a home from home. But the dangerous truth is, the likes of De Voe can see us coming. We don't truly fit in. We don't know how to play their game. So, don't be tempted to toy with De Voe; keep the relationship simple and keep your distance, because if he figures you for a copper, he'll kill you.'

Jack sat at the corner table in the bar of The Fox Hunters for another hour. Ridley's words of warning had fallen on deaf ears, as Ridley suspected they would. But . . . not because Ridley had got De Voe wrong – he'd got Jack wrong. Jack could fit into the criminal world undetected. He *did* know how to play that game. It was in him. He hadn't invited it or encouraged it, but he had allowed it, because it gave him a feeling of power that was intoxicating. It's what would allow him to control both Charlotte and De Voe, even though they were on opposite sides. Jack knew only too well that good and bad were more closely related than most people suspected.

CHAPTER 21

Everyone was waiting. It was the hardest part of any sting operation.

Barrowman's charity buffet was due to begin tomorrow at midday and would go on into the evening. The entire community would be there and, based on the new information from Charlotte, they now knew that all five burglaries would happen at some point after twelve noon and would happen simultaneously.

The five addresses, selected by Ridley, would all be under surveillance from the second they became vacant.

The targeted homeowners were unaware of what was about to happen. Hearst had decided that sharing this knowledge with them could compromise their safety and, in turn, the success of the operation: the gang had to be allowed to enter the properties and be caught in the act.

The police presence around the charity event itself was high profile. Uniformed officers mingled with thousands of locals and visitors in a show of force. Hearst wanted the gang to think that all resources were focussed in the wrong place; but the central location of Barrowman's event meant that these officers could be dispatched as backup in the blink of an eye.

* * *

Lee perched on the edge of the sink, staring at the single closed cubicle door. The toilet flushed, the door opened, and Mason stepped out. 'Jesus, Eamonn. You scared the life out of me.' As Mason washed his hands, Lee talked.

'He played you. But he didn't play me.' Mason immediately understood that Lee was talking about Jack. 'He went to meet Charlotte Miles in the middle of nowhere. They're plotting something.' Mason opened his mouth to object but was shut down before he could say a word. 'They could *both* be in De Voe's pocket for all we know! Still think your new best mate's the dog's bollocks? Still trust him?'

'Yes, I do.' But Mason's words now betrayed a tremor of doubt, fuelled by Lee's paranoia.

'Then where is he now, Colin? Here with the team, slogging his guts out to make sure every last detail is watertight? Or back in London "undercover" with De Voe? Undercover, my fucking arse!'

Mason dried his hands. 'Look, I know he isn't the easiest copper in the world to get along with, but he's not dodgy, Eamonn.' Mason suddenly felt the need to undo his top button, as the memory of being strangled by Jack in Mulhern's barn came flooding back. 'He's driven. And he's good – you can't deny that he's good.'

Lee shook his head in frustration. 'So why was he meeting with Charlotte in the middle of a field if they had nothing to hide?'

'Same reason we're meeting in a toilet, I expect,' Mason responded. 'Privacy. Sometimes people just need to vent their concerns to someone they trust ... and she picked a more pleasant place to do it than you did!'

* * *

In the squad room, a low hum filled the air as officers from Oxford and Chipping Norton nailed down the details of the plan to catch De Voe in the act. Davidson had not returned to the fold but had been left in Oxford working on the Mulhern murder. As predicted by Oaks, Davidson had not seen the light of day since being left behind and had been used as a desk-jockey, checking CCTV and cross-referencing case details on the HOLMES database. However, in a real turnup for the books, Davidson had proved to be exceptional at it. He'd developed a love of detail and was now another Bevan in the making. They were all proud of the youngest member of their team and Gifford even FaceTimed Davidson to tell him as much. Gifford wasn't going to suddenly turn into a great leader of men, but he was now enjoying the new achievements of his team, realising at last that these weren't new skills they were developing, but skills they'd always had that he'd never bothered to nurture before.

'Right!' Hearst got their attention at once. 'Uniform has reported that a set of temporary traffic lights has gone up on the B4437, just south of Chilson, and another two sets have appeared on the London Road near the Ascott-under-Wychwood train station. These lights are nothing to do with the council. So, ladies and gentlemen, it seems we may have just discovered this gang's route in and out. Emphasis on the word "may". Let's not take anything for granted. DI Gifford, if I divert six uniforms from the charity buffet, pop them into plain clothes and send them your way, can you get them up to speed, please? Deploy them in pairs to each traffic light location. Tell them not to approach any suspicious vehicle under any circumstances. This gang must be assumed to be armed and dangerous and I refuse to lose a single officer to them.' She paused, and all eyes remained on her, alert to every word. No officer in the Chipping Norton team had ever known her to actually lead a briefing, but she certainly knew how to keep their attention. 'De Voe remains under tight surveillance in London courtesy of DCI Ridley. Undercover officers have him in sight, his phone lines are tapped, and everyone who pauses for

a second in his general vicinity is photographed and checked.'
She paused again. 'We have this. We're ready.'

* * *

Ridley leant over the back of Laura's chair, looking at her computer
screen. She could smell his faintly musky masculine scent and
felt herself flushing. Ridley was reading a transcript from the last
recorded phone call between Michael De Voe and Alberto Barro.
Although neither man said anything in direct reference to what
was about to happen in the Cotswolds, they did mention that, on
completion of business, Alberto would get his usual 'goodie bag'
with a little extra as a going away present.

This audio would be added to the other 137 hours of recorded
evidence. When the case ultimately came to court, all of this seemingly innocent material would hopefully take on new meaning and
become the foundation of the prosecution. They would certainly
need every piece of evidence they could gather because, so far, De
Voe had still not put a foot wrong.

Once he'd finished reading, Ridley moved to his office without
looking back.

Laura watched him, silently telling him all of the things she
would never be able to say out loud. She sounded pathetic, even
to herself. Since her epiphany at the courthouse, she'd made two
clear decisions: that Ridley was the only man she wanted – and
that she'd never tell him, knowing he would never look at her in
the same way as she now looked at him. She'd never felt this level
of need before, along with the certainty that it could never be
satisfied. And that hurt.

* * *

Ridley looked out of his office window waiting for Jack to answer his mobile. Eventually, Maggie's voice whispered in his ear. Her low tone told Ridley that Hannah must be sleeping close by. 'Hi, Simon. Not sure where Jack is, but he's left his mobile in the kitchen drawer again.' This told Ridley exactly where Jack was – with De Voe! Ridley politely chatted to Maggie for another thirty seconds or so, before hanging up and leaving the squad room.

*   *   *

Jack leant casually with the palm of one hand flat on the desk, and his other hand pushed deep into the comfortable pocket of his £200 corduroy trousers. On his way to the emporium, he'd bought a £40 plain white T-shirt, as he knew he couldn't be seen wearing the same outfit the last time. He hoped it would pass muster.

He casually crossed his bare, fake-tanned ankles and chatted to Betina about horse breeds. He let her do most of the talking, so as not to betray his ignorance on the subject. It was all he could do to look interested. Last time they met, she'd been chatty enough; now, there was no stopping her.

Once it was Jack's turn to speak, he found himself starting a conversation that had no purpose other than to test his ability to lie convincingly. 'The girlfriend has gone cold on me, Betina. She's abroad with the family business, more than she's with me. I've got the yacht this weekend but, well, with no one to share it with, I may give the whole thing a miss. Monaco; did I mention that? Parked her right next door to Philip Green's. He's a card. Have you met him?'

Betina begin by saying that she hadn't had the pleasure of meeting Mr Green, although she had once seen him in a Monaco casino. 'If you're inviting me to your yacht, Richard, I'll have to say no. I'm out of town this weekend.'

'Anywhere nice?' Jack asked – instantly regretting it as it made him sound like a chatty hairdresser.

'Cheltenham way,' Betina said. 'And, from there I go straight to my family estate in Argentina for a couple of weeks. I'm due a long break.'

Jack was now sure that Betina was an active member of their gang of burglars and would be in the Cotswolds as of tomorrow. He also knew that if they failed to arrest her she'd be in Argentina before they could catch their breath, and subsequently impossible to extradite.

'Well, my loss.' Jack was beginning to realise how incredibly bad he was at flirting. But he'd not had much practice, seeing as he and Maggie had been together since their late teens. 'Tell Michael I'm sorry I missed him. And I'm looking forward to our day at the races.'

By the time Jack left shop twenty-one, he was feeling very pleased with himself. As the high-pitched brass bell marked Jack's exit, he was immediately faced down by Ridley pretending to do a little window-shopping. Ridley didn't say a word – he simply walked away, forcing Jack to follow at a discreet distance.

They finally came together on a bench near the Embankment Gardens.

'Give me the number of your burner phone,' Ridley said as soon as they were seated. 'You have to tell someone, always, when you're making contact with a suspect. You have to have that safety net of someone knowing where you are. You can't just . . . you can bend some rules, Jack, but not these. What if he'd sussed you? What if I hadn't called Maggie and what if she hadn't answered your regular mobile and I hadn't known that that meant you were with him? Go home.' Then he walked away, like a disappointed dad who was getting very close to the end of his tether.

CHAPTER 22

The journey back to Chipping Norton would have been an arduous one – half by train and half by bus – if Oaks hadn't agreed to drive to Banbury train station to collect Jack. The twenty-minute car journey covering the final leg began with Oaks regaling Jack about how Gifford and Lee were working hand-in-glove, whilst Mason pined for Jack's return; how Davidson had had a personality transplant and had become invaluable to the Jacob Mulhern murder investigation; and how Bevan was single-handedly responsible for making all of the whiteboards and case notes make sense. Oaks stopped talking when he realised that his own role had somewhat diminished and he'd fallen back into the routine of being a taxi-driver for DS Warr-from-the-Met. His blushes were saved by Jack's mobile ringing.

Charlotte, it seemed, was in a terrible state, as Jack listened to her anxious words. 'Jessica Yardley has fallen off her horse and is bedridden in a back brace.' Jack waited for Charlotte to take a breath and put this statement into some sort of context for him. 'She'll be at home tomorrow, DS Warr. She lives in one of the target addresses I gave to De Voe and now the whole family will be at home!' Jack's mind immediately went into overdrive in an endeavour to find the solution. 'Jess has got a four-year-old brother, Anthony, then there's the parents, David and Anne. I can't let De Voe go to that house now!'

Charlotte's use of the word 'I', rather than 'we' or 'you', grated on Jack's ears. It sounded like she was attempting to take control of the redemption stage of her involvement. Out of fear and desperation, she seemed to be putting her foot down. Jack took a deep breath, gave her the benefit of the doubt and decided just to deal with the immediate problem.

'We'll move them out, don't worry. We'll put them safely into a hotel and then their house will be empty.'

Charlotte wasn't mollified. 'No, no, no, you don't understand. He doesn't care that it's going to be occupied!'

A shiver ran down Jack's spine. She'd told him! Jesus Christ, why couldn't she just keep her thoughts to herself? She'd told De Voe about Barrowman's impromptu charity buffet and now she'd told him that one of the houses will be occupied.

'Charlotte . . .' Jack made a point of staying calm. 'When did you speak to De Voe?'

'I didn't mean to say anything, I swear I didn't. It just came out. He called me to . . . to thank me. He said it had been a pleasure working with me but after this week I'd never hear from him again. Then he said. "Goodbye, Miss Miles from Miles Farm near Little Compton," reminding me that he knows where I live! Anyway, that's when I said it. I said, "One of the houses has a poorly girl in it, so you can't . . ." And he cut me off saying that he didn't care. He said if they got hurt, it'd be my fault because I'm the one who gave him their address. He said I'm in this up to my neck. So, you have to do something, DS Warr. Not for me; for the Yardleys. Do something or I'll tell De Voe that it's all a trap and then he won't come at all!'

Jack sighed. 'Charlotte, calm down. I'll call you back within the hour. Don't do *anything* else, are you listening? Just wait for me to call.'

'One hour,' Charlotte agreed reluctantly. Then she ended the call. Oaks didn't know what had been said. And, seeing the frown on Jack's face, he didn't dare ask.

As they crawled through the centre of Chipping Norton, up the hill past the village notice board advertising everything from

evening classes to riding lessons, Jack could see how the popula-
tion of this area had suddenly swelled to bursting. Cafés and pubs
had spread onto pavements, buskers had come out of the woodwork, and the crowds of tourists moved as slowly as the traffic.

And Jack's gang of burglars could well be amongst these faces
already, making their preparations. As Jack's eyes scanned the
crowd, he imagined that he saw Betina seated outside a café
sipping a cappuccino. He couldn't help but think that this gang,
who'd got away with so much for so long, was mocking him.
And that uncomfortable feeling prompted him to come up with
an ingenious solution to the new problem Charlotte had just
presented him with.

* * *

The squad room was not designed to cater for the numbers of officers currently occupying it. As Jack and Oaks pushed past the extra
chairs and made their way to the front of the room, Jack could
see that CCTV from in and around Wychwood train station was
being fed to several large screens, and the B4437 temporary traffic
lights were now also covered by hidden cameras. He remembered
the wildlife survey done in Wimbledon Common, where cameras
had been rigged in trees and left to watch owls and kestrels come
and go from their nests. The same principle was now being used
here to watch the traffic lights.

Jack paused next to Bevan. She was hard at work, compiling a
spreadsheet of figures that would no doubt make sense to everyone else once complete. The source material was scattered across
her desk, comprising Betina's bank statements and a list of
passenger names, airports and flight numbers from Rio. These
had to be the extra hands she'd been asked to bring in, to carry

out the five burglaries in one evening. Bevan had even managed to get all of their passport images; although, in truth, after a good haircut and shave, they'd be unrecognisable.

Once at the front of the room, Jack asked to speak with Gifford, Lee and Mason in private. Oaks was allowed to join them, as he knew about the phone call from Charlotte. This 'summoning' immediately got Lee's back up; but he was determined to control his temper long enough to hear what lies Jack was going to come out with this time.

'Has Bevan ever done any undercover work?' Jack asked. The blank look shared by Gifford and Oaks said that she hadn't. 'The Yardley house will be occupied on the day of Barrowman's charity buffet. De Voe knows this and has said he doesn't care, so we can't give him another address . . .'

Lee couldn't hold his tongue a moment longer.

'You mean to say your snout's been chatting to our prime suspect, without your knowledge?'

'She's not a snout and he called her,' Jack said firmly. 'She's scared.'

'We only have her word for anything,' Lee shot back, 'because she isn't under our control. She isn't in police custody and her phone calls aren't being monitored.'

Jack ignored Lee's glare. For now, he was more concerned about sharing the solution he'd come up with. 'I say we put the Yardleys in a hotel, and leave Oaks and Bevan in their place, posing as the occupants.'

'Absolutely not.' Gifford's response was instantaneous. 'They're far too inexperienced to be put in harm's way like that.' Jack glanced at Oaks, suggesting that he was able to make up his own mind, but Gifford remained firm, holding Jack's gaze. 'The answer is no.' Jack couldn't believe it. What a time for Gifford to grow a backbone!

'I agree,' Lee added. 'I say that anything coming from Charlotte Miles can't be trusted. And I'm beginning to have my doubts about DS Warr.'

Up to now, Jack had been trying to avoid a confrontation, but Lee had just crossed a line.

'If you have something to say, DI Lee, say it! Or do you need DCI Hearst to fight your battles for you?'

Lee ignored Jack, turning to Gifford for support. 'He's been meeting Charlotte Miles in secret. Did he tell you that? She calls and he goes running.' Then to Jack: 'There's something going on and we demand to know what the hell it is. This isn't just protecting an informant; this is withholding evidence. This is collusion.'

'It's *control*!' Jack growled as his temper almost got away from him. 'I have to make her put helping us above instinctively protecting the most important person in her life. And I'm doing that by making her think that I'm taking risks too. So, if she only wants to speak to me, that's fine. And, if she wants to meet alone with me in the middle of a field, that's fine too. I've *never* withheld case-relevant information . . .'

Lee opened his mouth wide as if something had just occurred to him. 'You fucking her, Jack?'

Jack launched himself at Lee, landing one solid punch to his jaw that sent Lee tumbling backwards into Oaks. As Lee righted himself, Oaks held on to him long enough for Gifford to step in between and bellow, 'Stop!' In the heat of the moment, his Midlands accent came to the fore. 'If this is the waaay it's going to be, one of you is leaving my station, never to darken my door agaiiin?! You, Eamonn? Jack? 'Cos I am not having thiiis! I'd tell you to take it outside, but we haven't got tiiime for you children to have your schoolyard scrap. We were discussing which of my officers to put in harm's way and if that isn't deserving of your attention, you can all fuck off!' Gifford gave the room ten seconds of complete silence, his fierce glare daring anyone to break it. 'DI Lee, did DS Warr tell me that he'd met Charlotte in private? No, he didn't. DCI Hearst told me, after DCI Ridley told her. And DS Warr, put your thinking cap on and come up with an alternative to making DCs Bevan and Oaks into targets for murderers, because that, son, is not happening.'

The conclusion to this shambles came from an unexpected source, as Mason stepped forwards. 'De Voe's expecting occupants at the Yardleys' house, so that's what we need to give him. I've done numerous undercover operations. Why don't I go in with DC Bevan? I can keep her safe, Joe. You have my word.'

Gifford softened his glare while he thought about it and Oaks now deemed it safe to let go of Lee.

No more words were said, but Jack and Lee still stared daggers at each other. Lines had been crossed on both sides, and there was no going back. Gifford ignored them, making it clear that Mason was the only man in the room worthy of his time right now. 'All right. Ask Bevan if she's prepared to act as decoy inside the Yardley house. The decision has got to be hers.' He finally turned to Jack. 'DS Warr, send DC Bevan in. DI Mason, please stay to answer any questions she might have.' This was the first direct instruction Gifford had ever given Jack, and he followed it without hesitation. 'Oaks, be somewhere else, please. And close the door on your way out. And DCI Lee, I don't need you in my office right now, either.'

Lee and Oaks left, Bevan entered, and the next half an hour was spent calmly talking her through what would be expected of her, if she agreed to go undercover with Mason.

CHAPTER 23

The charity buffet was a lavish affair which was to take place partly indoors and partly beneath a marquee. The aroma of hog-roast and barbecues filled the outdoor air whilst, indoors, the air was kept as 'uncontaminated' as possible for the vegetarians and vegans.

And everywhere, indoors and out, was wheelchair accessible. Barrowman might have been an arrogant man in his business life, but in his private life he was acutely sensitive to people's diverse needs – his son had taught him that much.

Oaks, out of uniform, stood on a raised stage just outside the marquee, watching the relatively small crowd of around a hundred early-comers milling about the beer tent.

The stage was made up of sixteen blocks, normally arranged in an eight-by-two pattern in the church hall. Today they were in a two-layered four-by-two pattern, with stairs up the back, so that when Barrowman officially opened the charity buffet, he'd be visible above the three children selected from a local riding school entering on horseback.

Oaks had been relieved and disappointed in equal measure when Mason had taken the undercover job away from him. So Jack had put him front and centre at Barrowman's event. In truth, Jack didn't know if their gang would use this crowd as cover at all, but if there was a possibility, then they had to monitor it to keep the community safe.

If any one of the gang slipped through their hands, they could vanish into these crowds, never to be seen again. Thousands of strangers, gangs made up of people with no criminal record . . . one change of clothes and they'd disappear.

Beyond the hog-roasts and barbecues, dozens more marquees had been erected to act as shade for the horses. Several animals were already there, practising their jumps and getting used to the various noises they'd experience over the coming days: car horns, tannoy announcements, children screaming inside the fenced-off playground, and four local bands all revelling in their half hour of fame, twice a day, for four days.

In the main arena, Charlotte and Judas were cantering across the sawdust floor, kicking up a fine yellow spray as they went. To Jack, they looked wonderful. Judas was impressively tall and broad, with a powerful musculature that rippled beneath his immaculately groomed coat. For Charlotte to be in control of such a beast was deeply impressive, knowing that he'd come to trust her and surrender his independence. Their bond was clear to see. Jack watched, transfixed by Charlotte's power and authority: how could this amazing woman control a beast such as Judas, but fall foul of a low-life such as Michael De Voe? Jack concluded that it had something to do with the fact that animals were incapable of treacherous, deceitful cruelty; whereas human beings were capable of that and more. Jack quickly left before Charlotte noticed him.

Beyond the marquees for the horses, the church hall had been temporarily converted into a police and ambulance base. This was what always happened during large-scale local events, so seeing numerous police officers, paramedics and first aiders coming and going wasn't unusual. To all intents and purposes, this event had been organised like any other – and it had to be, because if this gang had been working the area, on and off, for the past three years, they could well have been around the annual equestrian event before. They would know what to expect, and would notice anything out of place.

The final area that Jack walked round was a field at the far end of the extensive site, away from the horses, that had been converted into a helicopter pad. This *was* something a little bit unusual: a helicopter from a flying school just south of Swindon had been privately hired at the last minute. Gifford had been able to discover that the client who booked the helicopter was a celebrity who wanted to treat their friends to an aerial view of the area. But Gifford didn't know who the celebrity was, nor where they were staying whilst in the Cotswolds. This was a perfect example of the problem with policing this area: privacy. People paid handsomely for it and therefore felt they were entitled to it. But there was an upside: the field was also going to be used by the police helicopter once it arrived.

Jack headed past the church hall, and out of the event space through one of the numerous fields that had been converted into car parks. Barrowman's charity buffet was due to open officially in thirty minutes, the crowds were building, and there was an atmosphere of excited anticipation.

Jack watched streams of cars being guided into makeshift parking spaces by teenagers in high-vis jackets. Hundreds of people, all in blissful ignorance, not suspecting that a coordinated series of simultaneous burglaries was about to occur.

* * *

Three rows from the front, seven cars from the left, Betina's white Mercedes blended in with the other vehicles. The aerial was up, and a red ribbon fluttered in the breeze. When the time came, Betina would be able to find her Merc and be gone before the police even knew what had happened.

* * *

There was one 'suite' in The Fox Hunters B&B. It was a bedroom twice the size of any other, with a sofa and chairs added to create a TV area. It was also south-facing and had patio doors leading into a private, walled area of manicured flowerbeds, an elegant fountain water feature and a netted trampoline, where four-year-old Anthony Yardley had spent every waking minute ever since the family had been installed there. He was having a whale of a time, whilst bedbound Jessica was kept entertained with computer games and room service. Only the parents were not treating this as a holiday: David and Anne Yardley silently worried about their house being turned upside down by strangers, even though they knew it would be keenly protected by police officers inside and out. In the end they trusted DI Gifford, and so relinquished their home to him, confident that it was in good hands.

David Yardley owned a chain of builders' merchants near Croydon. He left the day-to-day running of the business in the very capable hands of his two sons, both now in their mid-20s. Anne was David's second wife and he'd moved to the Cotswolds because it was where she needed to be for her career as a riding instructor. David was Jack in reverse: a man who'd followed his wife's career east to west, rather than west to east as Jack had done. But neither man regretted for a second their decision to follow their women across the country. They were both happily settled in their new homes with the people they loved most in the world. Jack had quickly come to know David and genuinely liked him; he was a smart, level-headed man who weighed up the risk and reward of every decision. He didn't, as with men like Barrowman, demand success at all times. David was a man who'd failed his way to the top, by learning from every knock-down and by getting up stronger.

David appreciated Jack popping in, even if it was just to reiterate his instructions. 'With police inside and out, your home will be safe. Please don't call anyone and please don't let slip what's going on. One of my officers will come and take you home as soon as possible.'

*   *   *

Mason and Bevan sat at the breakfast bar in the Yardleys' kitchen drinking from water bottles and eating shop-bought sandwiches. They were trying to leave no trace of themselves so that when all of this was over the Yardleys could have their home back seemingly untouched. Bevan had been full of questions about this assignment when Gifford and Mason first talked to her about it; not because she was frightened, but because she was a stickler for details and liked to know exactly what was expected of her. She'd openly asked Gifford if he thought she was 'good enough to not let them down' and he'd assured her that she was one of the most capable officers he'd ever served with, while he was privately convinced she was young and too inexperienced.

Mason and Bevan had settled into the kitchen because there were three exits from the room. An internal door led into the hallway, a double patio door led into the large enclosed back garden and a solid wood side door opened onto the side-alley – the most likely entry point for the gang as they'd be shielded from prying eyes. The most important door in this kitchen, however, was the glass patio door which provided clear lines of sight for the team of officers currently hiding in the back garden. It was already unlocked and slightly open, allowing for quick entry. Mason and Bevan's positions at the breakfast bar were also part of the plan: the second everything kicked off, they had been instructed to put this large, tiled kitchen island between themselves and the gang. They were not there to challenge, or arrest anyone. They were the decoys. Because whilst the gang were focused on frightening 'Mr and Mrs Yardley' into complying, the police would be entering via the patio doors behind them.

But for now, Mason and Bevan sipped water and ate sandwiches. 'So, what happened between you and DS Warr?' Bevan's question came out of the blue and Mason instinctively adopted a quizzical expression, as if he didn't know what she was talking about. 'You were different when you came back from Oxford,' Bevan continued. 'He'd got you on-side. With me, it was the fact that he spoke to me like I was working *with* him, not *for* him. He saw what I brought to the table and said that "you're great at the details, Bevan". No bullshit. That's what I like about him. There's no bullshit.' Bevan stuffed the last quarter of her sandwich into her mouth, indicating that she had now stopped talking and it was Mason's turn to speak.

'We had a difference of opinion.' Mason swigged from his water bottle to give himself time to choose his words carefully. 'He was right, I was wrong.' Then Mason laughed. 'I know that, because he told me.' When Mason laughed, deep crow's feet appeared around his eyes and his pure, unabashed smile turned him from a temporary colleague into a person Bevan felt herself wanting to know so much more about.

* * *

Barrowman's mic screeched into life, drawing everyone's attention in the marquee. From the church hall, Gifford could hear the reverberating echo of his opening words: 'Ladies and gentlemen, I won't bore you for long. As most of you will know, the annual charity auction held at the golf club two weeks ago was cut short when Sally and I had to leave unexpectedly. That event raises money for St Barnabas's special school which Mathew used to attend in Gloucester. But today's event is not meant as a fundraiser; today is a thank you for always being there for us when we needed you . . . though of course if you choose to pay £20 for a pint of beer, St Barnabas's will be most grateful. Most importantly, have fun. We've had some dark moments of late, so we all deserve a good day.'

* * *

All five target homes sat within a seven-kilometre radius of Ascott-under-Wychwood train station. And all five homes were under surveillance by teams of covert officers. Jack was part of the team based outside the Yardley house.

At the bottom of their back garden, the Yardleys had two hen houses. These were low, grey buildings, around three metres wide and seven metres long. They had no windows and two doors that led into a fenced-off area of grass, roughly the same size as the building itself; and one half-sized door at the back of the hut, used for egg collection whilst the hens were outside. Each building was home to a couple of dozen hens who were given the freedom to roam during the day and locked in at night to protect them from foxes and other carnivorous wildlife.

At this precise moment, the hens were all inside one of the huts, leaving plenty of room for Jack's team inside the other one. Although there were no windows, David Yardley had given them permission to make holes in the wooden side panels.

From his position inside the hen house, Jack could see Mason and Bevan chatting and laughing in the brightly lit kitchen. He noticed that they each looked genuinely interested in what the other had to say and were happily talking over each other, showing an easiness that normally only came with time. Jack couldn't help but think that they might make a nice couple, if Mason could ever live up to Bevan's fastidiously high standards.

At the front of this house, a single police officer watched the feed from the Yardleys' three external CCTV cameras that sat just beneath the guttering, rotating to cover the whole of the outside of the property.

It was another two hours before Jack, along with the other four covert teams, got the call they had been waiting for.

CCTV at Wychwood train station, and the hidden CCTV cameras mounted in the trees along the B4437 to monitor the unauthorised temporary traffic lights, had all picked up an intriguing sequence of images. Around 1 p.m., a silver Mercedes A-class collected three people, all wearing baseball caps, from the Oxford train. By the time this Mercedes passed the hidden cameras on the B4437, it was accompanied by two riders on a red Ducati Streetfighter V4 with custom-made saddle bags. This was noted, but not flagged as relevant until exactly the same thing happened around 2 p.m. A silver Mercedes A-class collected three people, all wearing baseball caps, off the Worcester train. Again, by the time this Mercedes passed the hidden cameras on the B4437, it was accompanied by two riders, on a red Ducati Streetfighter V4 with custom-made saddle bags. The rider of this second Ducati was very clearly wearing Adidas NMDs with red soles.

It was now 2.37 p.m., and twelve outsiders, sharing four getaway vehicles, were now somewhere inside the monitored zone around all five target homes. Jack suspected that neither Betina nor Alberto would have arrived with the hired hands, they'd more than likely been here for a couple of days already, so they would make the numbers up to fourteen. Jack sent out one final message before ordering radio silence: 'Assume other gang members are already here. Assume other vehicles will also be used. Take nothing as read. Stay in your teams. Don't get separated. Good luck.'

No one replied, as per protocol, but, inside the hen house, Jack's second-in-command, Sergeant McDermott, whispered a repeat of his final words – 'good luck' – triggering all other officers to whisper it back. Jack knew that every other team on this operation would have just done the same thing.

Then silence.

The officer watching the feed from the Yardleys' CCTV cameras reported that all was quiet at the front of the house, and down either side . . . and Jack had visual on the back.

But if the officer been watching the CCTV from the house next door, he'd have seen four shadows moving slowly forwards, using the extensive foliage as cover. They took their time. They climbed the side fence, under overhanging tree branches, and then slid along the fence, behind the trees, until they reached the side alley of the Yardley house. They were, to all intents and purposes, invisible. The swaying shadows from the branches concealed a set of heavy boots . . . an arm . . . a crowbar . . .

To the left of the kitchen door was a small opaque window twelve inches tall and half as wide. A light came on in this room and the distinctive sound of someone urinating could just be heard. Mason was using the toilet.

Inside the kitchen, Bevan was seated at the breakfast bar neatly folding her empty crisp packet and stuffing it inside the sandwich box. The door to the small toilet opened and Mason emerged, drying his hands on his trousers. In the same split second, the side door burst open and a tall, lean masked man brought a crowbar heavily down on the back of Mason's head, knocking him out cold.

The masked man then raced over to Bevan before she could work out what had happened, grabbed her by the throat and slammed her against the door of the fridge freezer with such force that it rocked back in its alcove.

Bevan's eyes were focussed on the man immediately in front of her, but in her peripheral vision, she could see a further three masked men dragging Mason's body out of the way so that they could close the side door – and then she saw Jack leading the charge across the lawn towards the unlocked patio doors, his radio transmitting the frantic voice of the officer watching the CCTV: 'They're in! Oh God, they're in! Four inside. I repeat, four inside.'

All of this seemed to happen in slow motion and, by the time Bevan's brain could assess the situation in full, she was standing with her back to the masked man, who had his forearm pushed into her throat and the crowbar pushed so hard into her side, it felt like it had pierced her skin and was now nestling between two of her ribs.

Three of the masked men ran back out of the side door, followed by all of Jack's team, bar one. Sergeant McDermott went straight to Mason, established signs of life, rolled him into the recovery position and then applied pressure to the gaping wound at the back of his skull. The growing pool of blood on the kitchen floor around Mason's head contained tiny white flecks that Bevan assumed to be skull fragments, and the look on her face told Jack that Mason was in dire trouble and needed to go to hospital . . . Now!

Jack stood in front of the open side door and spoke directly to the man in the mask behind Bevan. 'This is up to me and you now – because you're the one who can make this go completely tits-up, and I'm the one who can let you escape. We've got the other four gangs, so I'm happy. But if you want to be the one that got away, you're running out of time because backup will be here in seconds.' Although

Jack exuded an air of total confidence, he was fully aware that the man now standing with his arm pushed hard onto Bevan's throat could well be the same man who snapped a colleague's hyoid bone just eight months ago.

The masked man took a step towards the side door and Jack moved with him, blocking his exit. 'If you go, you go alone,' Jack said. 'There's no way you're leaving with her.'

Jack's dark, threatening eyes never blinked, while the eyes behind the mask flicked between Jack and the open door. Jack knew that this masked man had trapped himself in a corner, but he also knew that that was a dangerous place for any scared animal to be. If a mistake was going to be made, it would be now. Again, the masked man stepped towards the open side door, holding Bevan so tightly around the throat that she was on tiptoes as they moved as one. Bevan turned her head slightly, creating a tiny space between her windpipe and the crook of the man's elbow, so she could gulp a desperate mouthful of air.

The man raised his crowbar, extended it towards Jack and whispered three words: 'I'm the boss.' In that moment, Jack's blood ran cold, remembering Mathew's trembling voice as he spoke of being beaten, over and over, by 'Oberyn Martell'. His final words to Mathew had been 'I'm the boss'. This man, with his arm around Bevan's neck and a crowbar in his hand was Alberto Barro. This man was the weak link they needed to bring De Voe to his knees. Jack maintained his external calm for Bevan's sake.

The masked man slid his arm from round Bevan's neck and grabbed a fistful of her hair. The move took less than a second, but a more experienced field officer would have used it to break free. Instead, Bevan stood stock still, staring at Jack, waiting for him to tell her what to do. She had no copper's instinct – no survival instinct. She was totally relying on Jack to save her. Jack realised he'd misjudged her and wished she was still sitting at her computer surrounded by pastries.

The masked man pulled Bevan backwards and then, with one violent shove, he threw her forwards, still holding her firmly by the hair. She grimaced in pain as her scalp screamed in agony but she managed not to cry out.

Jack wasn't close enough to make a grab for her, or to make a grab for the man he now believed to be Alberto Barro. The masked man flicked the extended crowbar sideways, indicating that Jack should move out of the way of his exit. Jack seemingly started to do as he was told, but as well as moving left, he also edged forwards. Once the masked man could see a clear route out, he pulled Bevan fiercely towards his chest before throwing her forwards again, this time letting go of her hair. She lurched into Jack's arms, forcing him to catch her and giving the masked man time to escape. Jack got Bevan back onto her feet, steadied her, then dashed outside.

The Yardley house was at the end of a short gravel drive which Jack could clearly see down to the street at the far end. No one was running away in that direction. At the back of the house, a locked iron gate juddered as though someone had just vaulted over it. Jack leapt the gate and ran down the dirt track beyond. After running in a straight line for about thirty seconds, Jack realised that he was getting nowhere. He had no clue how far this road went and, to his left and right, the fields were scattered with huge rolls of hay, any of which would make a perfect hiding place. He was chasing ghosts.

Furious with himself, Jack started to walk back the way he came. He heard the rustle of bushes behind him one second too late and, as he turned, he walked straight into the heavy crowbar. Jack fell flat onto his back, staring up at the silhouetted masked man who now stood over him. The man spun the crowbar in his hand. He was playing, taunting – his favourite game. The man got out his mobile, found the name Betina and texted:

It's a trap. Get out.

Then, as the weapon was raised for the final kill, Jack breathed out what he thought might be his last words: 'Alberto Barro.' The words made the crowbar freeze, mid-strike. The man took off his mask and laughed. 'Good for you. What are you going to do . . . arrest me?'

As his head spun and his vision swirled, Jack's only hope of survival now was that Alberto loved the sound of his own voice so much, that he would keep taunting Jack until backup arrived. Alberto's mobile pinged. It was Betina:

Safe.

Alberto smiled. 'Know this before I kill you. You haven't got us all. What you've got is cannon fodder. Small fry who don't even know who they're working for.'

Jack's vision was becoming clearer and, with the adrenaline fiercely pumping, dulling the pain in his head, he said simply, 'Michael De Voe.' He saw the silhouette before him straighten and tense. Jack smiled. He couldn't see Alberto's expression, but he now knew that the police *did* know who the small fry were working for. And if they knew that, then they knew everything. Although Alberto was the one with a crowbar in his hand, it was his voice that now trembled in fear: 'Who are you?'

Jack's voice was deep and steady. 'Jack Warr.'

At this point, Jack still imagined that he was about to die, but he was determined that his name would be a ghost haunting

Alberto Barro's dreams for the rest of his life. As the crowbar was drawn back, time stood still long enough for Jack to clearly picture Maggie and Hannah. He smiled and focused on his beautiful, love-filled final memory.

Suddenly a voice shouted Jack's name, sending Alberto fleeing into the field, swiftly followed by adrenaline-fuelled police officers. Someone knelt by Jack's side – he had no idea who – and they assured him that he was going to be OK.

* * *

Barrowman's charity buffet was a loud, raucous event: exactly what this systematically victimised community needed. The beer tent was packed, the band was on stage belting out a classic pop number, and the low buzz of voices filled the air. Then all of this was abruptly drowned out by the sound of two different types of siren, coming from several directions. Police cars and ambulances. Everyone stopped in their tracks to watch dozens of blue lights flash past.

Barrowman intuitively ran towards the church hall – the only person moving amid the stunned crowds all speculating about what on earth was going on.

Half a mile away, in one of the fields, Betina, wearing tourist clothes, a headscarf and dark glasses, made her way through the sea of cars, towards an aerial sporting a red ribbon, blowing in the breeze.

As Barrowman marched in one direction, DC Oaks was running full-pelt in the other, through the dressage arena chasing a man dressed like a tourist, but wearing very distinctive, red-soled trainers. This man, when approached by Oaks because of the trainers he was wearing, had immediately bolted.

Oaks was transfixed by the flash of red he saw with each stride. This was Adidas Man!

Barrowman saw Oaks, changed direction and made a beeline for him. The arena was covered in a thick layer of coarse sawdust, with a barrier of hay bales to catch any riders who fell. Beyond the hay bales, metal crowd-control barriers were linked together with a hook-and-eye system. Every fifth barrier was left unlinked in order to facilitate the quick response of the St John's Ambulance if needed, and the Mayor when it came time to hand out the winners' medals. Barrowman knew where these unlinked barriers were, as he'd made certain he was chair of the health and safety committee. He slid through one of the gaps into the arena and walked calmly around the outside of the hay bales, in an arc that would see him intercept the man Oaks was chasing. When Adidas Man leapt onto the hay bale next to Barrowman, he was so focused on clearing the metal barrier in front of him that he didn't see Barrowman's fist until it slammed into his jaw. The man fell backwards into the sawdust, out cold. Oaks came to a stop, resting his hands on his knees as he tried to get his breath back. 'Is this them?' Barrowman was furious. Oaks nodded. Barrowman had no further questions for an underling like Oaks, so continued on his path towards the church hall. Gifford was going to be the one in the firing line for keeping Barrowman in the dark!

Adidas Man started to stir and groan, and he lifted one hand towards his head. Oaks quickly slapped the cuff onto the moving hand, spun him onto his front and secured both arms behind his back.

'What's your name?' Oaks said.

'No English,' the man replied.

'Good,' Oaks said. 'I'd hate you to report me for calling you an ugly little fuck.'

Adidas Man, in a sudden fury, brought one knee up and tried to turn onto his front, but Oaks kept his weight on the man's shoulders to hold him still. 'You understood that,' he grinned. Oaks then happily read him his rights, then waited for assistance to arrive, knowing he couldn't safely move him on his own.

The church hall was sectioned off into two areas. As Barrowman strode through the front door, he was met by a scene of calm efficiency as officers dealt with lost children, and first aiders dealt with mild sunstroke and elderly people who had had minor falls. But Barrowman could also hear a buzz of chatter from a second area towards the back of the room that was curtained off from prying eyes, and that was where he headed.

Pulling back the curtain, he saw a bank of screens linked to surrounding CCTV cameras, being monitored by a team of six officers, while Gifford stood in front of several whiteboards displaying an array of information. Barrowman couldn't make head nor tail of it all – until he spotted a map highlighting the five target properties and probable escape routes. Five properties were going to be burgled and no one had told him!

Barrowman was about to give Gifford a piece of his mind, but was stopped in his tracks by the sudden entrance of a bruised and bloody Jack. He had a blood-soaked bandage towards the back of his head, and blood on his shirt collar. 'Did we get Betina Barro?' he shouted. 'Who've we arrested? Names! Come on! And the Adidas NMD guy, did we get him?' He paused for a moment to get his breath while Barrowman and Gifford looked on in equal bemusement.

'Alberto escaped from my raid. He said we didn't get everyone . . . he texted . . .' Jack staggered on the spot, but quickly righted himself. 'He only cares about . . . he wouldn't text anyone else. It had to have been Betina.'

Gifford picked up a chair, took Jack by the arm and sat him down next to an officer seated in front of the CCTV screens. The officer pointed out where each target house was situated, and which ones had ended in arrests. With the exception of Alberto Barro, every other gang member who had arrived at a target home had been arrested.

'That doesn't make sense,' Jack mumbled to himself, desperate to put the pieces together. 'She was here. He texted her, I know he did. And she texted back. So, where was she? If not at any of the target homes, where the hell was Betina Barro?' Then a memory found its way to the surface and a terrible idea struck him. 'He called them "cannon fodder".' My God! Was it all just smoke and mirrors?'

*   *   *

Emil Borreson was a Swedish Bitcoin dealer who lived in a seven-bed mansion on five acres of land just outside Chipping Norton. He sat at his office desk, his fingers trembling as they hovered over the keyboard of his laptop. Stuck to the art nouveau shade of the desk lamp was a polaroid photograph of a terrified, crying woman seated on the floor of a dark room. Framed photos on the same desk suggested that this woman was Borreson's wife, or at least his partner. Also visible in the polaroid was a pair of feet, wearing Adidas NMDs. That same man now stood by Emil's side as together they watched the spinning circle in the middle of the laptop screen.

Betina stood a few yards away, mobile in hand, ignoring its buzzing. She had twelve voicemails from Alberto and she finally pressed play on one of them. 'Answer my calls! I've got away. Have you? You said you were safe – why aren't you answering me?' Then another: 'The police were waiting at every house, I just need to know that you're safe. Why aren't you . . . if this is the cops, pick up. Pick up or . . . I'll kill someone. Anyone. Where's my sister?!' And another: 'Betina, if you're not with the cops, and you are safe, pick up! Or have you betrayed me, Betina? Did you know they were coming? Please don't tell me that's it . . . please! This is that bastard De Voe's doing. And you let him! When did I become part of the fucking cannon fodder, you bitch? They have your name, Betina. They have his name, so you're not safe at all. You'd better hope the police find you before I do, darling sister. Because, blood or not, if you've betrayed me, I'll slit your fucking throat!' Betina listened to the voicemails without any expression on her face.

Adidas Man waved Betina across to the desk. Borreson's request to cash out his £20 million cryptocurrency account had been granted by the crypto exchange and the money was now on its way to a second bank account. Betina texted De Voe:

With you shortly.

'Please . . .' Borreson's voice was no more than a whisper. His armpits were dark with sweat. He stared at the image of his wife's terrified face. 'Please. Give her back to me.'

Betina assured Borreson that his wife was alive. After they left his home, they'd return to the place she was being held and let her go. Betina moved his laptop and his mobile out of reach, and placed a small camera on the desk in front of him, pointing in his direction. 'If you move from your desk before your wife walks through that door, I'll kill her. If you call the police, I'll kill her.'

Borreson said that he understood. He said it over and over.

'I know you do, Mr Borreson,' she said.

Outside Borreson's mansion, Betina and Adidas Man could hear distant sirens, but the surrounding foliage was too high for them to *see any accompanying blue lights. Betina instructed Adidas Man to bin the clothes he was wearing and head back to his bike. He asked about letting 'the woman' go, but Betina insisted that there was no time. 'They're on to us. We need to run. Now. Leave them both for the police to find.'*

* * *

The CCTV officer flicked from camera to camera, following the pre-determined escape route back past Ascott-under-Wychwood train station, via the temporary traffic lights.

Nothing.

Jack shook his head. 'No, they won't leave the same way they came in. Not now they know we're on to them.' All he could think of was that with every passing second Betina, Alberto and Adidas Man were getting further away. 'Find me another route out!' The cameras flicked between shots until – 'Stop!' Jack couldn't believe what he was seeing. Betina's white Mercedes! 'Track that car and keep sending the coordinates to my mobile. Have we got a helicopter?' Gifford looked sheepish and said that it had been diverted to a higher priority case at the last minute. 'Then contact the tourist helicopter that was using the far field,' Jack snapped. 'I need it on the ground by the time I get there!'

Jack ran as if his life depended on it. He was not going to be outsmarted by Betina and Alberto Barro, and whoever the hell Adidas Man turned out to be. He lurched from dizzy to clear-headed and back again as he ran. His skull throbbed beneath the bloodied bandage and his mind raced as fast as his body. How the hell did De Voe's gang get ahead of the police? Did they know they were being watched or was De Voe just playing the odds? What if Betina had seen Jack in the Cotswolds – not today, but days or even two weeks ago – and then recognised him when he went undercover as Richard Delaware? What if De Voe had always known that Jack was a copper and this fiasco was all his fault?

Up ahead, Jack saw the helicopter circling and turning into the wind before and smoothly descending in a vertical hover, until it danced to a halt on the grass.

* * *

A sky-blue Ducati Panigale approached a T-junction on an empty back road. To the rider's left was a sharp bend so even though he thought the road was clear, he had no option but to stop. Before he could pull away again, Alberto stepped into the road in front of him, with his hand in the air and a smile on his face. The rider instinctively lifted his visor, assuming Alberto needed help. Alberto looked apologetic, as though he was lost and needed to ask for directions, but when he got within arm's length of the rider, Alberto quickly punched through the open visor. The rider's body shuddered, as though having a seizure. When Alberto pulled his hand away, a small knife could be seen protruding from in between his forefinger and middle finger. Alberto deftly caught the bike as the rider slid lifelessly from it, then removed the helmet, shook the blood from inside it, climbed onto the bike and sped away.

* * *

In Jack's pocket, his mobile phone started pinging as the requested coordinates for the Merc updated. Jack climbed into the back of the helicopter and put on his headphones. The pilot had no clue what was going on: all he'd been told was that he'd been commandeered by the police and was to follow the instructions of the officer who'd meet him at the helipad. But Jack, with his head wound and blood-soaked collar, was not what he was expecting.

Jack handed over his mobile phone and said three words that, in seventeen years as a police officer, he'd never actually uttered before: 'Follow that car.'

CHAPTER 24

Bjarne Kristiansen was a Norwegian Army Reserve helicopter pilot who, in recent years, had earned his living from flying around the same patch of sky, repeating the same script about local landmarks and places of interest, or ferrying people from A to B like a taxi. He couldn't complain about the money, but he found it frustrating when his EC120 Colibri was capable of so much more. He was proud of his skills and could make her dance; he just never got the opportunity. Until tonight.

Bjarne tucked Jack's mobile securely between his thighs, so that he could see the screen, and took off, feeling a surge of adrenaline he hadn't experienced for a long time. As soon as he was off the ground, he tipped the nose down and accelerated forwards, flying so low that Jack could have sworn his blades were going to decapitate the crowd. Bjarne followed the constant positional updates along the back roads running parallel to the A429.

'I reckon they're headed for the M4,' he said.

'That's what we expected. But get a bit higher. I don't want them to know we're here,' Jack told him.

'Don't worry, she's as quiet as a mouse. They won't know what's hit them,' Bjarne reassured him.

Once Betina's Mercedes hit the M4, CCTV back at the church hall began to receive clearer footage of the car. Jack instructed Bjarne to share his own contact details with Gifford, so that Jack could take his mobile back in order to make a phone call.

Ridley was in one of four unmarked police cars near the west-side junctions of the M25. He'd also been getting updates relayed directly to him from Gifford, and although it was currently looking as if the Merc might stay on the M4 all the way to the M25, Ridley certainly wasn't committing all of his resources to that option until he knew for certain; there were simply too many opportunities for Betina to turn off and disappear. After their brief strategic catch-up, Jack swiftly changed the subject. 'Do me a favour please, sir . . .'

But Ridley already knew what Jack was going to ask him.

'DI Mason is in an induced coma. His skull's fractured – well, shattered really; it'll need a plate putting in. But he's stable. They'll keep him sedated until the swelling on the brain goes down, then they'll be able to see what's what. Bevan's with him. She's fine.'

*   *   *

From the doorway, Lee watched Mason being worked on in resus. Bevan was tucked into the corner, out of the way. An array of machines monitored Mason's vital signs, one pushing air into his lungs and another keeping him hydrated. His body didn't have to do anything except heal.

Lee's anger was impossible to hide. This case had got away from him because he'd been distracted by stupid personality clashes. That was all Jack's fault because . . . well, if it wasn't, then it was his own fault and Lee couldn't live with that. Mason almost dying could *not* be Lee's fault.

As a nurse scurried into resus with a portable X-ray machine, Lee spotted Hearst coming down the corridor towards him.

In an instant, Lee was back in professional mode. 'I'd better get back to the station,' he said as she approached. Hearst put a firm hand on his shoulder. 'I'm not here to drag you back. You stay as long as you need to.'

In truth, Lee didn't want to stay any longer with Mason, because it just made him feel guilty. And angry. He wanted to get back to work. He shook his head.

'Bevan's got the bedside vigil thing pretty much covered. I'm sure he'd rather wake up to her face than mine.'

Hearst nodded. 'OK then.' As they headed out together, Hearst brought Lee up to date. 'We have seven vans, each with two full cages, sitting in the car park waiting to be processed. We're having to double up in the cells, but what the hell. We've got a couple of runners, who we're following towards London. But between us and the Met, we'll scoop them up.'

'Who are the runners?' Lee asked.

'The Barros,' Hearst replied. 'And if I were a suspicious type, I might suspect that they planned it this way.' Lee's own suspicions again turned to Jack. His gut instinct simply would not let go of the idea that Jack was on the wrong side, or maybe just playing both sides.

Hearst could practically read Lee's mind. 'I check out the pedigree of everyone I let into my station, DI Lee. Including you and DI Mason. Jack Warr is from good stock. But you know how these London boys are: they don't know the meaning of the word diplomacy. Come on, I need a senior officer to get the ball rolling with these interviews.'

* * *

Ridley's rolling update to Jack took a serious turn for the worst. 'Hang on, Jack, something's coming through.' Jack waited, his heartbeat quickening. 'Jesus Christ. Jack, you there? Just got a report of a hijacked bike. The rider's dead.' Jack had never heard Ridley sound so despondent.

Jack let out a breath. 'That's Alberto. It has to be.'

'It's a sky-blue Ducati Panigale,' Ridley continued in a subdued tone. 'We're looking out for it now.'

'He's heading for De Voe,' Jack said. 'He knows De Voe's betrayed him, because I told him.'

'What about Betina?' Ridley asked.

'No, she's smarter than that. She'll be . . . she told me when I was at the shop, sir! She said she's heading for Argentina. If that was the truth, then she's going to Heathrow! Sir, you stop Betina; I'll get Alberto.'

On the ground, Ridley now started making his way towards Betina, whilst Bjarne was trying to gain permission to land at the London Helipad in Battersea.

Then another message on the radio: 'Ducati abandoned near Ealing Broadway Underground station. I repeat, Ducati abandoned near Ealing Broadway.' *Where was the nearest area car?* Jack wondered frantically. *Was anyone on the ground in Ealing?* He knew that as soon as Alberto went underground, they could lose him – CCTV or not.

Jack turned to Bjarne, desperate to get his hands on the man who had tried to kill him. 'Our target's going to jump on the District Line and head straight for Chelsea.

Bjarne frowned. 'Battersea Helipad is the best I can do, mate. That'll put you a fifteen-minute run away from Battersea Bridge.'

Jack's heart sank. Of course! He was in a bloody helicopter flying over a metropolis; Bjarne couldn't just land the helicopter in the middle of a busy street. Jack called Ridley and asked for a car, any car, to meet him at the helipad. He was still closer than any of Ridley's team, who were now all heading out of London towards Heathrow. Ridley dispatched the nearest patrol car to Battersea, just as Bjarne received his permission to land.

* * *

Alberto Barro sat on a District Line train, flirting with the stunning Eastern European woman sitting opposite him as she peered over her mobile phone. He slid his feet forwards across the aisle until his toes met hers, then his eyes moved slowly upwards towards her tantalisingly short skirt. Her strikingly long legs were smooth, slender and perfectly tanned.

* * *

Jack leapt from the helicopter, shouting his thanks to Bjarne as he hit the ground. Bjarne grinned, saluted and shouted back, 'Go get your man!' This had definitely been the most exciting day of his civilian life, he thought, as Jack jumped into an unmarked police car that, with blue lights flashing, instantly sped away.

The traffic was light until they got to the south side of Battersea Bridge. Here, they met gridlock. The driver gave two bursts on his siren, but nothing moved. For Jack, however, the noise of the siren seemed to go straight through his skull and agonisingly into his brain. Jack speculated that he'd probably burst an eardrum. He reached back and felt the bandage on his head. It moved so freely that he guessed it wasn't actually doing anything useful anymore. He pulled the last remaining sticky part away from his split scalp and threw it onto the dashboard. The driver stared at it in silent disgust.

'Sorry.' Jack dropped it into the footwell as the radio burst into life with a stream of updates . . .

'*White Mercedes taking the Heathrow turnoff. Still following. Heading for Terminal 5. That's the terminal for Argentina. Airport security is aware and will help with a stop . . . Approaching Terminal 5. The barrier is down. I can see four, correction, five airport security . . . Mercedes is doing a left, left, left, in an attempt to double back . . . Yeah, she seems to be trying to make her way back onto the road. Can a couple of vehicles hang back, to stop her, please?*'

More radios crackled into life and joined in the commentary as cars got into position to block Betina's escape.

'Stop, stop, stop . . . *Driver running! Driver running! Pursuing on foot.*'

Then there was an excruciatingly long pause. Jack opened the passenger door of the unmarked police car and stepped up onto the door frame, trying to assess exactly how far away they were from the Chelsea Emporium. In the distance, almost on the other side of the bridge, a black cab driver stood in the middle of the road arguing with two Community Support officers. They looked to have detained a drunk passenger who Jack guessed was probably refusing to pay. Jack stepped down into the road and listened to the radio. *Come on! Come on!*

'Driver in custody.'

Jack slammed the door shut behind him and ran across the bridge towards Chelsea.

Dishevelled, mud-spattered and bloody, Jack got his fair share of strange looks as he sprinted along the footpath. People glanced behind him, expecting to see the police hot on his heels. As his lungs burned, he thought, *If someone rugby-tackles me to the ground now, I'm never getting up!*

*　*　*

De Voe sat behind his half-desk flicking through a car magazine. He seemed particularly interested in the Bentley Continental GT Convertible. In front of him was a small, open black rucksack, with a blue cotton money bag inside it stuffed with bundles of £50 notes.

When the office door opened, De Voe glanced up and the colour immediately drained from his face. Alberto said nothing, waiting for De Voe to regain his composure. 'Is Betina safe?' De Voe finally asked.

Alberto shrugged. 'I honestly don't know.'

He pointed to the money. 'Was that for her? Is that how much I'm worth? Here's what I *do* know, Michael. I know that you lined up a series of robberies to occupy the police whilst Betina did the real job. I don't know what that was, but I'm guessing it was big enough to be worth the risk of betraying me. Did you actually tip the police off or did you simply assume that they'd be on to us by now?' Alberto watched De Voe's face grow pale. 'Not that it matters now. What matters is that at some point I became expendable.' He shook his head. 'And after all I've done for you, Michael.'

'After all you've . . .' De Voe got to his feet, though he was careful to keep the desk in between them. 'You beat a boy to within an inch of his life!'

'If he was a boy, he was a fucking big one,' Alberto smirked. 'With great taste in pizza, though.' He smiled to himself. 'What was I saying? Oh, yes . . . are you shagging my sister? Is that how you convinced her to leave me behind? By the way, if she does manage to escape the police, she will never, ever escape me. And nor will you.'

De Voe's jaw clenched and his nostrils flared as his breathing quickened. He made a split-second judgement that Alberto wasn't armed and moved towards the door. Alberto instantly lashed out, punching De Voe in the neck.

The speed of it shocked De Voe, but the lightness of the blow confused him – until he felt the wetness on his chest and saw the blood soaking the front of his shirt. Then he saw the small buckle knife, usually secreted in Alberto's belt, now clenched in his fist so that the blade protruded between his fingers.

De Voe clamped his hand around his throat and backed away, but Alberto didn't seem interested in stabbing him again. All Alberto wanted to do was watch the man he hated bleed to death. De Voe was pressing so hard onto his own neck, that his face was going bright red and he could hardly breathe. Alberto watched him stumble backwards, until he reached the door. De Voe grasped the handle and used his weight to push it down. Only then did Alberto move, punching De Voe several more times in rapid succession on the other side of his neck. De Voe clasped both hands to his throat and staggered back into the room, fountains of blood spurting through his fingers. He collapsed onto the floor and in seconds he was dead.

* * *

By the time Jack arrived at the emporium, he was close to passing out. He could feel his heart beating inside his skull as his head wound throbbed in excruciating pain.

He bypassed the main door and entered the underground car park. He was hoping to find a burly security guard seated in a dark corner somewhere but the car park was empty. *Shit!* Jack's only backup was now stuck behind a line of angry drivers on Battersea Bridge. Jack tried the door to the stairwell and found it was open. He paused briefly in a darkened gap between a ticket machine and the grey concrete wall, to get his breath back and to evaluate his options. De Voe's Ferrari was in its spot. Confused thoughts flashed in and out of Jack's mind: if Alberto was here, as Jack suspected, and he went in without backup, it'd be two against one. He needed that security guard! But what if he was on De Voe's payroll? Then it'd be three against one. Jack ventured into the stairwell alone and headed up to the second floor.

Alberto was in the tiny en suite toilet adjoining De Voe's office. Inside, on hangers, was a selection of fresh white shirts. He removed his own shirt, which was now patterned with arterial spray, and washed his hands and upper body. He then dressed in one of De Voe's clean shirts and, as he fastened the expensive pearl buttons, he watched a thick, red pool of blood around De Voe's upper body gradually congeal. Alberto regained his senses, snatched the rucksack of money from the desk and reached for the office door. But then he heard the familiar gentle noise of the shop door opening.

Jack pushed the shop door open just an inch, then reached up to silence the bell before entering. The office door was shut and a thin strip of light shone from beneath it.

Propped against the wall was a retractable metal window pole used for opening the skylight – Jack grabbed it, then opened the door cautiously, slowly revealing De Voe's body lying in a pool of his own blood. No doubt this was Alberto's work, but he didn't imagine that Alberto was still there; he'd surely be long gone, hopefully heading to Heathrow where he'd run straight into the hands of the waiting police.

Still, Jack remained wary as he pushed the office door wide until it was flat against the wall. The room was empty. Jack took a few moments to make certain it was safe to enter, then saw the open safe in the wall behind the desk. He thought he could see the diamond bracelet he'd stolen from the police evidence room and was so relieved at the thought of getting it back, he stepped across the room without even noticing the door to the tiny en suite. He laid the metal pole on the desk, reached into the safe and put the diamond bracelet into his pocket. The safe also contained a black velvet bag, and inside was a handful of large emeralds that Jack presumed to be from the stolen necklace that had once belonged to Barbara Hutton.

As Jack examined the emeralds, Alberto emerged silently from the en suite and stepped towards him, raising his hand with the buckle knife above his head. As Alberto prepared to strike, Jack heard an intake of breath and instinctively grabbed the metal pole, and spun round, swinging the pole at the blurry figure he now saw before him. The pole met thin air, sending Jack off-balance and making him see stars, as a wave of nausea hit him from the sudden movement. He stumbled against a low filing cabinet, catching his ankle painfully, but the throbbing in his head was so intense, he hardly noticed. As he turned to try and focus on his assailant again, he knew that although he'd evaded one attack, he was no match for Alberto in his current state.

Alberto smiled to himself as he took in Jack's weakened state, stepping forward confidently and aiming a thrust at Jack's throat. He wasn't prepared for the sudden flash of the pole as it crashed down onto his forearm, sending him staggering against the desk. But the force of the impact snatched the pole from Jack's hand, and it went skidding across the floor to the other side of the office.

Pain now added an edge to Alberto's blood-lust. 'Come on then, Jack Warr,' he shouted. 'Let's get this over with!'

Time slowed as Alberto charged again. Without a weapon, Jack knew he only had one option left. He raised his left forearm in front of him, hoping that Alberto would take the bait, then felt a searing pain as the knife plunged into the muscle. Ignoring the pain, Jack twisted his arm so Alberto's grip on the knife loosened, then grabbed it out of his hand before landing a solid punch squarely on the bastard's jaw. He heard the crack of bone as Alberto fell like a dead weight and Jack immediately knew that he was the kind of cocky, arrogant prick who was great at dishing it out, but no good at taking it. Jack crawled on top of Alberto and punched him again and again as the sound of distant sirens reached his ears.

Jack stopped, more from exhaustion than from any desire to spare Alberto further punishment. He closed his eyes, and the pain from his wounded forearm began to force itself into his consciousness. Suddenly he felt a hand closing around his throat. Alberto was not out for the count after all. He stabbed the knife into Alberto's shoulder and the pressure around his windpipe slackened, then suddenly his head exploded in pain as Alberto landed a punch on the wound from the crowbar. He felt himself rolling sideways onto the floor as fresh blood pulsed from the wound and a wave of blackness threatened to overwhelm him.

After what seemed like minutes, Jack managed to open his eyes and saw Alberto struggling to his knees. With a huge effort, Jack managed to do the same, until both men, exhausted and in varying degrees of pain, were kneeling on either side of De Voe's corpse. Alberto's mouth hung open, allowing blood to drip steadily onto his shirt that was now more red than white. He dragged himself to his feet, scooping up the discarded metal pole from the floor as he did so. Jack painfully followed suit, and the two men stood facing each other, both now armed with each other's weapons. Alberto raised the metal pole high above his head and charged forwards. Jack tried to raise the buckle knife but his arm didn't seem to be working. He braced himself for the impact, knowing that one more solid blow to his head would be the end of him . . .

Then Alberto suddenly went as stiff as a board and dropped to the floor like a ton of bricks. Two wires led from Alberto's shoulder blades to the taser in the hand of Jack's driver who, thankfully, was no longer stuck on Battersea Bridge.

* * *

Jack had assumed that Ridley was ensconced at Heathrow Airport, ready to arrest Alberto if he decided to follow his sister's escape route. In fact, within seven minutes of the 'all units', 'two ambulance' and 'coroner' call going out, Ridley was racing up the emporium stairs towards De Voe's office.

When he reached the top, Jack was seated on the floor in the corridor holding wads of gauze to the stab wound in his forearm. Beyond him, in the office, De Voe's body still lay centre stage, his eyes open and one hand still clutched at his throat. 'Alberto killed him.' Jack thought he'd clarify that detail straight away, in case Ridley thought that Jack had done it. Jack was white as a sheet, looking as if he might join De Voe at any moment, but he continued with his staccato handover. 'He's gone to the hospital. I stabbed him. He stabbed me. I'm fine.'

'You don't look bloody fine,' Ridley growled. 'Why the hell aren't you on the way to hospital, too?'

Jack grimaced. 'You'll have questions. I thought you . . . I think I . . .' He suddenly went from white to green. '. . . I might be sick.' Ridley helped Jack to his feet, and, before Ridley could stop him, he stumbled through the office door. 'There's a bathroom, where I can . . .'

From the en suite, Jack could hear Ridley shouting to him: 'I'll drive you to the hospital. You get checked out and I'll formally arrest Alberto. I'll be downstairs.'

Jack leant heavily on the rim of the basin watching the swirling water from the running tap take the contents of his stomach down into the drain. He felt so lightheaded he thought he was going to pass out. He lowered himself onto his haunches, still hanging onto the rim of the basin to stop himself from sliding all the way to the floor. He could feel something in his front trouser pocket pressing into him. Jack knelt on the floor, put his hand into his pocket and pulled out the diamond bracelet. Glancing round, Jack could see a dark shadow inside the shower cubicle. He opened the door and there, tucked into the corner, was the small black rucksack.

* * *

The conversation on the way to the hospital was one-sided, with Ridley filling Jack in on everything that had happened while he was chasing down Alberto Barro.

'You were right about all of the burglaries being decoys. The real target was a house belonging to an Emil Borreson and his wife. He's a bitcoin dealer. A very successful one.'

'Charlotte . . .' Jack was so tired that he couldn't get any more words out. His whole body felt as if he'd been kicked through a hedge and then trampled on, but he was still trying his best not to let the wound in his arm bleed onto Ridley's pale leather seat.

'She delivers their fruit and veg. Betina gave up Borreson's name and address as soon as she realised that we knew everything. She wanted us to know that she'd not hurt anyone, and never would. When Gifford got to Borreson's house, he was sitting at his desk in a puddle of urine, staring at a camera that wasn't even turned on, waiting for his wife to walk through the door. He'd been told that if he moved, she'd die. She's OK. Tied up in a disused barn on a neighbour's property.'

Jack let his head fall back and closed his eyes. He had so much still to think about.

First and foremost was the fact that with the man he respected most in the world sat next to him, between his feet, part hidden underneath his jacket, he had the small black rucksack with the stolen diamond bracelet in it along with a large amount of cash, although he didn't yet know how much.

'We got them all,' Ridley concluded. '*You* got them all, Jack. Well done. I've got a meeting with DCI Hearst tomorrow where I intend to tell her about the protection I promised Charlotte Miles.'

'*You* promised?' Jack said.

Ridley shrugged. 'It sounds less insubordinate than my DS doing it behind my back.'

Jack didn't say his next thought out loud: *And she likes you, so she'll forgive you.* Instead, he thanked Ridley for trusting him that Charlotte was an unwilling participant.

'DCI Hearst is a pragmatist, Jack. She'll be lenient with Charlotte, in the service of the greater good. Gifford will retire on a high, Oxford will get their killer and we . . . well, I'm not sure what we get other than a firm handshake and a warm feeling inside for having done an amazing job. But isn't that always the way?'

Ridley's genuine contentment at having done his job was written all over his face. It was admirable. Enviable. Ridley was a copper through and through. Jack started from the same place, had all of the same intentions and relished the wins just as much as Ridley; but he needed more.

Jack squeezed his ankles together, gripping the small black rucksack to make sure that taking it hadn't been some sort of hallucination brought on by the pain spreading through his body. It hadn't. The rucksack was definitely there.

Jack hadn't taken it because it contained a huge amount of money; he'd taken it because the world was wrong in the way it worked. The legal system would take this money and put it on a shelf in a police evidence room for the next God-knows-how-many years. It would probably never be needed as evidence, because they'd nailed everyone on so much else. And when the cash was finally released, it couldn't be used as victim compensation, because they would all have received their insurance pay-outs. It'd either be returned to the bank to be destroyed or end up in the Met's bank account and fed back into police services. Jack couldn't see the justice in any of those options when there were so many people in the world, who worked all the hours that God sent painting other people's nurseries, and still couldn't earn enough money to keep their own baby alive.

Life was unfair, and although Ridley would never bend the rules to put any of that right, Jack would. Life was *not* about settling for the firm handshake and a warm feeling inside; and it certainly wasn't about sitting back and waiting for your reward in heaven. Jack wanted his rewards now. But only the ones he'd earned.

CHAPTER 25

As Jack was pushed swiftly down the hospital corridor, the wheel-chair pulled naturally to the left, and he could feel the paramedic pulling on the right handle and pushing on the left one, just to keep the decrepit heap of junk in a straight line. This twisting motion moved Jack in his seat and made him feel even sicker than he did already, as did the bump and click on each rotation of the back wheel, while strip-lights on the ceiling were so bright that Jack kept his eyes almost closed, just to cope with the pain inside his head.

He tried to ignore it by listening to Ridley's handover to the ED doctor.

'He was hit in the head with a crowbar about five hours ago. He was checked by paramedics who said he had concussion and they couldn't rule out a fracture. Then he jumped in a helicopter and flew to London where he was in a physical, one-on-one confronta-tion with a suspect that resulted in his head injury re-opening, a stab wound to his forearm and, well, I don't know what else.'

Jack couldn't see the doctor's face, but he heard his heavy sigh.

In resus, Jack was helped onto a bed and his rucksack, which had been hanging on the back of the wheelchair, was put into a transparent property bag and placed underneath. He was then cut out of his clothes, while nurses attached various machines to his body. The doctor came out with a slew of letters that meant very little to Jack. He understood 'ECG' and 'BP', and he'd heard 'GCS', 'FBCs', and 'U&Es' said numerous times whilst watching *Casualty* with Maggie, but he had no clue what any of it actually meant. He wished she was here.

A male nurse wearing John Lennon glasses, who looked to Jack to be about 13 years old, leant in close by the side of Jack's head, as everyone else worked above him and around him. 'My name's Noah. So, what we're doing is we're making sure there are no obvious worries, such as internal bleeding. Then, we'll take you to CT to get a scan of your head. I need to ask you some questions, Jack. You up for that? Can I call you Jack?'

Jack had no idea how many hands were on him, but it felt like dozens. Someone was definitely pressing his abdomen and saying there was 'guarding on the left' and someone else was trying for a third time to insert a needle into the crook of his arm. He looked over Noah's head to Ridley who was wiggling his mobile in the air and mouthing 'Maggie'. Jack gave him the thumbs-up and Ridley left resus to make the call. Jack then heard Noah ask him if there was any history of medical problems in his family and Jack realised that he didn't know. He could hear himself saying, 'My dad died of cancer . . . no, no he was shot. My old mum was killed by a brain tumour. But my new mum's alive.'

At this point, Noah gave up. 'The morphine's kicked in. I'll get his notes instead.'

Ridley spoke so quietly and calmly that Maggie didn't feel worried, because he wasn't. 'Take your time, Maggie. He's in resus at the moment, and needs to go to CT before anyone will be allowed to see him, so . . . sorry, I forgot you work here. All you need to know is that he's fine and I'll not leave his side until you arrive.' Maggie asked nothing about Jack's injuries or how he acquired them. She didn't want to burden Ridley with the responsibility of trying to explain.

An hour later, Jack's bed was parked in an ED cubicle, where he was told he'd stay until the results of his CT scan had come back. He wore nothing but an open-backed gown and Noah, who was folding his ruined clothes into the transparent property bag on top of the small black rucksack, had an inexplicable smirk on his face. Jack, now on strong pain medication, was more comfortable. His head and body felt like lead, but there was far less pain. Noah couldn't keep his mouth shut any longer. 'We've all been admiring your tan, Detective.' Jack breathed out a weak laugh, which Noah took as permission to continue. 'Your head, hands and feet look like they've been on holiday!' Noah giggled as he put the property bag back underneath Jack's bed. 'OK, Jack, you've got a bit of a wait now till we get your results, but – sneak preview – Dr Okoya, our bang-on-the-head specialist, isn't unduly worried. I mean, you look like you've fallen down a mine shaft but, all things considered, you're in good nick.' Noah leant in close to Jack again and lowered his voice. 'That straight-lace in a suit who came in with you? That your boss?' Jack immediately recognised the description as being Ridley. 'Only I'm hearing all sorts of good things about that man from the nurses! Something about singing to babies?'

At that exact moment, Ridley approached. Noah stood bolt upright, put Jack's buzzer within reach and then walked away singing the same lullaby Ridley sang at Hannah's naming ceremony, the only difference being that Noah got all of the words right!

'I've just arrested Alberto for, amongst other things, your attempted murder,' Ridley announced. Now that he was sure Jack was going to live, Ridley had reverted to his official persona. 'I'll escort him to the station as soon as he's fit to move.'

'Don't let him see Betina,' Jack told him. 'She makes him strong. And wind him up, 'cos he's got a short fuse. But have someone in the room with you when you do.' Ridley nodded his understanding. Jack had never actually seen Ridley in a physical confrontation but imagined that most villains would probably underestimate him. Most people, in fact.

Jack then asked how Maggie took the news of him being in hospital. 'I didn't go into detail,' Ridley replied. 'I said you'd been injured but were OK. I mentioned the CT. You can tell her the rest when she gets here. I didn't want her overly worried while she was driving.'

'Did we get Adidas Man?' Jack asked.

Ridley chuckled. 'Oaks did. He can't wait to tell you all about it. Tomorrow, I'm going to head back to Chipping Norton to debrief with DCI Hearst.'

Jack smirked at the words 'debrief with DCI Hearst'. Ridley noticed but didn't seem to understand. He put Jack's grin down to the morphine and continued: 'I'll also talk to Hearst about setting your Judas Horse free.' Jack's smirk disappeared and, although he said nothing, his eyes betrayed his heartfelt gratitude. 'Charlotte won't get away scot free, I'm afraid. I'll do my best for her but . . . she gave target names to De Voe. I promise you this, though, Jack: the only person Charlotte will have to explain herself to is Annie. I'll protect her from any community backlash.'

Jack nodded. 'Thank you.' Life's moral grey area wasn't a natural or satisfying place for Ridley to be, but he'd go there for Jack.

The next thirty minutes were taken up by Jack talking Ridley through the events that had taken place in De Voe's office. It certainly wasn't an official statement, but Ridley knew that Jack might recall now something he could later forget. Especially if he ended up having full sedation for any reason. This conversation was brought to an end by Maggie arriving. She hugged Ridley for longer than she'd ever hugged him before.

'Thank you for looking after my Jack,' she said simply.

He nodded, then left them together.

Maggie's eyes explored Jack's body, taking in every cut and bruise, every dressing that hid an injury, every cannula sticking into him. By the time her eyes came to rest on his bruised and tired face, she knew all she needed to know. She lowered the bed rail, kissed his forehead, sat down on the low plastic chair next to him and held his hand. 'Want to see a video of Hannah smiling?'

With that image firmly in his mind, all of the pressure, stress and fear from the day disappeared, and Jack felt the overwhelming relief of being alive. The tears came quickly from both of them.

Two hours later, Noah arrived to take Jack up to a ward. As predicted, his CT scan had revealed nothing concerning – but Dr Okoya had admitted him for one night's observation. Maggie opened her shoulder bag and handed Noah a carrier bag filled with toiletries and a brand-new pair of pyjamas. Noah smiled to Maggie. 'Are you coming up with us, Doctor? Jack's on the same floor as Regina's poor little baby.'

CHAPTER 26

Jack swam in and out of sleep all night. There were so many sounds in the air, he didn't know what was real and what wasn't: buzzers, nurses whispering, doors creaking, shoe soles squeaking across vinyl floors. Every two hours, the patient in the bed next to him had his BP taken, and the humming noise made by the cuff inflating made Jack dream of Bjarne's 'quiet as a mouse' EC120 Colibri helicopter. And every four hours, Jack's own BP was taken. Every time, he part-woke and asked what time it was. And every time, the nurse would say, 'Too early for you to be awake, Jack.' Then he'd close his eyes and listen to her humming something gentle and soothing.

When Jack woke fully for the first time, Maggie was standing at the foot of his bed talking to Mario. 'Hey, there he is!' Mario beamed down at Jack. 'Mags told me what happened. Mate, I could never be Old Bill. Mad job! But a ride in a chopper. Nice!' Mario then gibbered on for a while longer about a bungie jump he'd chickened out of when he and Regina went to Victoria Falls. 'She was strapped to me, so couldn't jump either. Heights man! Turns out I don't like them.'

Jack, not thinking clearly, interpreted Mario's talkative mood as a good sign and tried to ask about Regina and the baby. But Mario was purposefully talking so much that nobody could get a word in and ask him any questions he didn't want to answer. Jack saw his mistake the instant Maggie put her hand gently on Mario's shoulder and the combination of Jack's clumsiness and Maggie's kindness made Mario cry.

'The name Princess has stuck,' he said through his tears. 'Her first operation is this afternoon, so we've got a meeting with the consultant this morning.' Mario looked at Maggie, knowing she would understand what he was talking about. 'By the time she's three months old, she'll have had two more operations. And that's if everything goes well! She's so tiny, Mags. But she smiles now, did Regina tell you? She smiles at everything, imagine that . . . I hear parents on the maternity ward saying things like, "I hope our baby is smart," or, "I hope she takes after her mum," or, "I hope he's tall." I just hope my baby lives. She doesn't have to be smart, or tall. She just has to stay with us.'

Mario wiped his face on his sleeve and, once again, beamed at Jack. 'Sorry, mate, sorry. I came here to ask how you are and listen to me, blubbing away. It's just the stress of today, you know. It's gonna be fine. It's just hard right now, 'cos we don't know stuff. I researched this amazing new treatment in the US that helps stimulate the parts of the brain that don't work. Brings them back to life. It costs six zeros! The medics may as well have said, "In order to cure your daughter, you need the still-beating heart of a unicorn."' Again, the tears welled up in Mario's eyes. 'It feels like it's *that* impossible. But not trying is more impossible. So, we're gonna sell everything we own.'

Mario, trying to joke, smiled at Jack and tapped the side of his nose. 'Maybe some things we don't own. Only joking, DS Warr. I'm on the internet every night learning physio for her arms 'cos . . .' Mario sucked air in through his teeth. 'You seen how much it costs, Mags? We'll need 24-hour support when Princess comes home. Regina's sister will move in with us and they'll do shifts. She's bought one of them camping beds so she can kip in the lounge, bless her.'

Jack was listening but he was miles away. He was with Hannah. Bathing her and fibbing about the noise an octopus makes. He imagined his baby girl *not* floating in his arms, *not* smiling up at him, *not* hanging on his every word. A tear rolled down Jack's cheek and onto his pillow. Neither Maggie nor Mario saw it.

'Anyway . . .' Mario took Maggie's hand. 'Now I've depressed you both, I'll head to the meeting. Say a little prayer for us, yeah?'

As Mario bounced out of the ward, waving furiously, Jack looked at Maggie. 'Is she going to die?'

'I don't know. Right now it's about keeping her alive this year, this month, this week. Actually, Jack, if you don't mind, I'd like to catch them before their meeting and wish them both good luck.'

'Go,' Jack said.

As Maggie left, the humming nurse appeared at Jack's side with the obs stand and announced that, for the final time this shift, she needed to take his BP. But before that job could be completed, Ridley appeared. The nurse looked at him with mock disapproval. 'And how did you get past the gatekeeper? might I ask. This is your third illegal visitor, Jack!' she began wheeling the obs stand away. 'Five minutes, Mr Singing Detective, then you're out.'

Ridley had walked down one long corridor and up two flights of stairs to get to Jack's ward, and this was the fourth 'Singing Detective' comment he'd heard. As the humming nurse gave him a wink and walked away with a smirk on her face, Ridley swore blind that he was never drinking Pimm's again.

Ridley remained standing as he explained that he'd signed Jack off work on medical grounds for one week. When he did come back, he'd be on desk duty for a minimum of one more week, at which point he'd have a fitness evaluation, before being allowed back to active duty. Jack, who knew all of this was coming, agreed without argument.

Then a memory suddenly surfaced, making Jack's skin go cold. He'd forgotten about the diamond necklace! If he wasn't allowed in the station for a week, there would be no way for him to return it to the evidence room.

Ridley squinted at him. 'You OK, Jack? You've gone very pale.'

Jack frantically tried to gather his thoughts. 'Sir . . .' Ridley sat down to show that he was listening. 'Sir, when I was going under-cover with De Voe, I needed a way in. I needed him to trust me. And I managed to do that. That's why he invited me to an all-expenses-paid trip to the races. Remember?' Jack then got to the crux of the matter, before he lost his bottle. 'I gained De Voe's trust by offering to sell him a stolen diamond bracelet.' Ridley's eyebrows shot up and his mouth opened slightly. 'I didn't steal a bracelet specifically for that purpose, of course,' Jack added quickly, 'but I did borrow one that I knew was stolen.'

Jack gave Ridley time to process his confession. Jack saw the look in Ridley's eyes and knew that he'd lost his alliance. Ridley had figured out that Jack must have taken the stolen bracelet from the evidence store, and that he had no option but to confess now, because now he needed someone to put it back for him.

Ridley then asked the one question Jack didn't want to answer. 'Would you have told me if you didn't have to?'

Jack couldn't say 'yes', as that would be an obvious lie. And he couldn't say 'no', as that would be insulting and disrespectful.

'My intention wasn't to involve you at all, sir. My intention was to insinuate myself into De Voe's life quickly because I didn't have time for anything else.'

Ridley sat back in his chair and shook his head, containing his frustration as best he could. 'Where's the bracelet now?'

Jack tried to lean down to open his bedside locker, but his back instantly seized up and he flinched in pain. Ridley pulled the locker door open, fished out the rucksack and started to unzip the main compartment. 'Front pocket!' Jack said quickly. Ridley's hands moved to the front pocket. He took out the diamond bracelet, stuffed the rucksack back into the bedside locker and stood up.

'Sir . . . thank you. I never meant to put you in this position. I hope you know that.'

'I do know that, yes.' Ridley closed his fist around the bracelet. 'Because I know that when you took this, you never actually gave me a second's thought. And that's a problem, Jack. Each time you step beyond the boundaries that guide us as police officers, you come back a little less like that man from Totnes who I employed two years ago.'

Jack, thinking he'd just made the biggest mistake of his career and now had nothing left to lose, spoke without his usual careful filter.

'Good. I don't want to be him. I'm better than him. Right from the off, you gave me shitty jobs, forcing me to realise that I wanted more. Then you made me fight for it. So, no, I'm not the man you employed two years ago, sir. But you have to take some of the blame for that. Or maybe the credit?'

Ridley remained statue-like, giving nothing away and Jack was certain that he'd blown it. There was no way Ridley was going to cover up the theft.

So Jack did the only thing he could: he hit below the belt. 'If you decide to get rid of me, sir, please make sure I'm sacked. Don't get me moved. If I'm going to continue to be a policeman, I don't want to be part of anyone else's team.'

Ridley's eyes smiled beneath his furrowed brow. 'Well . . . considering that moving teams would require a recommendation from me, it wouldn't be an option, would it?'

Ridley slid the diamond bracelet into his trouser pocket and left.

CHAPTER 27

Jack had relished his week's medical leave, although he'd driven Maggie demented by not resting anywhere near as much as he should have. On his second day home, she caught him finally building his office desk. Two hours earlier, he'd said he was going to lie down as his head was aching, and when she'd gone to wake him for lunch, he'd actually been in the spare room fixing the integral lock onto the desk drawer. As she gently chastised him, he tucked the trailing strap from the small black rucksack into the drawer, locked it, and added the tiny key to his keyring. He then kissed Maggie and she joined him for his long-overdue lie down.

Within minutes of lying down, Jack was snoring into the back of Maggie's neck. This deep sleep was something he currently managed to achieve very quickly. For these glorious few days, which Maggie knew would end as soon as he returned to work, Jack had slept soundly. Even the phone suddenly ringing didn't wake him.

Maggie picked up the phone and Regina instantly started a long, barely comprehensible story about the colour of Princess's baby-grow. 'I went to the shop on the ground floor, but they only had white and I wanted yellow. I knew there was a charity shop just two streets away – this was yesterday, did I say that? Anyway, I wanted a different colour, because I wanted a change, something brighter and less clinical, you know? Less "hospital". And I like yellow. So, yesterday I never opened the bedside cabinet because that's just full of white babygrows and I wanted yellow. I didn't open it all day yesterday, you see.' Maggie didn't see at all, but she said 'yes' and this prompted Regina to explain: 'I only opened it this morning.' Regina began to sob.

When Regina has first started babbling incoherently, Maggie had assumed the worst. But now she had no clue what to think. She couldn't make head nor tail of anything Regina had said so far. All she could do was wait and see if anything eventually made sense.

Regina regained her composure, took a deep breath and carried on. 'I opened the bedside cabinet to get the little collection tin so I could put it back on the nurses' station . . . they've been collecting for Princess, did you know that? I feel terrible begging, but I opened the cabinet to get the tin out and there it was . . . a carrier bag full of . . . I've never even seen one fifty-pound note, never mind this many! There's a note that says "For Princess". You should see it, Maggie. You should see what someone's done for our little girl!'

* * *

Jack's week of desk duty was only nine-to-five, designed to ease him back in, so by 5.30 each evening, he was back home with his feet up.

Jack and Maggie sat in old garden chairs on their wonky patio. They were pushed together so that Maggie was close enough to sit curled up with her head on Jack's shoulder.

The chairs had spent most of their lives on Charlie's allotment, so had definitely seen better days, Jack swore he could smell Charlie's aftershave on them, so couldn't bring himself to throw them away.

Hannah was lying on a blanket by their feet, as Penny finally planted the flowers that would clearly define the edges of Hannah's outdoor playground. 'We all need clear boundaries,' Penny insisted. 'They make us feel safe. And Hannah will always know that she's safe here.'

Jack's £40 T-shirt felt soft against Maggie's cheek. She had returned the corduroy trousers and the Hackett's shoes, but Jack had asked if he could keep the Paul Smith shirt – he'd begun to take more of an interest in his clothes, since discovering the feeling of authority they could give him. He was still the same man – just a slightly better-packaged version.

Maggie checked the wound that would soon become a scar on Jack's arm. She often did this, almost as a comfort, reminding her how lucky she was to still have the man she loved so much. 'Scars burn easily in the sun,' she said. Maggie's mind was now miles away, in St Lucia. On honeymoon. 'I'll buy you a Factor 50 sun-stick.'

Maggie lifted her head and told Jack that she loved him. 'No matter what,' she added.

Jack suddenly felt like he was being given permission to confess his sins, but he wasn't sure he was quite ready.

'I know the money was from you.' Maggie stared into Jack's eyes and read his thoughts. 'Actually, I didn't know for sure that it was from you. But the look in your eyes now says that I'm right. And then there's the honeymoon we didn't think we could afford until next year.'

Jack averted his eyes, before Maggie got too deep inside his head and saw something she wasn't supposed to.

'Me and you, Jack, the doctor and the policeman . . . we see so much go wrong in the lives of so many people. We know what loss and pain and unfairness looks like. We know that bad people can buy lives they don't deserve, whilst good people go hungry. Life, Jack . . . can be a fucker.' Maggie began to cry. 'What you did for Regina and Mario was beautiful.' Jack quickly wrapped Maggie in his arms and squeezed her tight. She whispered into his ear, 'Whatever you did, you never need to worry that I'll ask. I won't. I love you and I trust you.' Maggie pulled back from Jack, so that she could see his face. She ran her fingers down the deep furrow between his tearful eyes. 'This is him. This is Harry.' Her fingers lovingly moved to Jack's mouth and her touch made him smile. 'This is Charlie.' Maggie took Jack's face in her hands and kissed him. When she pulled away, a tear had rolled down his cheek. 'Never worry that I don't know who you are, Jack Warr. I see you both. And I love you both.'

Hannah's tiny hand grabbed Jack's bare foot and she looked up at him with a bright, smiling face. 'Well . . .' Penny looked exhausted. 'That'll do for today.' Penny scooped Hannah up. 'She's a bit ripe. I'll change her.' Penny looked up just as Jack tried to subtly wipe the tear from his cheek. 'My boy . . .' Penny said as she kissed his forehead and held back tears of her own. 'I'm so glad you're safe. There's no prouder mum, or dad anywhere in the world.' Then she went inside the house with Hannah.

Jack and Maggie sat together on the rickety garden chairs in perfect, contented silence. She was once again resting her head on his shoulder. 'I know you see me, Mags. For who I am. Who I need to be. You're the only person in the world who does.'

'I feel . . .' Maggie chose her words carefully. 'Not all the time, but every now and then, I feel the danger . . . of who you are. But that's OK, because we both know that life's not black and white. But if you ever bring danger to this door, Jack . . .'

Jack tightened his grip on her, and Maggie knew that she didn't need to finish her sentence. 'I swear on my life. I'll never do anything to hurt you. Or make you ashamed of me. Or make you doubt me.'

Jack felt her cheek lift on his shoulder as she smiled, and he could feel her cool tears soaking into his sleeve.

She laced her fingers into his and their perfect, contented silence returned.

Acknowledgements

I would like to thank all the staff at my publisher, Bonnier Books UK, with special thanks to Kate Parkin, Bill Massey, Stephen Dumughn, Ben Willis, Francesca Russell, Blake Brooks, Nick Stearn and Ruth Logan.

Thank you to my team at La Plante Global, Nigel Stoneman, Tory MacDonald and Cass Sutherland. Special thanks to Debbie Owen and Mick Randall, for all their help with *Judas Horse*.

Thanks also to the team at Allen and Unwin in Australia and New Zealand, and in South Africa, to all the staff at Jonathan Ball.

In Ireland, thanks to Simon Hess and Declan Heeney for all their hard work selling and publicising my books.

To all the booksellers and retailers, reviewers and bloggers who stock, read, review and promote my books, thank you again for your support, time and words.

Finally, thank you to my readers, who keep in touch via my social media and who I have met on Facebook Live in the past year. I hope you've enjoyed our chats as much as I have.

Lynda La Plante
Readers' Club

If you enjoyed *Judas Horse*, why not join the
LYNDA LA PLANTE READERS' CLUB by visiting
www.lyndalaplante.com?

Dear Reader,

Thank you very much for picking up *Judas Horse*, the second book in my new series featuring DC Jack Warr. I hope you enjoyed reading the book as much as I enjoyed writing it.

Jack is a character who has really taken hold of my imagination and I have loved returning to him in this new instalment in the series. He is a complex character who is still figuring out exactly who he wants to be. In *Judas Horse*, he is learning to navigate the challenges of new fatherhood alongside his career in the police force. This also allowed me to explore Jack's feelings about his own parents, and how he is shaped by both his biological father, Harry Rawlins, and Charlie Warr, the kind-hearted man who raised him.

If you enjoyed *Judas Horse*, then please do keep an eye out for news about the next book in the series, which will be coming soon. And in the meantime, later this year sees the publication of the next book in my Jane Tennison series, *Unholy Murder*, in which Jane must lift the lid on the most chilling murder case of her career to date . . .

The first six novels in the series, *Tennison, Hidden Killers, Good Friday, Murder Mile, The Dirty Dozen* and *Blunt Force* are all available in paperback, ebook and audio now. I've been so pleased by the response I've had from the many readers who have been curious about the beginnings of Jane's police career. It's been great fun for me to explore how she became the woman we know in middle and later life from the *Prime Suspect* series.

If you would like more information on what I'm working on, about the DC Jack Warr series or about the Jane Tennison thriller series, you can visit www.bit.ly/LyndaLaPlanteClub where you can join my Readers' Club. It only takes a few moments to sign up, there are no catches or costs and new members will automatically receive an exclusive message from me. Zaffre will keep your data private and confidential, and it will never be passed on to a third party. We won't spam you with loads of emails, just get in touch now and again with news about my books, and you can unsubscribe any time you want. And if you would like to get involved in a wider conversation about my books, please do review *Judas Horse* on Amazon, on Goodreads, on any other e-store, on your own blog and social media accounts, or talk about it with friends, family or reader groups! Sharing your thoughts helps other readers, and I always enjoy hearing about what people experience from my writing.

With many thanks again for reading *Judas Horse*, and I hope you'll return for the next in the series.

With my very best wishes,

Lynda

TENNISON
from the very beginning

TENNISON

HIDDEN KILLERS

GOOD FRIDAY

MURDER MILE

THE DIRTY DOZEN

BLUNT FORCE

and

UNHOLY MURDER